THE SAFEGUARD

A Novel of Georgia in 1864

Diana Wilder

Books By Diana Wilder:

The Memphis Cycle:
The City of Refuge
Mourningtide
Pharaoh's Son
A Killing Among the Dead

The American Civil War:
The Safeguard

Paris, 1834
The Orphan's Tale, Book I

RiverofWind

Book Layout © 2014 BookDesignTemplates.com

The Safeguard/Diana Wilder. – 2nd ed.
ISBN 978-0692548349

Dedication

To Captain James D. Wilder, USN, who served in the Judge Advocate General's Corps and retired as the Judge Advocate General for the 4th Naval District, headquartered in Philadelphia:

Thank you for your support and encouragement. Your input was invaluable, your insights very profound. And you have been the very best father a daughter could ever want.

This book is dedicated to you, with love.

CONTENTS

CHAPTER ONE

May 7, 1864

He stepped from dim cacophony into bright chaos, the pepper-sharp sting of drifting gunpowder catching at the back of his throat. He coughed, drew a deep breath, held it, and expelled it, feeling the sun-warmed air fill his lungs. It seemed, somehow, to lessen the noise behind him, screams, bitten-off curses and prayers. The dull rasp of a bone saw brought more shrieks, spiraling up higher than his ears could hear.

He grimaced and stepped farther into the sunlight.

The fighting had been hot and furious along this roadway, the artillery hurling shells into masses of gray-clad bodies that had turned to make a stand and then fallen back under the assault. Now the dead lay in rows as they had fallen, beneath the shattered branches of an alley of willows that led up to a house that seemed to stand empty and somehow silent in the hectic sunlight.

He drew another breath and looked down at his reddened hands. He would have to wash them before he returned. It didn't matter what the others said, clean hands led to better results, and he needed everything he could find to tip the scales in favor of the lives he was trying to save. He would need to find water, to have a bucket brigade set up to bring it to the hospital tent...

He turned to peer back over his shoulder at the hospital tent, caught a glimpse of the dim interior, more horrible than anything Dante could have conceived. He wouldn't return just yet. He needed the breather to give him some strength before he resumed command of the field hospital.

He raised his head and gazed down the alley of willows, his tired eyes fixing on the gracious lines of the house set between them. A house would most likely have a water source. A house this size would have a considerable water source; he only needed to send some men to find it.

Movement in the distance, somehow foreign to the carnage before him, made him pause to push his spectacles up on his nose and look more closely. Movement again, a flicker of color that resolved itself into a woman.

He stared, saying the word to himself. *A woman, here in the middle of hell.*

He could see her clearly now, the silhouette of a wide crinoline skirt, a small waist; a small woman, in fact, with a shawl draped over her shoulders. She was pale, disheveled, and clutching a bucket.

He watched her stoop to give water to a wounded man, touch him lightly on the forehead with a movement that spoke clearly of grace and compassion. She rose again to give more water, looking around her with a sort of dazed pity.

A lady, he thought.

He could see the men on the ground motioning to her, calling to her, and she turned to offer more water before straightening again. She motioned to one of the orderlies, who had paused before her. He could see her lips move. The orderly, inclining toward her in an attitude of respect, turned, looked toward the tent, and caught sight of him.

The orderly's expression eased. He turned back to the lady and spoke to her.

As he watched, she set the bucket down, gathered her skirts and, after one last glance over her shoulder at the big house, turned back toward him, squared her shoulders, fixed her eyes on his, and moved resolutely toward him.

He faced her, inclined his head to her, and waited as she approached him...

CHAPTER TWO

The Union Camp

The general looked up from the note in his hand to cast a quick glance around his encampment. His army with its three corps took up a lot of space; forests of white tents covered the hillsides, and the late spring air was filled with the smell of frying salt pork and stewing beans along with a tangy overlay of wood smoke from the cooking fires. He could hear the clink of tin utensils and general chatter. Soon he would be retiring within his own tent and dining on whatever his aide saw fit to fix for him.

He sighed. The past two weeks had been fast, fierce and furious, a running fight against a dogged opponent. They would be moving soon, heading farther south and east toward Atlanta, but for the moment they had time to rest and take care of matters, including some civilian concerns that had arisen in this corner of northwest Georgia.

"They're coming, sir," said the guard sergeant beside him.

He looked down along the main aisle of his camp and watched as a buggy approached, flanked by guards. The buggy creaked to a halt and stood swaying while the driver set the foot brake and clucked to the ancient white mule harnessed between the shafts. A smallish woman in a paisley shawl rose and started to descend from the vehicle. The afternoon sunlight glinted briefly from a pair of spectacles.

The general, watching from his headquarters tent, nodded to the sergeant, made sure the man hurried forward to offer his arm, and then turned his attention back to the paper he held in his hand.

May 13, 1864

To Miles G. Stanley, Maj. Gen. U.S.V.
Commander, Army of the Monongahela
   Sir:
   It is my pleasure to commend to you Miss Lavinia Wheeler, residing in this town, who has put my staff and, by extension, this entire army, considerably in her debt. I ask that you admit this lady to your presence and give full consideration to any request that she may make.

   Charles S. Haskell, Major, U.S.V.
   Chief Surgeon

Interesting, General Stanley thought. Major Haskell, a crusty physician of the old, Hippocratic School, was more lavish with his blame than with his praise. What could this lady have done to put the army in her debt?

Miles Stanley did not usually have much time to spare for the local citizenry. They were generally too strident in demanding rights that they had forfeited in his eyes by their support of an armed insurrection and too quick to take advantage of the mechanics of supply and demand by selling what supplies they had at exorbitant prices. But this woman was different: she seemed to have a claim on him.

He eyed the gaunt white mule, reflecting that the beast could have put armies to flight if someone had thought to put a skeleton on its back. And the venerable white-haired driver might have played the part of Uncle Tom without appreciable change. But the lady now—

He bowed as she approached on the sergeant's arm, nodded his dismissal to the man, and said, "Good evening, Miss Wheeler. I am Miles Stanley. I understand that you wish to speak with me."

The lady smiled at the sergeant and then directed a clear-eyed gaze at General Stanley. "Good evening, sir," she replied, motioning to her driver. Her voice was well-modulated with a cultured deep south inflection that contrasted oddly with the western Georgia drawls that he had heard lately. "It was kind of you to receive me. I am sure you must be very busy."

"It is no trouble," General Stanley said, hiding a smile at the formality of the exchange and entering into it almost unconsciously.

"Major Haskell was most complimentary in his note, and it is my pleasure to oblige someone who is described as having placed this army in her debt. How may I be of service?"

"You can look at this, sir," Miss Wheeler said, taking from the driver a blanket-wrapped bundle that was the approximate size and shape of a swaddled baby, and thrusting it into the General's arms.

Good God! General Stanley thought with weary resignation. *Another woman looking for the father of her child, probably long gone under the sod. 'Miss' Wheeler, no less. And she looking so virtuous.*

He took the strangely inert package into arms experienced in such actions, fingered the wrapping aside, and almost dropped the thing.

A face, half-hidden by a waving beard, peered up at him with a wry cynicism. It was a pottery jug rather than a baby; after a closer look, he rather wished that he had dropped it after all. It was an old face, an enigmatic face, and the potter who had shaped that face from dozens of tiny strips of clay had worked swiftly and surely. The face, and the pot-bellied jug beneath it, holding perhaps a gallon of liquid, were the brown-gray of the earth from which it had been taken, and one side had been blackened by the fire that had hardened and glazed it. The full, shaggy lips that seemed about to widen in a smile over what promised to be strong, even teeth, had been chipped slightly, adding to the jaunty effect.

General Stanley peered back at it with an expression compounded equally of amusement and disgust. Amusement won; he looked away from the clay face and set the jug upon the table with a slight clink.

"This is very interesting, Miss Wheeler," Stanley said. "But I fail to see what it has to do with me."

Miss Wheeler fingered the paisley shawl she had thrown about her shoulders. General Stanley could see at a glance that it was fine cashmere, probably a relic of more peaceful times. Her thin face flushed a little as she raised her head.

"Can't you see, General, how very old it is?" she asked.

The general lifted his eyebrows. "No, Miss Wheeler," he said. "I fear that I can't. I am not at all well-versed in jugs."

"This is early Colonial pottery!" she said. "A demijohn, to be precise." She looked at the jug, completely devoid of wicker and added quickly, "That is, this was a demijohn once."

Major General Miles Stanley, a fourth-generation Bostonian, was interested almost in spite of himself. "I am willing to concede the wicker, Miss Wheeler," he said. "You say this is early Colonial?"

Miss Wheeler's fine gray eyes sparkled behind her spectacles. "Yes, General," she said. "This came from Roanoke colony! It was discovered on the site a hundred years ago by my great-grandfather. Sir Walter Raleigh may even have drunk from it, himself." She looked up at him saw his skeptical expression, and added, "I am certain you do know who Sir Walter Raleigh is."

General Stanley bowed. "Sir Walter has enjoyed the gratitude of every tailor for the past two hundred and sixty years, Miss Wheeler," he said.

She surprised him: her eyes, set under arched, dark brows, sharpened and warmed with a quick comprehension of the joke. But her mouth did not move into a smile. "I doubt, sir, that he was concerned with his clothing there in Roanoke," she said. "And I can't imagine Queen Elizabeth giving a moment's serious thought to going there and stepping over mud puddles. At any rate, sir, you can see how very valuable it is. And there are other pieces. We-we have a museum here."

She colored slightly, obviously unwilling to tell a lie even to an enemy. "That is, sir, my family has an extensive collection dedicated to the relics of the past centuries. People come to see it from as far afield as Boston and New York. There are perhaps a hundred pieces, many salt-glazed and hand-wrought like this one." Her voice softened a little, "I brought you the oldest and finest piece, sir, so that you can see how it is."

General Stanley ran a finger down the side of the jug. "You do me great honor, Miss Wheeler," he said with a smile.

"I am glad that you feel that way General," Miss Wheeler said. Her voice was warmer now. "You see, it was made of clay from this land, fired in a kiln heated by wood from these forests, and it was scorched by the heat of the new world."

She picked it up in sure, reverent hands. "Only think: someone held this almost three hundred years ago, filled it from a stream, perhaps, and drank from it. Think how frightened and lonely they all must have been then! And how brave they were to leave all they loved to come here. I think they must have shivered in their rough-built cabins in the winter and thought longingly of England. And yet,

General, they found the strength and the courage to stay."

Her eyes lowered a little; General Stanley realized that she was very tired, with the sort of heart-deep fatigue that underlay everything. "I always wonder at the strength of courageous people, when I am such a coward, myself," she said.

General Stanley smiled at her. "My great-great grandfather survived that first terrible winter in Massachusetts," he said. "It's truly humbling to reflect how I might have fared if I had been there, away from modern amenities."

She flashed him a quick, happy smile. "Just so, sir," she said. "When I'm holding this jug in my own hands, as now, it's almost as though I'm touching those people who made it and drank from it. As though I can feel their courage and resolution." She looked up at him. "It is valuable, General," she said.

"In sentiment, certainly," he said with a touch of dryness. And then he relented. "And in fact, as well. Well, Miss Wheeler, our conversation has been a pleasure. Now what do you want me to do for you?"

She opened her eyes at him. Now that he really looked at her he could see that she had some claim to beauty. She had fine gray eyes that dominated her thin face behind their spectacles; she might have even been a taking little creature if she had not adopted a deplorably spinsterish style of skinning her hair back from her face in a way that emphasized her cheekbones and pointed chin. "Why, sir," she said, "I want it guarded, of course!"

"Guarded?" he repeated.

"Yes, sir. Your men came marching in here, tore things up—you yourself have said that this is valuable. I need to have this—to have these pieces—guarded."

General Stanley clasped his hands behind him and took a turn about his tent. "Miss Wheeler," he said over his shoulder, "You say my men 'tore things up' as you put it, and I admit the charge. But they thought themselves justified because this town had set some land mines that killed several of my men, and they didn't take kindly to it, especially since your town had reported itself as having surrendered. Your people can count themselves lucky my men didn't take a notion to raze the place. In all honesty, ma'am, I can't say I'd have exerted myself much to stop them."

She opened her eyes at him again. "I did not countenance any 'land mines', General," she said with the firm precision of an accountant. "Nor did I fire any guns or wield any swords: all that was the doing of the army, which didn't see fit to consult me or the town fathers, who most likely would have discouraged the land mines, at any rate. Nor, for that matter, did I sign any articles of secession, although—" she added with a flash of annoyance, "seeing the way your people have behaved, I'm not at all surprised to see that someone in this state did! Be that as it may, I helped to tend your wounded, as any of your surgeons will be happy to confirm. I still have bloodstains on my good parquet floors, and a few injured soldiers in my best parlor, none of whom seem to have anything seriously wrong with their appetites. I have asked that you protect something that must be of great value to any North American, whatever his allegiance. That is all. If this and its mates is smashed in some drunken revel, the nation will be the poorer!" She added "I would be loath to have that responsibility laid at my door, general, if I were in your place."

The general began to smile. The smile bloomed to a chuckle. 'Laid at his door', indeed! The nation would owe him a debt of gratitude for removing such an ugly specimen. "One question, Miss Wheeler," he said. "If this jug is so valuable, why didn't you just pack it up and send it with the Reb—I beg your pardon—the Confederate forces when they evacuated this town?"

"Because they were a pack of ruffians," she replied with more honesty than patriotism. "And they were in no danger from the—the 'Rebs', as you put it. They were too busy digging pits and such. I didn't dream of any danger until your men started charging about and whooping and firing their guns."

"I see," Stanley said.

"Will you take steps to guard it, sir?" she asked. "Please?"

The last hesitantly voiced word, coupled with the softening of her expression as she gazed up at him, disarmed General Stanley. He smiled down at her. "Let me give it some thought, Miss Wheeler," he said. "I have few men to spare."

He caught her quick, disbelieving glance at the forests of white tents scattered through the surrounding fields and hid a smile. "But I will issue an order for the time being that you're not to be molested," he said. "That's all I can do this evening. Will that satisfy you?"

Miss Wheeler sighed and wrapped the jug once more. "It must, sir," she said. "You are, as you said, a busy man. And I do thank you for your time. May I go now?"

"By all means, Miss Wheeler," he said. And watched her turn to leave with the bundle in her arms.

She hesitated, though, and turned back from his orderly, who had offered his arm to help her into her buggy. "General?" she said.

He heaved a silent sigh. "Yes, Miss Wheeler?"

"Would you like to have the loan of this, just for this evening? I am sure you appreciate its value, and it will remind you of your own brave ancestors. I know it would be safe with you."

General Stanley's heart melted beneath the double row of brass buttons that marched down the front of his jacket. "Thank you, Miss Wheeler," he said. "How can I refuse such a compliment and such an offer?" He took the jug from her, made a show of admiring it— ignoring the horrified expressions of his orderly and a regimental color-sergeant who had stopped by his tent with a message in his hand—and set it atop his camp desk.

He offered his own arm and escorted her to her carriage. "I will send further word to you when I can," he said as he handed her into the trap and then gave the reins over to her. "Good evening, Miss Wheeler. I will take good care of your demijohn."

CHAPTER THREE

Lavinia Wheeler stopped the buggy before her house to let off her driver, George. He stepped stiffly down from the buggy, cast a grim look at her, and started to climb the steps to the front door.

"You tell Callie and Bathsheba I'll be right in now, George!" she called after him.

His frown deepened. It had taken an argument followed by a twinge of his lumbago to convince him to allow her to take care of stabling the mule and putting the buggy away. Even with a pain that he described as a bar of hot iron across his back, it sat poorly with him.

Lavinia smiled at him and then drove her buggy to the stable behind her house. She unhitched the mule herself and led him in past the four cavalry mounts that had been quartered in the stable. At least one good thing had come of the town's occupation by the Federals, she thought as she rubbed the mule down with a handful of straw: her stable had more straw and fodder in it than it had had since her father's death two years before. She put an armful of hay in the feed trough before the mule, tweaked his ear, and went toward the house after pausing to pat the horses.

The evening sky had not yet darkened; sunset's glow lingered in the velvety, brilliant blue that still peeked out between the stars. If she looked westward she could just barely see the mountains. If she let her eyes drop slightly to the fields outside the town, she could see a constellation of campfires marking the Federals' campground. Someone was singing; she could hear the notes plainly upon the freshening breeze. She raised her head and listened, and in a moment she caught a snatch of softly voiced words.

...dying on the old camp ground...

The words made her shudder. She had seen too much of death in the past three years, death in her family, distant death touching those around her with sons, fathers and sweethearts fighting on battlefields whose names she could barely pronounce. In the past week she had smelled death, and in her own house had done her best to fight off death, for she didn't want anyone to feel the anguish that she had witnessed, no matter from what side of the Mason-Dixon line he might have come.

Her memories of the arrival of the armies and the battle seemed set, like motions in a dance glimpsed from a distance by fitful light. And yet, only a few days had passed.

General Dillon's Alabama troops had come streaming toward the town, and she had heard that there would be fighting. Women and men screamed, children ran about shrieking, weapons were checked and then tucked into belts or pockets. Her neighbors had loaded wagons with treasures chosen with the illogic of utter panic and left town.

She had chosen to remain: she was a Wheeler, after all. Even if that had not been so, her mule, Absalom, was old and easily tired now. He could not pull a cart loaded with her belongings even if she, working alone in the absence of her servants, all but three of which had run away, had been able to load it. She had left her house and gone to the town, moving among the empty buildings as though in a dream, staring around at the deserted houses and listening to the thunder from the north growing louder and deeper until it replaced her heartbeat.

Boom!

The sound had been followed by a crash and a fountain of earth surging skyward and then spattering about her like rain. She had picked up her skirts and run all the way back to her house. She had flung the door wide and run inside, calling for her people to gather up their things, especially the pottery, and hurry to the root cellar.

Lavinia sighed and leaned back against the doorpost, trying to remember. She had a confused impression of herself huddled against the wall with her best shawl about her head and her arms full of pots, wishing she had never left the safety of Savannah to come west to her summer home in Wheelerville. Callie and George, the two old servants who had been with her family since their births, huddled in beside her as the earth splintered and screamed about her with the sound of human voices. Bathsheba, Callie's fifteen-year-old granddaughter, had been with them, crying.

Somehow the hours had passed until she had looked around in the painful stillness and had known that it was over. She had climbed the steps from the cellar and emerged dazed and disheveled to the smell of iron and earth, raw meat and sweat.

The ground was ripped and red, sweet spring grass jagged with pieces of twisted, broken metal. The old willow tree she used to sit beneath was splintered, half of it split away from the trunk and leaning crazily toward the ground.

She had turned in a circle, her hand pressed against her mouth, her wide eyes taking in the damage, the dead and mutilated horses, the wreckage of human bodies, as the stillness faded horribly into shrieks of pain. She had blinked, looked down, and seen the men lying in the streets. To her dazed eyes they looked as though they had been bathed in blood and set in the sun to dry. People were moving among them, stooping now and then, speaking in tones barely audible above the din. She had begun to tremble.

"Water!"

The quavering word had broken the spell of horror that seemed to have been laid on her. She looked down to see a man lying almost at her feet, one leg twisted and useless behind him.

Her hand had gone to her mouth again; she had whirled and run for the well. The bucket had splashed in and emerged dripping, and she had given the man his drink.

She had straightened—she could feel the stretch of cramped muscles even now—and had looked around. Men were moving through the town, bending over the huddled forms.

She had felt George's hand on her elbow. He was telling her to go inside the house and lock the door, and she seemed to remember telling him to gather what supplies he could and throw the house wide open. And then she had gone to the surgeons, located their chief and spoken to him.

Lavinia blinked. The smells and sounds were gone, and she was standing in the peaceful twilight and looking at her house. All was well for the time being, and she could go inside.

The foyer was as gleamingly pristine as ever, the parquet floor glowing golden in the reflected light of the parlor fire, and the stairway paraded before her in a great sweep up to its landing, where it branched into two wings that curved around and up to the second floor. Callie came to her while she removed her hat and shawl, marched her into the dining salon and then stood there, grimly disapproving, while she ate the supper that had been set on the big mahogany table.

Lavinia speared a piece of sweet potato and eyed it thoughtfully. "Did you use honey on this, Callie?" she asked. "I thought I told you to keep it for the men."

"You may have done so," Callie said, "But I judged it best to give it to you. There's more where it came from, and you need strengthening. Do you want to faint in the middle of your work?"

"I don't think honey will keep me from fainting if I get sick," Lavinia said with a smile. "You pamper me too much." She picked up a fried chicken wing and bit into it.

"Someone's got to do it!" Callie said. "Well, you went to see that Yankee general, just as the doctor said. Did it accomplish anything?"

"Maybe," Lavinia answered, turning the bones over with her hand. "He said he'd consider setting a guard over the pottery, but nothing was decided tonight."

Callie frowned at her. "Pottery!" she sniffed. "He'd be better advised to assign a guard for you! I told you as much!"

"I'll be fine," Lavinia said. She ignored Callie's expression and ate the rest of her supper in silence. "Thank you, Callie," she said when she was finished. "Are our guests comfortable now?"

"They're as comfortable as they can be this side of the grave, Miss Lavinia," she said. She eyed Lavinia's tired face and said, "I'll tend them this night. You won't be needed."

"Thank you, Callie," Lavinia said. "I'll go upstairs now."

"See you do!" Callie snapped. "Get some sleep!" She watched as Lavinia gathered her skirts and set a foot on the stairs. "I've told Bathsheba to warm the sheets for you. Heaven alone knows what we'd have done if she'd run off like the rest!"

Lavinia smiled wearily at her. "We'd have managed," she said.

"Just barely," Callie said. "The good Lord said we wouldn't be overcome, but He didn't say we wouldn't be beaten half to death before we triumphed. Well." Her expression softened. "Good night, Lamb," she said.

Lavinia smiled back at her. "Sleep tight, Callie," she said, and went up the stairs to her bedroom.

She had moved into the large bedroom that her parents had once shared, leaving her narrow, whitewashed bed without a moment's regret.

A large armoire stood against the far wall. She went to it and opened it and looked within as though it held in its shadows the key to her strength.

The shelves that had once held lavender-scented linens and petticoats were now crowded with pottery of all shapes and heights, all the colors of the earth. A forest of faces gazed back at her, and ranked before and behind them were ramekins, plates, cups, tankards, all formed of the earth, and all very, very old.

She took the largest one and touched the rough glaze. One of the settlers had dipped this in the James River and drunk from it. He and his family had probably sat of an evening and gazed into the fire, and maybe set this jug on the hearth to warm the wine that was in it. It must have been a hard life, as she had said to General Stanley. Hard, exhausting, frightening at times. But surely, surely nothing like this time of trial that had overtaken her world and split it apart!

She sighed and held the jug closer. Everything had changed so terribly that she felt lost. All the set phrases, all the carefully choreographed motions of life had broken down and fled before the maelstrom. Now it was important to bring some ceremony, some sanity back to everyday living. One clung to what was decent, one did what was right. But it was proving to be a strain.

CHAPTER FOUR

It is early morning. The Army of the Monongahela, encamped at Wheelerville, Georgia, has been awake and moving since the first light of dawn. Patrols returning from their night shifts, shambling wearily along the lines of tents, speak quietly. You can hear the thud of logs being piled for cooking fires; here and there is the hiss of burning pitch pine logs. The metallic notes of reveille cuts through the sleepy air.

The sounds increase. Water splashes into buckets, tin plates rattle together, and now the scent of coffee and cooking meat fills the air.

Mounted messengers move like shadows through the lightening streets, the horses' hooves drumming upon the ground in an inverted echo of the drumbeat of 'assembly', rolling in increasing volume. Names being cried in the cool air, answers, laughter as the men break ranks to get their breakfasts.

** ** **

Major General Miles Stanley fastened the last button on his sack coat, smoothed his sleeves, and accepted a cup of coffee from his orderly with a smile and a word of thanks. After pausing long enough to toss a clean handkerchief over the hideous pottery jug that sat atop his camp desk, he drew his folding chair up to the edge of the tent fly, sat, and squinted up at the sky.

The day was starting out a fine one, he thought, though there was ra hint of approaching summer. He did not fare well in the southern heat, and it promised to be a busy summer, with the drive for Atlanta under way. The army of the Ohio was cutting off the railroads leading into Atlanta, and Hood's army looked as though it were heading toward Jonesboro to engage the Army of the Tennessee. And his Army of the Monongahela was being given a well-deserved rest after its swift push south from Brown's Ferry, Tennessee.

He drank his coffee, closed his eyes, and thought of Boston. His dearly loved wife would be awakening just about now, nodding to her maid's offer of a cup of tea. Presently she would arise, don her dressing-gown of Brussels lace, brought to the United States on one of Miles Stanley's fast clipper ships, and have her hair arranged in the smooth, glossy wings that suited her so well.

His smile deepened slightly into mischief. If he were home, now, he would be tapping on the door to her dressing room. She would look up, smile at him, dismiss her maid, and go to him with the secret smile of a woman who knows that her smooth hair is about to be disarranged and is looking forward to it.

A breeze rose and he caught the scent of flowers. He opened his eyes and gazed at the distant mountains, marveling as he always did at the fact that he had arrived at his current situation. Five years as the commander of a militia unit whose only prerequisite was a spot on Boston's social register would not seem to be much of a preparation for high command, but he had attained it against every expectation and, indeed, desire. He had fought with distinction at Shiloh and at Vicksburg and had commanded the land support for the misfortune-dogged Steele Bayou expedition. He had been given command of the Army of the Monongahela in January of the year and was, he had to admit, enjoying himself immensely. Boston, dear as it was and filled with his family and friends, would seem somehow flat after the war was over.

He heard the clatter of approaching hooves and looked up to see his Adjutant-General, Colonel Henry Schuyler, riding up on his tall roan gelding.

Stanley rose and lifted his cup of coffee. "Morning, Hank," he said with a smile. "Sleep well?"

Schuyler shrugged and swung down from his saddle. "Well enough," he said. "It's quieter today, that's for sure, though I had some rip-snorting dreams last night, a remnant, I guess, of that shell that burst two horses' lengths from me during the fighting."

Stanley smiled and sat back. "You'll have to tell me some time," he said, eyeing the papers in Schuyler's hands. "What do you have for me today? Any good news?"

"It's the usual mix," Schuyler said, handing Stanley the papers. "Rolls—you'll be interested to hear, Miles, that there were no desertions in the past week. After that lot of bounty boys came through, I was expecting more, but I was wrong."

"Hm. They probably figure they'll get their throats cut if they cut and run here," Stanley observed.

"Very possibly," Schuyler conceded. "Going along with that, it appears that most of the townsfolk have been trying to sneak back to their homes. From what our prisoners tell us, Dillon's actions started up a rare sauve-qui-peut among the good citizens of Wheelerville. The people coming in now are pretty shamefaced, though they're blustering a lot at having to stop and give an accounting to our pickets."

"How sad for them," General Stanley said.

"It does make a man's heart bleed," Schuyler said. "From some of the exchanges I heard, they all are red-hot rebels and have no hesitation about telling us so now that they know we aren't going to shoot them out of hand."

"I've seen the churchyards here," General Stanley said thoughtfully. "They certainly have contributed their complement of troops." He smiled wryly and sipped his coffee. "I guess I can't blame them for their sentiments. If it were Boston or New York that were menaced by southern troops, I would imagine there'd be a mass exodus of their good citizens and a certain amount of blustering once they had returned."

Colonel Schuyler lifted an eyebrow. "Maybe in Boston, Miles," he said. "Never New York. Well. Here are the latest statistics on the casualties from our last tussle. Things have stabilized, though twenty more died during the night—" He frowned at the paper. "Damnation! They forgot to note the two who've been discharged to return to their duties. Say, Miles, do you have a pencil I can use?"

"Look on the desk," Stanley said, nodding toward it. "Have you eaten yet? Chester's gone to fetch my breakfast, and he usually brings enough for two."

"Don't mind if I do," Schuyler said, frowning at the desk. He tweaked the handkerchief aside and stared at the unveiled jug. "Christ almighty!" he exclaimed. "What the hell's that?"

Miles Stanley had started at Schuyler's yelp of dismay. He sat back with a grin. "If you hadn't been so nosey, Hank, you wouldn't have suffered such a nasty turn. Lovely, isn't it? And yet its presence here's a signal honor conferred on me and my ancestors."

"Good God!" Schuyler said blankly, staring at the face as though it were a basilisk. "In what way?"

"An interesting little lady brought it in with a request... Hank, I want you to find out what you can about a Miss Wheeler, residing in the town. Anything of interest concerning her—"

Schuyler had lifted the jug and was staring at it.

"Careful," said Stanley. "It actually is valuable."

"That so? I'm always amazed at the way worth and beauty seldom match," Schuyler said, setting down the jug. "Miss Wheeler's name is in that report several times, by the way."

Stanley lifted his eyebrows. "Indeed?" he said.

"Yes. She has quite a few men quartered in her house at this moment, and she's helping to nurse and feed them."

"That's right," Stanley said after a moment's frowning thought. "I remember now: she told me she had a couple wounded soldiers. She insinuated that they were gluttons. How did they get there? Did Vogel commandeer her house against my orders like the last time?"

"No, sir," Schuyler replied. "She had them taken there. When the fighting started, everyone here made themselves scarce. Skirmishers moved through the town, then the guns came booming and roaring. You saw afterward how the dead lay in windrows along that road, didn't you? Well, that's the main thoroughfare leading to her home. The guns were throwing shells along that road, tearing trees up. A big willow in her front yard took a direct hit. You should have seen how it looked before the boys went and cut it down. Dead and wounded were lying all through the town, thickest near her house. And no one stirred during the fighting. Everyone thought the town had been evacuated.

"The head sawbones, Charlie Haskell, tells me that she showed up after the firing died down and the wounded were being collected. He caught sight of her picking her way along through the dead and the dismembered, giving water to those she could help. She spoke to several people, and one of them directed her to Haskell. She went to him and said that he could bring some of their most seriously wounded men into her house."

General Stanley was looking thoughtful. "She went through the hell of a battle's aftermath to offer her house as a shelter for the wounded," he said. He lifted his eyebrows at Colonel Schuyler, who continued.

"It's quite a house, Miles," he said. "You should see the place: white pillars, wings, a big, curving portico, beautifully furnished. It's known as 'Fairlawn', and the name's apt. Anyhow, she pitched in and worked alongside the surgeons at the field hospital. She was quite a trooper, from what they tell me. The ones remaining at her house are still badly off, but Dr. Haskell says they all would have died if she hadn't taken and cared for them." He smiled and added, "And she has a lot more than a couple, Miles. Try something like forty-two."

General Stanley lifted the jug and looked at it. "If she showed up so soon after the fighting," he mused, "then she was most likely here during that heavy bombardment. We kept it hot and fast for quite a while: she must have felt as though the earth were cracking apart. And to think she actually told me she envied brave people!"

"By all reports, she isn't lacking in courage," Schuyler said. "Interestingly enough, several of the men volunteered to make up a detail to go to her house and bury all the dead horses and move the debris. It was their idea. Quite a concession."

"Concession, nothing!" Stanley snorted. "It borders the miraculous!"

"There's more," said Schuyler. "She came to our people unasked and gave them permission to bury our dead on her grounds. She had picked out a quiet, shaded hillside for them. She told us to bury the dead there, and if we can identify them for her, she'll keep the records in case their families want to come and retrieve them after the fighting is over."

General Stanley's smile faded. "Generous heart! Did she do that, indeed?" he asked.

"Indeed she did," Schuyler replied. "Why do you want to know about her?"

"She interests me," Stanley said. "Especially after what you've told me. Have you met her, Hank? You say she's got a fine house. Her name's Wheeler, and this town is Wheelerville. You may draw your own conclusions from that. She's a small woman with bright eyes and a lot of energy, though I thought she seemed a little tired."

"Pretty?" Schuyler suggested with a smile.

"I'm a married man," Stanley returned. "Happily married. No, she's not exactly—Well, now, that's not quite accurate. Her eyes are very fine, a nice, clear gray. There was what looked like some pretty hair in evidence, though it was strained back so tight, and so securely hidden in a net, it was hard to tell. She could have been taking, I think, but now she fits the description of the quintessential spinster. My wife pointed out to me how sad it is for mature unmarried women in this society. If they aren't virtuous, they get abused and vilified, and if they're virtuous, they get sneered at, patronized, and told they're worthless."

Colonel Schuyler's expression was somber. "There'll be a whole generation of women facing that trouble after all the killing of this war," he said. "I just sent off another letter this morning."

Stanley's expression bleakened. "That's a type of letter I never want to write again," he said. "But this Miss Wheeler, now. That jug's old, from the first Virginia colonies. She stood here in this very tent with me, looked at it, spoke of the first settlers, and sighed and said she envied their courage. She called herself a coward..." He smiled and added, "I found her charming."

He fell silent and frowned into space for a moment.

Colonel Schuyler was familiar with that expression. He took out his pocket notebook and waited.

"I think I'm going to help Miss Wheeler," General Stanley said at last. "I have an assignment for you, Hank: I want you to find a man for me. Take your time and be sure you find the right person."

"Sir?"

"For starters, I want a senior noncommissioned officer. Not just company level: someone with considerable seniority. He must have a few years with the army in this war under his belt."

Schuyler nodded and wrote. He looked up when he was finished. "Very well, Miles," he said.

"I don't want a youngster, either. He must be older: late thirties to mid-forties, but vigorous and a good fighter if necessary. I'd prefer that he be unattached—"

"Unattached?" Schuyler queried.

"Unmarried or widowed," Stanley said. He continued, "He must be temperate in habits: I don't think I want a drinker for this assignment."

"Yes, sir."

Stanley frowned at the jug. "He should be responsible, steady and firm, not one to take any nonsense, no matter who's dishing it out. He should also be kind, someone his subordinates love as well as respect." His eyes flicked to meet Schuyler's. "Someone like you, I think," he said with the hint of a grin.

"Wrong rank," said Schuyler, writing busily. "But thanks just the same for thinking of me."

"Pity," Stanley said.

Schuyler scanned his notes. "From what I have here, you appear to want Michael the Archangel in a good mood."

Stanley smiled. "That's close," he said. "But two more things are needed. He must be presentable-neat, clean, orderly, well-favored if not handsome. But not too handsome, either." He added distastefully, "And not one to spend weeks in the same pair of drawers unless he has a damned good reason for it."

Schuyler set down his notebook. "I may have a man for you," he said. "He was the Sergeant Major from my old regiment, and I've known him well during the past three years. He fits everything so far: was one of the ninety-day men that signed up in April of '61, and re-upped twice, so he's senior, all right. Came with me when my old regiment was dissolved last year, which is why a New Yorker's in an Ohio cavalry regiment. In fact, he got special permission to send for his own horse from New York. He's in his early forties, a widower with three children."

"Sounds perfect so far," General Stanley said. "Though I'm surprised he isn't at least a lieutenant after all this time."

"It was all in the timing," Schuyler said. "The New York regiments were pretty political for a while there, and if you didn't push your connections, you didn't get anywhere. You know how it is. I wasn't in any position to help him much, only being a major up to the time of Vicksburg, and by the time I had any influence, the regiment's term had expired and they all went home."

"All but him."

"That's right," Schuyler said. "He told me he was in this fight until slavery was abolished and the Union restored. He could have gone for a commission in one of the new regiments they were forming, but he chose to transfer to a veteran group and went in as sergeant major. I think he was more concerned with doing his job well than with trying to get ahead in the army."

"What's he do in peacetime?"

"He's a cabinetmaker," Schuyler said. "A master cabinetmaker. The governor of New York has commissioned pieces by him. I found that out from the governor, by the way, not from him."

General Stanley lifted his eyebrows. "Interesting," he said. "But if he's so good, why are you suggesting him?"

"Ordinarily, he's indispensable," Schuyler said. "He's finally been approved for a captain's commission—he hasn't been told that yet—but there's been no confirmation yet. He's been cited for gallantry a few times, and General Quillan put him in for a formal commendation. You approved it, if you recall."

General Stanley sat back and frowned. "Really?" he said.

"It was that last engagement, just as we were leaving Tennessee," Schuyler said. "You'll remember: he'd overrun and captured a battery that was giving us considerable grief. He dismounted his men, turned the guns and began pepper the Rebs for all he was worth."

"I remember now," Stanley said. "He was wounded that day."

"Not badly," Schuyler said, "but enough to make him need to take a rest. He wouldn't stay at the field hospital: said he didn't want to be captured, and said he could ride and keep up with the rest. His colonel let him, but it's taken a toll. I can see he's exhausted. He could use a spell of light duty to get him back into shape. What is the last qualification?"

Stanley looked over at the jug. "He needs a good sense of humor," he said.

Schuyler closed his notebook. "Oh, well, if that's the case..." he said, "I'll send him to you as soon as I can. What do you need this paragon for?"

General Stanley tapped the side of the jug. "Miss Wheeler assisted my men out of the goodness of her heart," he said. "She has requested a Safeguard, and I've decided to grant her one."

CHAPTER FIVE

Lavinia turned as she always did to gaze back at her house. It had been built of brick made from the red clay of Georgia, with tall pillars of cypress carved and painted to look like marble columns. It was set in among gardens that had once been her family's pride, tended by eight slaves whose sole job had been to keep them flowering as long as possible.

The gardens lay tangled and wild now, the roses running riot in the May warmth, drowsy with the sound of bumblebees and birds. Lavinia tended a corner of the garden that contained her favorite rosebushes; they had been pruned before the fighting, but now they were crying for her attention.

But then so were the chickens.

She swung her split oak bucket from its rope handle and watched as the chickens came crowding about her. She caught the faintly sweet, faintly musty scent of their feathers. They moved with dancing deliberation, their staccato clucking punctuated and underscored by the plaintive peeping of the hordes of chicks that scurried about beneath their feet.

She dipped her hand into the bucket and scattered a handful of crumbs hoarded from the meals in her house. It was fortunate that the army had turned the rations for its wounded over to her; by skimping on her own share, she had managed to garner enough hard bread to feed the chickens each day.

It was odd, she reflected, how our dearest wishes always come true. She could remember watching the chickens as a child, fascinated by the glint of sunlight on shining feathers, by the dry, cool, grainy feel of the crushed corn in her hands, by the yellow arc it made when thrown, the sounds of the chickens strutting and clucking about her feet. She could remember begging to be allowed to feed them, herself, and she could remember her bewilderment and fury when she was told that it was field hands' work. She had cried and begged and ultimately been banished to her room for the endless length of a fine June day, but she had always wished...

Well, now she could feed the chickens any day she chose—and woe to her if they weren't fed, for there would be no chickens to eat! She scattered more crumbs and watched the birds scurry after them, led by the old russet-necked fighting cock who had ruled the yard for the past four years. A quick count showed that two were missing since their feeding the day before. Lavinia sighed and wondered if she would have any chickens left after the army was gone. It was fortunate that she had a goodly crop of peepers available to repopulate the henhouses.

For that matter, she wondered if she would have any livestock left. Her father's four fine thoroughbreds and her own hunter had been appropriated by the Confederate army in early 1862. The family's fat, elderly carriage horses had been the next to go, followed by her old pony. She had watched, dry-eyed, as they had been led off. She had stuffed the payment—a handful of worthless paper bills—into her pocket. Now all but three of the milch cows were gone, as well; she had taken the precaution of driving the remaining cows and their calves into the woods in the hope that it would keep them from being taken.

She looked back down at the chickens and upended the bucket. "That's all today," she said, dusting her hands upon her apron and then pushing back the strands of hair that had worked their way loose from the heavy, severe chignon at the base of her neck and were now tickling her lips.

She looked up at the sky; the sun was still low, so it was barely 9:00. In older days she would still have been luxuriously abed, drinking her morning chocolate. She didn't bother to calculate how long ago that had been. She had friends in Virginia and they corresponded regularly. Chocolate did not matter; she was grateful to have a bed at all, from what they told her.

She lifted her face into the wind and gathered her skirts. She knew she should be wearing her sunbonnet. Her mother had always told her that sun and wind would spoil a lady's complexion and scare away the beaux, but since there were no beaux to scare away and she was mistress of Wheelerville now, albeit a sadly diminished Wheelerville, she could do as she pleased. And anyhow, there was firewood to split, since she had barely enough wood to get her through the next two days, and something would have to be done quickly.

She did not like to think of that: she had never yet begged for help from anyone in the town, but she knew her own strength, and she also knew that Callie and George, both in their seventies, weren't strong enough to do any heavy work, nor was Callie's granddaughter, Bathsheba.

Along with managing her family's extensive business endeavors, she had had years of experience as the head lady of a large farming concern, but all but the last two of those years had been experienced while having a full complement of slaves at her command. Now there was no one there but herself and her three remaining servants. She thought the field hands would probably be returning within the next several days, but until then something would have to be done, and she did not quite know what. With badly wounded men quartered at her house, she needed hot water on a regular basis.

She pushed her hair out of her eyes again. It bore thought, but not a lot, not at this moment. She supposed she could appeal to General Stanley for help, but she had done so once already and she did not like the notion of repeating the appeal. If only she had thought to mention it the night before! She needed to pause and catch her breath. There was so much happening that required her to think and be strong for everyone. She looked up at the house again as she circled it, and when she was standing squarely in front of it, she turned away from the trees back toward the sun. And took an involuntary step backward.

A lone horseman was approaching her across the lawn. The rider sat still and square in the saddle with only a slight motion of his hips cushioning the movement of his mount. The sun, hovering behind his left shoulder, turned him to a black silhouette against the bright sky. He paused, then touched the horse lightly with his heels. His mount tucked its chin in and ambled toward her.

He drew rein before her. The tall chestnut mare, stretching down out of the sun to nuzzle her shoulder and then snuffle at her skirt, was firmly called to order and nudged sideways with a touch of the man's heel so that Lavinia did not have to peer up into the sun. He was no longer a shadow in the morning, but now the light picked out alarming details of brass, yellow braid, leather and steel.

A steel-sheathed saber was strapped to his saddle beneath his left thigh, and a carbine hung from a heavy leather strap at his right. His cap was adorned with a brass badge shaped like a pair of crossed swords, and the amount of yellow braid on his dark blue, high-necked jacket seemed to indicate some sort of rank: three rows of braid made a V just above his elbow, with three arcs of braid set above them. A diagonal stripe of red-edged yellow slanted across his right sleeve from the inner corner of his cuff to halfway up his forearm. A sling hid his left arm.

"Good morning, Ma'am," the man said, touching the leather visor of his cap with a gauntleted finger. His voice was deep and gentle, with the touch of a twang. "Is this the Wheeler house?"

She had been too busy staring to answer him; he repeated the question.

She blinked, pushed her hair out of her eyes once more, and looked up past the row of gilt buttons and the slanted leather strap into a lively pair of hazel eyes that were subjecting her to exactly the sort of appraisal she had been giving him. The man's straight mouth quirked as his eyes warmed in a way that Lavinia instinctively understood.

He was pleasant looking; Lavinia had no trouble applying the term 'handsome' to him. Her color rose. "Why-yes," she said. "Yes, it is." She added, "I am Lavinia Wheeler."

He nodded, slid his boot toes from the leather-hooded stirrups, swung his right leg across the cantle of the saddle, and dismounted. "Then Sergeant Major Asa Sheppard reports himself as arriving for duty, Miss," he said.

"What?" she gasped.

"By order of General Stanley, Miss," he said, taking out a folded paper from the breast of his jacket and offering it to her.

She took the note and opened it. The script was flowing and elegant, a gentleman's writing. She adjusted her spectacles and read:

By Authority of Miles G. Stanley, Major General, U.S.V.

A Safeguard is hereby granted to Miss Lavinia Wheeler, residing in the town of Wheelerville, Georgia, covering the person of Miss Wheeler and all properties and goods belonging to her, including a valuable collection of Early Colonial Pottery. All officers and soldiers belonging to the

Army of the United States are therefore commanded to respect this Safeguard and to afford, if necessary, protection to the person and property of Miss Lavinia Wheeler.

This instrument authorizes the Guard assigned to this duty to take whatever measures he deems appropriate to assure the safety of the person and property of Miss Lavinia Wheeler. This order can only be countermanded by myself or by one senior to me in rank.

Given at Headquarters this 14th day of May, 1864.
Miles G. Stanley Major General Commanding In Chief

She lowered the paper and looked at him. "What does this mean?" she demanded.

"The general has assigned you a Safeguard," he said.

"But I don't understand," she said.

"I've been stationed here to guard your property, Miss," he said. His voice gentled a little. "You can quarter me wherever will cause you the least trouble."

"I—I see," she said. She looked at him and he looked back at her as the silence lengthened. She realized that she couldn't spend the rest of the day standing on her front lawn and staring at him. "I am sorry, sir," she said. "Will you come into the house?"

"Thank you," he said. "Where would you like me to stable my horse?"

"The stables are behind the house," she said. "There's plenty of room for her, though fodder may be a problem."

"This haybelly wouldn't know what to do if you gave her proper fodder now," The sergeant said, loosening the mare's girth. "Once she's bestowed, I've a letter to you from the general."

"I'll take it now, Sergeant Major," she said, holding out her hand. "And then you can stable your horse and meet me indoors." He looked at her, then nodded and drew the letter out from his sling. She noticed the glistening white cloth as though for the first time. Now that she was actually looking at him, she could see that he was pale and a little heavy-eyed. "Why, you're hurt, sir!" she said, stepping forward to touch the sling with gentle fingertips. "I should have noticed it sooner. Forgive me! And you seem tired: no wonder, if you're wounded.

You'd best sit down on the porch. I'll have my butler see to unsaddling and stabling your horse. He can carry your packs inside, and I'll bring you some cooled water when you come in. Have you eaten yet this morning?"

The man's face was full of a strange, touched surprise before it eased into a slightly unsteady smile. He blinked twice and looked down and away. His voice was gentle and even a little hesitant when he spoke.

"Don't worry about me, Miss Wheeler," he said. "I'm here to worry about you. I'll take my horse to her stable and then you can show me my charges." He nodded toward a familiar, cloth-wrapped bundle strapped to the cantle of the saddle and plucked the knots loose one-handed. "And I'd best return this to you now with General Stanley's thanks," he said, offering it to her.

He watched her take it and added, "It's an odd sort of thing, isn't it? Did they put death masks on jugs back in colonial times?"

"What?" she demanded.

"Death masks," he repeated. "That's what it looks like to me at any rate. Maybe they did it to keep people from draining the tipple." And he met her affronted stare with those lively hazel eyes as he turned to lead his horse to the stable.

Lavinia gazed after him with narrowed eyes. Had he been daring to bait her? He had certainly given her a most detestable smile as he turned away. She opened the cloths about the jug and looked down into the face. Well, perhaps an untutored person might view it as a death mask; indeed, aside from all it signified to her of hopes followed and realized, hardships faced and conquered, it was not a beautiful piece.

She looked up again. The horse was moving easily, and Sergeant Sheppard's grip on the reins appeared to be reflexive rather than necessary. Both were well-groomed and well-set-up. If she must have another pair of mouths to provide for out of her sadly understaffed home, she thought, they might as well be presentable.

She started to look away, but the flash of white sling against the man's dark blue uniform jacket caught her attention again.

She shook her head and called herself a fool. She looked toward the house and saw George, who had been her family's butler since before her birth, standing in the doorway. She motioned him over.

"Miss Lavinia?" he said.

She smiled up at him. "George," she said, "Would you please follow Sergeant Sheppard to the stables and help him unsaddle and unpack his horse? He's wounded, and the harness looks heavy. Once that is done, please bring him to me in the good parlor.""Very good, Miss Vinnie," George said. "And Dr. Haskell's here."

Lavinia nodded and hurried toward the house, combing through her loosened hair with her fingers and praying that the mass would not come tumbling down about her shoulders.

CHAPTER SIX

"I was about to put my head in to take a quick look at the patients, Miss Wheeler," said Major Charles Haskell, chief surgeon for the Army of the Monongahela, as he bowed over Lavinia's hand. "I had wanted to wait until you arrived, though. If they continue to improve as they have up to now, I can leave them with you with an easy mind."

Lavinia smiled as he straightened, then nodded to the two hospital stewards who were flanking him. "You could have gone ahead, Major Haskell," she said. "You have been a welcome presence in this house any time this past week, as you well know. And are you improved today, yourself, sir?"

"I am well enough, dear Madam, for an old man," Haskell said as Lavinia took his arm and strolled with him into the ballroom. "And I am all the better for seeing a beautiful woman like yourself this beautiful day," he said

He was a courtly, silver-haired man in his late fifties. He had left a flourishing practice in Hartford, Connecticut, to serve in the armies because, he said, it was a surgeon's duty to ease suffering wherever it could be found, and he knew of no place where suffering could be found in greater abundance than in the armies of the United States of America and its enemy in this current conflict. Lavinia had watched him at work directing his team of physicians during the chaotic aftermath of the battle, and it had given her a profound respect for his skill as a physician and affection for him as a man.

Lavinia pushed a tendril of hair behind her ear. "You're too kind, sir," she said, looking down at the rows of cots that had been set up along the windows on the north side of the room. The occupants were watching the door with bright-eyed interest that broadened into smiles as she entered with Dr. Haskell.

Only Lavinia heard the slow, grieved intake of his breath before he stepped forward with his best smile. "Well, gentlemen," he said, "I see you're awake and aware. Which of you needs looking at first?"

** ** **

"It will get worse before it gets better, Miss Wheeler," Major Haskell said a little later over a cup of tea. "I can name about eight who will not see tomorrow's sunrise."

Lavinia looked down at her cup. "They're so young," she said. She looked up to see Major Haskell watching her with concern.

"You yourself are very little older than they, however weary you're feeling at this moment," he said. "Take heart, my dear lady: things will improve, no matter what happens."

Lavinia looked down again. "Will—will Corporal Higgins and Private Pierce improve, at least?" she asked.

Haskell looked thoughtful. Geoffrey Higgins was an artillery corporal in his late twenties. He had been brought into the house, all six feet and two hundred pounds of him. Pain and fever had whittled away sixty pounds almost overnight; he was heartbreakingly thin and pale now. He had been delirious with the pain of his shattered leg, and Lavinia had held him as he alternately cried for his wife and prayed for death. "He's doing much better," Haskell said at last. "He has a good, strong pulse, and the stump isn't oozing, though I could feel a little heat... But that's good, all in all. If we can hold off infection long enough to allow the healing to begin, he'll live. If we can salvage his knee joint, he'll walk again without much trouble. If, if, if. But his age and his condition are in his favor. But Private Pierce, now..."

Lavinia watched him anxiously. Private Pierce had been struck several times through the abdomen and chest, and he had been carried to her house with a collapsed lung and a badly perforated bowel that had necessitated a complicated operation removing five feet of bowel. The chest wounds made him susceptible to chills in the lung, and they were moving slowly with him for fear that he might suffer a fatal infection.

"Again, his age and his condition are in his favor," Haskell said. "But he is wounded in the bowels. He may well die." He respected Lavinia's silence for a moment and then said, "It's hard to keep from having favorites, I know. He was married so recently and his wife may be in a delicate condition... He may be inclined to despair, and that could kill him more quickly than the wounds. Let him speak of his wife since he loves her so much. She'll be his lodestar, and all the dearer when he gets home to her, which I dare say he will."

Lavinia smiled a little unsteadily. "You give me hope, Major," she said.

"That's something you should never allow yourself to lose," he said. "It's unnecessary and foolish. Did you send my note to General Stanley?"

Lavinia was touched by the concern in his voice. "I did, sir," she said. "He told me that he would give some thought to what could be done, and he issued an order that I am not to be molested." She frowned a little and added, "Though I don't believe the men of this army would molest me."

"You cannot tell, Madam," Dr. Haskell said. "The general's protection may serve a good purpose, and he's a man of his word: you will hear further from him."

"But I did, sir," she said. "A Safeguard was assigned to this house. He arrived just this morning, as I was coming into the house."

"That's very good to hear," Dr. Haskell said. His voice grew brisker. "I have ordered that you be brought some supplies that I think you'll need once the army moves out. Coffee, sugar, flour—several hundredweight of that should last you a while—and lengths of cloth and such. You will have a well-stocked dispensary. I personally selected some of the items for you, Ma'am, if you will come and see them."

"That is kind of you, Doctor," Lavinia said. She rose and walked beside him.

Dr. Haskell waved the comment away. "Oh, not at all," he said. "But more than that, I've left you a store of medicines, including morphia. But please be careful of it. It is so easy to abuse, especially by those in pain who have no vision beyond their current discomfort to understand that they are stepping into a worse hell than pain."

"I will keep it under lock and key, Doctor," Lavinia said, quietly closing the parlor door behind her. "If you will write up any instructions you may have, I will see that they are followed."

Dr. Haskell nodded. "It will be done, Miss Wheeler," he said. He hesitated and then added, "I have concocted a tonic for you, as well, and I have written down the formula. You aren't robust, yourself, madam, and I think it will strengthen you. The ingredients are easily found—spinach, for example, and other common herbs—and I strongly suggest, as a surgeon and as a man who has daughters of his own, that you avail yourself of the tonic and the recipe."

Lavinia lowered her eyes, touched by the wholeheartedness of his concern. "I thank you for your care, Doctor," she said. "I shall take some of that tonic this very evening."

"That's good," he said. "I thought to—" His sentence was interrupted by the sound of the front door closing, followed by George's cough.

"What is it, my good fellow?" Haskell asked, looking at George over his glasses.

"Begging your pardon, sir," George said, "Miss Lavinia asked me to tell her when the Sergeant Major came in."

"Sergeant Major-?" Haskell repeated. "Is he the man that General Stanley stationed here, then, Miss Wheeler?"

"That is correct, Doctor," Lavinia said, moving through the pocket doors and into the entry, where Sergeant Sheppard was waiting. "General Stanley was kind enough to assign him to me."

Although the sergeant's packs and weapons were set against the wall with his cap atop them, he was nowhere in immediate sight. She looked around and saw that he had mounted the staircase to the landing and was inspecting the carved mahogany banister with the delightedly intent expression of a man who has found a lost treasure against all hope or expectation. He straightened with a smile as he saw Lavinia come into the entry, and then stiffened to attention as Dr. Haskell followed her.

Haskell was frowning. "What the devil are you doing up there, sir?" he rasped. "Were you given permission to stroll through the house?"

"I couldn't help noticing this beautiful wood, sir," Sergeant Sheppard said. "It's Honduras mahogany. In fact, this house appears to be full of it—the finest I've ever seen. Look here: the workmanship is—"

"Never mind that, sir!" Haskell snapped. "Come down here at once!"

"Thank you, Sergeant," Lavinia interjected as the man descended to the hall. She caught a quick smile from him.

Haskell was subjecting Sergeant Sheppard to a comprehensive once-over, his eyes lingering on the sling, then raising to his face. "This is your Safeguard, madam?" he asked.

"Yes, Doctor," Lavinia replied. "This gentleman has been assigned to guard this house."

"His arm's in a sling," Haskell said. "And he looks to be running a fever. I wonder... May I see the order, madam?"

Lavinia handed it to him and watched him read. After a moment she looked over at the sergeant major, who was watching Dr. Haskell with a reserved expression. And no wonder, Lavinia thought, since she herself never liked to be discussed as though she were not there.

Dr. Haskell looked up when he was finished and handed the form back to Lavinia while eyeing Sergeant Sheppard. "Have you been passed as fit for this duty?" he demanded.

"Yes, sir," Sheppard replied. "My regimental surgeon gave me a paper to that effect."

"Your regimental surgeon?" Haskell mused. He flicked a glance at Sergeant Sheppard's cap. "Eighth Ohio Cavalry," he said. "Hm. Terence Bly: a contract surgeon." He said the words as though they were some sort of disease.

"Yes, sir," Sheppard replied. "I have the paper, if you'd like to see it."

"You'd do better to use it to wrap a smoke!" Dr. Haskell snorted. "The man's a thoroughgoing quack! Knowing him, I can't imagine he spent any time looking you over. Come here and let me look at you," he said. "Let me see that hand—no, don't take it out of the sling! You'll hurt yourself! Just hold still." He felt the fingers. "Warm, still, so the circulation's probably intact. Can you make a fist at all? Well, I suppose that's adequate. What do you have there?"

"It was a saber thrust, sir," Sheppard replied.

Major Haskell folded his arms and silently lifted his silver eyebrows.

Sergeant Major Sheppard returned the stare and then added, "It went into my shoulder, sir."

Haskell's eyebrows were still raised. "What kept you from bleeding to death, then, Sergeant?" he asked.

"Sir?"

Haskell's voice was crisp. "You've two major blood vessels that come together right at your shoulder," he said. "For that matter, you have an important joint right there: I would be very interested to learn why you still have an arm. Was it a slashing stroke? Or can you remember?"

Sergeant Major Sheppard's smile became a formidable frown. He said, with the touch of a drawl, "The saber entered here—" he lightly touched a spot on the sling about a hand's breadth in from the point of his shoulder. "—and was pulled out again."

"I see," said Haskell. "You were struck in the chest."

"My arm stopped working right after I was wounded," Sheppard said.

The two men traded stares. Haskell's mouth twitched. "Oh, very well, Sergeant," he said. "You're my match for mule-headedness. I'll concede the point. How long ago were you wounded?"

"It's been almost three weeks, sir," Sheppard said.

"Three—?" Haskell said. "That's all? And you've been returned to active duty? Hm. I'll lay a wager your scapula stopped the stroke and is bruised at the very least. And that's a saber wound—any sign of infection? No, wait. We're dealing with Dr. Bly. I'll have a look at you right away." He nodded to one of the stewards, who moved beside Sheppard. "Jones, undo his jacket and shirt and help him out of them. I don't want him moving that arm any more than he has to until I can be sure it's healing well."

Sergeant Sheppard twitched his sound shoulder away from the steward. "But sir," he began.

"I haven't all day to beat my gums with an impertinent fellow the age of my son, whom I'm half-inclined to send to a hospital after I give him a dressing-down," Haskell rapped out, peering at Sheppard over his glasses. "Now do as I order you!"

"Has the Major maybe forgotten that there's a lady present?" Sheppard said through his teeth.

Dr. Haskell blinked, looked over at Lavinia, and then bowed to her. "It appears that I have," he said. "I beg your pardon, Miss Wheeler. Jones, take the good Sergeant to the smaller sitting room and get him ready for me. I'll be in directly."

He nodded dismissal to the stewards and the sergeant and turned back to Lavinia. "Miss Wheeler," he said, "my apologies. I'll look the man over and tell you what I think. He's certainly got enough grit for the job: I haven't been so thoroughly sassed since I last was in Hartford with my grandchildren. But I don't want to add to your burdens by saddling you with another wounded man."

"Dr. Haskell, the sergeant is ready for you," said Jones. Haskell nodded to the man. "Excellent," he said. "Now take Miss Wheeler to the supplies and show her what we've brought."

** ** **

"He has a touch of fever, as I suspected," Dr. Haskell said later. "I've given him some quinine, which should help him. In fact," he said with the touch of a grin, "I gave him a good deal of quinine. I've left you some, by the way, which you may dispense to him and to the others as you see fit. Other than that, I've checked him out thoroughly, and he's healing well. He's a very healthy man in his mid-forties. Clean, outdoor life can often be very beneficial, and from what I can see, he's a sensible fellow who knows how to use his head."

He pulled his cuffs down. "Well, dear lady, I've given my full approval for Sergeant Sheppard to remain here, but with a few reservations. General Stanley personally picked this man to serve as your Safeguard. If it had been up to me, I'd have tried to send him home to New York to recuperate, but it would be all but impossible to accomplish here and now with this campaign on, so far from any base of operation. He'd be riding and marching with the army, and I think it would kill him. There've been enough good men killed already. At any rate, our good sergeant should take it easy for a couple of weeks. He should continue to use the sling for another three weeks, but gradually increase his use of that left arm. I've shown him a better way to tie a sling so there's more support for his wrist and he understands what he's to do. I've also ordered him to take a nap in the afternoons."

"I will keep that in mind, Doctor," Lavinia said with a smile.

"And now, Miss Wheeler, I'll make my adieux until tomorrow. The army will be moving on, as you know. I'll have a few days to show you what needs to be done with our wounded, here."

** ** **

Sergeant Major Asa Sheppard of the 8th Ohio Cavalry made his slow way up the stairs. His arm, firmly strapped and set into a businesslike sling, was not moving unless he took strong steps to make it. The quinine, which had been administered with a lavish hand, was making his ears ring, and all he wanted to do at the moment was to sit down and catch his breath.

Such a long time, such a hard road! He stopped at the landing, looked up at the stairs curving away before him in seemingly endless progression, and closed his eyes. When he opened them once more, it was to see a stern-faced old woman eyeing him. The white-haired man who had ushered him into Miss Wheeler's house was standing at her shoulder.

Sheppard pushed himself away from the wall, his sound hand to his head, and looked from the woman to the old man. "M-miss Wheeler..." he began.

The woman looked at the man and then at him. Her expression did not soften at all.

"I am assigned to guard Miss Wheeler," Sheppard said through the roaring in his ears. "Doctor Haskell—sent me—to—"

"Dr. Haskell?" The woman said in a surprisingly melodious voice. "What is he talking about, Brother?"

"He's the gentleman that general assigned to guard Miss Vinnie," The old man said. "Came to her this morning, Callie. He's been wounded—"

The woman tsked at him. "I can certainly see that, George," she said. "Poor lamb. Look at him, he's fevered. Take him along to the white room, the bed's newly made up there and the curtains are freshly washed. We'll put him to bed and I'll see what I can do to make him more at home."

The old man, George, set an arm about Sergeant Sheppard's waist and started up the stairs.

"No, wait," Sheppard said. "I can walk—I'm too heavy—"

"Don't be silly!" The old woman said. "Pay him no mind, George! And you, sir: do you have your things downstairs? I'll have Bathsheba bring them up for me." She lifted her head and peered up at the upper landing, where a pretty, dark-skinned young girl, about fifteen, was leaning over the railing and watching them with lifted eyebrows. "You heard me, child: get the man's gear and take it to the white room. And then come on up and give me a hand!"

The girl came nimbly down the stairs toward them. "But shouldn't he be with the other wounded, Grandma?" she asked.

"No, he shouldn't," George said, tightening his hold around Sheppard. "And you know very well why because you were cooling your heels and eavesdropping on your betters, Bathsheba! Go get the packs and come back up!"

"Right you are, Uncle George!" The girl said, and hurried down the stairs.

"There," said Callie. "Take him on up, George. And you, Sergeant—"

The question was very obvious. Sheppard smiled through the buzzing in his head and said, "Sheppard, Ma'am. Asa Sheppard."

She cocked her head at him. "Asa," she said. "A good, solid Bible name! Well, go on with you. Between and among us, we'll set you right!"

CHAPTER SEVEN

"You will be guarding these," Lavinia said, swinging the armoire doors wide to show the pottery collection. "They're the most valuable things in the house."

She stood aside and let Sergeant Major Sheppard take in the sight of the pottery arrayed by height on the shelves.

"They came from Roanoke colony," she said. "Formed out of the clay of Virginia and baked in the fires of the colonists—" She broke off at his expression, which was far from reverent. "Well?" she said.

"I've seen pottery like this before," Sheppard said.

"Oh?" she said. "Where? Massachusetts?"

He smiled at her. "They'd advanced beyond that sort of pottery by the time the pilgrims came over," he said. "No, I saw some like it in England once. It came from the wreckage of one of Henry VIII's palaces. It was found in a privy pit, as I recall. It hadn't been broken. Someone just threw it away, and no wonder."

"These are valuable, Sergeant!" she exclaimed. "Only think how old they are! Why, they used this sort of pottery in castles!"

"Udolpho, probably," he said.

Lavinia, who was known to read sensational novels when it suited her, understood the jibe and was not amused. "Sergeant!" she said. "This was made in Roanoke by the settlers!"

He lifted an eyebrow at the jug. "I wonder why," he mused. "I'd have thought they would have wanted to leave unpleasant things behind."

Lavinia frowned at him.

The frown had no effect. "So," he said. "The only use you have for me is to guard these pots?"

"Well, of course," Lavinia said. When he turned his hazel eyes on her and narrowed them thoughtfully, she widened her gray eyes at him and pushed her spectacles back on the bridge of her nose.

Lavinia had decided in the course of the morning that Sergeant

Major Asa Sheppard was a very vexatious man. He had said and done nothing offensive, but he had a very loud way of thinking, starting with the long, level look he had given her securely tidied hair when she had made her appearance at the breakfast table that morning.

He had been polite to the point of punctiliousness, rising to his feet whenever she or Callie stood or moved around until Callie, exasperated, had finally told him to stop hopping up and down like a flea on a griddle, for Heaven's sake, and behave himself.

He had come to their Spartan breakfast table fully dressed and impeccably washed and shaved even though George had reported that he had declined all offers of assistance. He had downed a cup of her dandelion root coffee without any appearance of relish, eyed the five eggs that Callie had fried up along with the few slivers of bacon sliced from their store, and then finally helped himself to exactly a fifth of what was on the platter. He had finished every last bit of it with an economy of movement that left Lavinia in no doubt that speed rather than enjoyment was his objective.

That had not been offensive in and of itself, but later, when she went to show him around the house and grounds, she had caught him quietly polishing off a square of hard army bread with every sign of relish.

He had listened to her protests in polite silence and then offered a piece to her with such a bland smile that she had itched to box his ears for him, and had thought she might actually be able to do so. She took it as a strong indication that Dr. Haskell's tonic was working.

She had restrained herself and taken him on the grand tour of the grounds, concluding with the pottery collection. He had listened with every appearance of interest, and had been flatteringly absorbed in her family's truly impressive collection of old furniture, but his reaction to the pottery had only confirmed her fears of the day before.

Well, he had his orders and it was too bad if he didn't like them.

"I've set up a chair for you," Lavinia said. "And here's a table where you can rest your musket, so your wounded arm won't get tired."

His brows drew together. "Miss Wheeler," he said.

She looked at him. "Yes, Sergeant?" she said.

"Do you mean to say you expect me to sit there from dawn to dusk and look at that collection of glorified mud p—that collection of pottery—with my carbine across my knees?"

"I have told you before, Sergeant, it's a valuable collection. General Stanley agreed with me on its value, and that's why you're here." She added with a touch of annoyance, "You may do as you wish with your gun."

"That's part of my assignment," Sergeant Sheppard said, "But there's a lot more to it than to sit here and gawk at a collection of ugly pots."

"They're very old, and their value is enhanced by their excellent condition!"

"I imagine no one wanted to touch them, and that's why they never got broken from being handled," Sheppard said.

She stared at him. "General Stanley sent you to guard those pots!" she stated.

"No, Miss Wheeler," he returned. "General Stanley sent me to guard you. You have better things to do with my time and your household's safety than having me sit with this collection of pottery."

She looked him up and down in exasperation. "I can't expect you to understand that these are quite the most valuable things on this entire plantation," she said in the tone of voice that always silenced argument.

It did not work with him. "Now that's a misstatement," he said. And then he added nothing else.

The flatness of the comment took her off-balance. "You are being impertinent, sir!" she snapped.

"Not impertinent," he said. "Just factual. That old man you call George is worth five hundred of those pots. So are any of the wounded fellows in your parlor—"

"I meant they were the most valuable of the objects on this plantation!"

"All right, then," he said. "If you want to talk about objects, then that big, black walnut Rhode Island highboy in the front bedroom is worth more than this entire collection or my name isn't Asa Sheppard and I didn't serve my apprenticeship in Philadelphia!"

"You are insolent, sir!" Lavinia said.

"I'm telling God's own truth," he said. "You don't need me to guard those things, Miss Wheeler. All you have to do is bury them in the yard. No one would dream of touching them even if they were found.

I'll bury them for you this afternoon, if you want."

She stared at him and he stared at her, and she suddenly realized that he was, after all, wounded and probably exhausted, and he had not had a chance to think things through. It must be infuriating for an active, lively man to be wounded and then cooped up in a room with a lot of inanimate objects. They could talk more later, and if he felt the pots were safe for the moment, why, they probably were.

"I shouldn't have expected so much of you right away, Sergeant," she began in a gentler voice than she had used before. "You are capable of walking around, and I tend to forget that you are recovering from a serious wound. Please forgive me."

His eyes flickered, and while he did not stand with his mouth open, his raised eyebrows were eloquent of surprise and even, oddly, disappointment.

Lavinia smiled and continued, "We can speak of guarding this collection another day. For now, some nice hot tea would probably sit well with you, and Callie can make some of her cornmeal and molasses biscuits. Come along downstairs, and I'll speak with her."

She swept toward the door.

"Now really, Miss Wheeler," he said.

She turned. "Did you say something, Sergeant?" she asked.

"Be honest, now," he said. "Was that fighting fair?"

She did not understand. "Fighting fair?" she repeated.

"That was taking unfair advantage of an opponent, Miss Wheeler," he said.

Her eyes met his, caught the spark of amusement, and kindled just as a knock sounded on the door: George, announcing General Stanley and his staff, come to pay his respects.

** ** **

"It's so green and peaceful here, with the wind coming through these old willows and sending the shadows racing across those green hills... Standing here, I can feel that this wasteful war is only the dregs of a bad dream." General Stanley let his eyes lower from the curtain of new-emerged willow leaves to the sweep of hills away to the west and finally the new-turned earth covering the rows of graves, each with its carved pine marker. He turned to Miss Wheeler. "It's generous of you, my dear ma'am, to give this beautiful land over to this purpose."

Lavinia gazed upon the lines of graves with shadowed eyes. "I saw so many of them die over the past days," she said. "There was so much courage, and so much pathos. How can I grudge them the little space they take up now, when their dreams and hopes once took up entire lifetimes, and their passing left other lives so empty? Some of them became dear to me during that short time, and I find that I mourn them just as much as those I knew and loved longer. I'll never forget them."

"But this was such a beautiful a spot!" Colonel Schuyler objected.

"I don't think it any less beautiful for their presence now," Lavinia said. "And in later years, when all quarrels are forgotten and their loved ones, from both sides, come here, they can take comfort and peace from the beauty of this spot." She turned away from the neat, quiet rows of mounded earth right into Sergeant Sheppard's hazel gaze. His unguarded expression made her pause before looking past him to General Stanley and his staff, ranged behind him.

"It is a humbling experience to encounter generosity and forgiveness when we are accustomed to encountering hatred and vengeance," General Stanley said. "You put me to shame, Miss Wheeler."

"But you and your force, General, have been generous to me and to my town," Lavinia said, gathering her skirts to step over one of the willow's roots.

Sergeant Sheppard moved forward to offer his arm. She took it with a smile at him and then nodded to the officers. "Well, gentlemen," she said with a resumption of briskness. "You have seen this place. As you can see, the names are carved into the headboards, and I have made a record of those buried here, as well. If their families contact me, I will be able to tell them where the remains of their loved ones are. It's little enough for me to do."

General Stanley nodded. "I am in your debt, Ma'am," he said. "And now, Miss Wheeler, with your leave, I'd like to see with my own eyes your collection of colonial pottery."

** ** **

General Stanley gazed across at the mountains, veiled by the rising mists of late afternoon. "We will be decamping within the next several days, Miss Wheeler," he said, raising the cup of coffee to his lips and then helping himself to one of Callie's cornmeal and molasses biscuits. "I would like to call upon you once again before I leave, but I have learned that haste is no respecter of persons, and I wouldn't have you thinking me remiss if I am unable to do so."

"I understand, General," Lavinia said.

They were sitting alone on her front porch. General Stanley had dismissed his staff, and Dr. Haskell had ordered that Sergeant Sheppard take his afternoon nap. The wind was rising, bringing a slight chill. Lavinia drew her shawl more closely about her shoulders.

General Stanley rose and strolled to one of the house's cypress columns and looked up at the capital. "I have sent word to the families of those who are convalescing here. They may try to send letters. In times like this, with all so unsure, I don't even know if they will reach me, but if they do, then I will do my utmost to send them on to Wheelerville."

Lavinia smoothed the fringe of her shawl and smiled up at him. "That would be splendid, General," she said. "News from loved ones is the best medicine I could offer my patients."

"Excellent," Stanley said. "And now as to yourself: I have given strict orders to all my forces and, through them, to the rest of the Federal forces. Wheelerville and Fairlawn are to be respected. No foragers are to come through and levy upon you, and there's to be no destruction of your property. You have seen for yourself that we have dismantled the defensive works, for the most part, and all the debris, of whatever sort, was cleared away or buried, as much as could be done."

"That's very generous of you, General," Lavinia said. "But you, sir: why do you do all this for me? I am sure that you must know that my family has supported the Confederacy."

Stanley went back to his chair. "To be honest, Miss Wheeler," he said, "I am not sure. From our first meeting, I felt as though— Well, Madam, as though I could welcome you as a friend. To be honest, again, you first made me laugh, and then you made me admire you. I believe my wife would feel the same. She's like you in many ways, a generous, kind, noble woman—and perhaps someday, when this dehumanizing war is over, I will be able to give her the pleasure of meeting you. For now, for her sake and my own, I would like to offer my services as your friend and protector, and I beg that you will not hesitate to accept them."

"Thank you, General," she said with a smile. "How can I possibly refuse so kind an offer?"

It was not until after he had left that she remembered she needed firewood.

CHAPTER EIGHT

The sound of firing rolls across the fields, muffled by the smoke to a continuous crackling, no more threatening than the sound of firecrackers on the Fourth of July. Blossoms of smoke blowing acrid and burning across his eyes as he gazes down at the row of brass cannon before him. The charge took the gun crews unawares; he sees five undamaged cannon with their caissons and limbers. Rammers and sponges lie abandoned on the ground among the wreckage of one of the teams.

He loosens his reins and looks beyond the blue-coated troopers who have followed him across the valley and through the hail of bullets to this commanding spot. The approaching glitter of light beyond them makes his brows drive together in a sudden frown. No time to waste. He motions to the men around him and jumps from the saddle, but another voice, shrill with panic, sounds before he can speak.

They're coming back, Sarge! They're coming back!

Let 'em come, he says. We'll turn these guns and give them a bellyful of their own grapeshot. Get the rest of the boys here on the double, and heave!

The white-eyed trooper before him gapes at the guns and at the lines of gray- and butternut-clad men whooping and yelling toward him. For Chrissakes, Sarge! We'll be killed for sure!

He chokes back the irritation building within him. God almighty, Renquist! Is there ever a time you DON'T panic? Get your butt off that damned nag and help me turn this gun! And the rest of you jackasses in pants stop gawking like a pack of hicks and do the same! I can see that half these guns are loaded. We can send a volley into them right away and reload at our leisure! Now come on!

It works. Booted feet thud to the ground, hands reach out to grip the wheels and pivot the guns. Some of the men start loading the empty pieces.

He watches with satisfaction. That's it. Now sight them—look right along the barrel, like you would a gun. Fire!

The brazen guns leap and bellow, belching flame. He peers through the thickening smoke and sees a swath of open field lying before them where the foe had stood thickest.

That's the way! He cries. Reload! Quickly now, quickly!

Hooves rattle on the ground, more felt than heard in the noise and the firing. The flash of a saber as it hisses into its sheath. What the devil are you doing, Sheppard?

He grins and wipes his forearm across his eyes and squints up at his regimental adjutant through the glare and the smoke. We captured this battery, Lieutenant, and now we're giving them a dose of their own medicine while we wait for the infantry to come up.

The Lieutenant nods and starts to speak. He flinches sharply sideways and sags as a flower of red blossoms at his side.

He moves forward to support the Lieutenant. Best get to the rear, sir! We'll hold them off! He nods to one of the troopers and watches the Lieutenant ride off, the man beside him. He turns his attention back to the guns.

The fight is heating up; minutes pass, endless in the glare and the noise. A bullet burns along his thigh; the wound bleeds sluggishly.

In the automatic motion of servicing the guns and shouting orders, some quiet, cool corner of his mind remembers warm summer evenings beside Seneca Lake in upstate New York, drilling with the militia and firing the city's three guns. Bands were playing then, drums providing a sort of thunder that is more than adequately supplied now by the rattle of musket fire.

Another bullet flattens itself on the barrel of his cannon. He flicks it off with a thumbnail and keeps shouting orders as his men move through the drill of the guns, each shot tearing holes through the enemy.

One of the new recruits turns to him. White teeth flash from his smoke-grimed face. By God, by God, they're putting up one hell of a scrap, Sarge!

He grins back, but then frowns at the field behind him. Never mind the scrap, Perkins! Where the hell's the infantry?

Here they come again!

He curses. We'll fire two of these guns. The rest of you, take cover and use your carbines. They don't have repeaters: we can keep up the rate of firing and mow 'em down. It'll be like shooting fish in a barrel. Move!

Forms surging toward them, wavering, melting into the earth before the force of their fire, and yet coming onward, as unstoppable as the tide.

He rams another charge home and takes the lanyard in his fist. If we can hold these guns, they won't be able to use them against the infantry—

A deep, booming cheer roars across the fields behind them. He looks and sees the blue ranks surging forward through the smoke, but the gray and butternut lines are closer. In the flash of a moment he sees the damage that could be wrought by the guns.

Hold tight! he shouts. Don't let them retake these! He turns to look at his own army; he hears hoofbeats behind him and the next moment a terrific blow sends him spinning to the ground.

Hooves thunder beside him; he rolls to his feet, shielding his head with his arms. He pulls at his pistol, bringing it up with his left hand as a bolt of curved, gleaming steel lances toward him.

He throws his arm up in an attempt to deflect the stroke and glimpses the face behind the blade, set mouth, cold, deadly eyes. Metal tears across cloth, clashes sickeningly against a button, and then drives deep into his chest.

The pistol falls from nerveless fingers. The lanyard's toggle grip is still in his right hand; he yanks it aside and down with the last of his strength. The cannon roars and leaps with the explosion, but he hears nothing as the world revolves with increasing slowness until it is still and dark.

Why, you're hurt, sir! It is a woman's soft voice that he hears, and when he struggles through the pain and the noise to gaze out through darkening eyes, he sees a woman's face bending over him: wide gray eyes behind spectacles, and a face framed by softly falling coils of mahogany hair; gentle fingertips are touching his bloody shoulder. I should have noticed it sooner. And you seem tired...

** ** **

Asa Sheppard opened his eyes to warmth and light and a faint, flower-scented breeze across his lips. He had been dreaming. It was mid-May now, he remembered. The battle had been over for more than two weeks. He remembered, as well, almost inconsequently, that it had been a victory.

He sighed, crossed one booted foot over the other and closed his eyes again. The afternoon sun was pleasantly warm across his shoulders. He could feel it through Major Haskell's workmanlike bandage, sinking into the wound, warming it, making the flesh renew itself and grow strong.

He sighed again and let himself sink more deeply into the healing warmth. He had been cold for so long, and exhausted for so much longer, it was a blessing beyond belief to be able to doze in the sun.

He looked down at his hand and moved his fingers. He was healing: he could move them without much pain now. But the pain had awakened him and there was such a thing as dozing too long.

He drew a long breath of the soft air and then reached inside the breast of his jacket for his pipe, tobacco and matches. He set the pipe between his drawn-up knees and tamped his last full measure of tobacco into it one-handed.

When it was filled to his satisfaction, he struck a match against the side seam of his trousers and then, when it flared, held pipe and match in one hand and brought them to his mouth. It worked this time without singeing his fingers. He blew out the match and carefully set it aside.

There. The day was warm and pleasant, his pipe was drawing nicely, and the only things lacking were the absence of pain in his shoulder and peace in the land. Well, at least he had found a small corner of relative serenity, away from the constant movement, noise and exhaustion that had nearly killed him. There had been no time to pause, to gather his strength, to allow his hurts to heal, and he had felt himself sinking downward into increasing weakness He probably would have died if it had continued.

All that had changed four days ago, when Colonel Schuyler had arrived at his tent and told him that the commander of the army wished to speak with him, and then had added that he would be personally packing Sheppard's gear while he was with General Stanley.

The interview had been an interesting one. General Stanley had offered him a chair. When he was seated, Stanley handed him one of the ugliest pieces of pottery that Sheppard had ever seen, and told him that he was being assigned to guard a valuable collection of pottery resembling it in every respect. The general had gone on to outline Sheppard's duties as he frowned at the piece.

He had been very precise as to the nature and scope of the assignment, and the sort of consideration and care he was to give to Miss Wheeler and the rest of her establishment. He had not played down the drawbacks and dangers of the situation, but he had pointed out that a good performance would certainly be rewarded. And then the talk had taken an odd twist.

General Stanley had fixed him with a considering gaze that seemed to miss nothing from Sheppard's tidy head of light brown hair to the polish of his boots and his clean white sling. He had folded his arms and said, "I've given your dossier a thorough review. You've been cited several times for gallantry and received two official commendations, with a third endorsed by me for that escapade with that captured battery in our last fight in Tennessee."

"Thank you, sir," Sheppard had said. "But I joined this army in order to fight against slavery and preserve the union, not to win commendations."

General Stanley had smiled again. "That was well said, Sergeant," he said. "We have the same motives." He had taken the jug back from Sheppard. "You're a widower, I understand," he said, setting the piece aside.

The question had been unexpected. Sheppard had frowned slightly. "Yes, sir," he had replied.

"I am truly sorry to hear of it," Stanley had said, turning back. "But I'd imagine that your experience with the married state has given you some knowledge of how to deal with women."

As though there's anything to it other than treating them like human beings,

Sheppard had thought wearily, shifting in his chair.

General Stanley had caught the motion. "I won't keep you much longer, Sergeant," he had said. "I consider this an important assignment and you come very highly recommended. You will find Miss Wheeler a charming lady who's experiencing some difficulties and needs someone she can rely on to protect her and hers. You need some light duty to give you a chance to get back on your feet, and I think this will answer very well for the two of you. Here's the order for —" he had handed it to Sheppard. "You'll see I've given you a good deal of latitude in the performance of your assignment. No one can crowd you or make you act with anything other than your own honor and good sense. And here's a letter from me to Miss Wheeler, which I ask you to give her after you have reported to her and shown her order. I'll do myself the honor of calling on her before this army pulls out, which shouldn't be for another couple of days."

Sheppard had taken the papers and tucked them into his sling. "Very well, sir," he had said. "I'll report to Miss Wheeler tomorrow morning."

General Stanley had nodded and tapped his fingers on the desk before him. "You can rest up during this stint of light duty in Wheelerville," he had said. "Do your best, and I'll see what I can do for you when this is all done."

The valediction and dismissal had been clear. Sheppard had gotten to his feet. "Thank you, sir," he had said.

"And give my respects to Miss Wheeler."

** ** **

Light duty.

Colonel Schuyler had described the assignment as 'light duty', as well, but Asa Sheppard had his doubts after looking into the situation over the past three days. There might not be much in the way of active fighting, but the place was understaffed, food was scarce, and the people in charge were obviously incapable of doing anything resembling heavy work.

As though you can, Asa, he thought.

He flexed his fingers again. How could a thin, narrow length of steel have done this much damage? Three more weeks in the sling, then at least a month trying to strengthen the arm. And how was he expected to be any sort of guard in this condition, weak as a kitten, heavy-eyed, and embarrassingly prone to getting choked up at the slightest thing?

He closed his eyes and leaned his head back. Dr. Haskell had said that an afternoon nap was just what he needed to help him think things through. He thought he might as well continue the one he had started. He sighed and began to relax in the afternoon warmth.

The sound of a door opening and then closing brought him fully awake again. He cocked his head, listening. A woman's light footsteps: probably Miss Wheeler's.

She was hard to figure. He could see that she knew how to use her tongue, but he had not yet heard her raise her voice. He had seen the way she dealt with those who were sick or injured, and had had a sample, himself, of her capabilities in that field. How had she come to run this large concern all by herself?

He had seen the graves in the family plot behind the house, and the headstone for one Gaylord Wheeler had been something of a revelation. A younger brother, in the army, dead in his mid-twenties. It gave him an impression of wasted youth, of talents brought to nothing. And there was Miss Wheeler herself, with that wealth of rich, red-brown hair screwed so tightly back into a knot after his first glimpse of it, as surely buried and forgotten in the eyes of this southern society as her brother.

As he thought this, he saw her moving almost stealthily down the garden path, something held in her hand and hidden in the folds of her skirt. Interesting, he thought, pushing his chair forward and getting to his feet. It was not a good time of day for anyone to be abroad in unsettled times with bushwhackers and looters scattered in the wake of the armies. He decided to follow her at a discreet distance and see what she was up to.

** ** **

Twenty minutes later, in possession of all the facts, he took a position in among the trees behind the house.

Chopping wood? Miss Wheeler? He'd had her pegged as a spunky little thing from their first meeting, but this beat all. The past few years must have been terribly hard for a lady born and bred, as she obviously was, and somehow she had managed to get by, but he doubted she was strong enough to chop the wood needed to fuel a fair-sized household, even if she had the courage to attempt it. If she wasn't careful she would end up killing herself.

He frowned and cocked his head. Look at that! She was holding the axe all wrong, and she didn't know enough to rub dirt on her hands to help avoid tearing her palms.

He shook his head and drew on his pipe one last time. He couldn't leave Miss Wheeler out here all by herself, especially so soon after an army had passed by. He had had all too much experience with the activities of the skulkers and raiders that rode afield from the armies, but by the same token he was beginning to get a good idea of Miss Wheeler's way of looking at things. From what he'd seen of her, she would order him back to his room if he offered to help her. She wouldn't take kindly to being spied on, and the smell of pipe tobacco was guaranteed to give him away.

With the pipe out he could keep an eye on her unbeknown until she came inside. Pity to waste his last full bowl of tobacco, but three hard years of campaigning had made him philosophical. This was the south, and they grew tobacco here. He could look into getting some more in the morning. In the meantime Miss Wheeler could no doubt cope with some gentle wood chopping; God knew, it would be the last for a good, long time if Asa Sheppard had any say in the matter.

He knocked his pipe out against the heel of his boot, blew in the bowl to make certain it was really out, then stowed it in the inner breast pocket of his jacket. He set his right shoulder against his tree, shoved his right hand into the pocket of his breeches, and settled himself in to stand guard.

CHAPTER NINE

The town of Wheelerville was uncomfortably aware that it had not done itself much credit during the recent fighting, even though their support of the Confederate war effort in supplies and men, some of whom now lay in the town's two churchyards, had been wholehearted. The citizens, who had almost to a man packed up and fled at the approach of the armies, were mostly returned now, but the streets still had an empty, somehow furtive look about them. It had been a time of acute humiliation, to spend a week huddling in the woods missing various items essential to comfort, for panic is not conducive to intelligent packing, and then to return to find the town overrun with the hated blue uniforms and be forced to run the gauntlet of insolently amused eyes and punctilious correctness.

The crowning blow had come with the news that Miss Lavinia Wheeler, who had been alone except for her two oldest servants and a teen-aged housemaid, had braved the bombardment and then opened her home to the wounded. Her courage and generosity were the reason that the town's neat brick and clapboard houses and buildings had been left unmolested and relatively clean, all dead horses disposed of, all bodies decently buried, all debris moved aside. They had even dismantled the *chevaux de frise* left by the retreating Confederate forces and piled them aside. All this should have been gratifying, but the townsfolk found it humiliating.

The two days since the departure of the Army of the Monongahela for the southeast and its projected rendezvous with the rest of Sherman's forces at Atlanta had been quiet, but everyone had a sense of waiting and watching. People looked out their windows, and whispers ran up and down the street.

** ** **

Asa Sheppard drew rein and looked around. He could almost feel the whispers stirring the heavy air as Dixie, his chestnut mare, ambled up the main street of the town. He could feel eyes peering at him through curtains; doors were cracked here and there, windows were slid shut as he approached. He could hear muttered words and the click of metal.

He took a deep breath. He had not expected this to be easy, but after the generous way the army had treated Wheelerville, he had hoped... There was nothing for it but to knock on a door and hope that someone would answer, and that that someone would not be holding a loaded, cocked firearm. A door opened down the street from him; a tall, stringy youngster, about fifteen, stepped onto his porch with a musket held muzzle-down in the crook of his arm.

Sheppard turned his mount with his knee and rode over to him. "Good morning," he said, raising his bridle hand to show that it was empty of weapons.

The boy eyed him in a reserved sort of way, but finally nodded. "Morning," he said in a voice that had only recently achieved depth and seemed about to squeak upward again. His musket remained where it was.

Sheppard said, "You can see my holster's securely buttoned and out of easy reach, and I'm not carrying anything in my hand. I'm not looking for any trouble. I just need some information."

The boy's somber expression eased a little. "Yeah," he said. "I noticed you're shy a wing. I guess I won't shoot you today. Not unless you try something pretty bad." He cocked his head and frowned at Sheppard's horse. "If you're looking for your fellow Yanks, they headed that way." He nodded southeast. "Going a good clip," he added. "You'll be able to catch up with them if you hurry."

Sheppard's hazel eyes lightened in a smile as he flexed the fingers that were half-hidden by his sling. "I'm not interested in catching up with them," he said.

"Then why're you here, Yank?" the boy asked.

"I'm assigned to stay in this town as a guard until your folks or mine come back," Sheppard said. "After that I'll be rejoining my unit."

The boy frowned at him.

"Are you the militia for this town?" Sheppard asked.

The boy's frown lightened a little. "Not hardly," he said. "I saw you and thought I'd best stick my head outside and see what you wanted."

"Fair enough," Sheppard said. "Now why don't you uncock that squirrel rifle and set it down so I can tell you what I want?"

The boy grinned suddenly. "My ma says my manners're pretty bad, and I guess she's right," he said, easing the hammer down and then setting the musket aside. "Though I don't rightly know what's owed to the enemy. But you aren't trying to kill me, so I don't know... There, it's down." He added, "I'm Abner Wigfall."

Sheppard nodded. "Asa Sheppard's my name," he said. "Sergeant Major of cavalry. I'm looking for the Justice of the Peace for this town, or whoever does a similar job. Can you tell me where to find him?"

"What do you want him for?" Abner asked. "Heck, you Yankees took over the town!"

Sheppard grinned at him. "Yes," he said, "And there sure are a lot of us running the place, aren't there?"

Abner blinked.

"Now let's be serious," Sheppard said. "For all that there's a war going on and a lot of people have been hurt and killed fighting it, I'm a law-abiding man. I'm in your town as a visitor and I want to report to the law in this town. I want to let him know whom I am and why I'm here. Now where is he?"

Abner considered. "You want to talk to Judge Prescott," he said. "We had a sheriff—that was my pa—but he's in Virginia at the moment and not likely to return any time soon."

Sheppard's expression shifted to understanding and sympathy. "In the army?" he asked.

Abner nodded silently.

"I came up against some Georgia cavalry a couple of fights back in Tennessee," he said. "They were tough. Very tough. One of them gave me this arm as a souvenir. He got clean away, too. He was probably just like your pa, if he's a trooper."

Abner's smile was unsteady, but it was there. "Thank you kindly for that," he said. "My dad's tough, all right, but he's an infantry lieutenant. He's with General Lee at the moment."

"Then he's a holy terror, and no doubt of it," Sheppard said. "He must be proud of you: from what I've seen, he's got a right to be."

The talk was welcome, but it was obvious that Abner wouldn't be able to continue along its track and still be able to speak. He said gruffly, through a constricted throat, "You'll want to talk to Judge

Prescott, like I said. Go to the right at the next street, and he's in the big stucco house painted brown."

"Excellent," said Sergeant Sheppard. "I'll go to him right away. And thanks."

"Any time, Yank," Abner said. He watched Sheppard gather his reins in his right hand. "Sergeant?" he said.

Sheppard looked at him.

"If you come again and give some warning, I'll give you some buttermilk."

** ** **

Alexander Prescott looked down at General Stanley's Safeguard order and then nodded. "Very well, sir," he said. "I'll make a note of your presence, and if you're needed I'll certainly contact you. I'll also take a moment to make a fair copy of this Safeguard order to put on record, if you don't object to it. If there's any trouble, I'll vouch for you, as will Miss Wheeler, I would imagine."

"That's good," Sergeant Sheppard said. He was seated in a comfortably upholstered chair with a glass of cool water at his elbow and a plate of bread and butter pickles beside it.

He had knocked on Judge Prescott's door twenty minutes before and been admitted by a tall, silver-haired gentleman with a soft way of speaking. The man had listened courteously to Sheppard's concern and then had admitted to being Judge Prescott. He had taken in Sheppard's sling and had insisted on escorting him to his well-appointed study and giving to him the most comfortable chair, waving aside Sheppard's protests with a smile.

Sheppard had taken the chair, outlined his duties as succinctly as possible, and shown Judge Prescott the paper. Refreshments had been offered, accepted and enjoyed, and now it was time to leave.

"Do you want me to report to you each week?" Sheppard asked.

Judge Prescott thought for a moment, and then shook his head. "No," he said. "I know your quality, and you know mine. As often as we encounter each other will be sufficient, and now that I think on it, you'll likely find it'll be more than weekly. And now, Sergeant, is there anything else I can do for you?"

Sheppard rose to his feet. "Direct me to your town's blacksmith," he said. "I need to get my hands on a maul."

****   **   ****

Wheelerville's forge was a tidy building set in the shade of some big maple trees. A long hitching rail fronted the forge, and a pile of scrap iron lay up against the side wall of the building. Sheppard noticed several broken, twisted musket barrels in among the other pieces of iron.

The smith had just taken a long, triangular piece of glowing iron from the fire and set it on the anvil. As Sheppard watched, he took a heavy pair of tongs, bent the wide end up and over a long, smooth bar of steel until it overlapped itself by two inches, and began to hammer the end. He looked up as Sheppard's shadow crossed the doorway; his lips tightened as he took in the uniform. "I'll be with you in a minute, if you don't mind," he said.

"I'm in no hurry," Sheppard replied, leaning his shoulder against the doorway and watching.

The smith nodded and bent to his hammering once more. When the weld was done to his satisfaction and the steel bar had been tapped out and set aside, he lifted the hinge from the anvil with a pair of tongs and dropped it into the water vat beside the forge. "I thought you folks had cleared out of Wheelerville," he said, turning to Sheppard at last.

"All but me," Sheppard replied. "I'm assigned to stay here as a Safeguard. My name's Asa Sheppard, and my unit's the 8th Ohio Cavalry."

"Sam Wallins," The blacksmith said. "A Safeguard, eh?" His eyes narrowed thoughtfully as he gazed through the rising clouds of steam from the water vat, and he paused to lift the hinge out again. "Doesn't appear you'll be able to do much guarding, the shape you're in at the moment."

"You might be surprised," Sheppard said.

Wallins eyed him and finally nodded. "I might, at that," he conceded, with a grudging smile. "Well, then, what are you guarding?"

"Anything belonging to Miss Wheeler," Sheppard replied. "You can look at General Stanley's order, if you like: I just showed it to Judge Prescott when I checked in with him."

"Wouldn't do me any good," Wallins said. "I can't read or write. Did your general know what he was letting you in for when he gave you the job?"

Sheppard lifted his eyebrows. "Guarding Miss Wheeler's property?" he said. "I don't think he had any doubts as to what he wanted me to do."

"I wonder," said Wallins.

"Why do you say that?" Sheppard asked. "What is there to guard beside her house and her property?"

"Nothing, really," Wallins said. "The problem lies in what is her house and her property. Miss Lavinia owns this entire town, lock, stock and barrel, including everyone's houses. Now she doesn't own what's in the houses, for the most part, but the houses and barns and outbuildings in Wheelerville are plenty in themselves. But then besides that, she's got a nice little plantation running about a thousand acres including slave quarters, plantation outbuildings like a well-set-up blacksmith shop, several smokehouses, a barn or two stuffed with bales of cotton, a sawmill with quite a few tons of good, seasoned timber, and a patch of hardwood forest that's another couple hundred acres."

"Good God!" Sheppard said. He leaned back against the wall and cradled his wounded arm against his chest. "They should have left a regiment!"

"I'd think so," Wallins said. "I'd say, in fact, that it appears to me, Yankee, that you've bitten off more than you can chew comfortably!"

Sheppard took a deep breath. "Well, they didn't leave a regiment," he said. "I've got the assignment, so I'd best do what I can. I've seen the horrors that happen where there's been fighting, and I'll keep it from happening here, if I can." He looked up at Wallins too late to catch the man's fleeting smile. "I came here to ask for the loan of a maul, master smith, if you have one," he said.

"A maul?" Wallins said, setting his hammer down. "Well, I do have one, and you're welcome to it, but it could stand sharpening. Is it urgent?"

"Not as urgent as it might be," Sheppard said. "Miss Wheeler's running short of firewood, and all her workers have run off. I'm the only one at the place strong enough to chop wood."

Wallins' eyes rested thoughtfully on Sheppard's wounded arm. "There's no one else there?" he asked.

"Just the two old folks named George and Callie, and a girl named Bathsheba," Sheppard said. "I can split kindling one-handed, so long as the big pieces are split first. I saw enough logs for kindling, but in about three days I'll need to split the bigger ones, and that'll take a maul."

Wallins nodded, but he still had some doubts. "I could come, myself," he said slowly. "There are a few strapping, healthy fellows right in the town, as well, who wouldn't be killed by a spell of hard work."

"No," said Sheppard. "Miss Wheeler's a proud woman. I don't think she'd look kindly on what she'd think of as charity. I'll split the wood for her."

"If it's charity coming from us, then why wouldn't it be coming from you?" Wallins demanded.

"I'd imagine she looks on me as a sort of servant," Sheppard said. "I'm a member of the household, and I'm eating at her table. She'd think I was earning my keep. I don't want to be taking advantage of her hospitality. Or anyone's here, come to that," he said. "It's been a rough couple of years, I'd imagine. No one deserves to suffer."

Wallins' expression contracted slightly. "Excuse me, Sergeant," he said, wiping his hand on his apron and holding it out. "I wasn't feeling too kindly toward you at first. I'd some close kin killed last year just about this time, but I don't imagine you're to blame for the cussedness of our two governments. You're a good man and I'd be glad to shake your hand."

Sheppard smiled at him. "Likewise," he said as they shook hands. "And thanks."

"Well, then," said Wallins. "Let me tell you that there's a goodly load of wood just outside town. Those defense things General Dillon put up were dismantled and piled aside. The logs with sharp branches set into them, I mean. Some of that wood is fit right at the moment for kindling, if you can get someone to haul it to Miss Wheeler's place."

"Fair enough," said Sheppard. "But I'll still need the maul."

"You'll have it," said Wallins. "But it needs sharpening, like I told you. Can I send it to you tomorrow?"

"That'll be soon enough," said Sheppard. "And I thank you. Now let me do you a good turn and warn you to be careful with those musket barrels you have in your scrap pile."

"What do you mean?" Wallins demanded.

"Most of the pieces you'll pick up on a battlefield are still loaded.

Get a 'worm' in there and work the charges out—and for God's sake do it far away from a fire! It could mean your life otherwise."

Wallins nodded. "I'll do that, Sergeant, and I'll thank you for the warning."

"No problem," said Sheppard. "Now you can do me a favor in return and tell me where I can find a store that sells some tobacco. I smoked my last pipe yesterday."

He wondered why Wallins suddenly looked so worried.

CHAPTER TEN

Sheppard understood Wallins' expression ten minutes later as he looked around the store. Barrels of supplies were clustered over at one end of the long room, with a counter behind them and shelves stocked with various yard goods and notions that had somehow survived the blockade. Closer to the door were several long trestle tables with stools. A tap was beyond that, and a long, low shelf crowded with pottery cups.

Several fellows in homespun breeches and checked shirts were standing before the tap, cups in hand, while three more sat at the tables, digging into a mess of rice and beans.

All conversation had stopped when he entered. It resumed almost immediately, but more quietly. The men at the bowl of rice and beans pushed their plates away and turned to look him over with an intentness that was not reassuring.

Sheppard nodded to the people before him and came farther into the room. He was glad he had left his carbine and pistol outside. "Afternoon," he said. "I'm Asa Sheppard, Sergeant Major of cavalry. I've been assigned to stay at Miss Wheeler's place as a Safeguard. I'm looking for the owner of this store."

An older man with a drooping mustache stepped from behind the bar and came forward, wiping his hands. "That's me," he said. "What do you want?"

"I came in town to get some supplies from the blacksmith," Sheppard said. "I told him I smoked my last pipe yesterday and he said I could maybe buy some tobacco from you."

The owner started to speak, but a tall, yellow-haired fellow with bare arms spoke over him. "We don't sell tobacco to Yankees."

Sheppard looked from the store owner to him. "Is this your place?" he asked.

"No," The man replied, "But I can speak—"

"I noticed," Sheppard said. "But I wasn't talking to you." He turned back to the owner. "Would you sell me any tobacco, sir?"

The owner's mouth pulled slightly askew, but he nodded. "I think I might," he said.

"What is your price?" Sheppard asked.

"A toast to the Confederacy's the price!" The yellow-haired man said.

"What is your name?" Sheppard asked.

"Al Townsend," The man replied. "What's it to you?"

"I'll be glad to tell you, Townsend," Sheppard said. "I'm working a deal with the owner of this store—"

"Ed Pickens," The owner interjected.

"Pickens," Sheppard repeated. "Mr. Pickens can refuse to sell me things, or he can tell me to get off his property, if he wants, and I won't mind obeying him. But from what I can see, you're butting into something that's none of your business. Now, Mr.—Pickens, I think you said," he said, turning back to the owner. "I've got two half-dollars here, silver. They're new minted and clean, if you want to look them over. If you'll take them and give me as much tobacco as they buy, I'll be grateful. If you're interested in an additional trade, I've got about two pounds of roasted coffee beans back where I'm staying that I'll be happy to trade for the same amount of tobacco."

Pickens' eyes brightened. "Coffee, you say?" he said.

"It isn't a whole lot," Sheppard said, "But I've enough to spare for a swap."

"You've got a deal, Mister!" Pickens said.

"Now hang on here a minute!" Townsend said.

"What do you want, Al?" Pickens demanded.

"You can't go trading with his kind! They overran the town, wrecked things up—"

"Dillon's fellows did more wrecking than they did," Pickens pointed out. Some of the rest nodded.

"Hell," said an older man with a seamed, leathery face, "Stanley's bluebellies cleaned everything up!"

"Yeah, well at least Dillon's men were southerners!" a younger man broke in. "This fellow's nothing but an invader!"

Sheppard flicked a glance to the door and spoke calmly. "My people had no quarrel with people who weren't fighting them. If you check things out, you'll see we left private property the way we found it—"

Al Townsend's retort was curt and crude.

Sheppard shrugged. "Whatever you say," he said. "Mr. Pickens, do you want to sell me that tobacco now, or is there something else we can arrange?"

"The silver's fine," Pickens said, "If you'll let me look it over first."

"Fair enough," Sheppard said. He took the two half-dollars from his pocket and set them on the counter top. He waited as Pickens lifted them, turned them over in his palm, and finally nodded.

"They're sound," Pickens said, setting four good-sized twists of rich brown tobacco on the counter. "And here's your smoke, sergeant: grown around here and cured in this town." He smiled as Sheppard lifted one and sniffed at it. "I think you'll find it to your liking," he said.

"Best I've seen in a while," Sheppard agreed. "I think you'll agree the coffee's the same."

"When can we arrange the trade?" Pickens asked.

"As soon as you want," Sheppard said. "Today, if you like."

"Now just a minute!" said the younger man. "You're buying and selling with this bluebelly?"

"You're damned straight, John Toombs!" Pickens snapped. "He's come in looking for no trouble from anybody and I guess I can be as polite as he is!"

"Did you forget my brother was killed at Antietam creek?" Toombs demanded.

"So was mine," Sheppard said. "And a cousin at Vicksburg. Let's let it drop. I didn't come here to fight anyone."

"As though you could!" Townsend sneered, eyeing Sheppard's arm.

"That's right," said Sheppard. He nodded to the people in the room. "Mr. Pickens: much obliged. Come to Miss Wheeler's place and I'll have your coffee ready for you."

"I'll bring the tobacco," Pickens said.

Sheppard nodded and started toward the door. In a few minutes he would be back at Fairlawn. His arm was paining him again, and the thought of sitting back and closing his eyes was becoming more inviting by the moment.

"Hey, Bluebelly!"

Sheppard stiffened for a moment. The voice was strident, filled with mocking hatred. He set his shoulders and kept walking.

"Sergeant!"

Sheppard turned to see Townsend close behind him with three others at his back.

"I don't like your hat," said Townsend.

Sheppard took off his forage cap and frowned at the cavalry insignia on it. "Neither do I," he said, setting it back on his head and tilting it slightly over one eye. "But until something's done so I don't have to wear it, it looks like I'm stuck with it. Good bye."

"I don't like you, either!"

"Gosh!" said Sheppard. "I just guess I'll have to live with it, now, won't I?"

"You're a coward!"

"Fine thing for a bomb-proof like you to talk," Sheppard said, keeping one eye on the door.

"What's a bomb-proof?" someone demanded of the room in general.

"'Invincible in peace, invisible in war,' " someone else supplied with a snicker.

There was a low growl of laughter. "Hell, Al, he's got you there!" said Pickens. "You were running as fast as any of us when Dillon's boys came through!"

Townsend's eyes narrowed. "I'll make you eat that!" he snarled as he strode forward.

Sheppard's fist drove into his solar plexus. Townsend doubled over, gasping like a landed fish; the next moment Sheppard's knee jerked upward driving his jaw shut with the sound of a slamming door.

Townsend's friends came lunging forward with a shout just as Sheppard sent Townsend spinning among them, bringing them down in a flailing, cursing tangle of arms and legs.

John Toombs, clutching wildly for support, caught Sheppard's ankle and sent him crashing against a table.

Sheppard wrenched his foot away and jumped to his feet, ashen-faced. His right hand, up against his wounded shoulder, was wet and red, and a large red stain was spreading across the white sling. He sprang for the door and was outside the next moment, jerking his mare's reins free. He was in the saddle a second later with his carbine in his hand.

Inside the tavern, Toombs had regained his feet. "Got him!" he exulted. He charged out the door followed by three others and was sent reeling back as the ironclad butt of Sheppard's carbine connected with the side of his head.

Dixie, spurred forward, rammed another man as he came bursting through the door. Sheppard wheeled her sharply, knocking a third spinning with her rump. A boot in the brisket felled another as he tried to grab for the mare's bridle.

Al Townsend staggered out into the street, yelling, and found himself suddenly silent and staring up into the black hole of the barrel of a cocked and leveled revolver. He could see the rounds in the cylinder; he stopped dead where he stood and moistened his lips.

"You cur," Sheppard said through his teeth. "You've had your free bite and now I'm warning you: the next time our paths cross, by God, I'll kill you! Now stand back and keep your hands where I can see them!"

He swung the gun toward the other attackers, who had lost all urge to fight and now were standing silently and watching. "On your faces with your hands behind your necks, the lot of you! Now!"

He watched as they obeyed and then slid the pistol back into its holster with his bloody right hand. "The rest of you: this was none of my doing, but I don't put up with bullies. Mr. Pickens, the coffee's yours whenever you want it. We can discuss it later. Now see to it that passel of bums keeps out of my way!"

He turned Dixie and rode straight down the street. He even managed to remain upright in his saddle until he was out of sight of the tavern.

✷✷ ✷✷ ✷✷

"He came into town to check in with me," Judge Prescott told Lavinia. "Some of the local ruffians took exception to his uniform and started a fight."

Lavinia frowned at the embroidery frame before her and set a stitch. She turned the frame, knotted the thread, and snipped it with the scissors that hung from the chatelaine at her waist. "A fight?" she said. "Who was it?"

She handed the threaded needle to Bathsheba, who sat demurely nearby with Lavinia's sewing box in her calico-clad lap.

"We don't know, Miss Vinnie," said Dr. Meacham, Wheelerville's physician. He had accompanied Judge Prescott to Lavinia's house that afternoon. "Sam Wallins went hurrying over to the judge, here, with word that the sergeant was walking right into Ed Pickens' store in search of tobacco. He was worried that something bad might happen since Al Townsend and John Toombs were there, and he wanted us to come help him if it was needed."

Lavinia had been reaching for a skein of pink silk. She paused and looked up at Dr. Meacham. "Sam Wallins?" she repeated. "What did Sergeant Sheppard want with a blacksmith?"

"He wanted to borrow a maul," Judge Prescott replied.

"A maul?" Lavinia demanded. "For what purpose?"

Bathsheba's eyes were wide and sparkling with interest. She lowered them and offered the thread when Lavinia turned back to her.

Judge Prescott cleared his throat. "He thought to use it to split firewood," he said.

Lavinia set the skein of silk in her lap and traded looks with the girl. "The man is wounded, with one arm in a sling!" she exclaimed. "Did he think he could split firewood one-handed?"

"He thought he could if he used a maul," Judge Prescott replied. "From what I've seen of the man, he may well be able to do so."

Lavinia scanned the thread and sniffed. "What gave him the notion of splitting wood in the first place?" she demanded, handing the thread back to the girl.

Judge Prescott reached over, gently took her left hand in his, turned it, and looked at the line of blisters across the edge of her palm. "He saw you doing it, Lavinia," he said. "Having done so, what choice did he have?"

Lavinia sighed and looked down at her hand. "I see," she said, drawing it away.

"Were you cutting wood, Miss Vinnie?" Bathsheba demanded, staring at Lavinia's hand. "Why, I'd have done it! I'm strong!"

"It isn't suitable work for a young lady," Lavinia said.

Bathsheba opened her mouth to protest, caught Lavinia's very direct stare, and subsided with a sigh.

"There's nothing wrong, Vinnie, with asking for help when it's needed," Judge Prescott said. "To refuse to do so is pride of the worst sort. Someone could have been hurt."

"My intent was not to hurt anyone," Lavinia said. "But please continue."

"Well, Miss Vinnie, we went with Wallins, but by the time we got there it had happened and was over. We saw most of it—"

The maidservant sat forward, her dimples deepening. "You did?" she said breathlessly. "Was there a fight?"

"Bathsheba," said Lavinia.

The girl sighed and sat back. "I'm sorry," she said, but with a notable lack of contrition.

Meacham suppressed a smile. "We saw it all," he said with a nod to Bathsheba. "That man can certainly take care of himself!"

Lavinia looked up, her eyes wide and startled. "Then there was fighting?" she said. "I hadn't been aware... Was the sergeant hurt?"

"He's well enough for the moment," Dr. Meacham said. "I wouldn't have come here if I'd thought otherwise."

"That is well enough for the moment, then," said Lavinia. She selected another threaded needle, positioned it, and took three stitches while Bathsheba watched. "Did Sergeant Sheppard do anything at all to provoke the quarrel?" she asked thoughtfully as she smoothed the thread and then turned the piece so that Bathsheba could see it clearly.

"Aside from being a Yankee in the middle of a group of Georgia Confederates during a time when our respective governments are at war, not at all, Miss Lavinia," Judge Prescott replied. "Those I spoke to said he was quiet-spoken and pleasant. In fact, a number of them said they had taken a liking to him and asked how he was doing."

Lavinia was suddenly frowning. She drew the thread through the canvas, knotted it, and then removed the needle and placed it in the ivory needle case in her sewing box. She took her scissors and trimmed a long end from the back of the piece, then looked up. "I received the impression that he was unhurt. And now I learn that he was hurt," she said. "How bad is it? Was that saber wound reopened?"

"I'm afraid it was," Dr. Meacham replied. "From what I could see, he was thrown backward and came up hard against something. The jolt tore the wound again. He was bleeding badly-the entire side of his shirt and jacket were soaked."

Lavinia was staring. "Dear heaven!" she exclaimed. "But I thought—"

Dr. Meacham spoke soothingly in the face of her concern. "It could have been much worse," he said. "We took him to my house and put him to bed. I tended the shoulder, and stopped the bleeding. He's in a lot of pain, but I don't think there'll be much danger of infection, since the wound was clean and bandaged when it was torn open again."

"Bleeding..." Lavinia repeated. Bathsheba looked from her to Dr. Meacham.

"He wanted to return here," Judge Prescott said. "He said you might worry, but Doc here wouldn't let him because he was afraid it would jar that arm."

"He was worried about my worrying?" Lavinia said. "That surpasses all! If I'd suspected... Is he out of danger?"

"He's doing well, Miss Vinnie," Dr. Meacham said. "But he'll be staying with me for at least a week, and more likely two weeks."

"Excellent," Lavinia said. "And I will go to see him, myself, right away. George will take the two of you to his room; you can select those things you may consider necessary for him, or that might give him some comfort while he's with you, Doctor. Bathsheba, I'd be grateful if you would ask your Uncle George to harness Absalom to the buggy and bring him, at his leisure, to Dr. Meacham's. Then, if you would, fetch my hat and bring it to me at the door."

She smoothed her shawl and then lifted the key ring from her chatelaine. "I have some medicines left by Dr. Haskell, the Federal surgeon, and there's some morphia among them. I will bring that along, Dr. Meacham, if you approve. It should serve to ease the sergeant's pain and allow him to get some rest. For myself, I will pay a visit to him, to set his mind at ease about what has happened." Her gray eyes narrowed slightly and she added, "After I have spoken with those brawlers at Mr. Pickens' establishment."

She saw that Bathsheba had not moved. "Run along, child, and do as I asked," she said.

"Yes, Miss Vinnie," Bathsheba said. "And if I wear my bonnet—"

"No, darling," Lavinia said. "A tavern is no place for a proper young lady. Your grandmother would never forgive me for taking you there."

"But you're going!" Bathsheba objected, "And you're a lady!"

"There's a difference," Lavinia said. "I am not a young lady."

"But that's not fair!" Bathsheba protested.

Lavinia's smile was grim. "You will learn, my dear," she said, "That it is you who must ensure the fairness of your life: fate isn't overly concerned with it. Now go and do as you were told."

CHAPTER ELEVEN

Ed Pickens' establishment was humming with activity, and the windows were thrown open to the late May breeze. People were laughing and chattering, and the air was full of the clink of eating utensils against pottery dishes. Lavinia could hear raucous laughter, oaths, and the reprehensible words of a very uncouth song bawled by a dozen voices.

The Judge hesitated at the door. "I can handle this for you, Lavinia," he said. "There's no need for you to deal with these folk."

She looked up at him with a half-smile. "Be honest with me now, Judge," she said. "Would you be saying this to Gaylord if it were him standing before this door?"

Prescott lowered his head.

"Maybe you would, come to that," Lavinia said. "My brother was always one to duck unpleasant necessities. You have seen that I do not, so we'd best get on with it. It should be interesting: I've never been in a taproom before. And to tell the truth," she added grimly, tucking her hand snugly into the crook of his arm," I have been looking forward to this. Now please knock for me."

She waited as he knocked on the door and then entered on his arm and stood just inside the door.

The taproom noise died away as the people became aware of her presence; by the time the room was silent, everyone was on his feet and staring.

"Good afternoon, gentlemen," Lavinia said, stepping forward and looking around with interest. "I hope all of you are in good health."

Ed Pickens had been staring. He dusted off a chair and offered it. "Good afternoon, Miss Lavinia," he said. "Would—would you like some sarsaparilla tea?"

"Why, that's very kind of you, Mr. Pickens," Lavinia said. "Thank you very much."

Judge Prescott escorted her to the chair, waited as she arranged her skirts, and then took her parasol.

Lavinia smiled her thanks and then, folding her gloved hands in her lap, turned her gaze on the men in the room. "I received some disturbing news about someone who is a part of my household at Fairlawn," she said. "I was told that he met with a mishap and is currently recovering from a new injury. I was surprised to hear this, since he was already convalescing from a severe wound. When I inquired into the circumstances surrounding this mishap, what I learned made me determined to come here at once."

Ed Pickens carefully set the cup of tea before her.

She thanked him, raised it to her lips, sipped, and then set it down with a nod. "Thank you, Mr. Pickens," she said. "The tea is excellent." She looked around the room. "Now," she said, "since I have an incomplete set of the facts, I would like to obtain the rest: I wish to speak with the heroes who joined in an attempt to overpower a wounded, one-armed man. Step forward, please."

No one moved.

Lavinia smiled. "Well, now?" she said. "Come forward. I won't hurt you." Her smile widened slightly. "You can see I am unarmed," she said.

There still was no answer. Her eyes swept through the crowd and narrowed as they encountered bruises.

"Very well," she said. "Alan Townsend, you will please come forward."

She watched as the man came to her. He was walking carefully, and seemed somehow hunched, as though it hurt to straighten up.

"Very good," she said. "Now let me see: who else do I wish to speak to? Luke Hartwell, you had best come up, too. John Toombs, I need to speak with you as well, and Rufus Russell, too."

She sipped her tea while they came up to stand before her, then looked them up and down. "What brave defenders of the Confederacy!" she said. "Such fine specimens of Wheelerville's manhood! How many of you attacked him? Four?"

"Please, Miss Lavinia," John Toombs began.

"I'll have a deal to say to you presently, John Toombs!" she said. "For the present, please hold your peace." She looked over the group again and then nodded.

"Mr. Townsend," she said, "You look as though you were dragged backward through a bush. From what I hear, the greatest portion of the blame for this deplorable incident rests with you. I am surprised at you: you always were something of a bully, but I had hoped that two years' service with the armies of our Confederacy might have caused you to grow up a little. From this day's work I see you haven't improved with age."

"That Yankee punched him in the gut," someone snickered behind her. "Felled him like a tree!"

Lavinia pushed her cup away. "Mr. Townsend was disabled by a one-armed man!" she said. "And is that when the rest of you valiant warriors decided to join in?"

"God a'mighty, Miss Lavinia!" Townsend burst out,"It was more than flesh and blood could bear, seeing that damned—"

She raised her eyebrows. "I beg your pardon?" she said.

"—the darn fool bluebelly!" Townsend finished.

Lavinia nodded to Pickens, who removed the cup of tea. "What, precisely, is a 'bluebelly'?" she asked, turning back to Townsend.

"A Yank," he said.

"A—Yank," she repeated. "A Federal soldier, regardless of rank?"

"Yes, Ma'am."

"I see. And I am sure there is an equally vulgar description of a Confederate soldier. What is it?"

"The term's 'grayback,' " Miss Lavinia," said Judge Prescott with the hint of a smile.

Lavinia looked at him for a long thoughtful moment. "'Grayback,' " she said distastefully. "That is a term commonly applied to lice, as I recall. Personally, I find the first term less offensive. So the sergeant was here in his uniform. Did he speak disrespectfully to you or anyone else? Did he offer you an insult?"

There was no answer. She turned and looked at the rest of the group. "Apparently not. Did he tell you all who he was?"

Ed Pickens said, "He came in here peaceably, without any guns or knives, and told us who he was. Stated his business pretty well, and we started talking, friendly enough, for all there was a little awkwardness at first. Those fellows butted right in." He considered for a moment and then added aggrievedly," They nearly spoiled a good swap!"

"You shut your mouth!" Townsend growled.

"Well, it's God's own truth!" Pickens snapped. "You stuck your noses in others' business and got them bitten off, and it serves you right!"

"Gentlemen, please," Lavinia said.

The room fell silent again.

"Now what else did he do to provoke an attack by four able-bodied men?" she asked.

"He wouldn't toast the Confederacy!" Toombs said.

"I find that hardly surprising," Lavinia said after considering for a moment. "He's at war with the Confederacy. Would you please tell me why the question even came up?"

None of the four answered.

"Very well," she said. "I will tell you why it came up. It came up because you heroes were ashamed that you had left this town when danger threatened. And you were embarrassed to learn that the danger had mostly been in your mind. So ashamed and angry were you that you decided to strike a blow for your manhood. And what better way than to attack someone who couldn't fight back?"

"He did pretty well," Toombs said.

"That may be, John Toombs," said one of the people there, "But I recall very well that Yank saying he wasn't looking to fight anyone. And then Al Townsend sneered something about how he couldn't fight anyhow, and the fellow said that was right. And then you all went ahead and picked a fight with him, and Al threw the first punch."

Townsend looked down.

"What heroes you are indeed, all of you!" Lavinia said. "'Throwing the first punch' at a wounded, unarmed, peaceable man! And he even beat you in fair fight!"

"He sure did," Pickens remarked. "He was pretty handy with things."

"I do not happen to think it an especially praiseworthy thing for a fighting man to triumph over a nest of lice!" Lavinia said. "For none of the ruffians who attacked Sergeant Sheppard are better than vermin! I am ashamed to be associated with them!"

"Now look here, Miss Lavinia—" Toombs began.

She turned and looked him up and down with a marked lack of approval. "I said I would have somewhat to say to you, John Toombs, and so I do!" she said. "You shiftless, cowardly ne'er-do-well! You are a shame and a disgrace to this town! The land your house is standing on, the timbers your house is built of, and the street along which your house is placed are all owned by me! Your family has a thirty year lease that is expiring in just about a month, and after this day's doings, I am inclined to tell you and your family to take your belongings and get off my land! And the rest of you: you call yourselves men! I've seen barnyard fowl with more brains and more courage than you! If you want to fight for the Confederacy, then you can very well go and join the armies and leave wounded, peaceable men alone!"

"Miss Lavinia!"

"Be silent!" she commanded. "I will say this once, and it had best be heard and heeded! Sergeant Major Sheppard was assigned to my lands to protect them and me from marauders and thieves, even against his own people, if they offer any harm! His presence is the result of an act of generosity, and not only is he to be looked upon as a keeper of the peace—which is what all of you ruffians and scoundrels should have been, yourselves!—but he is to be considered my guest and treated with respect! An insult offered to him is an insult to me, and believe me, gentlemen, I know how to deal with that! Now all of you brawlers get home this instant and do not let me hear of any more of this folly! Now go!"

John Toombs glared around the room. "Well, it's all well and good for the rest of you to snicker," he said. "What sort of man goes sniveling to a woman and hides behind her skirts, will you tell me that?"

Lavinia rose to her feet and went forward. "What did you say, Mr. Toombs?" she asked.

Toombs backed away from her.

"He said that Yankee went running to you," said Sam Wallins, who had just come in and was standing inside the door with his arms folded. "Shows what a jack-fool he is! Listen to me, Toombs, and the rest of you: the man never got back to Fairlawn. He was hurt pretty badly, and I was just coming up with the Judge here and Dr. Meacham. It was pretty obvious the sergeant wasn't in any shape to do much except lie down and get patched up, so we took him to Doc Meacham's place and took care of him. I've just come from there. Miss Lavinia here hasn't even had a chance to talk with him yet, so if you're thinking your embarrassment is due to anything other than your own stupidity, you'd better think again! I was there and watching when Doc took care of him. He didn't mention anyone's names. He's not one to go telling tales, or I'm much mistaken!" He nodded grimly. "And maybe you'd all better think to yourselves how you'd behave if the same thing happened to you. Might make you sober up a little."

The four men traded looks and were silent.

"If you have nothing else to say, you may leave," Lavinia said. She watched them go and then turned to the others in the room. "And as for the rest of you gentlemen," she said, "I hope I have made myself clear. Sergeant Sheppard is not an enemy. His assignment is to guard this town and keep all its residents from harm and insult. I suggest that we all consider how we can best assist him in this endeavor."

"Yes, Miss Lavinia," said Ed Pickens. He hesitated, and then picked up a parcel wrapped in brown paper and said, "Miss Lavinia?"

"Yes?"

"He was going to trade some coffee for some tobacco. Two pounds of coffee, he said, for two pounds of tobacco. Here's the tobacco, and he can bring the coffee when he can. I thought he was an honest fellow, and he sure was a fighter!"

Lavinia took the package from him. "I'll be sure he gets this," she said.

Another man said, "He was bleeding when he left. Is he all right?"

"Dr. Meacham has him in hand," Lavinia replied. "I'll be visiting him next."

"That was a shame," Pickens said.

"Yes, it was," Lavinia agreed. "And now, gentlemen, if you will excuse me, I will go to Dr. Meacham and see how the Sergeant is recovering."

CHAPTER TWELVE

"I gave him some quinine about a half hour ago," Dr. Meacham said as he led Lavinia down the hallway toward the guest room that he used for his patients. "I found that he's running a fever—not surprising, I grant, considering what's happened today—but from what I can see, he has done so since he arrived at your place. You say that Yankee doctor gave him quinine the first day he was with you?"

"That is right," Lavinia said. "And the doctor left a supply for me to use for the patients still at my house, and for the sergeant if he requested it."

"Hm," said Meacham. "And did the sergeant request any between then and now?"

Lavinia stopped and stared at him. "Why, no he did not," she said. "I should have realized!"

"There's no harm done," said Dr. Meacham, heading down the hall again. "This is just a temporary setback. He's a healthy man, and he'll do all right."

Lavinia had not moved. "I was so busy with the others... I never even thought of it. If I had been thinking-but he never asked for it."

Dr. Meacham stopped and frowned at her. "He wouldn't," he said. "He didn't let out a yip when I tended that tear in his shoulder, either. His type makes dangerous patients."

"Dangerous?" Lavinia repeated. "How so?"

"They don't complain until they're in the last extremes of pain, and by then it's usually too late. Unless you're pretty sharp-eyed, or know just what you're dealing with, you won't know that they're suffering."

"He said I wasn't to worry about him, that it was his assignment to worry about me," Lavinia said. "What are we to do with him?"

"The first thing you're to do is stop taking so much on yourself, Miss Lavinia, or you'll run yourself into the ground. You aren't to blame for his obstinacy, and you didn't know him well enough to guess what was afoot. Now you do know, it won't happen again."

Lavinia looked down.

Dr. Meacham smiled at her and continued. "And now I'll tell you what I plan to do," he said. "I plan to keep him abed for a week with that arm strapped in place so there's no chance of tearing it open again. Along with that, I'm going to dose him three times a day with quinine, and when I release him to your house, you're going to do the same until that fever is well and truly gone! He's a good man, Miss Lavinia, and I don't want those louts in this town to be responsible for his death!"

** ** **

Dr. Meacham's words gave Lavinia an uncomfortable deal to consider as she tapped on the sickroom door and then stepped inside.

Sergeant Sheppard had been put into a crisp, clean night shirt, and then tucked into a bed. He was propped up on three pillows, his sun-bleached hair was half in his eyes, and he looked pale and tired. Lavinia could see the outlines of a sturdy bandage on his left shoulder through the fabric of the night shirt; his left arm and hand lay under the covers.

At the moment he was gazing at a small, pasteboard-backed photograph. He looked up at the sound of the door opening and, seeing Lavinia, started to pull himself more upright.

"No, Sergeant," she said, closing the door behind her and then drawing her gloves off. "Please don't move. I heard what happened today, and I've spoken with Dr. Meacham—" She caught a glimpse of the faces in the photograph as she set her gloves on the dresser and put her shawl beside it. "Oh, may I see?" she asked.

He handed over the small rectangle of pasteboard and watched as she lifted it and pushed her glasses down her nose to peer at it.

Three children, dressed in what were obviously the outfits they wore strictly for church, gazed soberly back at her, though the oldest boy, on the left, proudly holding up a pearl-handled penknife, showed signs of an emerging dimple. They all had very firm chins and wide, interested eyes. The girl was holding a cloth doll, while the youngest had started to look away from the camera, probably toward a grownup out of range.

"What beautiful children!" she exclaimed. "Are they yours?"

His face eased into a proud smile. "Yes, they're my three," he said. "Jesse's the oldest: he's ten now, Lydia, in the center, is six, and the youngest, Caleb, is just turned two."

Lavinia turned the photograph. The back was stained and rusty, but she could see, through the discoloration, the imprint of names written in a childish scrawl, and the words 'for Papa'. "When did you last see them?" she asked.

"It's been nearly a year," he said. "I was given a furlough after Vicksburg was taken, and I went straight home. They sent this photograph at Christmas when I was in Tennessee."

"They're darling," Lavinia said. "Your eldest—Jesse?—seems very proud of that knife."

"It was given him by an act of God," Sheppard said. "It's nothing less than an answered prayer, and he prizes it more than anything else he owns."

"Oh?" said Lavinia, handing the photograph back.

"Exactly" he said. "He wanted a pearl-handled pocket knife so badly he could taste it. I went out and got him one, planning to give it to him on his eighth birthday. One Sunday my wife, Sarah, came to me as I was out in the wood shed looking over my lumber for some walnut logs. 'Come right away, Asa', she said. 'There's something you must hear.' So I followed her to the smaller barn and listened. I could hear Jesse crying, 'Lord, please give me a knife with a pearl handle: please!'"

Sheppard set the photograph on the table beside his bed. "He'd been learning about prayers in Sunday school," he said. "'Ask and ye shall receive' had been the lesson that week, and he decided to put it into practice. He went behind the barn and did just that.

"Sarah was smothering her laughter in her sleeve. 'You must give him that knife now, Asa,' she said, and when I pointed out that it was just a week till his birthday, she insisted. So I went back inside and got it.

"Jesse was still going at it when I came out again. I thought about it for a minute or two, and I decided to give the Lord credit for the knife. The shed was between me and Jesse, and I've always been good at throwing things. I frowned at the knife and weighed it in my hand.

"Sarah was watching me. 'What are you waiting for?' she demanded. 'Aren't you going to give it to him?'

"'No,' I said. 'Since he's asking the Lord for it, I guess I'll let the Lord get the credit.' And before Sarah could say anything more I lofted the knife.

"It went spinning over the roof, and Sarah and I heard a thud, a yelp, and the sound of someone falling.

"We went pelting back behind the shed and there was Jesse on his back, rubbing a goose egg that was springing up on his forehead. I threw myself on my knees beside him just as he sat up, grinning fit to split his face, and showed Sarah and me the knife. 'Look, Ma!' he said as I was busily feeling the knot on his head, 'the Lord sent me a knife, just like I asked for! Isn't it great?' And then he winced as I found the sore spot. 'Golly, Pa!' he said. 'I'm glad I didn't ask for a sled!' He slept with it under his pillow for the next week."

"He seems like a funny little fellow," Lavinia said with a smile. "How you must miss him. How you must miss them all! I know I would if they were mine."

His eyes were suddenly very bright. He closed them.

Seeing the glitter of moisture escaping beneath the arc of his lashes, she rose and made a show of unpinning her hat and setting it on a table by the door. By the time she had returned to stand by his bedside with her hands folded before her, he was lying quietly with his right hand relaxed on his chest. She said, "And how do you feel now?"

The hazel eyes, lacking a little of their liveliness, opened and lowered to the photograph again. "I'm well enough, Miss Wheeler," he said. "I'm sorry about all this."

She moved to the window and looked out at the willow leaves flickering in the breeze. "I spent a summer in Saratoga once, fifteen years ago," she said. "I remember it as a beautiful season. Before I went I had heard that northerners were a breed apart, prone to odd freaks. In fact, I discovered that I liked northerners as a group. They tend to be direct and to the point, traits I find admirable. I saw nothing terribly odd about them."

She drew the curtains aside and turned and smiled at him. "That is, Sergeant, until you came along," she said, returning to her chair. "I cannot imagine a more freakish thing than to hear someone apologize for having the rudeness to be attacked without provocation by what my father used to call barflies."

The sergeant's mouth curved into the shadow of a smile. "Then I am forgiven for all of this?" he said.

"Indeed you are, sir," she returned. "I have even managed to forgive you for standing in the way of a saber thrust from a Confederate soldier. Does that set your mind at rest, sir, is there anything more for which I must forgive you?"

"That's enough for now," he said, closing his eyes. "I don't want to be too happy: I'll have nothing to look forward to."

His voice sounded a little husky, and by the rhythm of his breathing, he was in pain. Lavinia remembered the morphia and sighed at herself for not giving it to Dr. Meacham during the drive to town. But that was easily remedied. She went to the water carafe and poured out half a glass. She then took the bottle of morphine from her pocket, unstoppered it, and by eye measured out a grain.

She looked over at him for a moment, seeing again the signs of pain in the set of his mouth and the rise and fall of his breathing. "Here, Sergeant," she said, stirring the morphine into the water. "This will help take away some of the pain and let you sleep. You should feel better when you awaken."

He opened his eyes, saw the bottle and the water, and frowned slightly as she set the glass to his lips. "What is it?" he asked.

"Morphia," she replied. "Dr. Haskell left it for me to use as I saw fit. Now drink it! Good heavens, Sergeant! One would think I was trying to poison you?"

He suddenly grinned. "My wife used to complain that I acted like it," he said.

Lavinia looked down at the plain gold ring on his left hand. "She must be worried about you," she said. "Drink this, and you'll be able to see her all the sooner."

The hazel eyes looked up at her with the touch of a wry smile in their depths. "That's not very reassuring, Miss Wheeler," Sheppard said. "Sarah died two years ago, giving birth to Caleb. I was busy fighting at Pittsburgh Landing."

Lavinia lifted her gaze to the window as Sheppard lowered his head and drank. "I am sorry, Sergeant," she said. "It is...so difficult, I know, losing someone you love. You know that time will help dull the ache, but time seems to drag so..." Her voice lowered slightly. "And these past three years, it seems that every time I turn round there is another loss and yet another..."

She looked down to see that Sheppard had finished drinking and was looking attentively up at her with the trace of a frown between his brows. The frown eased when he saw she was looking at him.

"There," he said, lying back. "All done. I hope there's more of this: those back at the house need it more than me."

"You need it most at the moment," Lavinia said, putting the bottle away. "And yes, Dr. Haskell left a goodly supply. He was very generous." She eyed the level of water in the carafe and said, "I'll get you more water, sir. Do you need anything else from the house, or did Dr. Meacham bring what you needed?"

"I am fine, Miss Wheeler," Sheppard said. "Don't worry about me."

"I am afraid you leave me no other choice," Lavinia said. "And it is not as much trouble as you seem to think."

She rested her hand against his brow for a moment. "You are still a little fevered, sir," she said, pushing his hair off his forehead with the absent gentleness she used with the plantation children. "Dr. Meacham told me he has given you quinine."

"He certainly did," Sheppard said. "I think it's beginning to work. My head's buzzing, but I don't ache as much."

"That's good news," Lavinia said, taking out the brown paper package. "And now, Sergeant: Mr. Pickens asked me to bring you these."

"The tobacco?" Sheppard said, brightening. "But he hasn't been paid yet."

"He said you could send the coffee whenever it suited you," Lavinia told him. "He seems to have taken a liking to you, Sergeant. So did a number of people."

"It was a mutual thing," Sheppard said. "They're good folk, most of them."

Lavinia set the tobacco on the table beside the bed. "Why didn't you tell me you were going into town for a maul?" she asked.

"Why didn't you tell me you needed firewood?" Sheppard countered. "Why did you try to chop your own wood?"

"You are wounded," Lavinia returned. "You might have insisted on chopping the wood for me."

"And you are not strong," Sheppard said. "I might have known ways to cut firewood that didn't take so much effort." He eyed her hands and added," I'd be willing to bet you have blisters."

"I would not take you up on it," Lavinia said. "Well, Sergeant, it appears you were watching me. Why didn't you let me know you were there?"

"Because I knew you'd have sent me back to my room to take a nap," Sheppard said.

"I might have," Lavinia admitted. "Or perhaps not. You've only just met me: how could you know for certain? You could have said something to find out. As it is, you nearly frightened me out of twenty years of life today."

"I'm sorry," Sheppard said again.

"No," said Lavinia. "It is I who should apologize. "I should have spoken to you—or to someone. It was foolish for me to think I could split the firewood by myself, and I should not have allowed my pride to get the better of me in this case. My greatest regret is that you paid the price."

"I've been worse off," he sighed.

"Is the pain better?" she asked.

He frowned and then nodded. "It's pretty much gone," he said. "I was getting so tired of it..."

"It wears you down," Lavinia said. "When you can't escape it, you tend to fret, and it's hard to put the pain aside..."

Sheppard closed his eyes. "I know," he said. "I'll tell you what, Miss Wheeler. I'll tell you the things I plan to do and the things I see. I won't try to hide them from you, I won't try to make them better than they are. I'll do it if you'll do the same for me. Maybe that way we can make this place run smoothly."

"I am agreeable to that, Sergeant," Lavinia said. "It'll be best if we work together." She added, "Tomorrow I'll ask some of the stronger men to come to my place and help with the firewood."

When she saw that he had opened his eyes once more and was smiling sleepily at her, she felt unaccountably eased.

CHAPTER THIRTEEN

The last two weeks of May had been exceptionally mild in Wheelerville, and several gentle, soaking rains had made the growing crops of corn and tobacco lush and green. The scars of the battle were disappearing, the last of the missing townsfolk and most of Lavinia's people had returned, a little the worse for wear and ashamed, but otherwise unhurt. Lavinia had greeted them all with a level look and a hot meal, and soon the fields were being tilled and weeded as before.

William Tecumseh Sherman's various forces were making their separate destructive ways down along the railroad lines that funneled into the city once named Terminus, then Marthasville, and then, finally, Atlanta.

South of Wheelerville, the Chattanooga railroad was secured and Sherman's supply lines lengthened when George Stoneman's Federal cavalry captured the important pass at Allatoona on the first day of June. Farther to the south, Miles Stanley's Army of the Monongahela was pressing toward Kennesaw Mountain against the stubborn resistance of Dillon's Alabamians, who were looking to join the shifting defensive lines of Joseph Johnston's Army of the Tennessee.

The long, warm days of June were unwinding into summer like beads dropping one by one from a necklace, each day bringing some new piece of news. And yet it all seemed distant to Wheelerville, left far behind in the wake of the armies. The guns at Allatoona were heard in Wheelerville, but the town had seen no further activity apart from a column of dark smoke that had risen to the southeast, just two days after the capture of the pass. A squall of rain had doused the smoke after some hours; no one thought of it once it was gone.

Sergeant Sheppard had spent two weeks at Dr. Meacham's private hospital, the first one abed and the second one quietly resting in the sitting room or the front porch. During that time an unusual number of townsfolk developed slight illnesses that required visits to Dr. Meacham's house, and while they were there they took the opportunity to sneak a look at Miss Wheeler's Yankee.

They were favorably impressed by what they saw. Sergeant Major Sheppard tolerated their sidelong looks with humorous equanimity, responded pleasantly when he was addressed, somehow endeared himself to the town's children, and showed himself generally to be a man of pleasing manners and good sense.

Once this impression became the consensus, Reverend Theophilus Porter, pastor of Wheelerville's church, paid a call at Dr. Meacham's with the object of ascertaining the status of Sergeant Sheppard's immortal soul.

He left after a rather lengthy visit and reported that far from being the rough-hewn heathen that had been feared, the sergeant was an elder in his church at home. He reported, further, that while the late Mrs. Sheppard had been the daughter of the Methodist pastor, the sergeant himself was a Presbyterian in good standing and served on the board of trustees for the Sabbath schools of Geneva, New York. The sergeant had asked Reverend Porter to pay a weekly call at Fairlawn, subject to Miss Wheeler's approval, and conduct some sort of divine services there.

Reverend Porter, pleased and flattered by the request, and more than half-inclined to view even Yankees with Christian indulgence, agreed to do so, resolutely ignoring the humbling recollection that Miss Wheeler, who admired straight speaking, had an unnerving habit of consulting her watch ten minutes into his sermon, and then every two minutes thereafter. The pastor's visit had been the first of many visits by various of the townsfolk, starting with Abner Wigfall's mother. Sergeant Sheppard was so well-liked, the townsfolk decided, hesitantly, that it might be appropriate for them to pay visits to the wounded at Fairlawn. There was some reluctance at first: the prospect of coming face to face with Yankee savages was not an inviting one, but the reality of the drawn-faced, suffering young men banished the monsters of the townsfolk's imagination. Within a week Lavinia noticed a change for the better among the men, most of whom had been pining for the sight of friendly faces other than fellow-sufferers.

Sheppard watched all of this without comment, dealt pleasantly with his visitors, and obeyed Dr. Meacham's instructions to the letter. The enforced physical inactivity had had its desired effect. By the time he had returned to Fairlawn just two days before, he was ready to tackle his duties in earnest.

**   **   **

"You take a good-sized pinch between your thumb and forefinger. That's right. Now cram it firmly into the bowl. Not too firmly, or you won't be able to light the pipe: you need some air space or the fire won't catch. Let me see."

Abner Wigfall handed Sergeant Sheppard the pipe and watched as he looked it over. "Did I do it right?" he asked.

"Looks fine to me," Sheppard said, setting the pipe between his teeth. "Now strike a match for me and hold it to the bowl while I get the thing to draw."

The match scratched along the tree bark beside Abner's knee and flared into sulphurous flame. He offered it to Sheppard, who raised his hand and held him off.

"Hold it a minute," Sheppard said. "If you don't let it burn a few seconds, whatever you smoke will taste like the fumes of hell. All right, now."

Abner held the match to the pipe and watched as the tobacco began to glow. He had escorted Judge Prescott to Fairlawn that afternoon. The judge was closeted with Lavinia, and Abner, who had all unintentionally become one of Asa Sheppard's friends and admirers, had gone in search of the sergeant. He had found him sitting at the foot of the large willow tree and gazing out over the newer graves with a thoughtful frown.

Sheppard had smiled at the boy and moved over for him, and the talk had turned to tobacco.

"Thanks," said Sheppard. "That's perfect." He sat back against the willow tree with a sigh and gazed out across the green fields to the mountains, lying to the northwest. Smoke trailed from the corner of his mouth to curl lazily up through the leaves above him. "There's nothing to match southern-grown tobacco," he said. "And nothing more annoying than not being able to light a pipe properly."

"You could try a segar," Abner suggested.

The sergeant cocked an eye at him. "They're a pain in the neck to carry about," he said. "They're always getting crushed or wet, and by the time you dry them out, or wrap them in paper like the Mexicans do, they're ruined. It's easier to carry a pipe."

Abner looked doubtful.

"And there's one other thing," Sheppard said.

"Yes, sir?"

"I'll kill you if I ever catch you with one of these blasted things in your mouth! Understand me?"

"But why-?"

"Because tobacco's a filthy, expensive habit and you're better off never starting, that's why!"

Abner grinned and drew his knees up. "You sound just like my pa," he said. The grin faded.

"Your pa's a wise man," Sheppard said, closing his eyes.

Abner watched as Sheppard blew out a puff of smoke. He followed it as it curled upward through the leaves, then looked down below the mountains and the sky to the neat mounds of earth, sprouting new, green grass. Three red gashes across it spoke of new graves. "It's a shame," he said, eyeing the new-turned earth.

Sheppard opened his eyes, followed Abner's gaze, and nodded. "Yes," he agreed. "A shame."

Abner was silent for a long time. "And yet it could happen to—" he burst out. He heard his own voice and stopped, then took a deep breath.

Sheppard drew on his pipe and cocked an eye at him.

Abner spoke slowly, frowning almost as though the effort to speak was too painful to be borne. "I mean, if you're old you know you'll die," he said. "You've only got so long to live. And babies have problems growing up, too. But—but someone who's young, someone who's not old shouldn't die!"

"I know," Sheppard said. "I know. It's hard to look into a coffin and see your own face."

"Or your pa's," Abner whispered.

Sheppard sat up, his eyes wide and grieved." Oh I'm sorry, son," he began. "I didn't know—"

"No, it's not that," Abner said." Pa's all right, or he was when he wrote his last letter. He said Grant's plowing on toward Richmond and Pa's brigade's in the way. They're in some place called Spotsylvania. He said there was movement, and the fighting's been going on for days, but they were going to move again... I don't know."

Sheppard gazed at the hills and was quiet.

Abner shivered and looked away from the new graves. "He said he sent his love," he said. "He told me to watch out for Ma and the little ones. Said I was the man of the family now..."

He broke off and frowned down at his toes. "But why did this war start? I don't suppose you wanted it! I know sure as fire Pa didn't want it!"

Sheppard took the pipe from his mouth and looked at the bowl. "Unfortunately," he said, "when you have a disagreement, sometimes fighting is the only way to settle it. Most people who fight in a war are doing it for something. Your father's no different. I don't know too many people who wanted this war."

Abner looped his hands about his knees and stared unseeingly across the new graves. "But why did it have to be a war?" he asked.

"Depends on what's at stake," Sheppard said. "Generally, the more important the outcome, the farther people are willing to go for it."

"But my pa's in it!" Abner said.

Sheppard eyed the boy's averted profile. Now was the moment that he was supposed to think of something bracing to say, something to cheer the boy up and assure him that everything would be fine, but he did not have the words.

"Your father has his duty to do, Abner," Sheppard said. "You can't expect him to turn his back on that, and I don't think you'd want him to, from what I've seen of you. But I'm sure he's also wise enough not to take any needless risks. You've got to trust him to do that. I know it's hard, but just remember this: he's trusting you to run the household while he's gone. You can do at least that much for him."

Abner nodded, tight-lipped. "Well, the Yanks've got Allatoona," he said. "What good that'll do escapes me."

Sheppard eyed his pipe. "If someone's always throwing rocks at you whenever you come near him, and you know he has them shipped to him from another town, the way to stop him throwing them at you is to make sure the shipments can't reach him. That's what's happening in the case of Allatoona: my army is cutting off your army's supplies."

"But how many people were killed while they tried to do it?" Abner demanded.

"Too many," Sheppard said. "You see the graves here, and there'll be more and more before the month is up. You see them, you see the torn-up land, the ruined houses, the trees blown apart or chopped down. People like Dr. Meacham doing without the medicines they need because there's a blockade on. Fine ladies like Miss Wheeler running themselves into the ground doing things that servants once performed for them... People like me far from their homes and their families for years. And when people like me go back to their homes on a furlough it's to find more graves and more empty homes." He smiled at Abner and added," Though you know, son, there've actually been times I've enjoyed being here, apart from the fighting and the dying."

Abner's lip quivered.

Sheppard climbed to his feet. "Can you get your hands on a riding animal other than a mule that should be six feet under rather than eating good fodder?" he asked.

"A—? Y—yes, I think so. Why?"

"I want to ride out westward and scout the area, and I'd be smart to have an escort." He smiled at Abner. "It'll shake the fidgets out of you. Come on: scare up a nag and meet me by the smokehouse. There are some things I want to look into."

** ** **

"I told you to get a horse, boy," Sheppard said as Abner tried to lift his mount, a calf-kneed bay gelding of indeterminate age, to a trot. "I wasn't looking to be disobeyed."

"You said you wanted a riding animal other than a mule," Abner said.

"I didn't expect you to come back with a jackass!" Sheppard returned. He considered and then added," A broken-winded jackass."

They had been riding for over an hour, going slowly, testing the lay of the land. Sheppard had ridden in a wide circle that curved to the southeast, and while he had talked easily with Abner, he had been constantly listening, his eyes moving across the landscape, missing nothing. They were moving along the edge of a pine wood. A stream rippled just at their horses' feet, spilling down from the northwest.

"This is my aunt Celie's favorite horse," Abner said with dignity. "She says he's comfortable."

"That's because he doesn't move," Sheppard said, flexing his left hand and settling the sling more comfortably. "What I want to know is, why doesn't she just sit on a sofa and save the cost and effort of feeding him?"

Abner grinned and kicked the animal again. "Besides," he said, "we can't all have nice horses this time of year, unlike some Yanks I've seen."

"Dixie's an exceptional animal," Sheppard said, slapping the chestnut mare's neck. His eyes narrowed as he turned to stare into the wood.

"She sure is," Abner said. He eyed Sheppard's mare and said, "Did you name her for the south?"

Sheppard looked back and smiled. "I guess it would be polite to say I did," he replied. "But the truth of the matter is that she was bred and trained by a friend of mine named Dixon. She's an Irish Draft/Thoroughbred cross. Her real name's 'Dixon's Darling'. I started calling her 'Dixie' for short after I got some funny looks when some folks caught me shouting 'Darling' after her."

"Whew!" said Abner. "I just guess so!"

Sheppard was looking away again. Abner could see that he was uneasy about something by the set of his shoulders, and his unease was being communicated to the mare, who was sidling and shaking her head in the rising wind. "Is she your own, then?" Abner asked.

"Yes," Sheppard said. "I got tired of the sorry remounts I was being given and thought it'd be nice to have a real horse to ride, so I cashed in a couple of favors some officers owed me, wrote home to Geneva, and had her sent down to me in Tennessee. That was at Christmas. She arrived along with a package from my sister and my children."

Abner nodded. "I see she's not gun-shy," he said.

"No, I used to take her hunting," Sheppard said. He was speaking almost absently, though he paused to smile at Abner.

"You hunt in New York?" Abner asked. "I thought it was a city!"

"There's more to New York than that," Sheppard said with a preoccupied smile as he stood in his stirrups and frowned southward. "It's larger than Georgia, I promise you."

"Yeah, but is it as pretty?" Abner asked.

Sheppard sat back down. "Just about," he said. "I think you'd like it if you ever came to visit me where I live."

"Maybe I could do that," Abner said. "When the war's over."

"When it's over," Sheppard agreed.

"After Grant's surrendered to Lee," Abner added.

That got Sheppard's full attention and garnered a grin from him.

"Right," he said.

Abner laughed and turned his face into the wind. "It's picking up a mite," he said. "Maybe we're due for a change of weather."

"Maybe," Sheppard said. His nose wrinkled as the wind sent the pine needles tapping and clattering softly about him. The sun was sifting down through the pine boughs, awakening a faint scent of turpentine that almost overlaid a strengthening odor of burnt wood and metal.

Abner hauled his shambling mount to a stop and sniffed. "What is it?" he asked.

Sheppard was frowning. "I'm not sure." he said. "If I didn't know better..." He stopped, his frown deepening.

"Smells like burnt, spoiled meat," Abner said. "That and rusty metal, maybe."

"That's a good way to put it," Sheppard said. He looked around at the trees. "Where's Wheelerville from here?"

"It's northwest," Abner replied. "We've made a circle to the south and east."

Sheppard nodded and turned his face into the wind.

Abner watched him lift his head and turn his head slowly from side to side. The chestnut mare's ears pricked and she snorted softly and backed a step.

Sheppard looked over at Abner. "Stay here and keep watch," he said. "I want to look things over, and I need you to stand guard. I'll be back." He turned Dixie and nudged her to a trot.

Abner watched him go and then turned away to listen to the wind sighing among the trees with the sound of mourners at a wake. Clouds were skittering overhead, pushed by the wind. The trees were showing their silver petticoats. Rain was coming, most likely, he thought. It would be a good growing season.

He heard the thrum of approaching hooves and looked up to see Sheppard riding toward him at a gallop, white-lipped and pale. He had lost his cap.

"Quickly!" Sheppard said, throwing himself from the saddle. "Change horses with me and mount up!"

"W—well, sure," Abner stammered, dismounting and taking the reins that were thrust into his hands. "But—"

"Get on the mare and ride back to town at a gallop!" Sheppard commanded. "Dixie can do it, and there's no time to waste! I'd go my-self, but lives are at stake and I'm not strong enough right now to do what needs to be done! And even if I were, I might get lost along the way! Listen to me: I want you to find Dr. Meacham and tell him to get things ready at Miss Wheeler's house. No delay, mind you: he'll need to have everything on hand and be ready to work fast! That's the most important part, and you must do it first. Then get together about a dozen able-bodied men and send them back to me, ready to do some hard work! Tell them they'll need strong stomachs!"

"B—but what's wrong?" Abner demanded.

"There's no time to explain," Sheppard said. "Mount up! Wait a minute, I'll help you adjust the stirrup leathers. There. Now tell Dr. Meacham you need shovels, axes, some sharp knives and a pile of blankets. Dear God! And send two wagons, too! Tell them to hurry! Meacham had best take his full kit to Miss Wheeler's. And tell the men to bring their guns with them, there's no saying who may be about."

"But what's happened?" Abner said.

"Bushwhackers," Sheppard said. "Remember that smoke everyone saw a while back? I've found the cause. Now get going!"

Abner gathered the reins.

"Abner! Wait!" Sheppard called.

"What is it, Sarge?" Abner said.

"You: when you're done, go to Miss Wheeler and tell her to get beds ready for two people. Stay with her and give her what help she needs. Warn her that it'll be really horrible. I'm depending on you: I know you won't let me down!"

"But you'll need me here!"

"She'll need you more there," Sheppard said. "Now go on. You can look another day, the wait won't kill you! Ride!"

CHAPTER FOURTEEN

"The burns and the exposure are the worst of it for the old man," said Dr. Meacham. "It's a miracle he survived this long."

Lavinia drew the sheet up to the old man's chin, gazing at the bandaged hands with shadowed eyes. She could feel the eyes of the woman on her, and she was not ready to meet her gaze yet. "You've bandaged and warmed him," Lavinia said. "Do you think he'll survive?"

"If he's survived this long, there's no reason for him not to continue if he wants to," Dr. Meacham said clearly, but Lavinia saw by his eyes that he was saying it for the woman's benefit.

Lavinia nodded and turned to the woman. She was visibly relaxing under the influence of the morphia that she had been given, her eyes softening, drooping. Lavinia could remember the terrible, unnatural brightness of her eyes as she was brought into the house. It was as though her well of tears had been burned away.

Lavinia had done everything she could do: the woman had been bathed and her bruises and cuts salved. Dr. Meacham had cleaned away the dried, crusted afterbirth, and carefully felt her abdomen and womb to make sure it was all expelled. She had been put into a soft, clean nightgown and set between clean sheets. Warm soup had been spooned into her slack mouth, water given to her. She had eaten a little and drunk a little, but she still gazed into the dark horrors of her mind, her eyes wide and unblinking in a once-pretty face stretched brittle and yellow as parchment over the planes of her skull.

She had spoken at first in the halting, mumbling voice of one drunk or sick. Random words about angels and vengeance, and a promise that had been made. The words had trailed into incoherence.

Lavinia took her hand. "You are safe now," she said gently. "It's over now and you are with friends. You can sleep now."

The woman's hand tightened in Lavinia's. "He promised," she said.

"He promised?" Lavinia repeated.

The grip grew painful. "The angel," she said. "My angel. If he promised— He'll keep his promise, won't he?"

"Go to sleep," Lavinia said. "Everything will be well."

"But the angel came to me and promised—"

Dr. Meacham bent over her and said, "If an angel gave his promise to you, then it will be done. You must sleep now and let him tend to things."

The woman closed her eyes.

Lavinia traded looks with Dr. Meacham and went out of the room. "How could this have happened?" she said once they were safely out of earshot.

"I'd heard of bushwhackers," Dr. Meacham said. "Whispers, like the stories we used to tell at night by the hearth to frighten ourselves when we were children. I had not heard half of it, and I wouldn't have believed it if I had."

"Do you think they were soldiers?" Lavinia asked.

"They might have been once," Dr. Meacham sighed. "But now? How can we say? One thing's certain: they were the sort who prey on the weak. Maybe not soldiers, but not far from an army."

Lavinia folded her arms and looked down.

"I remember the year I took the grand tour," Dr. Meacham said. "I liked to stand at the stern of the ship and watch the wake spilling out behind me, cutting into that deep green ocean. I couldn't stop gazing, it was so beautiful. And then one day one of the crew members pointed out something I'd never noticed before: sharks, following the ship. They hovered, came closer, snapped and retreated. Once they were pointed out to me, I saw them again and again." He smiled wryly and added," They were scavenging among the garbage and rubbish thrown overboard. It was a rich harvest, I guess. You know, the longer I live, the more I see that some people resemble sharks or wolves."

Lavinia shivered. "But a pregnant woman!" she said. "It's hard to credit."

"I think it was her condition that saved her from the worst of it," Dr. Meacham said. "I think— I'm not sure—what she saw made her abort spontaneously, and then the rains started. It was enough to turn those monsters' minds from her."

"But not from the baby," Lavinia said. "Not from the baby." She closed her eyes upon the memory of herself trying to pry the poor, ruined body from the woman's arms.

Who would have guessed what horrors lay in store when Abner Wigfall came galloping into the town on Sergeant Sheppard's big chestnut mare, shouting for help on the double?

The men had assembled, the supplies had been sent, and Lavinia had hurried about her house, readying it for two wounded people. Nothing had prepared her for the nature of the wounds on the corpses or the condition of the survivors: an old man who had been tortured with fire and hanged until he was nearly dead. And there had been a woman, bloody and bruised, clutching the battered corpse of a still-born baby. The rescuers had brought the mutilated corpses of two men and of another woman who had been raped and then strangled. Lavinia had stared in shock at the woman's shattered jaw. Who could have done such things to other human beings?

The horror had galvanized the people around her. Abner, frozen with shock when the two wounded had arrived, had shaken himself free and then helped her throughout the afternoon, fetching water and tearing bandages. He had been white-mouthed, with enormous eyes, but he had not wavered. Lavinia had finally sent him home.

The word had somehow reached the wounded soldiers in the house. Corporal Higgins, weak and sickly with his amputated leg, had somehow managed to rise from his bed and dress himself. He had presented himself, wobbling on crutches, before Lavinia, pleading to help any way he could. Lavinia had set him to work alongside Abner, assembling bandages and keeping the water hot.

The men had started coming back by late afternoon, telling a tale of finding burned wagons, smashed liquor bottles, ransacked belongings, and other horrors. They told her that Sergeant Sheppard had found the scene and sent Abner for help. He had returned to cut down the bodies and then do what he could to help the woman and the old man and make them comfortable, speaking to them, reassuring them until help came.

"They were refugees, probably fleeing from Allatoona," Ed Pickens had said. "They were trying to make their way here, from what I could see."

"Do you know who they were?" Lavinia had asked.

Pickens had shaken his head. The wagons had been burned, their belongings stolen or smashed. There was nothing to tell anyone their names, and the people themselves were incoherent.

When Lavinia had asked who could have done the atrocity, he had only shaken his head again. "Not Yankees, seemingly," he had said "They didn't turn a hair at the sergeant's uniform."

Lavinia looked at Dr. Meacham. "I told them to bring the dead back here to be buried," she said. She was standing on the front porch and gazing south. "I remember wondering at the cause of the smoke. It was gone after the rains, and I forgot all about it..."

"I think the rains must have saved their lives," Dr. Meacham said again.

"They must have," Lavinia agreed with a shiver. She said, "And yet they couldn't put names to their attackers."

"Are you surprised?" Meacham asked.

"I guess not," Lavinia said. She shivered again. "I am sickened when I imagine what they went through. Dear God!"

"It's not through yet, Lavinia," Dr. Meacham said.

Lavinia looked up at him.

"They're dying," he said. "You've been mistress of a household long enough to know the signs, yourself just looking in their faces. The woman was left with the afterbirth in her womb, in the dirt and the rain. Her womb is badly infected. It's only a matter of time. Hours at the most. The old man is no better off. If the exposure doesn't kill him, his burns will turn septic and that will finish him. The first death would be kinder."

"I can give them more morphia," Lavinia said.

"Yes," Dr. Meacham said, frowning out toward the hills. "I am ashamed to reflect that it's only through the kindness of an enemy that we can do even that for them."

An enemy. Lavinia turned toward the house and gazed up at its massive white pillars, marveling that they had remained unchanged while everything else in her life had altered until they were all but un-recognizable. Bloodshed, rape, robbery—they had never touched her before this terrible war had come right into her yard. Now they seemed to be wherever she looked.

The clop of hooves made her look up from her abstraction of horror.

Al Townsend was riding down the alley of trees toward her. He had volunteered to go help the rescuers when Abner had burst into

Pickens' establishment. He had sneered that a bluebelly wasn't going to go him one better, and while he had been the only one who had voiced the thought openly, Lavinia was certain that many others had shared it. His sneer was completely gone now, his normally high-colored face pale and pinched. He spoke calmly enough, though, when he reined in.

"They're all heading back now, Miss Lavinia," he said.

"Where is Sergeant Sheppard?" Lavinia asked. "He's wounded: is he coming back?"

Al Townsend shook his head. "He's looking for the little girl," he said.

"The little girl?" Dr. Meacham repeated.

"The woman's little girl," Townsend said. "He was sitting with her and that old man when we came up. Holding their hands, kind as a mother, talking to them low and sweet, telling them everything would be all right, smiling at them, though the look in his eyes when he looked up at us like to have torn our hearts out."

Townsend drew a strand of his horse's mane through his fingers and continued with anguished slowness. "She was clutching that dead baby in her arms, and the two were talking like people in a fever. Anyone could see they were sinking fast, especially that old man. He was bleeding from his nose and some clear, bloody liquid coming out his ears, but the two of them were hanging onto his voice and his face like it was their last sight of happiness. God, when I think of all—"

He stopped and drew a ragged breath. "The old man blacked out soon after I arrived, and the woman was losing her grip, too. I heard her saying, 'My little girl' over and over, each time like she was fighting to come awake from a nightmare. And each time he said, gentle as a brother, 'I'll find her for you, I promise'. When she was loaded onto that cart, he stayed with her, and she kept her eyes on his face, wide open and kind of terrible, but there was a glory and a hope in them that would have broken your heart to see. The last thing she said to him as they took her off was 'Your promise', and he said 'I'll find her'. And then he bent to kiss that bloody, torn hand of hers. She kept looking at him as they drove away.

He went looking for the girl, once they were out of sight. Said he wasn't going to let any babe wander alone and terrified. I tried to get him to go back, he looked like one of the wounded, himself, but he said no, he had given his promise, and he wasn't going back on his word for anything."

Townsend lowered his head; Lavinia could see the glitter of tears on his cheeks. He cleared his throat. "Miss Lavinia," he said, low and quiet. "That fellow's a better man than me, and no mistake. I should have never tangled with him. I wish I hadn't: it was stupid and mean of me. He's got more grit than I could ever have. I forgot what's really important and thought it was me. I'm a jackass, sometimes."

"You certainly are that," Meacham agreed acidly. "Did someone at least stay with him?"

Townsend nodded. "Sam Wallins did," he said. "Wouldn't take no for an answer, him and Judge Prescott. I would have, too, but they told me to git."

"Better and better," said Dr. Meacham. "Judge Prescott's an old man and he isn't up to gallivanting about."

"They weren't gallivanting," Townsend said. He dismounted and eased the reins over his mount's head. "Sergeant Sheppard was earnest as death, and he knew what he was looking for. He was crossing back and forth through the woods when I left, calling softly, like a father calling a baby back to him." He wiped his eyes with the back of his hand. "If I was little again, lost and alone and scared in the woods, I'd run for that voice," he said. "I wouldn't even have to think about it."

Lavinia looked at Dr. Meacham. "Angels keep their promises," she sighed. "Mr. Townsend, would you be good enough to pull that big whitewashed rocker to the center of the porch for me? And then go into the house and ask Callie to feed you."

"I've food at home, Miss Wheeler," Townsend said as he wrestled the heavy chair into place.

"Eat it when you get there," Lavinia said. "But have some here, as well. You need feeding. It's the least I can do. And you, too, Dr. Meacham. You must be exhausted: a good meal won't hurt you. Our patients are sleeping, and there's nothing more we can do. The dead are waiting to be buried, and that's enough. Now go on inside."

She watched them enter the house, then gathered her skirts, went to the rocker and sat down. The wood creaked reassuringly; she arranged her skirts, drew her shawl more closely around herself, and began to rock.

** ** **

The sunlight faded into dusk, the wind rose and fell and then died away. The stars paled before the moon as it stepped free of the eastern skyline. Above it, the evening star seemed to glow in its own light. A flight of meteors, dim as will-o'-the-wisps against the deepening night, arced low in the sky. The first fireflies of the year flared, sparkled, raised higher and higher in the sky, and then sank down into the grass to flicker like a carpet of stars.

Lavinia watched it all in silence broken only by the distant sounds of the spring evening and the rhythmic creak of the chair's runners upon the floor of the porch. Her thoughts flickered like the fireflies, darting backward and forward through the moments in her memory, touching the parchment-pale faces of those inside the house, remembering the blood, the fear, the despair.

Abner Wigfall's young, wide-eyed face above a basin of dirty, red-stained water, Dr. Meacham's mobile mouth drawn down in pain. Corporal Higgins hauling himself about on crutches, making himself silently useful. The halting voice of the woman speaking of angels and promises.

Where was the sense of it? How could people do such things to each other? What kind of soul lay behind the eyes that could see helpless people and reduce them to the bloody, ruined travesties of life that she had salved and soothed with her hands that day? Or did such monsters even have souls?

She had tended heartbreak, she had eased death, she had assisted lives in their entries into the world during the twenty years that she had run Fairlawn plantation. She had seen wounds and suffering, and while she did not like it, she freely acknowledged that there was no guarantee, in a world of free souls, that one of them might not abuse its freedom by killing and torturing and robbing. She understood all this and she accepted it, but her world had been wrenched awry that day and her body was too exhausted and her mind too dazed to make the effort to wrestle it back into its proper place.

She closed her eyes and lifted her face toward the stars, trying to find in their silent passage a salve for her own disquiet. Voices sounded in the house: Dr. Meacham speaking urgently with Callie.

Grieved whispers: the old man was dead, and the woman was sinking swiftly now.

Her fingers tightened on the arms of the rocker.

Death and birth and death again. For every opening life another closes. What is the point of committing your heart when heartbreak is the inevitable end? What is the use of striving for honor or decency when all lives pass away with the speed and anonymity of a log consumed by flames?

The slow, weary clop of hooves, seeming to underscore her doubt and despair in the night's growing stillness made her open her eyes and gaze down along the alley of maples to where a heavy-headed horse plodded toward her with as slow and deliberate a motion as though it had done nothing else through eternity.

Weariness and defeat lay in all its movements: the beast's head lolled at the end of its neck, bobbing dispiritedly with the swaying rhythm of its walk. Its hooves barely cleared the ground before sinking once more into the earth with a finality that seemed to speak of exhaustion and despair more eloquently than words.

Lavinia raised her eyes from the animal's gaunt and dejected form and saw its rider for the first time. Asa Sheppard was approaching her. He was slumped in the saddle, gray-faced with fatigue. His sling was gone, his uniform was torn and dirty, and his gloveless hands were cut and bruised. His sound arm was hidden within his jacket, which seemed to be twisted awry, and his head was lowered, but at least he was alive.

Warmed by a faint spark of relief, Lavinia pushed to her feet, descended the veranda steps to the road, and went toward him.

Sheppard raised his head; his eyes, meeting hers, shone with an exultation that made her catch her breath. He shifted his sound arm to show her what he was carrying as she came alongside his stirrup.

A little girl was sleeping within the shelter of his jacket, her smudged, dirty cheek pillowed against his heart. One thumb was in her mouth while her other arm circled him. As Lavinia watched, breathless and trembling with emotion, the child opened sleep-blurred eyes to gaze at her without fear, and then closed them with a sigh and snuggled closer within Sergeant Sheppard's torn, dirty jacket.

The world tilted and fell into place once more. Lavinia could see that a great light lay behind every shadow that was cast, more powerful than the shadows could ever be. Like the movement of a great dance, another life arose for every one that departed, and the heart always had room for another love.

"Welcome back, Sergeant," Lavinia said through the glad tightness in her throat. "Let me carry her now, she's probably heavy and you're still convalescent. We'll take her in to her mother while there's time for her mother to understand that you kept your promise."

CHAPTER FIFTEEN

...Seventy-eight...seventy-nine...eighty...

The brush sighed through the long strands of hair with a slow, soothing rhythm. From crown to ends, over and over again, the creamy bristles burnished the mahogany brown hair to an even richer gloss.

...Ninety-two...ninety-three...

The hair tumbled warm and soft across bare shoulders, trailed along the back of the low boudoir chair in a river of bronze to hang, at full length, barely a foot above the floor.

...Ninety-nine...one hundred...

Lavinia lowered the brush, savoring the flash of morning sunlight upon its rose-embossed silver and rich emerald enamel. The colors were repeated on the powder box, the tortoiseshell comb, the bottles and boxes arrayed on the dresser before her, all part of the set that she had purchased from the New York jeweler named Tiffany during the summer she had traveled to Saratoga, when the war was just a thundering beyond the horizon. It had been part of her morning routine for the past fifteen years, part of the ritual that began with her first sleepy-eyed awakening to a new day and ended with her emergence from her rooms, impeccably dressed and ready to deal with the world and its troubles.

She had felt an increasing need for such armoring rituals, lately. Who knew what new disaster might overtake her and those she loved? How could she guess what demands might be placed upon her at any moment? The peaceful hour spent brushing out her hair and donning her garments afforded her a chance to prepare herself for the coming day.

She took up the comb and carefully maneuvered the teeth through the bristles of her brush, working the strands of shed hair loose and pulling them away. A porcelain hair-receiver, made to store hair until it was needed to puff out coiffures, lay to one side. Lavinia had not

used it since it was first given her by a middle-aged beau who had pro-
fessed to admire her hair to the point of distraction. Lavinia, who had
seen at once that his admiration of her hair was exceeded only by his
admiration of the fortune she was expected to inherit, had given him
short shrift.

The ritual was nearly complete: she raised her eyes to the mirror
before her and saw, dimly, the face of the girl she had been twenty
years before. Wide gray eyes in a pale blur of face, imperfectly
glimpsed, framed by a torrent of red-brown hair. *Not pretty*, she
thought, but with a certain distinction.

She gazed reflectively, then reached for her spectacles. The shad-
owy image of departed youth sharpened into the present as Lavinia
settled the spectacles in place. Now the years were visible, though she
thought that several weeks of taking Dr. Haskell's tonic, and taking
half an hour a day to sit with her feet up had helped to lessen the lines
of fatigue and smudges of exhaustion.

The hair-receiver lay before her; Lavinia lifted a disdainful eyebrow at it, bunched the hair, tossed it into the fire, and turned her
attention to her gown.

The pieces of her dress, cut and sewn in two independent parts,
were separated by the width of her room. She donned the bodice and
hooked it up the front, then paused to frown thoughtfully down at it.

She had sewn the garment herself ten years before, using a light,
cotton fabric that had come all the way from India. The plaid contained all her favorite colors, jade green, sage and dusty lilac, and over
the years it had softened and faded to a silky bloom. The dress had
been one of her favorites, and it had survived her shift to dull, dark
colors. The weskit-edged bodice, currently fitted with pagoda sleeves,
was piped with hunter green velvet, with matching covered buttons
sewn down the front.

She rose, stepped into her wire-hooped crinoline, tied it at the waist
and donned another petticoat. The skirt was lying on her bed, where
Callie had placed it after fastening Lavinia's laces. She lifted it and
eased it over her shoulders, shaking its folds out over the hoop skirt.
She settled the skirt at her waist and hooked the waistband, then adjusted the bodice and gave her crinoline a twitch.

Lavinia had four 'cage' crinolines; she reflected that the patriotic
thing to do, in view of the shortage of metal in the Confederacy,

would be to turn them in to the authorities, but she dismissed the thought without any trouble.

The Confederacy had enacted, in April of 1863, a tax in kind that relieved her already beleaguered plantation of one tenth of its corn and tobacco crops each year. They had compounded the injury by sanctioning the use of force in collecting the taxes. They had also done away with enlistment terms, requiring that all men currently serving in the armies remain until war's end. With all those wrongs, Lavinia had decided that the Confederacy could do without her extra crinolines.

She sat down at her dressing table once more, took up her comb and opened one of the enameled silver boxes. From her dwindling store she carefully counted out eight hairpins, the number required to fasten her hair securely in its chignon. She set the pins to one side and gathered her hair with both hands. Her usually severe style was unbecoming, she thought. She had found a softer way of arranging it, one that might be prettier around her face. She thought she might try it that morning.

Her mind went back to the Confederacy. Where was the logic, she wondered, in a sovereign state's seceding from a union of similar states because that union's government infringed upon its rights, and then immediately placing itself in subjection to another central government that was less organized and more limiting than the first one and was growing increasingly despotic?

Just like Matthew 12:45, Lavinia thought with a quiver of wry amusement. *Then goeth he, and taketh with himself seven other spirits more wicked than himself, and they enter in and dwell there: and the last state of that man is worse than the first. Even so shall it be unto this wicked generation*

"Wicked," she said aloud, gathering the mass of her hair and coiling it. It came spilling out of her hands. The new style was going to take some practice—

"Vinnie? Are you dressed yet?"

Lavinia blinked, her reverie disturbed. She turned toward the door. "What is it, Callie?" she called.

"That poor little mite is calling for her mother, and won't take any comfort from me. I thought, since you are like the woman in most respects, she might cotton to you."

Most respects except about fifteen years of age, Lavinia thought with a sigh, putting the hairpins back in their box. There was no time to pin her hair up; she braided it quickly, tied the end with a length of ribbon and went into the hallway.

Callie was waiting, her grim mouth tight with distress. The distant sound of weeping was coming from the east side of the house.

"She was coughing all night, off and on," Callie said. "Running a slight fever, too."

"Oh dear," Lavinia said. "I was expecting it, but I'd hoped... Did you give her any willow tea?"

"She took a little," Callie said. "And then she spat it right out in a temper." She eyed Lavinia's braid. "Would you like me to pin up your hair?" she asked.

"There'll be time later," Lavinia said, gathering her skirts and hurrying down the hallway. "I'd wanted to try something new. It's in Godey's from a year or so before the war. Well," as she heard another yell," There's nothing wrong with her lungs, seemingly: I can hear her from where we stand, and the sooner I get to her the better."

"I shudder to think what she'll do when we try to give her quinine," Callie said, hurrying after her.

"Well she can't be all that sick if she's in a rousing temper," Lavinia said. "And if she's in that temper, then it stands to reason she most likely hasn't had any terrible nightmares. God bless Sergeant Sheppard for finding her!"

Silence fell as they reached the nursery door. Lavinia could hear snatches of words and sobs, and then a deep, reassuring voice. She took a deep breath and opened the door.

Sergeant Sheppard was there before her. He was still heavy-eyed from the day before, but he was smiling as he held the little girl with the sure confidence of an experienced father.

Her head was buried in his shoulder and she was whimpering with weary fretfulness.

Lavinia watched them for a moment, her eyes taking in his torn jacket. It looked as though he had crawled through a bramble thicket: one of the chevrons on the left sleeve was half pulled away, and the sleeves were dotted here and there with holes. She reflected that that, at least, was something that could be easily dealt with as she quietly closed the door behind her and came into the room.

Sergeant Sheppard looked up at her and smiled as his hand

smoothed the girl's hair. "She was crying for her mother," he said. "I thought I could help; she's quieted a little, but she'll be all the better for having a woman to hold her."

The girl looked up at Lavinia, her eyes wide and eager. "Mama!" she cried. And then she saw Lavinia as though for the first time. Her face fell.

"Poor little thing," Lavinia said, drawing up a chair and sitting down. Sheppard waited as she adjusted her skirts and pushed her braid out of the way. "Here," she said, "Give her to me."

The girl was as solid as a little log. She snuggled against Lavinia and raised tear-drenched brown eyes to her. "Where's Mama?" she asked.

Lavinia stroked the little girl's back with grieving hands. "Your Mama has gone to Heaven," she said. "She kissed you goodbye last night: do you remember?"

The girl looked up at Lavinia. "Did she die?" she asked.

"Yes, sweetheart," Lavinia said. "She was very sick."

The girl was shaken by a renewed fit of sobbing. "But she was having a baby!" she wept, burrowing against Lavinia's velvet buttons. "Did she die from having the baby?"

Sergeant Sheppard pushed himself to his feet and went to stand at the window.

Lavinia watched helplessly as Sergeant Sheppard drew his sleeve across his eyes and turned back to her. He knelt beside them and cleared his throat. "No, darling," he said. "Your mama got sick along the way, and when it rained she became worse and she died. She talked about you when she was sick, she said how much she loved you, and she was happy when she found out that you were safe."

"But the baby—"

"Listen to me," Sheppard said. "Sometimes, when the mother is terribly sick, the baby inside her gets sick, too. If the mother dies, so does the baby."

The girl was whimpering again. Sheppard took her from Lavinia and held her tightly. "I know," he said. "You want to see her and talk to her and you can't. But I'll tell you a secret that I found out when my own little girl's mama died: your mama's an angel now, your very own angel, and you'll never lose her. She's here with you, watching out for you, loving you more even than she could when she was here alive."

The girl drew back a little, her wet eyes wide open and fastened on Sheppard's. "Promise?" she asked.

"Honor bright?"

"Honor bright," he said.

** ** **

"Her name's Meg, for Margaret," Sheppard said. "Her mother told me while she was still lucid last night. I wish she'd been able to tell me her family's name. But she said Meg had been walking barefoot by the wagon while her mother rode. She panicked when she heard the shouting and the firing, and she ran away just as those bushwhackers came bursting through the trees."

"It's a good thing that she did," Lavinia said. She gathered her horse's reins and settled herself more comfortably in the sidesaddle that had lain unused since her horses had been confiscated three years before.

Her mount, a light-mouthed bay gelding with some thoroughbred in him, had been found wandering through the woods near the spot where the renegades had performed their butchery. He had been wearing an army-type saddle, twisted awry. Aside from a recent collar gall, there were no brands or other marks to identify him, and Judge Prescott, judging him a spoil of war, had brought him back to Wheelerville. He had presented him to Lavinia after breakfast that morning.

Three years. Lavinia had always been happiest on horseback, and the sheer delight of being in a saddle upon a mettlesome horse once again and wearing her Paris-made riding habit of bottle-green velvet was enough to put her in high spirits that even yesterday's tragedy could not quite cast down. And the horse was obviously accustomed to carrying a lady side-saddle. Her cup was running over.

It had been an odd day. Meg had sobbed her way into quietude and then, in the manner of children, had managed to tuck into a respectable breakfast upon being taken down to the kitchen. She had whimpered once or twice, thinking of her mother and her family, but Lavinia had been heartened to see that she had been lively and bright-eyed all in all, and happy to be left in Callie's experienced care.

She had taken Sergeant Sheppard on a tour of her holdings, a long journey even by horseback. They had visited most of the major out-buildings on the plantation proper, and she had introduced him to

Toby, her overseer, and the rest of the farm hands. Now they were skirting the fields of growing tobacco and corn on their way back toward the house. The tour of Lavinia's lands had taken up most of the day. She and Sheppard had paused at the plantation smithy to speak with Caesar, Fairlawn's chief blacksmith. While they were there, Caesar's wife had offered them a lunch of hoppin' John and greens, and they had accepted gratefully.

Caesar, who had been the last to return from his flight before the fighting at Wheelerville, had been full of news about the battles to the southeast. He was a large, laughing man with a boisterous sense of humor and a gift for remembering detail. Lavinia had caught Sergeant Sheppard looking thoughtfully from her to Caesar several times, but he had held his peace.

Caesar had listened with a frown to Sheppard's account of finding the murdered family, and then had nodded. "I heard tell of a group of folk hanging round here," he said. "Horrible stories. They're enough to put the fear of God into you, and make you want to keep a lookout."

"Well, tell everyone to stay close together," Sheppard said. "Don't let anyone venture out alone."

Caesar had nodded and watched as they rode away. Now they were returning to Wheelerville through the thick, golden light of late afternoon that slanted across the fields. Their conversation had come full circle and they were speaking of the morning's sorrows in the waning afternoon light.

Sergeant Sheppard gazed out across the sea of tossing corn to the line of trees marking the downward sweep of the hills into the valley. "I think Meg was trying to get back to her mother," he said. "But she had gotten lost. From what I could tell, she was sighting on common landmarks like tree fungus, bushes... She was drawn farther and farther into the woods. Then the rains came and she took shelter in a hollow log and, surprisingly, had the sense to stay there."

Lavinia drew a long breath. "She could not have seen anything, then" she said.

"Nothing," Sheppard agreed, his eyes shadowed. "Dear God."

Lavinia watched as Sheppard wiped at his forehead with the back of his right hand. "God was watching over that child," she said. "But I am sorry that it was you who had to encounter all that filth and horror, wounded and tired out as you are."

"As well me as another," Sheppard said.

Lavinia spoke with careful gentleness. "I think this tragedy touched some remembered pain in your own life, Sergeant. I am truly sorry."

"It was nothing," Sheppard said. "Anyone else..."

Lavinia smiled at Sheppard and let the disclaimer pass. "She died blessing you, you know," she said. "She thought you were an angel toward the end, nor was she far wrong."

Sheppard was silent.

Lavinia gathered her horse's reins. "But it's over now," she said with a return to briskness. "Since we can't change the past, it's best to bend our energies to what we can do."

"You're right," Sheppard sighed.

"I was thinking things through last night," Lavinia said. "The family may well have come from around Allatoona. At any rate they were obviously trying to move out of the armies' path. I have friends in the government: I'll make inquiries. We'll bury the dead here and care for Meg while we see what happens. It'll be good for her: she looks to you, I've noticed. And it'll be good for you, too, I think. And Sergeant," she said.

As he raised his eyes to hers, smiling, she saw the mark of remembered grief once more and saw, as well, his torn, ragged jacket.

"If you do nothing else good during this war," she said, "This one act of yours marks you as being one of the best and kindest men I have met."

CHAPTER SIXTEEN

"She'll need to meet children her own age," Sheppard said as they approached the house along the alley of pines. "Someone she can play with and chatter with.

"I set up a school for Fairlawn's children ten years ago," Lavinia said. "I teach there, myself, off and on."

They rode along in silence for a few paces while Sergeant Sheppard frowned at two horses tethered to the hitching ring before the house. "I see Judge Prescott's brown gelding," he said. "And there's the judge, sitting on the porch. I don't know the other horse."

Lavinia squinted through her spectacles at the two horses, and then gave it up and turned back to find Sergeant Sheppard smiling at her with an unexplained touch of amusement. The expression puzzled her, but not too much. "If the person's with Judge Prescott," she said, "he's welcome, whoever he is."

Sheppard waved to the Judge. "He's a good man," he agreed, urging Dixie forward until he was riding stirrup to stirrup with Lavinia. "How many children do you have on this plantation?" he asked after a moment.

Lavinia heard the question through a sudden surge of delight as her horse, still lively after a long day's ride, tossed his head and curveted sideways. She made a mental note to allow him time to get accustomed to a side-saddle again. "Now?" she asked after she had brought the gelding back under control. "We have about thirty children between the ages of two and twelve, with others on the way. Before my father's death we had three times that number, but all but thirty are gone now."

She smiled and smoothed the gelding's neck with one gloved hand. "Most of the families fled before the fighting around here, but they are all back now." She remembered the refugees and shivered. "I thank God they've all returned safely," she said.

"They all came back willingly?" Sheppard said. He seemed surprised.

"Of course they did!" Lavinia said. "Where else would they go? This is their home, after all."

Sheppard did not answer. Instead, he said thoughtfully," And the children are allowed to run and play?"

"Well, of course!" Lavinia laughed. "I can hardly stop them: they're children, after all! They do work in the fields after they reach twelve, though.

Don't worry, Sergeant: Meg will have plenty of playmates."

"What about the town children?" Sheppard asked. "Will she see any of them?"

"They are welcome to come to the school," Lavinia said. "Most of them do. All the children play together."

"I'm surprised to hear it," Sheppard said, turning away from Lavinia to look up at the pillared facade of the house and nod to Judge Prescott. "From what I'd heard before about slave—" He stiffened and let the sentence drop. "Good God!" he said through his teeth. "What is he doing here?"

Lavinia, who had been smiling a greeting to Judge Prescott, saw Al Townsend standing on the veranda beside the judge.

"Good afternoon, Miss Vinnie," Prescott said. "It's good to see you riding again."

"Thank you, Judge," Lavinia said, stroking the gelding's neck. "He's beautiful!"

"Afternoon, Miss Lavinia," Al Townsend said from the veranda. He had been sitting in one of the porch rockers, half-hidden behind one of the columns as they approached. He had risen and pulled off his hat as they reached the steps and now was standing quietly with his hat in his hands and his head slightly lowered. Lavinia could see that he was wearing his best suit of clothing and a new cravat.

"Mr. Townsend asked to accompany me," Judge Prescott said. "I saw no harm in it, and here he is."

"Good afternoon, Sergeant," Townsend said.

Sheppard reined Dixie to a halt and frowned at the man. "Afternoon," he said. His voice was uncharacteristically clipped. "If you're calling on Miss Wheeler, here she is. It's up to her whether she wants to receive you."

Townsend nodded. "Afternoon, Miss Lavinia," he said again. "I came to see the sergeant, if it's all right with you."

"I have no objection, Mr. Townsend," Lavinia said, easing her right knee from the fixed head of her sidesaddle. Al Townsend hurried to her side and offered his arm as she dismounted. She caught up the trailing hem of her habit and thanked him, then added," But it's up to the sergeant to say if he has any objection."

Judge Prescott smiled and said nothing.

Sheppard had been watching in silence. "It depends on what he has to say, Miss Wheeler," he said.

Townsend nodded once. He was kneading the brim of his hat between his fingers. His brows were knit and Lavinia could see that he was speaking with difficulty. "Well, it's this," he said." I saw what you did yesterday."

Sheppard's frown eased. He slid his feet from the stirrups and swung down to the ground. "And I saw what you did yesterday, yourself," he said. "I admit it was a help."

Townsend's anguished expression had deepened and his fingers were even more busy with the hat. "Well, if it was a help, I can't rightly take credit for it," he said. "I was in a snit, pure and simple. I went along because I didn't want any bluebelly making me look cheap. Well, I found out that no one has to make me look cheap, I'm good at doing it myself. I saw—"

Townsend broke off. "Well," he said, "The fact is, I wanted to say I'm sorry for my part of things when you came into town that time. The whole thing was my fault. I knew you couldn't fight—that is, I thought you couldn't—and I pushed things. I was too busy feeling pretty small for running away when the fighting came to this town. I fought in the armies for two years, and I thought I had more gumption than I showed. Anyhow, I'd had some harebrained notion of showing I wasn't so yellow as all that. It didn't work, and I'm sorry I tried it and you got hurt."

Sheppard was eyeing Townsend with a reserved expression, but he said nothing.

Townsend took a deep breath. "Anyhow, Yank," he said, "you whipped me fair and square first time we met, and I don't mind saying I deserved it. It was a lesson I needed to learn. If you can see it clear to say you'll be good enough to put it out of your mind, I'd surely be obliged to you."

Sheppard held out his hand. "It's forgotten," he said. "For all I know, I might have done the same if a Reb had come sashaying down the main street of Geneva, New York and started getting chummy."

"Well, thank you kindly then, Sergeant," Townsend said. "You've put my mind to rest and I'm obliged."

The silence following this pronouncement threatened to grow into minutes. Judge Prescott cleared his throat and said, "Sergeant Sheppard, why don't the two of you take the horses to the stable and make them comfortable?"

"That is an excellent idea, Judge," Lavinia said. "I'll go inside and ask Callie to bring out some refreshments."

"None for me, Vinnie," Prescott said. "I was just bearing Mr. Townsend company, and I would have spoken up for him if necessary. He has a proposal for the sergeant that I think he would be interested in hearing. Once he puts it to the sergeant, I'll go tend some business at home."

"Thank you, Judge," said Lavinia. "Mr. Townsend, you can accompany Sergeant Sheppard to the stable and make yourself useful there. When you return, there'll be biscuits and something to drink."

Sheppard sketched a salute and led Dixie off, closely followed by Townsend leading Lavinia's mount.

Lavinia watched them go, and then turned back to Judge Prescott. "How did you talk him into this, Judge?" she asked.

Prescott smiled and sat down again. "Didn't have to do any talking, Vinnie," he said. "He came to me unasked."

Lavinia looked toward the stable. Both men were moving easily beside the horses, and they were talking quietly. It would be all right, she decided. Al Townsend was the sort who acted without thinking at times. He was so big and strong, people seldom dared to come up against him. Well, it had happened this time and he had been stopped. Maybe he had learned a lesson.

** ** **

Lavinia paused before the attic door and lifted the ring of keys from her belt. She had heard the musical jingle of brass and silver so often in the past years, it was now almost inaudible to her. The key to the door was smooth and bright with a rose embossed on the head. She set it in the escutcheon, turned it, and pushed the attic door open.

The scents of lavender, camphor and cedar came billowing out toward her, overlaying a lighter scent of old wool and silk. The shapes of boxes and cupboards were slightly outlined in the dim light; the windows had been closed in the past and the shutters drawn and locked. She crossed the cluttered floor with purposeful steps, wrestled open the windows, unlocked the shutters and flung them wide, bringing a flood of light and air.

The room was crowded with trunks and cupboards, each bearing a paper label in Lavinia's copperplate handwriting from the inventory she had performed in 1860 when the sound of war had begun to rise on the horizon, her mother was lying on the point of death, and her brother had come to Fairlawn from the Wheelers' Savannah house with the woman who, he had announced, would be his wife.

Writing out the lists had helped to steady Lavinia's mind during those difficult days. It was easier and better to frown at the piles of silks, alpacas and kerseys than to snap at her father and brother, and try to be cordial with her brother's silk-tongued fiancée. Better to weep over the almost endless task of folding and packing than over her own exhaustion and pain and fear for the future.

And see what it had accomplished! All the castoff clothing, all the good fabric that had been purchased against future need and lain unused, the ball dresses of her youth, the draperies, the good woolen pelisses, the finely tailored suits of clothes-all were awaiting her with their wealth of scent, color and memory.

She consulted the small ivory-leafed silver notebook that hung at her chatelaine. She needed at least three yards of fine dark blue wool fabric, and as many of sky blue kersey. Yellow tape or braid of varying widths: four yards should suffice for that, and two feet of red tape or fabric. Brass buttons might pose a problem, of course, but she thought she might be able to locate the proper number.

She went to the nearest armoire, pushed her spectacles down on her nose and peered at the label. Yes, it was all there: the fabric needed to clothe someone just under six feet tall and about one hundred and eighty pounds. Fabric, trim, buttons: all that was needed was a pattern and her sewing machine, so carefully packed away at the start of the war.

She closed the notebook and fingered the dark blue wool pelisse that her mother had often worn. It would do for the dark blue fabric, though to be safe she would have to find some more, along with good, sturdy cotton twill for lining.

She moved down the line of trunks, frowning at the labels. If she had stopped to think, she would have known to write larger, but as it was— Yes, there: she could read her brother's name.

She gathered her skirts into a pad and knelt, then unlocked the chest and heaved the lid open. It fell back with a thud and she savored the clean, sharp smell of cedar. The top compartment of the chest held undergarments, drawers, shirts, suspenders, all washed and pressed and neatly folded.

She took out a pile of drawers, shook one out, and eyed it thoughtfully. Sergeant Sheppard was an inch or two taller than Gaylord had been, she thought, and Gaylord had been a little stockier. Sheppard had more leg to him, but that should not make any difference in the fit of the drawers, unless the waist was too small, which she doubted. It could be managed. The shirts should fit, since they had been cut and sewn with a generous hand. She refolded the garments and set them aside. A pile of socks joined them a moment later, and two sets of men's braces.

Her eye caught a folded piece of paper tucked into one of the cubbyholes in the partition. She twitched it out, opened it with a frown, and scanned it. After a moment she replaced it with a reminiscent smile. It was a copy of her carefully encoded directions to the gold she had purchased and hidden late in 1861 when it had become apparent that the war was going to drag on far longer than everyone had originally thought.

Since her father had been so consumed by his grief at Gaylord's death in 1861, Lavinia had decided not to trouble him with the family's business concerns, which she had been handling in fact for the past several years. She had authorized the sale of the family's Confederate bonds at thirty percent below their face value and bought gold with the proceeds, sacks of Federal twenty-dollar gold pieces. Now the gold had tripled in value, and there was enough there to pay the back taxes on Fairlawn if the Union prevailed, or to ransom the life of a loved one, if worse came to worse.

Lavinia had made several copies of the directions and had hidden them throughout the house and buried them on the grounds of Fairlawn. She replaced the directions, lifted the partition out and frowned at the stacks of carefully folded clothes within the chest. Gaylord

Wheeler had owned trunks and trunks of clothes, all made of the most expensive fabric and cut in the finest style. He had had a regrettable penchant for checks, encouraged by his fiancée, Louise: Lavinia doubted that the natty brown hound's-tooth frock coat she was holding in her hands would take indigo dye very well. But the military-cut riding jackets of dark blue superfine cloth, now, would be another matter. She would have to cut off the wide-skirted tails in order to match Sergeant Sheppard's short jacket, but it would not be difficult.

Lavinia sorted through the garments without finding what she sought, then sat back on her heels with a frown. Her father, James Wheeler, had been taller and more broad-shouldered than Gaylord, who had taken after his mother. She would do well to go through the trunks containing his clothing. Heaven knew, he had spent enough time in the saddle to merit a whole dozen riding coats!

Lavinia replaced the partitions in Gaylord's chest, got to her feet, and dusted her dress. She would open her father's trunks, she thought, and see what she found. And while she was at it, she could look through her own trunks. She had put aside all the pretty, vibrant colors that she had loved in favor of black and maroon and dark brown, all colors she had never liked, once she had reached her thirty-fourth birthday.

Now that she thought of it, she was surprised at her own folly. The idea had been Louise's, and Lavinia, exhausted after a five month stay by the girl that had finished with her mother's death, had somehow found herself agreeing that she was too old to wear bright, lively colors. Now that Gaylord's death had scotched all chance of him marrying Louise, Lavinia was astonished at her own timidity.

What was the point of wearing dark colors all the time? It was not as though she were a widow, after all! What had planted that notion in her head? Louise, walking about the plantation, commenting on various deficiencies of the house and Lavinia's person in her sweet, clear voice, speaking of the changes she would make until Lavinia had itched to slap her.

Drab colors indeed! Hadn't she earned the right to please herself?

She thought so, and she could remember a beautiful sage-green watered silk dress that was just waiting to be refurbished and donned once more. And while she was at it, maybe she could see what was there in the way of ribbons and lace to use in her hair, now that she had decided to abandon her severe chignon.

CHAPTER SEVENTEEN

Was it possible to form an effective militia unit with only twenty-three able-bodied men, most of whom were well over fifty? The question occupied Sergeant Sheppard as he walked slowly back down the alley of willows toward the house. Twenty-three able-bodied men and half again as many squirrel rifles, old dragoon pistols and small derringers. And maybe twelve serviceable horses under the age of twenty.

Sheppard stopped and frowned back over his shoulder toward the town, mentally tallying the buildings, scanning the terrain, placing sharpshooters, and then sending a group of bloodthirsty renegades in to tangle with them. He reviewed the picture formed by his mind and frowned thoughtfully. Well, maybe it could work, but there would be little margin for error. Miss Wheeler lived a fair distance from the center of the town, and that house, with its tall windows and wide double galleries, would need a full company of men to defend it adequately. An attacker could break the glass and climb into any window that suited him. Protecting the outlying farm families would pose a problem, as well. And yet, the murder of that family of refugees had shown everyone very clearly that something would have to be done quickly.

He pulled off his forage cap and ran his hand through his hair in an absentminded gesture that predated his army service by several decades. The June evening was mild for the mountains of Georgia; he did not replace the cap. Crickets were beginning to chirp in the underbrush, the fireflies were sparkling in the grass, and the stars seemed to shimmer in the light wind that trailed across the deep blue evening sky.

Outlying farm families and Miss Wheeler's field hands. Sheppard's mind circled the memory of Caesar's children playing in the yard. What if they were attacked? Who would protect them?

Or, Sheppard thought, could THEY perhaps help to protect everyone else? It bore thought; he had heard of Negro troops serving in the eastern theater. By all reports they were good fighters. It did not surprise him: he was a firm abolitionist, and it was the slavery issue that had prompted his enlistment in the early summer of 1861, with his wife's full support. He had known former slaves and had found them as articulate and intelligent as anyone else he had met. Caesar, Miss Wheeler's blacksmith, and Toby, her overseer, were certainly intelligent and strong men—though it was odd the way they reminded him of Miss Wheeler.

He tried to estimate the number of slaves in Wheelerville. Miss Wheeler had said there were thirty children under the age of twelve: there were probably at least fifteen men of an age to beget children, and probably at least that number again of men able to handle a gun. But what would the townsfolk think?

And what would the army think of him raising and training a company of militia?

He turned the question over in his mind as he lifted his face to the evening breeze. His orders were very specific: protect Miss Wheeler and all her property. The property included all of Wheelerville. That being the case, where was the problem with helping Wheelerville form a militia unit? If he served in an advisory capacity, no one could complain, least of all General Stanley, whose primary aim in giving Sheppard the assignment in the first place had very obviously been that of protecting Miss Wheeler.

But not helping to raise a group of soldiers who might fight against his country.

Sheppard sighed. He would have to do some steady thinking. No one had pressed him, and that was good, but the memory of the ring of faces anxiously watching him, waiting for a reply, was unsettling.

The house loomed before him, warm and somehow welcoming. He had felt it the first time he had seen the place, as though someone had spoken a quiet greeting. It had been morning then, the long, new light gilding the lines of the woman who stood in the yard and gazed back at the house as he was doing now. He had felt the morning sun warm upon his shoulders then; now, in the evening, it glowed behind the house and gilded his cheekbones.

It was as though he were seeing an exact, but opposite, copy of his first sight of the house. It only lacked a mahogany-haired woman in a plain, windblown calico dress to make the illusion complete. He shook his head with a wry smile. Time passes and moments of magic seldom repeat themselves.

He mounted the four steps to the front entry, settling his sling more comfortably. It wasn't working; he shifted his shoulders after a moment and then pulled the sling off with a flash of irritation. The arm was healing well, and keeping it motionless irked him now. The wound itself itched damnably, and it took all his self-control to keep from giving in to the urge to scratch.

Callie was waiting inside the door as he came in. She eyed the sling he had in his hand, but said nothing.

"Where's Miss Wheeler?" Sheppard asked, bunching the sling and stuffing it in the breast of his jacket.

"She's in the main parlor, Sergeant," Callie replied. "She wanted me to bring you to her once you returned. I'll take you in and then get you some food."

"How's little Meg doing?" Sheppard asked.

Callie's grim face softened. "She watched me cooking all afternoon and then she took a nap."

"How's her fever?"

"Pretty much gone, praise the Lord," Callie replied. "She was asking for her mother again."

"She will do it," Sheppard said. "There's no stopping it, and I don't think it's kind to tell children pretty lies about some of life's realities. My little Lydia cried for her mama, and we kept telling her that her mama was dead and in heaven. It hurt for everyone, but in the end I think we did right."

"'Ye shall learn the truth,' " Callie quoted solemnly, "'And the truth shall set ye free.' "

"Exactly," said Sheppard. "But we'd better be selective about the truth that's told. Meg mustn't know everything about how her mother or her other kinfolk died. When she gets older it will be enough for her to learn that they were killed by raiders."

Callie frowned but then thought better of it. "You're right, Sergeant," she said. "Well, Miss Vinnie was calling for you, and I'm to bring you to her.

** ** **

Tallow candles cast a circle of warm light in a corner of the parlor.

The rest of the room was dimly lit by a small fire that touched the gilding of picture frames and the carved lines of furniture and left the rest wreathed in shadows. A cascade of pink flowered muslin lay like a drift of rose petals across Lavinia's lap and pooled on the floor. Her hands were moving nimbly in the folds of cloth, and Sheppard caught the flash of a gold thimble.

"Callie said you wished to see me," Sheppard said.

Lavinia smoothed the muslin, straightened the thread in the needle, and took several stitches. "I have something to discuss with you, Sergeant," she said. "I hadn't thought Mr. Townsend would keep you quite so long."

"I apologize, Ma'am," Sheppard said, enjoying the warm play of firelight upon her hair. He had noticed that she was wearing it in a looser, prettier style; it suited her better. "I didn't know you were waiting for me. A group of townsfolk had a proposition to put to me, and I heard them out and gave an answer."

Lavinia nodded and tied off the thread. "That's nice to hear," she said.

"They asked me to help them organize a militia," Sheppard said.

"Mm," said Lavinia.

Sheppard eyed Lavinia's downturned head and said slowly, "I'm not sure what I should do. I'm not allowed to give aid and comfort to an enemy, but I can't believe that protecting civilians would be considered that. Then there's the problem of numbers. Short of arming the slaves here, I don't think we have enough people. But we'll all be slaughtered if we don't do something."

After a long silence, he looked to see Lavinia tying off the thread.

She felt his eyes on her and raised her head. "That is excellent news, Sergeant," she said comfortably, setting the muslin aside with a preoccupied smile and taking up a pile of white garments. "I am very glad to hear it."

"*What* did you—" Sheppard began.

Lavinia offered one of the garments. "I would like you to try this right away, Sergeant, and see if it fits," she said, holding it up.

Sheppard, staring, saw that it was a pair of drawers.

"I suspect the fit will be satisfactory," Lavinia said, eyeing Sheppard's legs and then lifting her gaze to his waist, "but it's best to make certain. Here, take it, sir."

Sheppard was speechless as she thrust the drawers into his hands.

"There are two pairs of trousers here, as well, which you must try," Lavinia said. "Pay special attention to the length of the inseam and the fit about the seat. All this being equal, I will require your clothing for a time, especially your trousers and your jacket—"

"Miss Wheeler!"

Lavinia blinked and looked up at him. "What is it, Sergeant?" she asked.

"You can't mean— Why, these are drawers!"

"I should hope they are," Lavinia said. "At least, they are what Georgia men wear as drawers. For all I know, New Yorkers wear them to church in the summer with nothing but their undervests over them." Her gray eyes narrowed thoughtfully behind their spectacles. "It must be very diverting to travel through New York in the summer," she said. "At any rate, we're in Georgia at the moment, and I'd be obliged if you would keep these beneath your trousers."

She looked up and saw his dumbfounded expression for the first time. "For heaven's sake, sir!" she exclaimed. "Why are you standing there like a pillar of salt with your mouth open? You have the drawers: they are fine ones, and impeccably clean. I believe I have estimated your measure correctly, but there's only one way to tell, and the sooner it's done the less time will be wasted."

Sheppard raised the drawers and looked from them to her.

Lavinia consulted her silver-bound ivory notebook. "Drawers, shirts and stockins. I don't know if you wear braces, Sergeant, but there are two pair of those, as well. Now do tell me if the fit is satisfactory."

"Here?" Sheppard demanded.

Lavinia blinked. "Of course not!" she sniffed. "I've better things to do than watch men prance around naked—" She caught herself up and continued with slightly heightened color. "Your uniform is torn and dirty, and you must have a replacement. I have placed some garments in your room that may be altered to suit you. I would be obliged if you would try them on at once and advise me of their fit. If they're suitable for the moment, you may leave your old jacket and trousers with me for repair. I can use them as patterns, as well, when I sew their replacements."

Sheppard, who had been standing flatfootedly staring at her with his hands full of drawers, suddenly sat down on one of the overstuffed settees and succumbed to a boisterous, satisfying fit of laughter.

Lavinia eyed him. "No doubt, Sergeant, you will tell me in your own good time what you find so amusing."

"Oh Lord!" Sheppard gasped.

"What is it?" Lavinia demanded.

"I thought-I thought you w-wanted me to try them on here!" Sheppard said, holding his sides and trying to wipe tears from his eyes.

"Of all the silly—!" Lavinia began. She stopped and frowned. "And perhaps, Sergeant," she said frostily, "you can tell me where your sling is."

"At the moment it's crumpled in a ball in my jacket," Sheppard replied.

Lavinia closed her notebook, smoothed the chains of her chatelaine, and eyed Sheppard's shoulder. "Dr. Haskell gave orders that you were to wear that sling for three weeks," she said.

"Three weeks have come and gone, Miss Wheeler," Sheppard said. "I've obeyed his orders and I don't need the sling any more."

"Dr. Haskell didn't know that you would have that shoulder torn open again," Lavinia pointed out. "Two of the weeks were spent abed, and you're still healing. You would be well advised to wear that sling for another two weeks, Sergeant."

"I am afraid, Miss Wheeler, that I don't see the need for it," Sheppard said, folding his arms.

"But I do see the need, Sergeant, and it is best that you comply." Lavinia took up the pink muslin dress again with an air of finality, then set it down with an exclamation of annoyance as Sheppard did not move. "May I ask what you are staring at, Sergeant?" she demanded.

"Beg pardon, Ma'am," Sheppard said. "I'm trying to find your shoulder-straps."

"*What* are you trying to find, Sergeant?"

"Your insignia," Sheppard repeated. "From your tone, I thought I'd surely find at least a pair of eagles there, but it appears I'm wrong. Maybe you can tell me, Ma'am, what your rank is."

Lavinia rose, bringing Sheppard to his feet as well. She pushed her spectacles back on the bridge of her nose and looked up into Sergeant Sheppard's hazel eyes. "I am the mistress of this plantation, sir," she said. "And you are living under my roof and eating at my table. As long as I am mistress of Fairlawn, I expect those who live here to do as I ask them. I don't think my request was outrageous, and your levity in response is most reprehensible, sir."

Sheppard made no comment, though he folded his arms behind his back and lifted his eyebrows at her.

Lavinia looked him over, exasperated. "And as for you Sergeant: from the way this exchange has gone, I would expect to find foam around your mouth from having it washed out with laundry soap for impertinence!"

Sheppard gazed down at her and she gazed up at him. "One more week," he said.

"I beg your pardon?"

"I'll wear it another week," Sheppard said.

"You should wear it another two," Lavinia said.

"One week will be sufficient," Sheppard said.

"You're in danger of bodily harm, Sergeant," Lavinia said. "If you were one of the little boys on this plantation, you certainly would be thumped on the head. You will wear that sling for two weeks."

They traded a long look. Sheppard's mouth crooked slightly; Lavinia's eyes began to dance before she dropped them.

"One, then," Lavinia said. "But then you will have Dr. Meacham look you over and make his recommendation. Now try on those drawers—in the privacy of your rooms!"

She turned away toward the muslin dress, then straightened with a yelp of surprise as Sheppard snapped to a heel-clicking salute, scooped up the garments, and marched from the room and up the stairs

CHAPTER EIGHTEEN

The raw, red earth of the newly dug graves contrasted oddly with the pallor of the plain pine coffins and the rich green of the grass beyond them. Each coffin lay atop its grave, kept level with the earth by two sturdy ropes passed beneath it and held by two men. The sighing wind stirred the petals of the bouquets laid atop the pine boxes, sifted through the hair of the men standing bareheaded by the graves, and ruffled the skirts of the women present.

The air was alive with glances. Wide eyes moved from face to face, lifted to the hills to the west, to the leaves above, to Rev. Porter in his black robes, his face raised to the skies, his worn prayer book open in his hands, anywhere but to the coffins. The horror was too new to be faced, and while only a few people in Wheelerville had actually seen and touched the six victims waiting to be buried, their shocked pity and horror had overwhelmed the town like a flood. They were waiting to bury neighbors, countrymen, people who could have been sisters or brothers or a father, people who had spent their final hours in unimaginable terror and pain and died nameless, leaving as their survivor a child who could not understand the enormity of her loss.

The glances flickered to the four year old girl standing beside Sergeant Major Sheppard with her hand tucked into his. Her hair had been combed and set into ringlets, and she was wearing a pink dress produced from Miss Wheeler's capacious trunks. She looked down from Sergeant Sheppard and stared at the coffins. Her eyes, which up to that moment had held only a vast puzzlement, moved from one coffin to the next.

The words were said, the prayers offered and finished. Reverend Porter closed his prayer book and nodded to the ten men. The coffins were lowered into their graves and the ropes pulled back up.

Meg watched all this in silence, though her lower lip was beginning to quiver. She took a step forward to look down into the nearest grave, keeping her grip on Sheppard's hand as though it were a lifeline.

"Mamma?" she faltered.

No one spoke. Several people lowered their heads. Lavinia looked up and met Sergeant Sheppard's eyes.

"Where's Mamma?" Meg said on a rising note of desolation, her eyes moving from the coffin back to his face.

Sergeant Sheppard pulled his left arm from his sling and took her hand in both of his. "Your mama is not in that box," he said quietly. "She's in Heaven."

"But I want her here!" she cried, clinging to the hand and then, turning blindly for comfort, to him as he went to one knee and put his arms around her and held her while she wept. "I want her here!"

** ** **

"We need to talk with you, Sergeant," Sam Wallins said later that afternoon. He and the others had come upon Sheppard as he stood with one shoulder propped against a tall oak tree that overhung the new graves. He was smoking his pipe. His eyes had been fixed on the sky, his expression uncharacteristically grim, but he took the pipe from his mouth and nodded to them when he saw them approaching.

"I'm here," he said. "What do you want?"

"It's about Al Townsend's suggestion that we talked about yesterday," Wallins said. "We need to talk about it again, especially in view of what happened today."

Sheppard knocked his pipe out against the trunk of the tree, ground the smoldering tobacco out with his heel, and said "Yes?"

Wallins nodded at the graves. "We just can't let it happen again," he said. "We can't let our womenfolk be raped and butchered by those monsters." When Sheppard was silent he said, "Damn it, Sergeant, you saw it more than any of us! You saw it all! We've got to do something! How can we just sit and let things go on?"

Sheppard eyed the pipe. "I don't have an answer yet," he said. "I'm not sure I can give you an answer."

"What is there to answer?" Wallins demanded.

"If it's a question of pay," Ed Pickens began.

"It's got nothing to do with pay," Sheppard said. "I don't want any pay. But I'm not sure I can do what you ask."

"Why not?" demanded Al Townsend. "Damn it—" He stopped and looked around. Not seeing Lavinia, he continued, "Damn it all, you're a soldier! We've seen you can fight! And with those monsters on the prowl, we need all the fighters we can get!"

"That's true enough," Sheppard said, frowning down at the graves. "But these were a small band of refugees. Two able-bodied men, two women—one pregnant—and an old man. They were a perfect target for their killers. This town, now, is different. I don't think it'd be a likely target, considering its size."

"There might be larger groups," Ed Pickens objected. "I've heard tell of it: people being attacked and whole towns laid waste."

"It's happening now, south toward Atlanta," Haller Reeves, the publisher of the town's newspaper, threw in. "I hear tell of raiding parties. Women insulted, people riding away with hams and hogs and valuables slung over their saddles."

Sheppard frowned at him. "South of here, you say?" he asked.

"Yes," said Reeves. "I've heard no end of it. It's all those curst, thieving Yankees overrunning the land!" He broke off as someone hissed to him to be quiet.

Sheppard's expression contracted slightly at the last comment. He shoved the pipe deep into his trouser pocket, straightened, and turned to face the others. It was obvious that he had made up his mind.

"Well?" said Wallins. "What do you say, Sergeant? Will you help us?"

** ** **

"So he refused to have anything to do with forming a militia," Lavinia repeated thoughtfully, settling the thimble more firmly on her ring finger. "Well, I can't say that I am surprised. But what do you think I can do about it?"

"You can order him!" Ed Pickens said.

Lavinia arched her eyebrows and pulled the needle through the fine blue fabric of the jacket sleeve, took a turn through the yellow braid that formed the lowest chevron, anchored it, and knotted it. "But I can't do that," she said, taking another stitch. "I have no power over him."

"He's staying here!" Pickens objected.

Lavinia traded a thoughtful glance with Judge Prescott as she smoothed the braid with a fingertip. She was holding a post-funeral reception that afternoon, and everything was set up and ready. Her guests would be arriving shortly, but she had a few minutes to finish up Sergeant Sheppard's jacket.

She had thought it would be easy to cut down one of her father's worsted blue riding coats to make a shell jacket like Sergeant Sheppard's, but she had encountered some unexpected difficulties, and she wasn't entirely happy with the result. She had enough resources to make two more jackets, though, and she had thought of several ways to improve the garment.

"Sergeant Major Sheppard is not under my orders," Lavinia said, testing the tautness of the thread. "He was assigned to guard my valuables—"

"You own Wheelerville!" Ed Pickens objected. Encountering a sardonic look from Judge Prescott he said, "Well, she does, Judge! If Sergeant Sheppard was assigned to guard Miss Lavinia's valuables, then that includes the whole of Wheelerville, lock, stock and barrel!"

"That may be the case with the property, Mr. Pickens," Lavinia pointed out, "but I don't own any people."

"That to the side," said Dr. Meacham, "There are some of us who think the people of Wheelerville are worthless!"

"That's a fine, smart-aleck thing for you to say, you quack!" Pickens said hotly. "But the fact remains—"

"Why aren't you surprised, Vinnie?" Judge Prescott interrupted.

Lavinia shook the jacket out and eyed it thoughtfully. "It stands to reason," she said, fingering a button. "Sergeant Sheppard is a non-commissioned officer in the Federal army. He has been asked to help organize and train a militia composed of enemy citizens in enemy territory. I am surprised the men of this town had the nerve even to put the question to him. I'm sure he was, too."

"Well, he knows we wouldn't be fighting him!" Wallins objected.

"What if a force of northern soldiers came through here?" Lavinia asked. "Would you fire on them?"

"They as much as said they would," Dr. Meacham said.

"We did not!"

"Haller Reeves spoke of raiding parties and then talked of 'those curst, thieving Yankees'! Sergeant Sheppard had been looking interested, up till Reeves shot his mouth off. Then he iced over like a pond in winter!" Meacham shook his head and said, "Comes of printing a scandal sheet that has an editorial column each week. He's shot off his mouth in print for so long, he's forgotten that you shouldn't do it in person."

"The Sergeant took it all wrong!"

"How was he supposed to take it?" Judge Prescott asked. "It doesn't sound like a compliment to me! Good lord, where are your brains? If you wanted his help, you've just spoiled your chances of getting it! I hope someone has the sense to horsewhip Haller Reeves while we're talking! Now Sergeant Sheppard probably thinks taking you under his wing is tantamount to treason!" He pursed his lips and added, "Come to that, he's right!"

Lavinia cut the thread and folded the jacket. "That is why he won't help you, gentlemen," she said. "I can't say that I blame him, though I hope he will reconsider. And now, if you will excuse me, I must tend to the wounded before my guests arrive."

** ** **

Twenty minutes later, smiling broadly, Lavinia was heading for the burial ground with the new jacket over her arm. Corporal Higgins was getting around more easily now on his crutches, though he was still weak. She thought another two weeks would serve to strengthen him, and then he could perhaps be fitted with a wooden leg.

She always enjoyed talking with Higgins, whose glib Irish tongue tended to run to fulsome compliments when he was around anything in a skirt. It cheered him up, and it kept Lavinia and Callie in an unaccustomed ripple of amusement. He was a lively conversationalist and a good-hearted man with a lot of common sense and the ability to make the other wounded men smile even as they obeyed him. She would miss him when he was gone.

He had listened to Lavinia's humorized account of the afternoon's fiasco and then had said, "You could talk to him yourself: I've seen he's a reasonable fellow with a good heart. For a sergeant! Maybe he could just help out a little. Depends on how you ask him. It's worth a try."

Lavinia smoothed the jacket sleeve and frowned at the trees. Sergeant Sheppard was still there by the graves, as though, having won the honors of the field, he was determined not to quit it. His pipe was in his sound hand, his tobacco pouch held awkwardly in the other, and as she watched he took a pinch from the pouch, put it in the bowl, and pushed it firmly in. He frowned at the unlit pipe, upended it over the pouch, knocked the tobacco out, and then put both away.

He sighed and leaned back against the tree. After a moment he reached into his pocket, took out a shiny object, and gazed thoughtfully at it. As she watched, his expression grew sad.

Those curst, thieving Yankees.

Men! Lavinia thought, gathering her rose muslin skirts with one hand and approaching him.

He saw the flicker of her skirt out of the corner of his eye and straightened, his cap in his hand. The flash of welcome in his eyes and the sudden warming of his chill, remote expression drew an answering smile from her.

"Good afternoon, Sergeant," she said when she was beside him. "I suspected you'd be here. I came here a lot in years past when I wanted quiet to think."

"It's a beautiful spot," he said.

"I think it's my favorite spot in the entire plantation," Lavinia said. "So green and peaceful..."

"I'm surprised you gave it for a cemetery, then," he said, replacing his cap.

"I was, too, at first," she said, looking at the new graves. "But then I thought after all the struggle and hardship they saw, and the horrors, how can I grudge them the peace and the greenness when I have this whole sweet earth to roam through until I die?"

He had turned and was watching her with light-filled eyes. He said slowly, "Miss Wheeler, there are times I think you must be an angel."

She smiled up at him. "I know of someone who was convinced that you are one, Sergeant," she said. "She wasn't far wrong about you, either."

His eyes looked a question, but he did not speak.

"It was her," she said, nodding at the nearest grave.

Sheppard looked down at his hand, lying quietly in the sling.

Lavinia folded her hands before her after a moment and leaned back against the tree. "What were you thinking of as I came up?" she asked.

"What was I thinking of?" he repeated.

"You had something in your hand," she said. "You seemed sad."

He reached into his pocket and handed it to her, a disk of silver, warm from his hand. "It was this," he said.

Lavinia turned it over in her palm and saw the once-familiar shape of Liberty, seated, with a shield to her right and an arch of thirteen stars over her head and about her shoulders. A spread-winged eagle was on the reverse side, clutching an olive branch in one talon and a bundle of arrows in the other. The words UNITED STATES OF AMERICA formed a half-circle about it, and beneath it were the words HALF DOL.

Since the start of the war three years before, she had had very few of those coins pass through her hands. She saw as though for the first time Liberty's gracefully lounging pose above the date, 1846. She handed the coin back to him. "A half dollar?" she said.

He held the coin between his thumb and forefinger. "The date," he said. "1846. I was thinking how things were when this coin was first minted. This war was no more than a nightmare thought, easily ignored by all but the hotheads. The United States were rubbing along pretty well; no one would have dreamed we'd be seeing this wasteful, painful—" He stopped and looked at the half-dollar again. "Eighteen years," he said. "That poor woman in her grave was most likely Meg's age, with no more thought of being a mother, or of dying, than Meg herself had until a day or two ago. I was just returned to Geneva after serving my apprenticeship and producing my masterpiece."

"Your masterpiece?" Lavinia repeated.

Sheppard smiled reminiscently. "It was the finest mahogany I could afford. A chest-on-chest in the old style, with a carved pediment and a bonnet top that took me weeks to do right. It's in the Governor's mansion in Albany now."

"I thought you were—" Lavinia began. "How long have you been in the army?"

"Three years," Sheppard replied.

"Then this isn't your career?" Lavinia asked.

"Good lord, no! If I'd wanted an army career, I'd have gotten an appointment to West Point and been an officer. No, Miss Wheeler, I've been a cabinetmaker for over twenty years."

"That's why you were looking at the banister when you first came into the house," Lavinia said. "And if your work is in the governor's mansion—" She did not finish the sentence.

Sheppard smiled at the half-dollar. "Eighteen years," he said. "I had just met Sarah, too. My wife. She was the daughter of the Methodist pastor in Geneva, and I chanced to pass the church just as she came out from the service. I fell in love straightaway. It took her six years to decide she loved me back."

Lavinia looked up at him. "You know, Sergeant," she said, "Sometimes people can't see their own good fortune because they're too caught up in their own wishes and hopes. Sometimes it takes years to understand that the love of their lives is standing right before them, close enough to touch."

He returned her look. "And sometimes a man knows his own heart from the first," he said, putting the coin back in his pocket.

His voice had been almost neutral, but Lavinia sensed an intentness in his words. She looked down at her folded hands. "I have another thing I want to discuss with you," she said.

He groaned. "Oh Lord," he said. "I might have guessed there'd be something more! If it's about what those fools suggested—"

"No," Lavinia interrupted briskly, holding the jacket up. "It is about your clothing. Take off your jacket and try this on. I'll be making two more, and I think this will do until they're sewn. I am not satisfied with the insignia or the waist, but I think it'll do for now."

Sheppard eyed the jacket. "I can't try it on," he said.

"And why not, pray?" she countered. "If it's modesty that stops you, I'll turn my back."

"It's this sling, Miss Wheeler," Sheppard said. "I'd have to take it off to try the jacket on, and you threatened to thump me on the head if I did."

"I'll forego the pleasure this time," Lavinia said. "Here, I'll take this, and you can unbuckle your belt—" She took the sling from him and waited while he unbuckled his cartridge belt and set it at the foot of the tree. She took his old jacket when he had doffed it, and then watched as he donned the new one and fumbled one-handed with the buttons.

He was fastening them awry. Lavinia tsked and pushed his hands aside. "Here, allow me," she said. "There, you see? That arm isn't healed enough to do without that sling."

"It's clumsy because it's out of practice," Sheppard said, lifting his chin like a little boy to let her get to the hooks and eyes at the high collar. "If you'd let me use this arm we wouldn't have this problem. As it is, it'll probably ato— atro—" He frowned at her.

"Atrophy," Lavinia supplied.

He looked her in the eyes and then grinned. "That's it," he said. "Thank you. Atrophy. I'm only wearing the sling to oblige you, and you should know it's doing me considerable harm."

"You are a handful, Sergeant, and that is God's own truth!" Lavinia said. "I'd be tempted to do you some harm myself by thumping you on the head after all, except that I promised I wouldn't!" The buttons finished, she stood back and looked him up and down. "Well," she said, "how do you like it?"

He smoothed the fabric with respectful fingertips. "It's beautiful!"

"It does suit you," Lavinia agreed, picking up the belt. "Now turn around: how's the fit across the shoulders?"

"There's enough room," he said, shifting his shoulders.

"Hm," Lavinia said, tracing the side seams with a light fingertip and then running her hand around the collar seam. "Bend over a moment, I want to see how the collar is set in, and you're too tall for me to see properly from here."

He turned his back and went to one knee before her. "Here," he said over his shoulder. "Is this better?"

"Much better," she said, tugging at the high collar. He could not see her smile. "This gave me no end of trouble," she said. "Lower your head a moment." She eyed the line of the collar seam. His hair, darker where the sun had not reached it, grew to a V at the nape of his neck, and his shirt was startlingly white against his sun-browned skin. She firmly suppressed an urge to trace the line of his hair with a fingertip and said, "You can get up now: it seems fine. There could stand to be a little less fabric here, maybe, though some looseness is necessary if you plan to do any hard exercise in it. The jacket was one of my father's, and while he matched you in height and breadth of shoulder, he had some extra flesh on him. I tried to make allowances... Well, it seems to fit fairly well at any rate. You can wear that while I use this one as a pattern."

Sheppard took her hand lightly in his for a moment. "Miss Wheeler," he said.

She looked up at him.

"This was very kind of you," Sheppard said. "I don't know how to thank you."

Lavinia drew her hand away. "You'll be swearing at me after I make you put your sling back on," she said, offering the length of fabric.

"Not swearing," he said. "Never at you."

She lowered her eyes before his expression. "Well, it fits," she said again.

"It isn't as breezy as the other," he said.

"Those tears were cause for pride, Sergeant," Lavinia said. "I'd keep that jacket as a memento of a charge faithfully carried out."

He looked quizzically at her.

"You saved Meg's mother from madness," she said. "She kept speaking of you, thinking of you, saying that you had promised. You kept your promise, and I think it caused you some pain to do so."

"I gave my word," he said.

"Yes," she agreed. "You did, and that was that." She handed him the belt and watched him fasten it, then looked at the graves. "Well, it's been a sad day," she said. "I only wish—Anyway, we've done our best."

Sheppard nodded.

"And Sergeant—" Lavinia said. "I would like to apologize for the boorishness of my menfolk. It caused you some distress, I think, and I would not have had that, much though I would have been glad for your help. No one was thinking of you as a 'thieving Yankee', and I think everyone there knew the comment for what it was."

"-The bitterness of someone who's lived through a war," Sheppard supplied.

"That is it," Lavinia said. "I only wish there were some way you could help them without doing anything against your conscience."

"There may be a way, Miss Wheeler," he said slowly, pushing away from the tree. He took his old jacket from her and offered his arm.

"What would that be?" she asked. Her eyebrows raised when he told her.

CHAPTER NINETEEN

"Giving aid and comfort to the enemy!" Ed Pickens snorted. "I like that! After all we did for him!"

The funeral reception was in full swing. The men were standing in a haze of tobacco smoke and speaking of the day's events. Their voices, which had been discreetly lowered at first, had risen over the course of the discussion, bringing quizzical glances their way from the women, who were clustered at the other end of the ballroom.

Abner Wigfall had joined the group of men after assembling some refreshments for his mother. He stood a little to one side, painfully conscious of his status as the youngest man present. He had been listening to the talk with flashing eyes, but he kept quiet.

Al Townsend had also been silent, but his expression had grown darker as the volume escalated. Now he set his fists on his hips and eyed Ed Pickens. "You keep blabbing about that, Ed," he said, "But you haven't told us just what it was you did for him."

"I sold him tobacco!" Pickens snapped. "Everyone here saw me do it!"

"That's supposed to be a favor?" Townsend demanded. "You chiseler! You sold it all right! For ten times the going rate! He paid you in silver, too! And then he swapped some coffee for the next batch. We'd all heard you say just two days before that you were ready to kill for a drink of coffee!"

"A deserter like you's a fine one to talk!" Haller Reeves snarled.

"My enlistment expired!" Townsend retorted. "I served more than my time—and got no pay for the extra—and I didn't ask for any, either! You're hiding behind that rag you call a 'newspaper, scared that they'll call you up nevertheless!"

"And we're to think you a brave soldier!" Reeves sneered. "Picking a fight with a wounded man!"

"Well I got my ass kicked for my pains," Townsend said. "I deserved it. The point is, none of us did him any favors and I'm honest

enough to admit it! Heck, he stuck his neck out helping us! That refu-
gee family— And if you tell me he wasn't feeling sick as a horse, I'll
call you a liar! You all saw him! Why, Sam Wallins and Judge Prescott stayed with him when he was going through the woods after that
poor little mite, calling her name, crossing and recrossing his trail,
white and unsteady in his saddle, going on through sheer pluck!"

"You don't know anything about it, you half-wit!" Reeves snarled.
"He wiped the street with you!"

"At least it knocked some sense into my head!" Townsend said.
"You're expecting a soldier, who's been fighting our armies, to teach
us to fight so we can take a pot-shot at his armies? You've got wind-
mills in your head!" He glared at Reeves for a moment and then added
with fine sarcasm, "And considering it was you, you loose-lipped
booby, who opened his fat trap and spoiled everything, you're a fine
one to talk! If brains were gunpowder you wouldn't have enough to
snap your suspenders!"

"You're sure singing a different tune!" John Toombs said.

"Well shee-yit!" Townsend said. "You noticed!"

"He's a damned Yankee!" Reeves said. "He's better off shot!"

"You keep saying that and it isn't fair!" Abner said. His voice
squeaked upward and cracked, and he subsided with a blush.

Sam Wallins had been listening quietly with his arms folded. He
hoisted an eyebrow at Abner.

"Going to be a Yankee, yourself, bantam?" Toombs sneered. "Your
pa'll be proud of you for sure!"

Abner doubled his fists. "You take that back!" he said.

"Run along home, little britches!" Toombs said. "Come back when
you're dry behind the ears!"

"You're a—"

"Cut it out!" Wallins said. "Pick on someone your own size, Jack."

"Are we going to let that bluebelly sit here and eat our food and
drink our water and not pay for his keep?" Reeves demanded.

"Ah for Chrissakes, Haller," Townsend began. "You keep saying-"

"But Sergeant Major Sheppard is eating *my* food and drinking *my*
water, Mr. Reeves," Lavinia Wheeler said behind him. She had entered the room on Sergeant Sheppard's arm half a minute before and
had been waiting for a moment of silence before speaking. "Did you
have some complaint about what he eats?"

Sheppard, beside her, was standing with the rigidity of someone who has just realized that he has stepped into a trap and is looking for a way out without betraying his unease. His eyes moved from Reeves' face to Toombs and then flicked about the room.

"I do have a complaint, Miss Wheeler!" Reeves said. "I've seen the rascally acts of these cowardly Yankees—"

Al Townsend let out a groan. "God help us!" he said. "He's starting up again!"

"—of which this fellow's a perfect specimen," Reeves continued. "We have just finished burying the bloody, abused handiwork of his kind—"

Sheppard's eyes blazed and he took a half-step forward. Lavinia's left hand, tucked into the crook of his right arm, tightened its grip as she brought her right hand to join it. Abner Wigfall, watching, realized that she was holding him by main force, although her expression had not altered from its calm smile.

"You windbag!" Townsend sneered. "Do you deal in anything besides lies? Who found those folk and saw to it they were cared for? Who rescued that little—" He stopped speaking as Lavinia's quiet voice spoke over him.

"The 'handiwork of his kind', Mr. Reeves?" Lavinia asked gently. "I fear you are misinformed! I spoke at length with the unfortunate creatures he rescued, and neither of them saw any blue uniforms. Indeed, they had been fleeing the federal armies when they were set upon. Had they stayed with Sergeant Sheppard's kind, they would have been quite safe."

She smiled at Reeves and added softly, "That is something you would have been better aware of, sir, if you had gone with the rest of these good people to assist at the scene of the disaster rather than staying safely in Wheelerville."

Her words fell into utter silence. She looked around the room at the people gathered there, at Callie and George standing discreetly in the doorway, Callie's hands hidden in her apron, at the women moving forward in silence. "I don't understand why tempers are so high now," she said. "The danger and the horror are past, and we have cause to be happy."

"The danger is not past, Miss Wheeler!" Ed Pickens said. "Reeves here has heard tell of marauders—"

"Oh hell!" Townsend interjected. "We've seen marauders!" He caught Lavinia's slightly frosty look. "Begging your pardon, Miss Lavinia," he said.

Pickens was bristling. "Will you shut your fat—"

"I beg your pardon?" Lavinia said. When Pickens did not speak she smiled up at Sheppard. "Would you be so good, Sergeant, as to get me a plate of some of the refreshments and bring them to that chair by the window?" she asked.

Sheppard's eyes were still flashing, but he nodded.

"Now, gentlemen," Lavinia said, moving toward the chair she had indicated. "Let us discuss matters calmly. Why are you all so upset?"

"We've already told you, Miss Lavinia," Haller Reeves said. "This—this fellow—" he eyed Sheppard, who was returning with a cup of spring water and a plate of corn biscuits balanced carefully atop it. "—has flatly refused to help us."

Lavinia took the plate and cup from Sheppard and nodded to a spot beside her chair. "But he hasn't refused, sir," she said. "Indeed, we were just discussing matters as we approached the house. He has told me that he can help you within certain parameters."

"What's a perimeter?" Pickens demanded.

"Parameter," Lavinia said. "It is a guideline, or a limit. The sergeant can assist you if certain problems can be overcome and certain conditions met."

Reeves' eyes narrowed. "What conditions?" he demanded.

Lavinia sat back. "Sergeant?" she said.

Sheppard shifted on his feet. "You don't have enough weapons," he said. "You don't have enough men, either. Even using the boys of this town—which I don't like to do—you can maybe put twenty or twenty-five in the field. You need more than the assortment of squirrel rifles and old pocket pistols you have now. Why, there's barely enough to go around."

"He has a point," Wallins said wryly to no one in particular.

"It's quality, we're looking at, not quantity," Pickens said.

"Quality!" Townsend snorted.

"Quality doesn't count for much if there are only thirty of you and you're facing five hundred," Judge Prescott pointed out. "All the courage and pluck in the world won't even the odds if the enemy's armed with rifles and all you have is a broom. What is the solution, Sergeant?"

"Go where there's been some fighting and pick up firearms and horses. You'll need horses, too," Sheppard said. "You'll find all sorts of weapons thrown away for want of a little cleaning or refurbishing. And you'll find some good animals wandering that only need a little rest and care to be fit again."

"That's a good idea," Toombs said. "What do you suggest doing about the people?"

"Two things," Sheppard said slowly with a glance at Lavinia. "You could train the ladies of this town to fight—" he paused at the uproar that greeted his words. "Which I'd recommend, since you may not be around when they need defending. And you could arm the slaves of Wheelerville."

"The slaves?" Pickens demanded.

"Toby and Caesar and the rest," Sheppard said.

Lavinia looked down at her hands as the room went into an uproar.

"Sergeant," said Judge Prescott, "I don't believe you have been told—"

"There, what did I say?" Reeves demanded. "He's nothing but a goddamn nigger-loving abolitionist!"

Callie and George traded looks and withdrew.

Sheppard's brows drove together, but he did not try to speak over the rising voices.

"—Put guns in niggers' hands—!

"—Arm the darkies—!

"—I'm not fighting beside any nigger—"

Lavinia touched Sheppard's arm and nodded toward a nearby serving spoon, sitting in a bowl of spoonbread. He retrieved it and then winced as she rapped it sharply on the table beside her.

When everyone was silent she said, "I give you all notice here and now that I will not tolerate that word in this house. Sergeant Sheppard has told you part of what he told me. There is more. Sergeant, please tell them the final condition for you to work with them in setting up a militia."

Sheppard lowered his eyes. "You must—" he began. He cleared his throat and began again. "As a soldier in the armies of the United States of America, I am forbidden to give any assistance to enemy citizens outside the scope of my assignment." He took a breath.

"But—"

Lavinia looked up at him. "Sergeant?" she said.

He continued after an uncomfortable pause, "—but if the people of this town first agree freely to take an oath of allegiance to the United States of America, and then take that oath, I can do all within my power to assist them. Anything other than that is treason."

He lowered his head as the storm of protest broke over him. Even Dr. Meacham and Judge Prescott seemed upset, while Abner Wigfall stood in mute misery.

Lavinia rapped again with the spoon. "Those, gentlemen, are the conditions within which Sergeant Major Sheppard of the United States Army is permitted to help us raise and train a militia—"

"Tyranny!" Reeves shouted.

Lavinia looked him up and down until he closed his mouth. When he was finally silent she said, "Are you quite finished, sir? Or must I expect another mannerless outburst?"

Haller Reeves flushed and looked down.

"Well, I'm not fighting beside any nigger!" Toombs snarled. He cast a contemptuous glance at Sheppard. "Or any crawling bluebelly, come to that!"

Lavinia lifted her eyebrows but said nothing.

"There's no crawling bluebelly here!" Abner exclaimed. "You take it back or we fight!"

"Your pa'd really be proud to hear you!" Reeves said.

"He sure would!" Abner retorted. "He respects an honest enemy, and he knows honor! He always said you were a pack of jackasses, and I guess he's right! And if he were in the sergeant's place, he'd do the exact same thing! You're squawking like a flock of geese because the sergeant won't help us! Well, he's given some suggestions, and I think they're good ones, and so would my pa! Get some guns, arm some people who can fight, and put something together yourselves! How can you ask him to do the work for you? For that matter, how can you expect him to do it? Pa told of people in Pennsylvania expecting him to guard them against his own kind on the way to Gettysburg, and he said it was awful awkward! If he were here, he'd say you were stupid! I don't think—"

Sheppard quieted Abner with a hand on his shoulder. "Thank you, son," he said. "But it's no use your arguing with your folks and your friends. I've told them what I am allowed to do, and that's that. With Miss Wheeler's permission I'll go now."

He left, taking with him the stares of all the people in that room. The talk started up again after the door closed behind him.

** ** **

Sheppard sat down on the top step of the back porch with a sigh and gazed west toward the mountains, still outlined by sunset's pale afterglow. The hardest truth he had learned in the three years since the war's beginning was the ease with which hatred replaced liking, and the way a well-liked acquaintance could one day turn his eyes upon you and see not the man that you were, but the group to which you belonged, and direct his hatred at you for that membership.

He sighed and drew up one knee. It might be a fact of life, but that did not make it right. He eased his left arm from its sling and carefully rubbed at the healing wound. It hurt, but at least it was a hurt of the flesh and not of the heart. He closed his eyes and continued the motion.

"Sergeant."

The voice was close by. He opened his eyes, turned and saw George standing on the step beside him. The rising moon glittered on his white hair and turned his eyes to barely glimpsed shadows. He was holding a plate that was giving off wonderful smells.

Sheppard straightened.

"I brought you some food," George said, coming closer. "Spoon-bread and chicken and some greens. It's part of our supper, Callie's and mine, and you haven't eaten anything."

"I'm not sure I want anything," Sheppard said.

"Come on now," George said, speaking from the humorous distance of nearly eighty years of life. "Sure you need food-young fellow like yourself, just getting over being hurt. Even if you don't feel hungry, you'd best eat."

"That's right," Callie said, coming up behind them. "And I brought some buttermilk from the dairy. It builds good, sturdy bones, Sergeant. You eat some of this food and drink up and you'll find things are looking a whole sight better."

Sheppard smiled and took the plate, then sat back as George set a napkin about his shoulders.

"Wouldn't do for you to go messing up Miss Vinnie's fine needlework," George said. He watched Sheppard pick up a piece of fried chicken and take a bite. "Well, now," he said after Sheppard had chewed and swallowed. "Feeling better?"

The chicken tasted good and the spoonbread, buttery and hot, was delicious. Sheppard said so.

"A meal will set you up every time," Callie said. "Somehow, chewing something good gets the bad sounds out of your ears: niggerlovers, crawling bluebellies—all of it."

Sheppard sighed and looked down. "I'm sorry you had to hear all that," he said.

Callie and George traded amused looks. "We've been hearing it all our lives, Sergeant," George said. "I just consider the source, and I remember there's a wind blowing through this land, that'll sweep all the things away that shouldn't remain."

Sheppard put down the bare chicken bone and turned away from George to reach for another piece. He saw that the back porch was surrounded by people. George and Callie were standing beside Toby and Caesar, and there were others from the group of field hands that Sheppard had met some days ago, all watching and listening.

Toby came into the reflected light from the window and nodded to Sheppard. "I heard the news," he said to George.

"Did you hear all of it, Toby?" Callie asked.

"All of it," the plantation overseer said. "I even heard we're dealing with a 'nigger-loving abolitionist' here." His voice was very dry even as he smiled at Sheppard.

"That was Haller Reeves shooting off his mouth again," Caesar, the plantation blacksmith, remarked, folding impressively muscled arms. "Point is, there are things that have to be done, and I don't feel right about leaving them be until those folks in there can get their thoughts untangled."

George nodded. "The point is, Sergeant," he said, "We want you to help us form a militia."

"I don't know if I can do that," Sheppard said. "We're on shaky ground. Much though I'd like to, there's a lot that could stop me."

"What, for instance?" asked Caesar.

"For starters," Sheppard said, "Your state doesn't recognize the right of slaves to bear arms."

George shook his head. On the back porch, among his own people, he was self-assured and decisive. "We don't recognize Georgia's right to regulate us at all, Sergeant," he said.

Toby spoke up. "That's right," he said. "President Lincoln made a proclamation over a year ago freeing all slaves. What's to keep us from bearing arms?"

"Georgia might take a different view," Sheppard pointed out. "And we're in Georgia at the moment."

"I don't see where it makes any difference," said Caesar. "The question is: will you train us to fight?"

Sheppard frowned and set the piece of chicken down. He wiped his fingers after a moment. "I was ordered to protect Miss Wheeler and her property," he said. "I was told to take whatever steps I thought were necessary. If she's in danger—" He paused and then said, "And by the laws of the United States of America, you're free. But I can't arm or train you unless you take an oath of allegiance."

"Where's the problem with that?" Callie asked. "Get the Book out and I'll take it now! We all will!"

"You understand that you'd be protecting Miss Wheeler," Sheppard said. "That's one thing that must be kept in mind."

"I've no problem with that," Toby said. "She's one of God's own saints! I'd protect her if it meant my life. So would anyone here!"

Sheppard frowned. "And the state of Georgia might take a dim view of what you're doing."

George had been eyeing him with a measure of puzzlement. His expression cleared suddenly. "He doesn't know," he said to the group.

Sheppard looked at him. "I don't know what?" he asked.

"Listen, Sergeant," Caesar said. "Georgia's got no say in what we can do with our lives, and even if it did, protecting Miss Lavinia's a good thing to do. She's an angel."

"Look at him," said Callie to the rest. "He still doesn't understand, and the way everyone's beating around the bush, it's no wonder at all." She leaned over Sheppard. "Listen to me, Lamb," she said. "We aren't slaves. We haven't been since Miss Vinnie's father died."

Sheppard blinked. "Then I've been assuming since I came—" he began. "But Miss Wheeler's father freed—"

"That whited old sepulcher never did a Christian thing in his life!" Toby burst out. "Free anyone? Not him! No, sir! Not him and not that strutting peacock of a son of his! I thank God they're both dead! No,

Sergeant, it was Miss Lavinia. The minute her father was in the ground, she drove straight to Judge Prescott and wrote up everything legal and proper, making us all free. She called us all together and said that we weren't slaves any more, but that this was still our home if we wanted to stay. She said she'd pay our way across the Ohio River, if we wanted. And she said that if we stayed here, we could farm her land and she'd give us a fair share, and so she has. Why Sergeant, she paid the taxes out of her own pocket, rather than cut into our shares! And my brother–my brother Antoine—he was sold into Mississippi by old Mr. Wheeler six years before he died–Miss Lavinia tracked him down and bought his freedom too and said it was all she could do, and little enough. I swear to God, Sergeant, I'd die for her, and I'd thank God for giving me the chance! She's got a heart of gold even if she does have a tongue like vinegar at times. Ask any of her people! For that matter, Sergeant, I've seen her dealings with you, how she cared for you and fussed over your comfort: you know how she is!"

"That's right, Sergeant," Callie said. "Miss Lavinia freed us all. We're loyal citizens of the United States, and we don't have any problems fighting, even if that means protecting some white trash at times! There's a Bible in the library: get it out. We'll take that oath of allegiance here and now, and you can start training us tomorrow!"

** ** **

Sheppard administered the oath of allegiance to fifty of the Fairlawn people, field hands and housefolk alike, the next morning and set about training them at once. The field hands were all strong, intelligent men, especially compared to some the raw city boys he had dealt with in the past three years who had not known one end of a horse from the other. Sheppard had been unprepared for their skill with firearms and horses, and by the end of the first day he was cautiously confident that things would work out well.

The townsfolk were silent, which worried Sheppard. He had an uneasy feeling that people were thinking things over and making plans.

CHAPTER TWENTY

Al Townsend arrived the fourth morning after Sheppard had sworn in Toby and his people. He was pale and controlled, with a simple request and a simple reason for making it.

"I saw the things those bastards did," Townsend said. "I don't want that to happen here, and I'll do what I can to stop them."

"You'll even take an oath to support an enemy government?"

Townsend's brows were knit. "I don't know that it's an enemy government," he said. "It was my government until 1861, and I wasn't the one who suggested we secede. I wasn't happy when we did, though I...I forgot about it with all the fuss about the war. I guess-I joined in April for a two year stint and came home when my term was up... Hell, Sergeant, I don't know. I don't hate the stars and stripes, but my kinfolk died in the armies. All I know is my home's Wheelerville and I want to protect it. Here I am if you can use me, and I'll do whatever's needed."

"You'd even swear allegiance to the Union?"

"That's right, Sergeant," Townsend said.

"You don't mind being branded a traitor by your friends and neighbors?"

"If it keeps them alive, I don't care," said Townsend.

"I wonder," said Sheppard. He reached into the breast of his jacket and took out his pocket Testament. "I don't understand why you're doing this, Townsend," he said.

Townsend eyed the Bible. "Can I swear on that?" he asked.

"It's just a New Testament and Psalms," Sheppard said, turning it over in his hand. "I suppose it'd be all right, though I think you'd need a complete Bible for it to be legal, but that's a question for the lawyers."

"All right, then," Townsend said. "Let's do it. I'll swear, and I'll stand by it and do my best."

Sheppard held the Testament aside as Townsend reached for it.

"No," he said, "I'm not taking your oath."

Townsend stared at him.

Sheppard spoke more seriously. "You're talking a lot differently from our first meeting," he said. "What's made you change your mind?"

"I got a whiff of myself and I didn't like the smell," Townsend said. "Look, Sergeant, can't I—"

"No," said Sheppard. His inflection was a little odd. "And I'll tell you something else: I drill my group each morning from nine till noon in the clearing by the small woods. I don't want to see anyone skulking around watching while I'm doing it. Do you understand me?"

Townsend stared at him and then wordlessly held out his hand to Sheppard.

** ** **

Abner Wigfall came to Fairlawn that afternoon right after Sheppard had returned from performing a sweep patrol with Caesar. He was carrying his shotgun and walking with as brisk a step as he could manage with an obviously heavy heart. He found Sheppard sitting on the back porch and watching the sunset. Callie had given him a cup of buttermilk, and he had unfastened his jacket and propped his feet on the railing.

Sheppard set his feet on the floor and sat up with a welcoming smile when he saw Abner. "I'm glad to see you, lad," he said, nodding to another chair. "What brings you here?"

Abner looked down. "The windbags came here to talk to Miss Lavinia about you and about—things. I didn't feel like hanging around and listening to them shouting about bluebellies, niggers and half-wits, and I wanted to talk to you, so here I am."

"Well, you've come at a good time," Sheppard said. "There's buttermilk enough for the two of us, and the day's getting cooler. Sit down!"

Abner obeyed and set the musket between his knees. "Are you training that group now?" he asked.

Sheppard cocked an eye at him and tilted his chair back. "Yes, we've started," he said quietly as he set his feet on the railing again.

"Oh," said Abner. He started when Sheppard handed him a cup of buttermilk, but he took the cup and then held it on his lap. "Are—are they any good?" he asked at last.

"Drink your buttermilk," Sheppard said. "Yes, they're pretty good, or they will be. They're a little awkward right now, but they're strong, smart and willing." He smiled and added, "Give them a little practice and they'll be very good."

Abner traced the rim of his cup with a fingertip. "I hear Negroes make poor soldiers," he said. "Shiftless, they say."

Sheppard frowned. "Who told you that?" he asked. "They're humans like everyone else. What do you think they do in Africa? Play drums and lie under trees? The African people are a warrior race. They have lions there, and other tribes that they fight. Just like the Europeans and just like the Indians here. There are quite a few colored regiments in my army: they're holding their own in the fights they've been in, and I've seen them in your army as well, off and on."

"I didn't know," Abner said. "No one ever told me." He sighed, sipped at the buttermilk in his cup, and then sat back. "Well, I'm here," he said.

Sheppard looked at him, the easy smile gone from his expression.

"I've brought my own gun, too, Sergeant," he said, offering his shotgun.

"I remember the gun," Sheppard said, frowning at it. "You looked as though you were planning to use it to blow a hole through me the first time we met. Why did you bring it this time?"

"Why, to volunteer, Sarge," Abner said.

Sheppard's frown changed to a scowl. "To volunteer?" he said.

"Well, I can't let those monsters attack here and do nothing about it other than shout about niggers and bluebellies! Someone's got to fight, and it can be me!"

"You want to take the oath of allegiance?" Sheppard said.

"That's right, Sarge," Abner said. "Can we get it over with, and then you can start training me?"

Sheppard unfastened the top button of his shirt and took off his cap. "You sure you want to do this?" he asked.

"Yes, sir."

"This is your idea?" Sheppard persisted. "No one put you up to it?"

Abner looked at him. "I said I'd take the oath," he said. "What's the problem? You've overrun us, we surrendered. There's some renegades out there need to be handled, and I guess I'll help with it."

"I'm not a garrison in a conquered town," Sheppard pointed out.

"I'm just a lone Safeguard assigned to protect Miss Wheeler and her property. Has it occurred to you that your people could easily overrun me?"

"So what?" Abner said. "You're a soldier and you're ready to fight to protect Wheelerville. I want to help."

Sheppard was smiling again, but he shook his head. "Put your shotgun away," he said, "And finish your buttermilk."

"Are you going to help me swear that oath?" Abner asked.

"No, son, I'm not," Sheppard said. "I don't want your oath, and I'm not going to train you. It wouldn't be fair to you or to your pa."

"But someone's got to protect this town!" Abner cried.

"Relax, Abner. I've got a full squadron of able-bodied men here, and while some people around here might not approve of the color of their skins, I'll say here and now that they're a likely lot and they've as much right to defend this town as anyone else."

"But don't you want me?"

"No, I don't," Sheppard said. "You'd feel bad about swearing the oath, and your pa would be hurt when he heard of it. Take your musket and go home, and tell your ma to stop worrying."

Abner stared at him. "But—"

Sheppard crossed his ankles and grinned up at him. "You heard me, son," he said. "I don't want you to swear, and I won't take you any other way."

Abner rose and shouldered his shotgun. "I don't understand you," he said. "I say I'm willing to do what you want, I offer to help, and I'm honest about it, and you tell me you don't want me after all."

"You got that right," said Sheppard.

Abner stared at him. "I thought you—" he began. His voice cracked. He took a slow, deep breath and tried again. "I thought you were a friend," he said bitterly. "You seemed to want to help—"

"I still do," said Sheppard.

"Do you?" Abner asked. When Sheppard gave no answer, he slowly turned away and started along the back path toward the town.

Sheppard's voice stopped him. "Abner!"

He halted and looked over his shoulder.

"You people make things too difficult," Sheppard said, setting his cup of buttermilk on the floor beside his chair. "Look here: there's nothing on earth to stop you from coming and watching my group drill. I'm surprised I have to point it out to you."

CHAPTER TWENTY-ONE

Was there ever such a plague of windbags? Lavinia thought. *Enough to make Pharaoh weep!* She reflected that if the Lord had seen fit to afflict the Egyptians with the patriotic political leaders of Wheelerville at the first try, the Chosen People would have been able to leave for the Promised Land nine plagues earlier than they had.

Haller Reeves, Edward Pickens and several of the other vociferous patriots had come to her looking for Judge Prescott on what they termed an urgent legal question. They had been going round and round the issue for the past hour, and nothing had been said until just now when, it appeared, they were ready to get down to brass tacks. She smoothed her expression to polite interest and smothered a sigh.

"You're the legal man," Haller Reeves said, peering at Judge Prescott as though he were a piece of defective type. "We need to know about this oath" he broke off and looked around. "Say, Miss Wheeler, is that Yank anywhere about?"

Lavinia had taken out her embroidery frame after the first twenty minutes of fruitless conversation because she found jabbing cloth with a needle a diplomatic alternative to jabbing human flesh. She was sorting colors of embroidery silk at the moment. She separated a strand of royal blue and carefully set the others aside. "Sergeant Sheppard is away from the house," she said. "I don't expect him to return for a while."

"Arming the darkies, no doubt!" Reeves said with an air of suppressed anger. "Training them to kill us while we sleep!"

Judge Prescott laced his fingers together and stared at Reeves with pursed lips.

Lavinia plunged her needle into the center of a flower with as much zest as though it were Haller Reeves' backside. "That is patent nonsense, gentlemen," she said. "I can't believe that you came to talk about it. Did you plan to discuss something sensible? Or shall I ring for refreshments and then see you on your way?"

Judge Prescott met her gaze and smiled at her as the others shifted in their chairs and muttered.

"All right then," Reeves said. "Here's the question: the Yank won't help us unless we take an oath."

Judge Prescott said, "Sergeant Sheppard's not a man to beat around the bush. He certainly made it clear enough to me when I heard it. Was there anything else that you wanted to know?"

"Just this," said Reeves. "Say we did take that oath like he suggests. What's to make us abide by it?"

Lavinia looked up at Reeves and then at Judge Prescott.

The judge lifted his white eyebrows and said, "What is to keep you? Honor, for one thing. I hope you would be giving your word in good faith."

"Well, I don't exactly know," said Reeves. "He won't help us unless we swear an oath. That sounds an awful lot like coercion—"

"Don't take the oath," Judge Prescott said. "That's the simplest answer anyone can give you."

"But he won't help us if we don't."

"Then go help yourself," Prescott said. "Nothing's stopping you from finding your own book about drill and such, and start drilling. My god, man! It isn't as though you've never seen it done! Al Townsend could do it for you! He served in the army—"

"That deserter!"

"He served all his time and didn't ask for pay," Judge Prescott pointed out. "In my view he was in the right."

Reeves dismissed Townsend with a grimace. "That Yankee's holding a knife to our throats!" he said. "We have no choice! How binding is an oath taken that way?"

Prescott sighed. "You know the answer already," he said. "An oath taken under duress is not binding—"

"That's what we wanted to know," said Reeves.

"—but this doesn't fit the definition of duress," Prescott finished. "What are you planning to do?"

"Why, go to the Yank and offer to swear just like he said."

Lavinia peered at him through her spectacles. "Then you'll be lying," she said.

"What choice do we have?" Reeves demanded.

"You can choose not to do it," Judge Prescott pointed out. "There are other options." He raised his voice over the exclamations of protest and said, "I mean it, gentlemen. Georgia has supplied troops to the Confederacy, raised and trained them herself. There have been militia units here before there was a war. We all know how to defend ourselves—"

"He's a soldier!" Pickens cried.

"He wasn't always a soldier," Lavinia said. "Nor was my brother, or any of the other men of the Confederate armies. Can't you teach yourselves, as they did?"

"I beg your pardon, Miss Wheeler," Reeves said. "But it's obvious that you're unfamiliar with such matters. It's hardly a subject to interest a lady. Suffice it to say that it's impossible for us to do without the Yankee, and he has us in a cleft stick—"

"Like rattlesnakes, perhaps?" Lavinia suggested. She met Reeves' affronted gaze for a demure moment before pointedly returning her attention to the canvas before her.

Judge Prescott stared and then burst into laughter.

Lavinia smiled and drew the thread through the canvas. A slight sound, just as she was tying off the stitch, made her look toward the window in time to catch a flash of light.

She frowned and looked more closely, but the movement had ceased. What had it been? Light on something dark and glossy, perhaps-like the heel of a polished leather boot? What time was it?

She lifted her watch from its clip at her belt: 7:00 PM. Time for Sergeant Sheppard to return. She froze at a soft scraping sound, and then smiled and raised her voice. "All this is very interesting, gentlemen," she said, "But I cannot say too strongly how ill-advised and dishonorable it is. Let us think of another way to learn to defend ourselves."

** ** **

It took another half hour for Lavinia's guests to depart, and then only after she had been forced to exclaim at the time and apologize for keeping them so long. She had seen them to the door and then returned to the parlor to work on her embroidery. The visit had given her a great deal to consider, and while she regretted what had been said and what had been resolved upon, she was looking forward to the next days' developments with curiosity tinged with amusement. Sergeant Sheppard would be seeing Dr. Meacham shortly about his healing arm; she would drop a word in the doctor's ear so that Sheppard would not be taken unawares.

She snipped off her thread and set the needle in its case. It was getting too dim to work comfortably; there was always tomorrow. For now she would take a leisurely stroll through the house and then go to see Meg, who should be in bed by now. They had a routine: Lavinia would cuddle her on her lap and listen to her prayers, then tuck her in and kiss her good night. Sergeant Sheppard always looked in when he returned, and sometimes he would tell bedtime stories, but he was late this night.

Lavinia knew she was foolish to allow that little waif to steal her heart the way she had. Meg's time at Fairlawn was probably limited; Lavinia had sent inquiries off to Allatoona, but with the Federal armies pressing on toward Atlanta in the growing summer heat, and the resulting unrest, she doubted there would be a reply very soon. But at some point there would be a reply, and she would have to let Meg go to her family.

The thought was painful. Dear little poppet! She chirped like a bird and smiled every time she saw Lavinia or Sergeant Sheppard, who she thought was her father. She had the run of the place and the smiles of everyone. She was already quite a pet with the recovering wounded and the plantation workers.

Lavinia took off her spectacles, polished them with a corner of her apron, and turned her thoughts to more fruitful channels. Meg's departure would not come for a while, so there was no use thinking of it. In the meantime, she had to confer with Callie as to the next day's tasks, and then eat a light supper. She rose, shook out her skirts, and unclipped the chatelaine from her belt. The keys jingled as she set them on the marble-topped pier table in the hallway and bent to pull the drawer open.

The door opened behind her and she heard footsteps in the hallway. She stiffened as they approached, then relaxed when she caught a glimpse of their owner.

"Oh, it's you, Sergeant!" she said, turning to smile at Sergeant Sheppard as he came up behind her. "Welcome back! Did the patrol go well?"

"It went well enough," Sheppard answered. "Toby and his people are born riders."

Lavinia nodded. "They come by it honestly," she said. "They've been on horseback ever since I can remember, accompanying my menfolk and their friends when they went hunting, ranging afield with their fowling pieces and squirrel rifles. They're splendid shots." She frowned and added, "You know, Sergeant, I've often wondered why the Confederate states don't enlist Negro soldiers on a larger scale."

"There are a great many fools in this world, Miss Wheeler," Sheppard said.

Lavinia could sense a depth of meaning behind the words, and there was a shadow in Sheppard's expression. "There are a great many fools who choose to cling to their folly even when they know it for what it is," Lavinia said. "I was about to take some supper, Sergeant. Have you dined yet?"

"I'll sit with you, if I may," Sheppard said. "But I had something at Caesar's cabin just now. His wife is an excellent cook."

"Callie taught her," Lavinia said. "Callie's a wonderful cook. Even with the shortages we have now, she does wonders. But before the war—! Oh, Sergeant, it was splendid! I remember how my mother and Callie would be in the kitchen together-Mother was part French, and she had recipes from the time of Louis XV. In summertime, when we came here, the house would be filled with the scent of spices and roasting meats—we always seemed to have guests from Richmond, from Savannah and Charleston, and cousins from New York, in the winter, when we kept house in Savannah..."

Her smile warmed. Those had been wonderful times, and maybe they could come again, who knew? She raised her eyes to Sheppard's just as he looked down at her.

The shadow was gone from his expression. His eyes were wide and smiling; the cool evening air had put color in his cheeks, and the scent of mown fields seemed to cling to him.

He gazed down into her eyes for a long, heart-catching moment before he dropped his gaze. "The day's falling toward a pretty sunset, Miss Wheeler," he said. "The fireflies are out, and the crickets, too. I just heard a mockingbird in the willow tree out back, singing his heart out. It's a shame to waste it all. Would you care to take a stroll with me after you've eaten?"

"I think I would," Lavinia said, taking her shawl from the hook by the door. "And we can go walking first. Heavens! I haven't taken time to listen to a mockingbird's song in years! Nor," she added with a smile, "Have I had the pleasure of a handsome man's company in a long time! It will be like old times. You can tell me how the militia is coming along, and maybe we can prevail on Callie to make us some tea afterward."

CHAPTER TWENTY-TWO

As he rode down Ash Street the next day, Sheppard found himself wondering if it had really been over a month since he had first done so. Nothing had changed. He could almost feel the whispers stirring the heavy air as Dixie ambled up the street. He drew rein and looked around, frowning. He could feel eyes peering at him through curtains; doors were cracked here and there, windows were slid shut as he approached. He could hear muttered words and the click of metal.

"For heaven's sake!" he said aloud. "What d'you think I'm going to do? Set a torch to this town?" He hadn't expected an answer, and he did not get one. He added under his breath, "Not that you don't deserve it!"

Dr. Meacham's house was on the corner. He swept his gaze down the street once again and then dismounted. Dixie nuzzled his shoulder and snuffled at his cap while he snapped the tether ring to her halter and looped it to the doctor's hitching post. He could see that people were openly watching him from their windows. He considered briefly and then swept a bow to the gazes, rapped smartly on Meacham's door, and marched inside when it was opened.

** ** **

"Squeeze my hand as hard as you can," said Dr. Meacham, holding out his hand. He winced as Sheppard did so, then said wryly, "Well, I must say I can't find anything wrong with your grip, but then I hadn't expected there to be, considering all you've been able to do in the past week. Take off your jacket and shirt and we'll see how everything looks.

Sheppard nodded and began to unbutton his jacket.

Meacham went to the window and stood gazing out at the street. "You can lie down on the cot when you're ready," he said without turning around. "I didn't expect to see you today," he said after a pause.

Sheppard folded his jacket and set it across a nearby chair back. "Why not?" he asked. "I was told to come here in a week; a week's gone and here I am."

"Some things have happened since then," Dr. Meacham said.

Sheppard paused in the act of unbuttoning the placket of his shirt. "We buried Meg's family," he said. "I can't think why that would keep me from coming here."

"People here asked your help in raising and training a militia unit," Dr. Meacham said. "You refused, but then you started training the Wheeler slaves instead."

Sergeant Sheppard pulled the last button from its hole and started to ease the shirt over his head. "You're off in some particulars," he said. "Such as the fact that the town refused to work with me."

Meacham turned and looked at him.

"I'm a soldier in enemy territory with an assignment," said Sheppard. "There are things I can't do as a loyal U.S. citizen, and training enemy civilians to fight, when they might take their weapons and use their training against my people, is one of them. The only way to get around it is for them to swear an oath of allegiance. I told this to everyone right up front, and they refused to take the oath. The Negroes didn't refuse, I'm working with them, and they're doing very well."

"Nevertheless—"

Sheppard pulled his sound arm out of the sleeve. "Look," he said. "Why hasn't this town had the gumption to do something for itself? I can't train enemy civilians to fight, but that doesn't mean I'm going to stop them from teaching themselves, like thousands of small towns throughout this country did before the war. Why do they expect me to do it all?"

Meacham finally turned and went over to him. "You're arming former slaves," he said, helping Sheppard doff the shirt.

Sheppard sat down on the edge of the cot. "So?" he said. "What is Wheelerville afraid of? Another rebellion like Nat Turner's in '28?"

Dr. Meacham was silent.

Sheppard, seeing his expression, exclaimed, "Good God! That is what they're scared of! Where are their brains? The Negroes all had firearms and knives long before they were freed. Caesar's a dead shot, and so's Toby. I hear they go to market each week with birds and squirrels they've shot. If they can drop a squirrel at fifty paces, they can certainly hit a man. And if they'd wanted to rise up and slaughter the people of this town they could have done so years ago when they were slaves. From what I've heard of him, old man Wheeler would have been a prime target."

"Try telling that to the town," Dr. Meacham said, eyeing the healing wound.

"No, thanks," Sheppard said with a flash of impatience. "I've already had a sample of their way of thinking. I don't suffer fools gladly. Do the folk here honestly think I'd have had anything to do with those people if I thought there was the slightest chance they might harm Miss Wheeler?"

Dr. Meacham looked up from the wound. "She's the main reason for what you do, isn't she?" he asked.

His tone made Sheppard frown. "Yes," he said. "Her protection is my assignment."

Dr. Meacham carefully traced the line of the scar. "Hm," he said. "I wonder, though—"

Sheppard eyes were snapping as he half-raised himself on one elbow. "What do you wonder, Doctor?" he asked.

Meacham's eyebrows were slightly raised. "Never mind, Sergeant," he said, pushing Sheppard back on the cot. "Idle speculation is useless. Let me get a good look at you. Well, you're healing pretty well by all appearances. Scab's going away, though I wager it itches. Does it hurt when I touch it—like this?"

"Yes, damn it!" Sheppard said through his teeth, wincing as the doctor's long, sensitive fingers explored the area around the wound.

"Definitely painful," Meacham agreed. "Hm. Do I feel some heat, maybe? No, maybe not... Let me see what I can find. Put your arm down along your side and try to relax. This may hurt a little..."

Sheppard complied and lay with his eyes closed as Dr. Meacham gently probed the wound, felt the underlying ribs, tested the layers of muscle. The pain was there, but it was bearable, and the cot was comfortable. A finger of breeze pushed in through the open window and stroked his hair away from his face. Dr. Meacham's low, soft voice faded to a murmur, and he caught the scent of herbs and sweet oil...

"...I can see it's been a long haul for you..."

The voice came pushing into his mind through a memory of Seneca Lake sparkling in the sun of New York State's late, breezy spring. It almost seemed to be a part of the dream. He opened his eyes and looked up at Dr. Meacham for an uncomprehending moment. His gaze shifted beyond Meacham's shoulder until it encountered the starched white curtains fluttering in the window. He closed his eyes.

"You're healing but you're still tired," Meacham said. "This was a serious wound."

"I've had worse," Sheppard sighed. He raised his head and saw that his shoulder was bandaged. "What did you just do?" he asked.

"I rubbed some balm well in," Meacham said. "And then I bandaged you." He smiled and added, "You were asleep for a good half hour."

Sheppard closed his eyes and lay back against the pillow. "I'm sorry," he said. "I never meant to—"

"If you fell asleep it was because you needed the rest," Meacham said. "Miss Wheeler could tell you that."

Sheppard touched the bandage and then lay back again.

"Speaking of Miss Wheeler," Dr. Meacham began, "There's something I think you should know."

Sheppard looked at him.

"The people here, led by some folks...want their own militia and aren't particular how they get it."

Sheppard smiled and closed his eyes again. "Yes," he said. "I heard."

** ** **

The light breeze stirred the pine boughs overhead, filling the air with a faint scent of turpentine. Splashes of sunshine glinted like scattered coins upon the fallen needles, slanted across names and numbers half-hidden by lush, high grass.

Sheppard paused and gazed down at one date showing crisp and new in its surround of cold stone, before raising his eyes to the name.

"Edward Toombs, September 17, 1862," he said softly. "So you were there, too." He straightened and gazed out across the massed stones toward the gate.

He was in Wheelerville's cemetery, standing among the newer graves. Rosebushes, planted atop some of the older ones, were budding. Banks of wild pansies lined the encircling brick wall in splashes of purple, blue and yellow. He could see evergreen bushes and, here and there, bouquets withering in the warmth. Dixie, tethered at the gate and nibbling at the thick grass beside the gateposts, lifted her head to snuffle at the air; she pricked her ears and nickered as he turned toward her.

Sheppard looked around the graveyard. It was a peaceful and cool there under the overhanging pine trees, with the breeze rustling their needles overhead. He looked back at the tombstone, then turned and went to the wall, bending down to pick a bunch of the wild pansies and gather them into a bouquet.

He went to one knee by the grave and set the flowers just below the headstone. "Edward Toombs," he said. "So you were there at Antietam creek. I wonder if you came anywhere near my baby brother, Adam. You'd have liked him if you had."

Dixie whinnied just as Sheppard was getting to his feet. He looked up and saw that a group of townsfolk were waiting just outside the gate. He could see Haller Reeves, Ed Pickens and John Toombs. Al Townsend stood beyond them, his arms folded and his expression dark and ominous. He looked up as Sheppard watched and frowned as though he were trying to convey an idea.

Sheppard looked back and then away. Where will it end? He sighed mentally, setting his cap on his head and heading to the gate. He nodded to the gathered people and started to move through them toward Dixie.

"Sergeant Sheppard," said Reeves.

Sheppard turned.

"We need a word with you."

"Here I am," Sheppard said.

"What were you doing with my brother's grave?" Toombs demanded.

"Putting a bunch of flowers on it," Sheppard answered. He watched as Toombs pushed past him into the graveyard and then turned to Reeves. "What do you want, Mr. Reeves?" he said.

"We want to talk about the militia," Reeves said.

Sheppard looked at him. "Yes?" he said.

"You said you'd train us," Reeves began.

"—If we'd take an oath of allegiance," Pickens said.

"That's right," said Sheppard.

"Flowers?" said Toombs, kneeling beside his brother's grave.

"I lost a brother at Antietam, too," Sheppard said. "I thought—Yes, I put flowers there. It seemed right."

Toombs looked down at the wild pansies and suddenly covered his face.

"To hell with those flowers!" Reeves snapped. "Look, Sergeant, you said you'd train us if we'd take an oath of allegiance. We said we'd think it over—"

"Did you, now?" Sheppard asked.

"—and in the meantime you went ahead and started training those niggers to fight!"

"'Niggers' isn't the word," Sheppard said. "And if you keep using it, I'm leaving. They already know how to fight. So do all of you. But they took the oath."

"They'll kill us in our beds!" Pickens exclaimed.

"Using what weapons?" Sheppard demanded. "The same squirrel rifles and knives they've had to hand any time these past thirty years? You're scared of a turnip ghost."

"He's got a point," said Sam Wallins, who was standing a little to the side and watching quietly.

Reeves threw him an annoyed look. "Well, you've made things pretty clear," he said to Sheppard. "And we've thought things through. Since you've made it a condition, we'll take that oath and then you can teach us to fight as well."

Sheppard was frowning thoughtfully as he scanned the faces surrounding him. "Many of you lent a hand with those refugees," he said after a moment of silence. "It was hard, heartbreaking work, and I saw your quality. You've seen my way of operating, as well. Is this man speaking for all of you?"

No specific man answered, but the fragmented replies were clear enough. Sheppard moved through the crowd and took Dixie's reins. "All right," he said. "So you say you'll take the oath now?"

"That's right."

"An oath of loyalty to the United States of America?" Sheppard persisted. "Given on your word of honor? Sworn on a Bible?"

Some of the people shifted their feet, but Reeves nodded.

"I see," said Sheppard. "And you'll swear down with the Confederacy and death to Jeff Davis?"

"Whatever you require, Sergeant," Reeves said.

Sheppard frowned at Dixie and rubbed her gray muzzle with his sound hand. "Very good," he said. "When do you want to take this oath?"

"Whenever you require," Reeves repeated.

"I don't require any specific time," Sheppard said. "But there are some serious problems..."

"I don't understand you," said Reeves.

"I didn't think you would," Sheppard said. "Well, men, you seem set on this. Follow me, if you please."

"What are you doing?" Pickens demanded as Sheppard led his mare into the graveyard.

"Wait and see," Sheppard said, threading his way through the gravestones until he was beside John Toombs, who was still kneeling at his brother's grave. "Come here," he said. He waited until the others had come up, then said, "I'll administer the oath here."

"What are you talking about?" Wallins demanded.

Sheppard shot him a level look. "You said you wanted to take an oath of allegiance," he said. "You said you'd swear death to Jefferson Davis and down with the Confederacy. Well, then, you can swear it here and now, along with the oath a soldier takes when he joins the army, surrounded by the soldiers of the Confederacy, who died fighting the army you want to join."

He scanned the names and then pointed to one tombstone. "Look here," he said. "April 7, 1862. This man fell at Pittsburgh landing. I was there: maybe we came face to face. I'm sure you all knew him. I wonder what he'd think of all this. Or what Edward Toombs over there thinks."

Toombs looked up, wet-eyed and shaken.

Pickens looked around himself. Reeves had grown pale.

"But I shouldn't be delaying things," said Sheppard, holding up his pocket testament. "You say you want to be soldiers under me, then swear. I've my own Bible here, given to me by my wife when I first joined the army in April of 1861. The New Testament and the Psalms. I've carried it into battle and read it. I've even bled on it: it'll do for your oath. Each of you can come up in turn, put your hand on it and swear. I know the words: I've administered them often enough to new recruits. Do you want to hear them?"

There was no answer.

Sheppard fronted them. "Come now," he said. "They're the words you've agreed to speak. Listen to them!"

He lifted his head and quoted:

I do solemnly swear that I will bear true allegiance to the United States of America, and that I will serve them honestly and faithfully against all their enemies and opposers whatsoever, and observe and obey the orders of the President of the United States, and the orders of the officers appointed over me according to the rules and articles for the government of the armies of the United States, so help me God.

Sheppard looked around as his words faded into the stillness. "Well?" he said. "What's stopping you? You say you're willing to swear: then swear!"

No one moved until Reeves took a half-step forward. He met Sheppard's eyes and took a long step backward.

"So I was right!" Sheppard said through his teeth. "I didn't want to believe my ears last night when I heard you talking to Miss Wheeler. I thought you had more honor and more sense, but you have neither. So you'll swear the oath, will you? And learn what little I can teach you that you can't find out for yourself, and then throw your pledged word aside on some legal quibble manufactured by you, one that even a pettifogging New York lawyer would scorn to use!"

"Wait, Sergeant!" Wallins said.

Sheppard set his foot in the stirrup and swung up into his saddle. "You pack of blackguards!" he said, reining the mare in a circle. "I'm not taking your oaths! I wouldn't have any of you at my back if I were facing a charging brigade alone! I'd rather be killed by an honest foe than stabbed in the back by you! You're a disgrace even to the Confederacy! I expected better of all of you, but I'm especially disappointed to see *you* here, Sam Wallins!"

Toombs scrambled to his feet, the flowers in his hand.

Sheppard eyed him scornfully and then nodded toward the new tombstones. "It's a crying shame to think that all these good men threw their lives away for the likes of you, however mistaken their cause! I won't subject them to this insult! God knows, they deserve better!"

He turned Dixie and spurred her to a canter through the center of the cemetery. She cleared the brick wall in an effortless leap and clattered away down the road toward Fairlawn.

John Toombs knelt down again and put the flowers on his brother's grave.

"Of all the—" Haller Reeves began.

"Oh shut up," said Sam Wallins.

CHAPTER TWENTY-THREE

A day that had promised to be exhausting and crammed with sadness and effort had been surprisingly enjoyable, Lavinia thought. Her morning visit to the wounded had been easy and pleasant, and she had been pleased to see that Corporal Higgins was ready to try walking on his wooden leg any time she said he could. The other wounded had been greatly improved, though it had saddened her to think that only eighteen remained where she had started with sixty. But those eighteen were bright-faced and cheerful, some ready to be up and about and doing what they termed 'chores'. She would have to think of things to give them to do.

Callie's rheumatism, which usually acted up this time of year, was giving her no trouble, and she was going around the house singing, shadowed by Meg, who looked upon her and George as grandparents. Meg herself was busy getting into mischief with the plantation children and those of the town who came to Lavinia's thrice-weekly classes. The pottery collection had been easily dusted, and Lavinia was considering moving it to more fitting quarters in one of the sitting rooms.

She had finished her afternoon's tasks early. The chickens were thriving, the cows were giving plenty of milk. Sergeant Sheppard's work with the field hands seemed to be going well after only one week, and the sweep patrols he had ordered were bringing in new livestock and goods each day. Toby's top hands had come in with three more cows that they had found wandering in the fields east of her land.

And now Lavinia was in the back paddock with the bay gelding Judge Prescott had found for her, feeding him some dry gingerbread and making much of him. He had seemed such a dandy, with his neat white feet and the blaze down his face, she had named him Beau Brummel–Beau for short–and was planning to teach him to jump.

Who knew? Perhaps, come autumn, she would be able to hunt him.

He nibbled at the palmful of bread she offered him and then, hearing the quick beat of approaching hooves, blew the crumbs across her skirt with an explosive snort and raised his head to peer down the road past Lavinia.

Lavinia turned as well, dusting her hand on her skirt, and saw Sergeant Major Sheppard coming along at a spanking canter. It seemed Dixie had been keeping up the pace since leaving town. Lavinia could see lather on the mare's neck, and specks of foam from her bit spattering her forequarters.

Lavinia bestowed one final pat to Beau's arched neck and turned to watch Sheppard come up.

"Good afternoon, Sergeant," she said as he brought Dixie to a balanced stop. "Welcome back! Isn't it a lovely day?"

He touched his cap to her and said, "It certainly is, Miss Wheeler."

His tone was preoccupied, and Lavinia saw that he was scowling. "Is anything wrong, Sergeant?" she asked. "You are well, aren't you?"

He looked full at her and his frown faded a little. "I'm well enough, Miss Wheeler," he said through his teeth. "For all that I had a run-in with a pack of rats."

Lavinia raised her head and looked carefully at him. "Why, Sergeant," she said. "You're angry!"

"You could say that," said Sheppard. His mouth was set in a straight, hard line as he dismounted and loosened Dixie's girth. He looked over at her after a moment. "In fact, that's just about right," he said a little more gently. "Though maybe 'angry' isn't the right word."

Lavinia pushed the wide brim of her sun hat aside and smiled up at him. "Well, if you're enraged, then it's a good sign," she said. "I can never work up a good fit of temper when I feel poorly. Tell me what's upset you. It wasn't something I did or left undone, was it?"

The use of the word 'upset' so completely inappropriate to his emotions, sent a short-lived quiver of amusement across Sheppard's lips. "No, it's not your fault at all," he said. "And how you of all people would come to the conclusion that it might be–" He broke off with a shake of his head. "Well, it wasn't you or anyone here." His frown grew deeper. "But of all the disgusting, dishonorable—!"

"There," said Lavinia, her head tilted. "I made you smile for a moment at least. Here, Sergeant, I'll walk with you to the paddock and you can tell me about it." She took Sheppard's arm, ran a finger down the edge of the sling and said, "I'm sorry you are still wearing this."

"I'd have thought you'd say 'I told you so,' " Sheppard said. "Most women would jump at the chance."

"Another time, perhaps," Lavinia said. "And on something less serious than the health of a friend. How long do you wear it, sir?"

"Another week," Sheppard said. "And only when I'm doing something strenuous. I can remove it other times."

"Hm. By 'strenuous', I imagine Dr. Meacham meant physically strenuous," Lavinia said. "Restraining your sense of mischief is probably arduous, but I doubt it would strain your shoulder."

They were at the paddock gate now. Sheppard stared at her for a moment and then began to laugh.

"Well!" said Lavinia. "I've made you laugh. Now you needn't be in a temper. Tell me what happened while I unsaddle Miss Dixie."

"No," said Sheppard as she began unfastening buckles. "I'll do that!"

But Lavinia had already undone the girth and was trying to pull the saddle off the mare's back. "Don't be foolish!" she said. "There's nothing to it!"

"She's seventeen hands, Miss Wheeler," Sheppard objected, trying to reach the girth. "I'll do it."

"Don't be foolish!" Lavinia said again, tugging at buckles. "You just—have to know—when to pull!" She was a short woman and Dixie was a tall horse; she gave the saddle a purposeful heave, bringing it over the mare's back and sliding down toward her head.

Sheppard gasped "Miss Wheeler!" and lunged forward as she lost her balance and went over.

When the noise and dust had settled Lavinia found herself in Sheppard's arms on the fresh, springy grass with the saddle beneath her left shoulder. She was clutching at the breast of his jacket and staring wide-eyed up at him with her spectacles askew and half off her face.

He stared down at her and she stared up at him for the space of two unsteady breaths. From this close a vantage point, without the distortion of her spectacles, she could see that his eyes were flecked with brown.

"Are you all right, Miss Wheeler?"

Lavinia blinked and saw that he had pushed to his knees and was looking down at her with real worry. Her cheeks flamed. "There!" she said breathlessly, sitting up. "You see? I've made you laugh even more!"

Their eyes met again and they burst into laughter simultaneously as he got to his feet and then helped her up.

"Well, it worked, Miss Wheeler," he said, heaving the saddle to the fence. He turned to unbuckle Dixie's throat latch and ease the bridle over her ears. "I'll let one of the two-armed fellows carry it into the tackroom."

Lavinia took a handful of hay and quickly rubbed the mare down. Dixie rewarded her with a friendly shove to the midriff that nearly sent her flying. She patted the mare's neck and then looked up at Sheppard. "Now," she said. "What happened in town? Did they come to take the oath today, then?"

"How did you know?"

"I heard you last night outside the window," she said. "I knew you were listening. It was all I could do not to laugh."

He stared down at her.

"Smile, Sergeant," she said. "I knew you were aware of things. I was wondering when they would approach you, and what you would say when they did. It was what you wanted, wasn't it?"

"Not a lying oath," Sheppard said. "If they're going to come to me with that attitude, then I don't want them."

"That's what I told them," Lavinia said. "They wouldn't listen. Did you bite their heads off?"

"You amaze me, Miss Wheeler," Sheppard said.

Lavinia smiled at him. "It isn't so amazing," she said. "I just allow for the commonsense that I know you have. I'm sure you do the same for me when you aren't busy being amazed by me. Or do you merely find me puzzling?"

Sheppard offered his arm again. "I find you..." he began, and then stopped.

"Yes?" said Lavinia, smiling up at him. "What do you find me, Sergeant? Annoying? Admirable?"

Sheppard tucked her hand in his elbow. "Adorable," he said with a smile.

Lavinia transferred her gaze from his eyes to the second false buttonhole of his high collar. She had had light-hearted exchanges like this in the past years, but it had been a long time, and she had an odd, breathless feeling that this conversation was serious.

Sheppard looked down at her. "I was going to say 'admirable', too," he said, and then added nothing more.

Lavinia's eyes met his and lingered, then warmed in a happy smile that brightened her thin face and softened her pointed chin. "Addle-pated," she said. She lifted her eyebrows at him. "I mean you, of course," she added. Her eyes widened a little as he lifted his sound hand and touched her hair. The expression shifted to amusement as he presented her with a long strand of grass.

"Yours, I think," he said.

"Thank you, sir," she returned, taking it from him. "Well, they came to you and you consigned them to Gehenna, from your expression."

"I was angry," he said.

"Maybe 'angry' isn't the right word," Lavinia said, gathering her skirts. "Come on, Sergeant, let's stroll through the rose gardens. Heavens, it's been so long since I did so in a moment of leisure with a friend! And they've been so fragrant this year!"

He looked down at her and then bowed. "I'm honored," he said.

"To see the roses?" she queried. "They're there for anyone to see!"

"Honored with your friendship, Miss Wheeler," he said.

"It isn't such an honor," she said, smiling. "I begin to think it was inevitable. I like angels. Come, Sergeant: this way."

** ** **

"Did they know that Mr. Townsend and Abner had come to you?" Lavinia asked some time later as she cut a bright yellow rose and raised it to her face. "I didn't tell them," Sheppard said. "I don't imagine Abner or Al said anything, either."

"Why not?"

"They offered to take the oath," Sheppard said. "I don't think they wanted the others to know."

"Why not?" Lavinia asked. "The others offered to swear, as well."

"Yes, but with a notion of weaseling out of it when the time came. Abner and Al were sincere."

Lavinia frowned and snapped the thorns off the stem. "Now that is a terrible thought!" she said. "To reflect that sincerity is somehow despicable while two-faced hypocrisy is not!"

"That's the way it is," Sheppard said.

"Despicable!" said Lavinia. She looked up at him and, smiling, sniffed at the rose. "But that doesn't touch you, Abner or Mr. Townsend."

"Or Sam Wallins," Sheppard said. "For all that he was there. I think he may have been trying to stop things."

"What will they do now?" Lavinia asked.

Sheppard gave a one-shouldered shrug. "I imagine they'll find out sooner or later that Abner and Al are spying on me—"

"Spying-!" Lavinia began. "No, really! Of all the deplorable— Don't let them!"

"It was my suggestion," Sheppard said. "I can't let this town go helpless—though Toby and Caesar and their people are doing well— and there's nothing to stop someone from watching me and learning from me. I just can't teach them."

"That sounds a little dubious to me," Lavinia said.

"It's the best I can do," said Sheppard. "And maybe it'll calm them down a little. I got tired of hearing how the 'niggers' would murder them in their beds."

"They know better," Lavinia said.

"I should hope so," Sheppard agreed. "But they aren't thinking too clearly just now."

"They are in no danger from any of the Fairlawn people," Lavinia said.

Sheppard lifted his eyebrows.

Lavinia looked down at the rose. "They aren't slaves, Sergeant," she said.

"They told me," Sheppard said. "Why didn't you, especially after I spoke of them as slaves several times?"

She turned away from him and went over to a bush of bright red cabbage roses.

"Why?" Sheppard repeated. "They said you freed them out of your own generosity."

"Generosity," Lavinia said almost in a whisper. "Did they tell you why I freed them?"

"No," he said. "But I think I can guess."

She turned and faced him. "Can you?" she asked.

"Yes," he said. "I've seen Toby and Caesar, and I've seen the others, and their children. They're your blood kin, aren't they?"

She lowered her head. "I never guessed," she said. "I was blind, I suppose, but I didn't suspect until the day my father died, when I went to write his death date in our large Bible. I opened to the pages of births and deaths, and there were his name, and Gaylord's—my brother's—and my grandfather's. But my mother's name was not there, or my grandmother's. I read, and I understood suddenly that the names there were slaves, and the names below them were children—my half-brothers and half-sisters, my nieces and nephews— Even Callie and George were—were my uncle and aunt. How could I keep them in captivity? And when I saw that they were my brothers, I saw that others were, as well—all people—how could I keep them?"

Sheppard did not speak as she turned away from him and paced down the path to stand with her head lowered.

Lavinia was silent for a long time. She finally raised her head and turned, taking a deep breath. "Well," she said. "I freed them. It was the least I could do."

"I heard," Sheppard said again. "You gave them their freedom and free passage across the Ohio. And you found Toby's brother and bought his freedom, as well."

"It's the least I could do after learning of my family's wickedness!" she said.

"You have to be careful judging people," Sheppard said, touching a pink rose. "You can't just look at what they did. You also have to think of where and when they lived and who they were. Something that would be a rip-snorting sin for me might be no more than a mistake for someone raised without any sense of conscience. And something that would be common courtesy for you or me might be an act of heroism for someone else who grew up without our benefits."

Lavinia was frowning. "For someone who was never taught right from wrong, perhaps," she said. "But my father—and Gaylord— They had my upbringing!"

"Yes," said Sheppard. "But were either of them as smart as you? And did they really have the same upbringing?"

"What do you mean?" Lavinia demanded. "Of course they did!"

"I wonder," said Sheppard, lightly stroking the bunched petals at the center of the rose. "I suspect your father grew up with a notion that it was lawful and proper to do as he wished with the women he owned—"

"Human beings!" Lavinia exclaimed.

"That's what you say," Sheppard said. "But he might not have viewed it quite that way. Some people view slaves as livestock, to be bred as they see fit. Now don't be glaring at me," he added with a smile. "I don't hold that view. I joined this fight because I want to see this whole evil situation stopped. I'm just saying that that's how they claim to feel.

"They and hundreds of others like them grew up viewing their slaves as so much cattle and treating them so. Your father saw men taking concubines all his life: it was done, no one thought anything of it, or not in public."

"It's desperately wicked!" Lavinia flashed.

Sheppard smiled at her. "Have some charity, Miss Wheeler," he said. "I imagine your menfolk weren't deep thinkers. They saw a common practice and followed it. If somewhere in the depths of their souls they had a flicker of doubt, it was easily quenched by the thought that they were following an old, established practice. "'If a man does ill, not knowing it to be so, his stripes are less'. Let it go, Miss Wheeler. God's a better judge than you or me."

"But such a legacy of sin!"

"Let it go," Sheppard said again. "That's what you've done for the slaves, do it for yourself. And if you're going to speak of sin, then maybe you'd best read from the nineteenth chapter of Ezekiel, verse 19, where it says that the sin of the father is not visited on the children who have followed righteousness."

Lavinia was still gazing at the yellow rose in her hands. "Is that what you truly believe, Sergeant?" she asked.

"It's what I truly believe, Miss Wheeler," Sheppard said.

"Thank you," Lavinia said. She raised her eyes from the rose to his. "Thank you," she said again, and went to him. She did not speak as she set the rose in the top buttonhole of his jacket, but she reached for the knot of the sling when she had finished. "This isn't strenuous, sir," she said. "You may remove this."

She was busy untying the cloth as she spoke. She pulled it free, folded it with a few deft movements of her fingers, and presented it to Sheppard.

He straightened his arm with a grimace.

"Does it hurt?" she asked.

"Some pain isn't bad," he said. "This is...like exercising after a long rest."

"Then it is a good sign," she said. "And now tell me, Sergeant. Is that mockingbird singing tonight?"

His expression brightened. "He seems to be making a habit of it, Miss Wheeler," he said.

"Excellent," Lavinia said. "We will listen to him tonight. And Sergeant—my name is Lavinia."

CHAPTER TWENTY-FOUR

The mockingbird's song livened the warm evenings over the next two months. During that time the Fairlawn Free Militia headed by Sergeant Sheppard, drilled and did maneuvers. A counterpart, the Wheelerville Guards, was raised by Al Townsend, who was elected their captain with Sam Wallins as his second.

Townsend, who had left the Confederate army as an ordnance sergeant the year before, proved to be a commander with a gift for finding and using the skills of his men. He and Sheppard met often to discuss the results of their separate patrols. This led, during the second month, to a division of duties that benefitted both Wheelerville and Fairlawn.

During this time, Sherman's forces laid siege to Atlanta. Lavinia, with kinfolk in the city, waited anxiously for news as he and circled south of the great railroad terminus in a series of devastating raids that culminated in the fall of the city on September 2, 1864.

Refugees streamed away from Sherman's armies, some of them passing through Wheelerville with tales of destruction and privation. Lavinia sent them on their way with such food as she could spare while Sheppard and Townsend, remembering Meg's family, tightened patrols around the town and its outlying settlements. The townsfolk were showing some of the strain, but spirits were high there and at Fairlawn, especially after two forays by irregulars were beaten back before they reached the town.

The mockingbird sang, the roses bloomed, and the air grew rich with the scent of honeysuckle and magnolia. And Lavinia and Sergeant Sheppard found a refuge from the fatigue and worry of the succeeding days in their evening strolls.

** ** **

"If you don't milk those cows now, there'll be no telling what'll happen to you!"

Bathsheba turned from contemplating her pretty face in the triangle of mirror set over her wash basin, and pulled a grimace at the door. "I'll be right out, Mama!" she called, and turned back to her reflection.

"You'll be gored for sure, girl, if you wait any longer!"

It was her father's voice this time. Bathsheba grinned and smoothed her hair, then went to the door. Her bright skirts swished satisfyingly about her ankles, plumped out by the crinoline she had fashioned herself out of green willow branches.

Her father was waiting for her with a bucket of grain in his hand. "For someone as pretty as you are, 'Sheba," he said, "it's a puzzlement to me why it takes you so long to get out of that room in the morning!" His voice was proud for all that he was scowling at her.

She dropped a smacking kiss on his cheek. "I have to make myself pretty for my pa," she said, and took the pail.

"Be careful, now," her mother said. "There's bad folks about. You see anything wrong, you run straight to your pa!"

"Yes, Ma," Bathsheba said. She paused and then added with an impudent grin, "Or maybe to Sergeant Sheppard. He's got a repeating musket!" She scooted out the door before her mother could say anything else.

Two minutes later she was strolling through the golden morning mist toward the cowshed, swinging the pail of grain and thinking of the day's coming events. Her life had settled into a comfortable routine over the past several years. She would feed and milk the cows, carry the milk to the springhouse, and then go to the big house where Miss Lavinia was teaching her to embroider and to sew. There were other lessons, as well: reading and writing, deportment—though Miss Lavinia didn't know she was teaching that. Bathsheba was an observant fifteen year old: she learned by watching, and she was an excellent mimic.

Later that afternoon Bathsheba would help to teach the younger children in the thrice-weekly class that Miss Lavinia ran on the plantation grounds. That was always a lively affair, and Bathsheba enjoyed sitting with the littler ones. Later still, there might be time for a stroll through Miss Lavinia's rose gardens with one of her beaux. She had three of them, and she couldn't make up her mind which one she preferred.

She tossed her head, thinking of the last dance she had been to, where a fistfight had actually broken out over the question of who would dance with her. It had all been very exciting, and she couldn't wait for the next one.

She dipped a curtsey to an imaginary partner and then grimaced at the pail. The cows were probably in the shed before her, waiting for their morning treat, a handful of grain apiece. She had been following this comfortable routine since she was old enough to carry a full milk pail, and now it served to set each day in its placid path and bring her thoughts into order.

And it was such a lovely day, she thought, with the mist rolling across the fields from the stream, soft and cool against her face. Glowing golden in the long morning sun, it softened sound and sight until Bathsheba could almost imagine that she was moving through a dream. Familiar landmarks flickered into being as she approached them, two-dimensional at first, but gaining definition and detail as she drew near, and then softening into nothing as she moved past them.

The silence grew as she approached the shed, changing from the muffled stillness of a misty morning to the ominous silence of threat. The cows were not lowing, as they usually did, and she could hear none of their usual bustle and stamping.

Bathsheba hesitated, moving the bucket from one hand to the other. Something was wrong, but what? She took a step forward and then another—

A line of men in worn, dusty blue loomed out of the bright haze with the suddenness of shadow puppets. She gasped and backed away, the bucket held protectively before her. Rough arms seized her from behind and she heard a gabble of voices, their accent incomprehensible to her in her shock.

"Let me go!" she gasped.

The arms loosened. "Relax, girl!" said a voice in her ear. "We aren't trying to hurt you!"

She pulled free, trembling, to see that she was in the center of a knot of rough-looking, staring men. Her heart thundering with fright, she wondered how Miss Lavinia would behave in this situation. The thought steadied her, a little. She lifted her chin and faced the men squarely.

"W—what are you doing here?" she demanded.

"We're just passing through," one of them said. "We're on foraging detail."

"We're looking for food," said another, a tall man with bright blue eyes and a bronzed face framed by a rough beard. "You have any?"

"N—none to spare," she said through chattering teeth.

"That's what they all say," the bearded man said to the others. He spoke with a slight accent that Bathsheba could not quite place, and he had a stripe on his lower sleeve. "Listen, missy: we've got orders to take what we need—"

The stripe on the man's sleeve made Bathsheba think of the sergeant and the militia. She said, "Maybe I should ask Sergeant Sheppard if—"

"Sergeant?" said one of them. "You have troops here?"

The faces were somehow harsh and threatening now. Bathsheba gathered her skirts and backed away. "There's cows in the shed yonder," she said, pointing. "They need milking, and there's buckets there."

As the men turned to peer through the haze where she had pointed, she picked up her skirts and ran away toward the big house as fast as her feet could carry her.

** ** **

"For an animal that doesn't roll in the mud, girl," Sheppard said, working the snarled hair loose from Dixie's mane with his fingers, "You're a rare chore to keep clean."

The mare turned to nudge him and then lip at his shoulder. Sheppard's further comments were forestalled as Bathsheba burst from the woods clutching a pail of grain in one hand and pressing the other against her side.

"Sergeant—!" she gasped. "I saw soldiers! A whole passel of them!"

"What?" Sheppard demanded.

"Soldiers!" Bathsheba repeated. "I just got away from them!"

Sheppard caught her by the elbows and steadied her. "Did they lay hands on you?" he demanded.

"They grabbed me—" Bathsheba began. She faltered a little at the sudden blackness of his scowl. "Oh no, Sergeant," she said. "They startled me. I turned and started to run away. They stopped me, that's all. I told them to let me go, and they did."

"Then you weren't hurt or insulted in any way?" Sheppard persisted. His scowl lessened as Bathsheba shook her head breathlessly, but he set his hands on her shoulders. "Look at me, child," he said.

She lifted her face to his without fear.

He gazed into her eyes for a long moment and then nodded and released her.

Bathsheba watched as he turned away. "They behaved pretty nice, though they looked rough," she said. She drew a deep breath at his eased expression, and tried to speak more calmly. "There were maybe thirty of them," she said. "They were at the cowshed, out beyond my house. From the look of them, they were heading toward town."

Sheppard shot her a level look for a split second, then nodded. "Very good," he said. "Were they bluecoats?"

"Yes, Sergeant!"

"Mounted?" Sheppard asked.

"Not that I saw," Bathsheba said.

Sheppard considered and then went toward the stable with Bathsheba following him. "Did you see any bugles on their caps?" he asked at the door of the tackroom.

Bathsheba frowned and then nodded. "Bugles for sure," she said. They also had letters on their hats. The same letter for each of them. I think it was an 'H.' "

Sheppard's saddle was slung over one of the racks. He cast her a considering look as he looped the stirrups across the seat and slid his arm underneath. "You sure noticed a lot for a youngster who's had a scare," he said. "All right, then: did you see any noncoms there— sergeants or corporals with stripes on their sleeves?"

"There was one fellow with stripes like those near your wrists," Bathsheba said. "They were edged with red but they were blue."

"That means he was fool enough to reenlist," Sheppard said. "If he didn't have anything higher up on his sleeve, then he's a private. Did you see any stripes on anyone's upper sleeves?"

"I—I think I did," Bathsheba said. "I was busy trying to get away, though."

"Just as well," said Sheppard, lifting the saddle with a grunt. "From what you say, it sounds like a company on foraging detail."

"Foraging," Bathsheba said. "They used that word."

Sheppard looked thoughtful. "I see," he said.

"What can we do?" Bathsheba asked.

Sheppard nodded toward Dixie's bridle on its peg. "Carry that out for me, will you?" he said, and shouldered the saddle.

They headed back outside in silence. "There's a couple of things to do," Sheppard said at last, settling the saddle blanket on Dixie's withers and sliding it back, then putting the saddle atop it. "And you're going to have to handle some of them. Listen: go to Miss Wheeler and tell her what you saw. Tell her I need the order at once, and ask her to bring it out to me. I'll be by the front step. While you're inside, I need you to ask George to bring my weapons to the porch, along with enough ammunition for a reload on both. He knows where they are. I'll finish saddling Dixie and meet him by the front porch."

He reached under Dixie's belly for the girth and frowned at Bathsheba. "Do you have all that?" he asked.

"Yes sir. Anything else?"

"Yes," said Sheppard, taking the bridle from Bathsheba. "I need you to tell Corporal Higgins to put on his jacket and trousers and get on the veranda with a gun. Tell him to get all the men who can get around, more or less, to go out there, too. The more Union troops they see in evidence the better."

"Y—yes, Sergeant!"

"And one last thing, Bathsheba," Sheppard said. "Send one of the young men to your father and another to town. Tell your father and Al Townsend that on no account are they to try to tangle with these fellows! They can gather everyone in a safe place, but I want them out of sight! One false move and they might just have the entire Union army all over this town! Now go—and thank you!"

Bathsheba hesitated as Sheppard buckled the bridle's throat latch. "But what're you going to do, Sergeant?" she asked.

"I'm going to stop them," Sheppard said. "I don't think it'll be much trouble, but I don't want to take any chances. Now go on in, and don't forget what I told you."

**   **   **

"It would have been better if we'd been given horses," Joseph Myers said through his teeth as he used his bayonet to saw at the cord securing a nicely cured ham to one of the rafters. "The problem with foraging when you don't have a horse is you have to carry the stuff yourself!"

"Fat chance we'll ever get horses!" snorted Jim Sturgis.

"They mounted the 97th Illinois!" Myers said. The rope parted and the ham dropped satisfyingly into his arms. "There!" he exulted. "I'm done for the day! See you on the road!"

He stepped outside, caught sight of his First Sergeant, and went up to him. "There's a few more left in there, Sarge," he said. "If you want to send four more boys in, they can clean the place out."

Sergeant Greene nodded. "Good idea," he said. "Pity to waste good ham." He nodded toward four men who were lounging under a tree and chewing stalks of grass. "You there!" he sang out, "Root, Watson, Leary and Diggins! Yes, I mean you! What do you think this is? An ice cream social? Go inside and help out, and be quick about it!"

Myers watched the four get to their feet and go into the smoke-house, then squinted through the mist.

Sergeant Greene followed his gaze. "I wish this fog would lift," he said. "Makes it hard to see what's nearby."

Myers nodded and took out his pocket knife. He opened it, wiped it on his trouser leg, and meditatively cut a slice of the ham. He was a tall man, just completing his twenty-fifth year on earth and his fifteenth year in the United States. He could remember life in Alsace, before the unrest in Europe had caused his family to decide to travel to America, but that time was long ago and far away, and there was nothing about him, aside from the slight remnant of an accent, to betray the fact that he was not a native-born American.

He frowned at the sliver of ham and then set his teeth into it.

Sergeant Greene was watching him. "How is it?" he asked.

"Good," said Myers. "Needs soaking, but it sure beats marching rations."

Greene nodded. The past two months had been an almost endless round of marching and fighting. In that respect, they had been a logical continuation of his regiment's service, starting with Shiloh, Morning Sun, Wolf Creek Bridge and Chickasaw bayou in 1862, following through Vicksburg, Jackson and Mission Ridge the next year and continuing to the present. At the moment the 57th Ohio Volunteer Infantry, along with the rest of the XVth Corps under the command of Black Jack Logan, was heading toward Kennesaw Mountain in the face of increasing resistance. He was beginning to see rebel sharp-shooters behind every tree, and this forage detail assigned to Company

H had come as something of a relief.

"Give me a slice of that, Joe," he said. He took the ham, tried a bite, and raised his eyebrows in appreciation. "Very good!" he said. "These Georgia Rebs do know how to cure a ham!"

"Not bad," Myers conceded. He frowned across the fields. "Do you think that girl gave the alarm?" he asked, cutting another slice of ham and offering it to Greene."

"The way she went tearing off?" Greene said. "I guess so."

The drum of approaching hooves made both of them straighten and frown toward the sound.

"Skilton," said Myers. "Never rides slower than a canter. How many horses has he worn out since he got those shoulder straps?"

The others around them were watching as well, but they relaxed as the hoofbeats resolved themselves into the form of Lieutenant Skilton on his rawboned brown gelding.

"Lieutenant Lybarger says there's a town up ahead!" Skilton said. "Get your packs and supplies and move out! We've got to be back with the rest by sundown." His light eyes swung toward Private Myers, who was munching on his slice of ham.

Skilton rode over. "All right," he said. "Cut me a piece and then let's get moving."

"What a mooch!" said Sergeant Greene when Skilton was out of sight. He came from the same small Ohio town as Joe Myers, and had just been promoted to first sergeant. "Too young for his rank and too big for his goddamn britches! He can get his own food from here on, and he can tote it, too! Well, let's move out! Maybe we'll come upon Lybarger and we won't have to deal with that shavetail!"

CHAPTER TWENTY-FIVE

Lavinia peered over the tops of her spectacles at the tiny stitches running the length of the cuff. She had sewn the seam herself twenty years before, twelve perfect stitches to the inch. She sighed. That was when she had had time to be perfect. She had been eighteen, in the first blush of youth, accomplished and innocent enough almost to be able to believe that the suitors who came riding to Fairlawn in the summer, and Savannah in the winter, loved her for herself and not the portion she stood to inherit.

Ah, the good old days. Lavinia's mouth tightened at the corners as she carefully matched the tiny stitches. The years had not robbed her of her skill, and they had given her some wisdom, besides. Hers had been as happy a childhood as could be expected for one whose father had been a heedless, weak pleasure-seeker whose only virtue, in Lavinia's eyes, was his superb horsemanship. Lavinia's mother had been the mainstay of her young life, the woman who had shown Lavinia what it meant to be a great lady, whose death still caused an ache in her heart after four years.

Ordinarily, the past was past for Lavinia; she was too busy to allow herself to be caught in old longings and griefs. She would not go back in time if she could, not for all the tea in China. Or perhaps, more accurately, all the coffee in Yankeedom.

The seam was finished. She set the fine lawn sleeve aside with a sigh and polished her spectacles on her spotless handkerchief. She had found herself thinking of the past just this morning, a sort of brooding, pensive emotion heightened by the mist that crowded up against her window and blurred all the familiar features around her. It made her remember a nightmare that had haunted her years before, born of the turbulent emotions and half-understood urges that plague any child emerging into adulthood.

Her home had been enveloped in a mist that obscured sound and sight and even altered touch so that what seemed to be the corner of a table turned out to have thick, warm fur, and windows would open into blackness only to disclose distorted, leering faces. She had gone from room to room in the dream, frantically searching for her own bedroom, where she would be safe from the looming sounds and faces. But when she reached her room and opened the door, sobbing with relief, she would face something so horrible something so appalling in its corruption that she would be sent spinning into wakefulness, gasping with fright and trying to remember what it was that had frightened her so. She had thought, time and again, that if she could remember what it was and face it, the dream would lose its terror.

The dream had faded as Lavinia grew up, and she had forgotten it until this morning. She called herself fanciful, but she had felt a whisper within her all morning that something terrible was about to happen.

She clicked her tongue against her teeth and mentally thumbed her nose at her dream in a gesture she had seen Toby's youngest child use. Work was a good cure for anything; she would get to work. She set the threaded needle in her pincushion and reached for a spool of thread.

"Miss Lavinia!"

She turned to see Bathsheba running down the hallway toward her, her skirts bunched in both hands. Her hair was blown and drifting like a dark cloud about her smooth, flushed face. She came to a halt before Lavinia, skidding a little on the polished floor.

The sense of doom returned with a shudder. Lavinia steadied the girl. "Catch your breath, Bathsheba," she said with an effort at calmness. "Then tell me what is wrong."

Bathsheba leaned up against the hand-blocked scenic paper with a hand pressed to her side. "Sergeant Sheppard needs that guard form right away!" she panted. "The one that Yankee general sent to you! He needs you to bring it out to the front porch, please and thank you!"

"The form?" Lavinia said. "What are you talking about, child? The Order?"

"That's it, Miss Lavinia! He needs it now in a powerful hurry!"

"I'll get it," Lavinia said. "Is it urgent?"

"Urgent as death, Miss Lavinia!" Bathsheba said, pushing away from the wall and hurrying off toward the back of the house.

"Death?" Lavinia repeated. "Why, what has happened?"

"I can't stop!" Bathsheba called over her shoulder. "Sergeant Sheppard needs that paper, and he's got a pile of other things he needs for me to do. I've got to find Uncle George and then send Isaiah out to the town!"

"To the town?" Lavinia repeated. "What is going on?"

"I can't stop!" Bathsheba said again. "I'll tell you later!"

Lavinia shook her head in exasperation as Bathsheba ran off, calling for George. Whatever else could be said about Bathsheba, who shared the virtues and vices of other fifteen year old girls, she certainly had a good helping of sauce.

She went to the pearl-inlaid escritoire that her father had sent back from New Orleans, opened the slanted top, and slid the secret drawer open. The Order was there along with other important papers, including another copy of the encoded directions to the hidden gold.

General Stanley's order was neatly folded beside the directions. Lavinia took it out and tapped it against her palm, reflecting as she did that it would be a good idea to forge a copy to use instead of the original. Who knew? It might save the original for a more important time.

She closed the hidden drawer, slid the locking pin home, and put the order in her pocket. She reached the front porch just as Sergeant Sheppard came riding up on Dixie.

He seemed somehow taut and grim, but he touched his cap when he saw her and rode up to the balustrade. "Do you have the order, Miss Lavinia?" he asked.

"It's right here, Sergeant," she said, taking the paper from her pocket and handing it to him and then patting Dixie, who was nosing her sleeve and begging for a treat.

Sheppard scanned the order, folded it, and tucked it away in the breast of his jacket.

"Why do you need it, Sergeant?" Lavinia asked. "Is something wrong?"

"I'm not sure yet," Sheppard replied. "But Bathsheba came running to tell me she met a detachment of soldiers on her way to one of the cow sheds."

"Soldiers?" Lavinia repeated.

"That's right," Sheppard said, buttoning the inside pocket of his jacket. "She ran into a company, from what she said. She thought there were about thirty. If that's the case, they might be an advance guard, with the rest of the force coming along behind them."

Lavinia felt the blood drain from her cheeks. Childhood terrors are one thing; adult fears, rooted in the here and now, are far worse. "Do you—do you think they could have been the ones that killed Meg's family?" she asked.

Sheppard had been sitting restlessly in his saddle, eyeing the doorway and then turning to peer down the road toward the town. He looked up in time to see Lavinia clutch at the porch railing. "It isn't as bad as all that, Miss Lavinia," he said. "They sounded like a foraging patrol. Not bushwhackers. She wasn't hurt or insulted in any way, and they let her go when she decided to run. They could have caught up with her easily if they'd meant any harm."

Lavinia relaxed, a hand against her throat. "Then if they're—" she began. A sudden thought stopped her cold. "Are they-Sergeant, are they Confederates?" she asked, thinking how she had come to enjoy their twilight walks, and how she would miss him when he left.

Sheppard had risen in his stirrups and was staring toward town. He looked over at her and grinned with a sudden touch of mischief. "They're Union, sorry to say, Miss Wheeler," he said. "Looks like you're stuck with me a while longer."

George came through the front door carrying the sergeant's carbine and sling and a box of reloads. The Remington revolver was tucked into the waistband of his trousers, lending a piratical air to his usually benign appearance. "Here, Sergeant," he said, offering the carbine sling. "I'll hand you the gun in a moment. I hope I brought enough ammunition. There's seven of these tube things—seven rounds each makes just about fifty, give or take what you've got in there already, and I brought the spare cylinders for your pistol, too."

"That should be more than enough," Sheppard said, settling the wide leather carbine sling across his chest and then clipping the carbine to it.

Hearing an uneven clump on the floorboards, Lavinia turned to see Corporal Higgins and two of the other convalescents come out.

"You wanted us, Sarge?" Higgins said.

"That's right, Higgins," Sheppard said. "Bathsheba ran into a foraging party by the dairy. From what she says, they're probably heading toward the town with the aim of stopping at every henhouse and smokehouse between them and it. They seemed orderly enough, reading between the lines, but I think I'd best to get strict with them right away."

"What do you want us to do?" Higgins asked.

"I want as many men as possible to go and sit on each porch," Sheppard said. "In uniform, if they can. If anyone comes here, I want it to be clear that this place is a hospital and it's hands off. It isn't going to be so easy with the rest of the town."

"What are you going to do?" Lavinia demanded.

"I'll just tell them to put back what they've taken and go somewhere else," Sheppard said. He looked over at Higgins. "I sent Isaiah off after Caesar to tell him to make the Fairlawn militia lie low. He's to go to Al Townsend with the same word. The last thing I want is to have the people of Wheelerville fighting the Union army."

Lavinia closed her eyes for a moment. The situation was not getting any better. "Do you think it may come to that?" she asked, looking up at Sheppard.

He was frowning down at his stirrup leathers. "Not if I can help it," he said grimly, shortening them.

"But you are taking someone with you, surely!" Lavinia exclaimed.

"No," said Sheppard. "It'll just be me and the Order. It'll be enough, if things don't get ugly."

"Here she comes," said Higgins, nodding off toward the garden path, where they could see Bathsheba running toward them.

"I did everything you said, Sergeant," she panted. "Everyone's been and gone, and the people are coming to take shelter at the house. My pa said to tell you they hit the smokehouses and cleared out the dairy."

"I was afraid of that," said Sheppard, gathering his reins. "The only good thing I can say is that they aren't cavalry. They'd be carrying off four times the supplies."

"Is there anything else you want me to do, Sergeant?" Bathsheba asked.

"Just keep yourself safe," Sheppard said. "And see that you watch out for your mistress."

Lavinia stopped him with a hand on his knee. "Sergeant," she said. He looked down at her.

"Let me come along with you. This is my town. I can talk to them. It'll only take a minute to have Beau harnessed to the buggy."

"It is no place right now for anyone who isn't a soldier," Sheppard said. "You might get hurt. What happens to me isn't important."

"Maybe it's not important to your assignment," Lavinia said through the foreboding tightness in her throat. "But it is to those who wish you well. You are foolish to take unnecessary risks."

Sheppard lifted her hand from his knee and raised it to his lips. "The foolishness of the risks depends on who is taking them," he said, smiling down into her wide eyes. "I must be certain that you're safe. That is the reason General Stanley assigned me here. Stay with the rest and make sure they don't panic. If anyone asks, say that these fellows aren't the ones who killed Meg's family. You can talk to them later, if things go well. But not now."

He looked up at the group behind Lavinia. "Corporal Higgins," he said, "do as I told you. The more who can come out, the better.

"Yes, sir!"

Sheppard nodded and spurred Dixie forward.

Lavinia took a step after him. "Sergeant!" she called.

He reined in and looked back at her.

"Please be careful."

CHAPTER TWENTY-SIX

By the time Company H's point men reached the town, the mist had cleared enough for them to see that it was a neat place. A sign announced the date of establishment of the town, named Wheelerville, and the town itself was a fair-sized cluster of clapboard and brick houses with trim walkways lining the dirt streets. There were two main streets that the point men could see, and several intersecting roadways. It looked to be a prosperous community and, by the smells coming into the streets from the houses, a well fed one.

Joseph Myers, who had been assigned to point duty with the usual two others, Sergeant Greene and Private Leary, sniffed appreciatively. He thought some bacon and eggs would taste fine. There would be time for that shortly, but for now—

A report and the zing of a bullet across his path stopped Myers in his tracks and sent him grabbing for his musket. As he straightened he saw a rider emerge from one of the side streets, his carbine held across his chest at the ready. The man was Union by his uniform, a Sergeant Major of cavalry with red-edged service stripes on his sleeves. His expression was forbidding, and he was holding his carbine as though he were ready to use it.

"Stop there!" the sergeant major called. "State your unit and your business!"

"Company H, 57th Ohio!" Greene replied. "We're on forage detail. And who the hell are you?"

The man nudged his horse a little closer, though he still held his carbine ready. "Asa Sheppard, Sergeant Major of the 8th Ohio Cavalry," he replied. "This town is under Union protection."

"What?" demanded Joseph Myers.

"You heard me, private," the man said. He scanned the three. "You're a point patrol, aren't you?" he said. "Where's your commander?"

"He should be coming up," Myers said, quietly cocking his piece.

The Sergeant Major's eyes swung toward him at the sound. "Put that musket down," he said. "I mean you no harm as long as you honor the Order. Where's the rest of your unit? Are they far behind?"

Since he could hear the approaching clatter of Lieutenant Skilton's horse, Myers did not think he had to answer.

Sergeant Sheppard lifted his head and turned toward the sound, his eyes narrowed.

Skilton came galloping up. "I heard a shot!" he exclaimed, reining his horse hard on its haunches in a spray of dust. He saw Sergeant Sheppard and reached for his pistol, then relaxed as he saw the uniform. "What is all this?" he demanded. "Did you fire upon my men?"

Sheppard cast a quick glance over the young man and then saluted. "I stopped them with a shot across the path and well in front, sir," he replied. He took a paper from the breast of his short jacket. "This town is under Union protection by order of General Miles Stanley of the Army of the Monongahela. Here's the order, signed by the general himself. I am assigned to act as Safeguard here until I am relieved."

"I don't understand this," said Lieutenant Skilton. "You say you're a guard?"

"Yes, sir," Sheppard said. He looked the group over and said, "The town is off limits to foragers. I must ask that your group return what it's taken and go on its way."

The lieutenant frowned at Sergeant Sheppard. "Let me see that," he said, holding out his hand. He took the paper from Sheppard, scanned it, and then read it aloud.

By Authority of Miles G. Stanley, Major General, U.S.V.

A Safeguard is hereby granted to Miss Lavinia Wheeler, residing in the town of Wheelerville, Georgia, covering the person of Miss Wheeler and all properties and goods belonging to her, including a valuable collection of Early Colonial Pottery. All officers and soldiers belonging to the Army of the United States are therefore commanded to respect this Safeguard and to afford, if necessary, protection to the person and property of Miss Lavinia Wheeler.

This instrument authorizes the Guard assigned to this duty to take whatever measures he deems appropriate to

*assure the safety of the person and property of Miss Lavinia
Wheeler. This order can only be countermanded by myself or
by one senior to me in rank.*

> *Given at Headquarters this 14th day of May, 1864.
> Miles G. Stanley Major General Commanding In Chief*

He lowered the paper. "I've never heard of this sort of thing!" he
said scornfully.

"You've seen the order, sir, and you've seen the signature," Sheppard said. "With all respect, I must ask that you honor the order, return
the goods your men have taken, and leave this place."

"I'm under orders from General Logan to act as forage detail for
my brigade," Lieutenant Skilton said. "I'm afraid that cancels your
order. And when was it given, anyway? May? It's out of date!"

"Look again, Lieutenant," Sheppard said. "The order is very specific. It can't be countermanded except by General Stanley, or an officer
senior to him."

"That's the most ridiculous thing I've heard!" Skilton said disgustedly, handing it back. "It talks about a collection of pottery! We aren't
taking any pottery!"

"The Order also commands that the property of Miss Wheeler be
honored," Sheppard pointed out.

"Show me her property and I'll honor it!" Skilton said.

Sergeant Sheppard motioned around him. "This whole town be-
longs to her," he said. "Lock, stock and barrel!"

"Do you expect me to believe that?" Lieutenant Skilton demanded.

"You may believe what you wish, Lieutenant," Sheppard said. "I'll
show you the deeds in the town hall, if you want. But I have my orders and General Stanley made them very clear. I must ask that you
call your men off and tell them to give back the supplies they've tak-
en."

Myers, watching, saw Skilton's eyes narrow. He took a good grip
of his musket.

"I've never heard of a Safeguard," said Lieutenant Skilton. "And I
don't know what a lone soldier would be doing here if there is so much
to protect. And if Miss Wheeler is so rich that there is so much to pro-

tect, then she can spare enough to feed my group. Frankly, Sergeant, I think you're lying. I'm placing you under arrest and ordering my men to go about their duties!"

Sheppard's gaze did not waver. "You are mistaken in that order, Lieutenant," he said. "And my instructions are to stop looters at all cost."

"I've told you, the order is countermanded!"

"Let me remind you, Lieutenant, that my orders can only be countermanded by Major General Stanley, or someone who ranks him. For the last time, with all respect, I must ask that you tell your men to give back the food and goods they have taken and leave this town alone."

Skilton did not answer, but his hand tightened on the grip of his pistol.

Sheppard saw the slight motion and reined his mare across the road.

Myers took a deep breath and held it.

** ** **

Lavinia stood gazing after Sergeant Sheppard, her cheek against her hand, where he had kissed it, until he had dwindled a blur of dark blue glimpsed among the tossing beech leaves. She turned back toward the house when even that blur was finally gone.

The sight was gone, but not the fear. Something terrible was about to happen. Lavinia could feel it as clearly as a blow to the heart. She Lavinia could feel a sense of approaching disaster. It had to be the soldiers' arrival: that was all it could be. What could she do?

She took a deep breath and looked up at the veranda. Things had happened while she had been gazing. The most mobile of the invalids were on the porch as Sergeant Sheppard had directed. Most of them were armed, and they all had the strange look of men who had awakened from a dream and were facing a reality that disturbed and frightened them.

The ebbing of all the excitement had left Bathsheba at loose ends. She was twisting her skirts in her hands. "M—Miss Lavinia?" she said. "What do you want me to do?"

Lavinia straightened and squared her shoulders, turning her mind from her sense of foreboding. "We have a household to run, Bathsheba," she said with a crispness made sharper by worry. "You know your schedule of chores: the best thing to do is make certain they get done. Take care of your current duty and you'll have time to take care of the next as it arises. Now get to work."

Bathsheba grimaced and sketched a curtsey. "Yes, Miss Lavinia," she said, and hurried off in the direction of the linen press.

Lavinia watched her go, nodded absently to Corporal Higgins, and went into the house.

Do your current duty and you'll have time to take care of the next as it arises. Excellent advice, she thought, gazing up the sweep of the grand staircase, but it was not helping her.

She set her foot on the steps and forced her mind to run in its usual lines: chores, plans, things to consider.

She moved through the house over the next twenty minutes, calm and capable, giving directions to Bathsheba, who was doing an inventory of the linen, consulting with Callie, who was planning the day's meals. But she was restless even as she saw to the smooth operation of her household; nothing could hold her constant attention.

From the kitchen she went up to inspect the cisterns let into the roof to collect rainwater. Not surprisingly, they were filled. She descended to the cellar, where she examined Fairlawn's extensive collection of cookpots that were too worn out to use but too good to discard. There was good metal there: the Confederacy could use it, she thought. But then she thought that whatever use her worn out cookpots might find in later years, they would almost certainly be used to fight men like Sergeant Sheppard or Corporal Higgins.

The thought was not to be borne, and the feeling of oppression was lingering. Why was she so fanciful? She shook her head and went back upstairs.

Al Townsend was awaiting her in the parlor. "Everyone's been yanked off the streets, Miss Wheeler," he said. "Just as the Sergeant ordered."

"That is good," Lavinia said, pulling her embroidery frame forward. She slid the needle from its hiding place and checked the tautness of the thread.

Townsend looked at his hands, folded before him with unaccustomed docility. "They look like they mean business," he said.

She looked up from the frame. "Did you see them, then?" she asked.

"Yes, ma'am," Townsend said. "Thirty of them that I could see, but

I think there were more. Armed and moving quickly, but loaded with hams and meats and bags of grain."

Thirty of them. Veterans. And Sheppard was only one against them. She rose, bringing Townsend to his feet as well. "Excuse me, Mr. Townsend," she said. "There are things I must do quickly. Stay here as long as you want, but keep out of sight. That is what the Sergeant said."

She did now wait to see if Townsend obeyed her, but left the parlor, calling for George.

"Harness Beau to the buggy, George," she said as he came to her. "Callie! Would you fetch me my good paisley shawl and the straw hat with the roses that came through the blockade?"

George and Callie traded surprised looks and left.

Lavinia went out to the porch. "Mr. Hayes," she said, "You are getting around well. Would you please go into the wards and see what is needful, and give orders for it to be done? Water, bandages, perhaps some tea? I'll leave it to you, and thank you."

Private Hayes looked startled, but he got to his feet and went inside.

The buggy arrived soon after with Beau snorting and prancing between the shafts.

Lavinia took the hat from Callie and set it on her smoothly coiffed hair, then settled the shawl about her shoulders. "Thank you, Callie," she said. "Would you please tell Toby to make sure his people are busy? If nothing else, the tobacco sheds are nearby and they can count the drying bunches."

"Yes, Miss Vinnie," Callie said. "But what are you going to do?"

Lavinia gathered her skirts and descended the steps. "I'm going in town," she said. "Someone's got to stand with the sergeant, and it had best be me. They won't fire on a woman—"

"Don't you believe it for a minute, Miss!"

Lavinia turned to see Higgins lever himself to his feet and reach for his crutches.

"Corporal?"

"If you'd seen what I've seen— Boys, tell her: it isn't safe!"

"Nonsense," Lavinia said over the chorus of agreement. She nodded to George. "Would you hand me in, please?" she said.

George did not look happy, but he offered his arm. "Maybe I

should come with you," he began.

Higgins slowly descended the steps and came limping over to her. "You can't go now!" he exclaimed. "Miss Wheeler, it's dangerous right now! Those soldiers are coming through!"

"I know that, Corporal," she said, accepting a boost from George and reaching for the reins. "That is why I'm needed there."

Higgins seized the off rein. "Miss Wheeler!"

"Corporal," she said.

"You can't go in town, Miss Wheeler," Higgins insisted. "The Sergeant forbade it."

"But I don't take my orders from Sergeant Sheppard, Corporal," she said. "Now if you will stand aside..."

"But Miss Wheeler—"

Lavinia's tone dropped a degree. "I mean it, sir," she said, taking up the whip. "Please stand aside."

Higgins kept his hold on the reins. "If you're going to take the bit in your teeth and go against everything the sergeant ordered, then I'm coming with you," he said.

"No you are not," Lavinia said. "Let go of the reins."

Higgins eyed the whip and then met her gaze. "If you're going, then so am I," he said. "He'll kill me if I stay here, that's for sure!"

Lavinia frowned at his crutches. "The jolting will hurt you," she said. "You'd be wiser to stay behind. I'll be fine, truly I will, and Sergeant Sheppard won't have any reason to complain."

"Then take Caesar or Toby with you."

"They must stay here," Lavinia said. "I'll be fine."

"Then I'll come with you, Miss Wheeler," he said again. "My word may not amount to much with a gang of foragers, but I can teach them to keep a civil tongue in their heads when they're dealing with a lady."

"Don't be foolish, Corporal," she said. "Get back on the veranda."

"No, Miss Wheeler. I'm coming with you." He raised a hand to stop her exclamation. "And if you don't take me with you, I'll cut the reins, and then where'll you be?"

"I'll simply saddle this horse and ride him into town," Lavinia said. "I'd prefer it at any rate."

She gazed at him and he gazed back at her. "Oh very well," she said, taking pity on his white face. "Get in the buggy. George, would you please fetch some of the down pillows from the house? I don't want Corporal Higgins to be jolted any more than is necessary." When George had gone and returned with the pillows, and arranged them, she shook out the whip and said, "There, see? I hope you're happy. Now let's go help the sergeant."

CHAPTER TWENTY-SEVEN

Lieutenant Skilton looked at the point patrol. "I'm going back to the company and telling them to come here," he said. "We'll commandeer a wagon. They'll take any supplies they can carry, then head out of here. And as for you, Sergeant—" He turned back and recoiled at the sight of the black barrel of Sheppard's carbine leveled at him and the sound of its loading lever being snapped forward and back. "Now by what—" he began.

"You have read the order, Lieutenant," Sheppard said. "And I have warned you. Drop your reins and raise your hands. Now!"

The lieutenant did not move. Sheppard raised the weapon. "You heard me!" he said.

Skilton slowly obeyed.

Sheppard nudged Dixie into an amble. He took Skilton's reins when he was beside him and then unbuttoned the flap of his holster, removed the pistol, and thrust it into his belt after glancing at it.

"Now," said Sheppard, "turn and face your men. And be sure to keep your hands where I can see them."

Skilton's eyes were blazing, but he did as he was told.

Sheppard edged Dixie slightly behind Skilton and directed a level stare at the three men before him. "Now, soldiers," he said, "The lieutenant will hand me back the order and you will hear it read aloud again, then I will tell you some things that had best be done at once. Listen:"

He read the Order in an even, clear voice. "Did you all hear me?" he asked as he folded the order. "And did you all understand it?"

Myers looked from Sergeant Greene to Private Leary and then nodded.

"Good," said Sheppard. "You have heard that I have General Stanley's authority to take whatever steps are necessary to protect Miss Lavinia Wheeler's property, and that is what I am doing now. And the first thing I am going to do is relieve the lieutenant, here."

He nodded to Sergeant Greene. "First Sergeant," he said. "Go find your outfit and tell them to stop where they are. And you—" nodding to Myers. "You look like a steady fellow. I assume your captain is somewhere about: I need to speak with him right away. You will bring him here on the double. Tell him I respectfully request his presence—"

"Company H's captain is wounded," Skilton said.

"I see," said Sheppard. "And are you commanding in his absence?"

"Lieutenant Lybarger is in command for the time being, Sergeant," Greene said. "He's our regimental quartermaster, usually."

"Good," said Sheppard. "Find him and bring him here, if you please."

Lieutenant Skilton was fidgeting in his saddle. "This is an outrage!" he burst out. "I demand—"

"I'm sorry, Lieutenant," Sheppard said firmly, "But you've been relieved. I am acting within my authority. You read General Stanley's order. I have General Stanley's permission to do whatever is necessary to make sure it is obeyed, and that's exactly what I'm doing right now."

He nodded to Myers and Greene. "The two of you: go!"

"What about me?" asked Leary.

"You can sit down and keep out of mischief," Sheppard said. He looked back at Skilton. "That goes for you, too. Dismount and tether your horse to that railing there, then sit down beside your man."

Lieutenant Skilton slowly took his right foot from the stirrup. "You won't get away with this!" he said as he swung his leg over the cantle of the saddle and landed on the ground with a thump.

"You watch me, Lieutenant," said Sheppard. "And see how well you do, disobeying a clear, written order from a major general!"

** ** **

"He's holding Lieutenant Skilton at gunpoint?" First Lieutenant Edwin Lybarger demanded. He was sitting against the bole of a tree, frowning at a worn map and worrying at a piece of well-cured ham with his teeth. The rest of Company H was standing around him, and his horse was cropping nearby with one ear cocked forward.

"That's right, sir," said Myers. "The fellow showed Lieutenant Skilton a note that he said was signed by General Stanley—"

Lieutenant Lybarger swallowed his mouthful and frowned at the slice of ham in his hand. "General Miles Stanley?" he asked.

"Yes, sir. It was an order for a Safeguard. Lieutenant Skilton said he'd never heard of one—"

"Sweet Jesus, what an idiot!" said Lybarger, scrambling to his feet and brushing at the crumbs of ham scattered down his dusty front. "And where's Leary?"

"He's back in the town, too."

"Is he being held at gunpoint?"

"No, sir," said Sergeant Greene. "At least I didn't think so. I think that sergeant's on the up-and-up. He was polite about everything, and I guess he just figured he didn't have anything for Leary to do so Leary might just as well stay put. Anyhow, from what I saw Skilton's only getting what he's been asking for all this time. He's a jackass."

"You said that right," said Lieutenant Lybarger. "Trust a shavetail to foul up! I'll be polite when I deal with this sergeant, but I don't take kindly to people who hold my men hostage. Get to your feet, everybody!"

"That sergeant said the boys were to stay where they are," Myers said.

"A First Lieutenant might be a small fish in the scheme of things," Lybarger said through his teeth. "But he still outranks a sergeant in most armies I've heard of. I'll get to the bottom of this. Come on, boys."

** ** **

Lawrence Skilton had never been so baffled and infuriated in his life. The only, late-come son of elderly parents, he had grown to manhood in the sunshine of everyone's approval. His enlistment in late 1863, after months of prayer and thought, had been an act of pure patriotism. His family had exerted some of its influence and secured for him a commission as second lieutenant. As a result, he found himself among people who seemed to view him with contempt.

He was considered an interloper, he had taken a position that had rightly belonged to another, and nothing he had done to ingratiate himself had helped. He was disliked, obeyed with reluctance and mocked behind his back. He wanted to be—not beloved, maybe, but accepted as a veteran among veterans, but the fulfillment of that desire had eluded him.

Now he glared at Sheppard. "I'm not being unreasonable," he said aggrievedly. "How can I be sure that signature is General Stanley's? For all I know it's a forgery!"

Sergeant Major Sheppard cocked an eye at him. "How can you be sure?" he repeated. "Why, the same way I can be sure you aren't all a pack of renegades after rape and murder."

He watched Skilton draw himself up. "Made a point, didn't I?" he said. "Maybe you should chew on it a bit. And you might want to consider that there's nothing to keep me from shooting you out of hand after the way you acted. I don't think anyone'd criticize me, either."

"If you're going to insult—"

"Forget it, Lieutenant," Sheppard said. He nodded to Leary. "Think about it," he said. "Is it so unlikely General Stanley would be giving out orders to protect this place? It's a pretty enough town, I'll admit, but nothing out of the ordinary that would make desperadoes want to forge a Safeguard order for a woman and her collection of pots."

"Then why did he assign a guard?" Leary asked.

"He's protecting the property and person of a lady who helped him and his men," Sheppard replied. "The property happens to be the whole town of Wheelerville, and the lady happens to be Miss Wheeler."

"Well, who is this Miss Wheeler?" Skilton demanded.

Sheppard adjusted his grip on the carbine. "She is a lady," he said. "Good and kind with a heart of gold. She opened her house to us to use as a hospital. Still has wounded there, for that matter, and she running the place single-handed. She's a very fine lady."

Skilton attempted a sneer. "You seem to be sweet on her!" he said.

Sheppard paused to consider the suggestion. "Could be," he conceded. "She's certainly an angel. You see how you feel about a lady who takes her enemies in, sick, wounded, hungry and exhausted, and cares for them."

Skilton looped his arms about his drawn-up knees. "You were wounded?" he asked.

Sheppard's gaze sharpened. "Don't try anything," he said. "And you—" This to Leary, "The sun's shifted: get in the shade. It shouldn't be much longer."

"I asked you a question, Sergeant," Skilton said.

Sheppard shot him a level look and then nodded. "I was wounded," he said. "Here—" He unbuttoned his jacket one-handed, followed up with his shirt, and pulled both aside from his shoulder while keeping his carbine trained on Skilton. The scar from the saber stroke was angry and red against the paler skin around it.

Skilton eyed the scar and then looked up at Sheppard. "I'm sorry, Sergeant," he said. "Maybe I was wrong—"

"You were wrong," Sheppard agreed.

"I've never heard of a Safeguard," Skilton said. "I just joined in November."

Sheppard frowned at him.

"Say, Lieutenant, there're people staring at us from the windows!" Leary exclaimed.

"What?" demanded Skilton.

"They're the townsfolk here," Sheppard said. "I told them to stay indoors and not try anything."

"They look as though they'd as soon hang us as look at us," Leary said.

"They're Confederates," Sheppard said. "Why should they be friendly to people they view as invaders? Or as thieves?"

Skilton's color rose. "They're wrong about that," he said.

"I agree," Sheppard said. "But that's neither here nor there. Stay quiet and they'll have no reason to come out. You'll both be fine."

Skilton frowned down the street and then looked back at Sheppard. "Let my man go," he said. "I'll stay here till the others come."

Leary stared at him. "Of all the—" he began. "No, damn it all, Lieutenant, you can't do that!"

"I can and I will," Skilton said. "He has no quarrel with you: he won't keep you in danger. You can get out of here and—"

"I'm staying with you, Lieutenant!" Leary burst out.

"Don't be a fool," Skilton said. He looked back at Sheppard, who was eyeing him with a touch of approval. "Will you let him go?" he asked. "I'll agree to—"

"What the devil is going on, Skilton?" It was Lieutenant Lybarger, riding his roan gelding and followed by five of the company's men in skirmishing order.

"I'll handle this, Sergeant," Skilton said. He pushed to his feet and turned to face Lieutenant Lybarger. "Sir, I can explain," he said.

Lybarger's eyes flicked over Skilton and then came to rest on

Sheppard and narrowed. "I'll deal with you in a minute, Lieutenant," he said. "I've business to tend to with this man. How dare you hold my men hostage, Sergeant?" he demanded. "Lower that carbine right now!"

Sheppard obeyed, but he kept the weapon at the ready and reached into the breast of his jacket. "With respect, sir," he said, "this order provides protection to this town."

Lieutenant Skilton said, "Sir, the point patrol came into this town and were stopped by this man. He has an order signed by General Stanley—"

"So I heard!" Lybarger said grimly. "Let's see it." The words came out simultaneous with the sound of a wheeled vehicle approaching. Lieutenant Lybarger, sitting his horse with his hand imperiously outstretched to receive the Order, saw Sergeant Sheppard turn toward the sound with an exclamation of dismay. He turned, as well, his hand still extended.

Private Leary, still sitting in the shade, craned his neck and then grinned. "Well I'll be damned!" he said.

** ** **

"I hope I'm not too late," Lavinia said as she turned the buggy down Ash Street. "If something's happened— I've had the most terrible feeling all day!" Corporal Higgins levered himself more upright. "Give me the reins, Miss Wheeler," he said. "Don't be foolish, Corporal," Lavinia said. "I can drive. Just you sit back and try to relax."

"No," said Higgins. "If you're supposed to be under Union protection, you'd best have a soldier driving you. Come on, hand the reins over." Lavinia eyed his white face. "No," she said. "You'll hurt yourself, ill as you are. I'll drive."

"Do as I say!" Higgins snapped. He looked immediately contrite. "I'm sorry, Miss Wheeler, but I'm just missing a leg. There's nothing wrong with my arms."

Lavinia gave the reins over to him. "You'd best slow down," she said as Beau broke into a spanking trot. "This jolting—"

"I'll be fine, Miss Wheeler!" he gasped, urging the bay to a canter. "You just worry about your own safety!"

"At least go over the smooth parts!" Lavinia pleaded, one hand to her hat.

"This road doesn't have any smooth parts!" Higgins said grimly as they turned onto Main Street. "Here we are! Holy Christmas!"

Lavinia stared. Sergeant Sheppard, who was holding two Union soldiers at gunpoint, one seated, was facing another, who was mounted and followed by five others with muskets at the ready. Everyone was frowning.

"Dear heavens!" she gasped. "He's got two officers angry with him! And there's a whole crowd of soldiers coming down the side street! I was afraid this would happen!" She turned to Higgins. "Drive right up to them, and let me do all the talking."

"Yes ma'am!" Higgins said with the hint of a smile.

Lavinia willed herself to composure and folded her gloved hands before her as Corporal Higgins, properly wooden-faced, brought the buggy right up to the mounted officer.

She nodded to the man, who doffed his hat, and then turned to Sheppard. "You shouldn't have met our visitors alone, Sergeant," she said. "I asked you to wait for me."

She smiled as the dismounted officer clawed his hat from his head. "Would you please present me to these gentlemen?" she asked Sheppard.

The sergeant shot an ominously eloquent look at Higgins as he bowed. "Miss Wheeler," he said, "allow me to present—"

"Edwin Lybarger, Ma'am," the mounted officer supplied with a creditable bow. "I am acting as the commander of Company H, 57th Ohio Infantry. And these—" indicating the officer who had been seated on the ground until just a moment before, "—are Lieutenant Skilton, and Private Leary."

"It is a pleasure, gentlemen," Lavinia said. "I am Lavinia Wheeler. Let me welcome you to Wheelerville in behalf of its citizens." She turned to Sheppard. "Sergeant, did these gentlemen require anything?" she asked.

"They don't need a thing," Sheppard said. "I was just showing them General Stanley's order and suggesting they return what they have taken and go on their way." He handed the paper to Lieutenant Lybarger, who scanned it, nodded, and gave it back.

"Had they not seen it before?" Lavinia asked.

"The Lieutenant had not," Sheppard said. "Now that he has...?"

"Very well, Sergeant," Lybarger said. "It's pretty clear. You have my apologies. If—"

"Sir," said the young man, Lieutenant Skilton. "This whole affair was my fault. Nothing the men did had any bearing on any of this, and I accept full responsibility. I acted hastily."

Lybarger's expression was unreadable. "We can discuss that later," he said.

"But why later, sir?" Lavinia asked with a smile. "Your men are tired, and I see that they are loaded down with goods."

"Goods that are going to be returned right away," Sheppard said.

"Just so, Sergeant," Lybarger said.

"Why can't your men bring their goods to Fairlawn?" Lavinia asked. "It's not far from here, and you can take some refreshment. I'll be glad to show you where your wounded have been cared for."

"Our wounded?" Lybarger asked with another look at Skilton. "I wasn't aware..." he saw Corporal Higgins' stump for the first time. "I beg your pardon, Ma'am," he said.

"Do come to Fairlawn, Lieutenant," Lavinia said. "All your men are welcome. You can rest before you continue your journey." She smiled at Sergeant Sheppard, who was looking narrowly from Lieutenant Lybarger to Corporal Higgins, and said, "The good Sergeant will be happy to lead your men to my house; I will have refreshments awaiting you there."

CHAPTER TWENTY-EIGHT

Lavinia drew Beau's reins through her gloved hands and gazed anxiously up the road toward Wheelerville. Sergeant Sheppard should be returning at any moment along that road, and if the look he had flashed at her as he rode off at the head of the foragers was any indication of things, she was in for a scolding at the very least. It had been a pleasant day, for all that the beginning had been frightening, but Lavinia would have found it more pleasant if she could have shed the conviction that Sergeant Sheppard was angry with her. Angry, indeed! Furious, rather! And maybe, she thought wryly, she deserved it.

After he had been shown around Fairlawn, Lieutenant Lybarger had offered to take with him any letters the wounded soldiers wanted to have sent home. While he and Sergeant Sheppard had ridden off to supervise the return of the supplies the 57th Ohio had taken, the others of the foraging party had helped the wounded to write and address their letters.

When the foraging party had finally departed, Lavinia had sent it on its way with a gift of four hams and as many bushels of shelled corn, as well as a large barrel of cured tobacco.

She had then gone through the motions of performing her various daily tasks, but her mind had been distracted, still caught by the nagging feeling of impending disaster.

She had finally decided to face it. If she was to get a scolding, then she preferred that it be as private as possible, and if disaster was to come through a friend, then the sooner she faced it, the better it would be. She had ordered that Beau be saddled, and had ridden out to intercept Sergeant Sheppard. Twilight's increasing mist cloaked the passage of time; Lavinia, caught up in her unease, remained where she was, waiting.

Beau had grown weary of standing still. He stretched his neck down to snuffle at the grass by the wayside. Lavinia dismounted, loosened her reins and watched as his ears flicked back and forth. She reflected for a moment how much easier it would be if she were an animal. There would be no concerns except the question of where the next meal was coming from and whether the sun was shining. If she were a horse, now, like Beau, all she would need would be food, warmth, and a congenial neighbor's backbone upon which to scratch an itching chin.

The thought made her smile. The smile remained as she heard the lazy cadence of hooves upon the packed dirt of the road and turned toward it. Beau raised his head and pricked his ears forward.

Sergeant Sheppard, bareheaded and windblown, was approaching at an amble. His jacket was open and the neck of his shirt unbuttoned. His forage cap was folded and tucked beneath one of the straps of his saddle. He was looking back over his shoulder; as Lavinia watched, he turned back toward her.

The shift in his expression as he caught sight of her made the smile fade from Lavinia's lips. Disaster was upon her, she thought with a twinge of regret for the pleasant, friendly days past, but she raised her chin and looked steadily back at him.

He drew rein, his left hand going awkwardly up to the buttons at the front of his jacket.

"No, Sergeant," Lavinia said. "You need not stand upon formality today. It's warm and you've been exercising. Please be comfortable."

Sheppard nodded and lowered his hand again.

"I've been waiting for you," Lavinia said. "You were gone quite a long time."

"I stopped in town to talk with Caesar and Al Townsend," Sheppard said. "I wanted everyone to know what they are expected to do if foragers or bushwhackers come again."

Lavinia pushed her sense of fear aside and looked up at him. "Did you decide on a plan?" she asked.

Sheppard drew a strand of Dixie's mane through his fingers and nodded. "We did," he said. "It'll have to be practiced until everyone knows what to do without thinking, of course, but it'll be a help in future."

"What are we supposed to do?" Lavinia asked.

Sheppard raised his head and looked directly at her. "Pretty much what I told everyone to do this morning," he said. "Those in outlying houses stay together; those in town gather at a spot they'll be choosing this week, one that can be fortified. They're to see how the intruders act, and then react in whatever way is appropriate."

Lavinia lifted her chin. "'Pretty much what I told everyone to do this morning,' " she repeated. "I gather that includes what you told me."

Sheppard was silent for a moment, weighing his reply. "Yes," he said finally. "Specifically what I told you."

Beau began to nibble at the tussock of grass. Lavinia tightened the reins and brought his head up. "I see," she said. "You are angry with me, aren't you, Sergeant?"

Sheppard's gaze had been distant; it shortened, rested on her as the moment stretched out, thin and cutting. "Yes, Miss Wheeler," he said. "I guess I am. You ignored my clear instructions. And even after I told you that the situation was dangerous and I wanted you to stay where you could be protected, you chose to interfere with things."

"'Interfere'!" Lavinia exclaimed, remembering her fears for him. "Then you think it was nothing but interference that brought me into town?" Sheppard folded his arms and frowned at her. "Do you have a better name for it?" he asked. "'Meddling', maybe?"

"There was a great deal at stake," Lavinia said. "I did what I thought was justified. I don't think it takes any imagination to understand why I felt that way, or why I did what I did."

"That's beside the point," Sheppard said. "You asked for a Safeguard and you have one! I told you to stay where you were until it was safe. You heard me, you understood me, and you chose to ignore me. If you want your life and your property guarded, then you'd damned—" He broke off. "I beg your pardon," he said. "You'd darned well better listen to me! The next time I give an order, I expect it to be obeyed!"

"I'm not a soldier, Sergeant! I don't take orders from you or from any man! Besides that, you worried to no purpose. Those men were charming!"

Sheppard lifted his eyebrows at her. "I wonder how charming you'd have found that crowd of roughnecks if they'd taken a notion to shoot me and all the other men here, clear out your henhouses and smokehouses, fire all your crops, and then burn the town to the ground," he said.

"Oh fiddlesticks!" Lavinia said.

"Those folk exist, Miss Wheeler: I've seen them. Men who aren't above raping a helpless woman and torturing an old man! Just remember how Meg came to live with us!"

"But it didn't happen in this case!" Lavinia pointed out.

"It could have! I had thought you an intelligent woman before this, but now I wonder if you have even half a brain inside your head! That was the most inexcusable, pigheaded disregard of orders I've ever seen!"

"Now you're being foolish," Lavinia said. "And rude."

"No, I'm not!"

"Yes you are!" Lavinia could not suppress a smile.

Sheppard drew a deep, exasperated breath. "Don't you realize what you stepped into?" he demanded.

"Of course I do," Lavinia said.

"There were men coming down the side streets of the town."

"Pooh!" Lavinia said. "The townsfolk were all watching, and they had guns!"

"They were inside their houses, where I'd ordered them to be!" Sheppard said. "What if those Federal troops had opened fire on me?"

"They'd have been killed by the people of Wheelerville," Lavinia said.

"With you and your buggy in the way?" Sheppard demanded. "How many of the Wheelerville citizens do you really think would have started shooting as long as there was a chance of hitting you?"

Lavinia opened her eyes at him.

"Hang it all, woman!" Sheppard said, exasperated. "I'm supposed to be protecting you! You could have been killed! You placed yourself in terrible danger, and I was powerless to help you! And you did it against everything I asked you to do! I haven't told you how to run your plantation, Miss Wheeler. Why did you decide to tell me how to fight a battle?"

"You were facing at least three men, and more were coming against you," Lavinia said.

"There was a company coming," Sheppard said. "More than three by a long shot! I was expecting them!"

"You didn't tell me that," Lavinia said. "All I knew was that it was dangerous."

"I had the situation under control," Sheppard said through his teeth.

"I was in no danger!"

"I didn't know that," Lavinia said. "And I couldn't let you face them alone. I was afraid you might be hurt, and I couldn't bear the thought."

Sheppard stared at her. "Of all the mean-spirited—" he exclaimed.

"Sergeant?"

"You don't fight fair! I've had some choice words waiting for you, and now I can't say them without sounding like an ungrateful blockhead!"

Lavinia laughed up at him. "You can go ahead and say them now, Sergeant," she said through the emerging warmth of a happy smile.

"No, it's no use! Why did I ever— Confound it all!"

"Then I'm forgiven?" Lavinia asked. "I never meant to put you in danger."

He looked at her. "Oh hang it all," he said. "There was nothing to forgive. I lost my temper. I do it once in a while." He dismounted and took Dixie's reins in his left hand. "Miss Lavinia," he said. "Please. Don't do it again. Promise me."

"I can only promise to do what I think best," Lavinia said.

He hesitated as he looked down at her. "I can't have you in danger," he said.

"Nor I you," Lavinia said.

A rising wind, carrying the scent of distant rain, stirred the magnolias. "Were you really worried about me?" he asked.

She slipped her hand into the bend of his elbow and smiled at him. "I was," she said. "I realized that I—" And then she stopped, unsure if she could finish the sentence, or if she wanted to.

The words lingered in the magnolia scented air. Her hand raised slowly toward his cheek; she caught the flash of hazel as his eyes flickered toward it and then returned to her face. The next moment he had her hand gripped between his.

"Please," he said again. "You don't know the danger you were in. Promise me. Please."

The pleading in his expression startled her. "Why, Sergeant," she said. "You really were worried. You didn't have to be." A motion of his hand stopped her. "Oh very well," she said. "I'll be more careful in future. I promise."

He smiled at her and released her hand.

The sense of waiting snapped when Dixie, who had been standing patiently behind Sheppard as the tension grew, stamped and blew down her nose, drawing an answering whinny from Beau.

"I'll race you home!" Sheppard said.

"Done!" Lavinia said breathlessly, gathering her skirts. "We'll go across the fields! There are some grand fences!" She laughed down at him as he lifted her into her saddle and then mounted his mare. "The last one into the fenced yard is a rotten egg!"

** ** **

"That's not fair!" Sheppard said ten minutes later as he reined Dixie to a halt. "You're riding a racing colt and I'm heavier than you!" He thought and then added, "And my horse was carrying an army saddle and my weapons!"

"Dixie's longer-legged and two hands taller!" Lavinia countered through breathless laughter as she thrust her riding crop through her belt and loosened her reins. "You suggested the race! Be glad I didn't insist on a handicap!"

"It wasn't fair!" Sheppard repeated as he dismounted and then reached up to lift Lavinia down from her saddle. The crickets were beginning to sing in the bushes, sunset's deepening rose was staining the low clouds to the west, and the windows of the big old house were glowing in the softening shadows. His hands lingered at her waist, hers at his shoulders, just for a moment.

His smile deepened and his hands curved more warmly about her waist in an almost unconscious caress. "Lavinia," he said.

Her breath caught in her throat and her eyes widened upon his in half-delighted alarm as he raised his hands to cover hers, bring them down to his heart, and hold them there. "Oh Lavinia," he began. "If I could—"

"Miss Vinnie! Did you find the Sergeant? Supper's waiting!"

Callie's voice, sounding from the house, might as well have been a thunderbolt. Lavinia started and drew one hand away. "Land sakes!" she gasped, pushing a wisp of hair out of her face. "I'm a sight! But that gallop was worth it!"

Sheppard raised her other hand to his lips and kissed it. "You're pretty as a picture," he said. "Go on ahead in; I'll walk the horses to the stable and ask someone to see they're properly cooled."

"Done," said Lavinia. "Supper will be waiting by the time you return and wash up, or I don't know Callie."

** ** **

The dying sun was glittering along the balustrade as Lavinia flung her habit's trailing skirts over her arm and mounted Fairlawn's front steps. She turned to smile at Sheppard and watched him lead the two horses back toward the stables.

Such a lovely evening! The sun was flooding the misty outlines of the world with golden light while stars were beginning to glint at the very top of the sky. A rising breeze promised to sweep the night air clear. Fireflies sparkled in the grass, and behind her Lavinia could catch the scent of cornbread and butter.

How could she be so happy, so at ease? Was she really in the middle of an invaded state? Or were her memories of war and heartbreak only the lingering traces of a tragic dream?

She loosened her riding gloves as she turned and went into the house, drawing the left one from her hand. China clinked somewhere in the house; supper was ready, no doubt. She stepped into the vestibule and then faltered to a stop as she sensed eyes upon her.

She looked around, her heartbeat quickening. Once, on a picnic organized by her church, she had strolled alone through a grove of magnolia trees bounding a stream and felt the same half-ticklish sensation. She had turned and found herself facing a coiled copperhead's flat, yellow gaze.

She lifted her chin. There were no copperheads in her house. Of that, at least, she was very sure. "Very well," she said, raising her voice. "Who is there?"

No answer, and the doorway leading toward the hall was dark. She frowned at the darkness, took up a lamp, and stepped into a hallway filled with shadows.

"Lavinia?"

The voice, coming from the shadows, was low and soft, but it sparked in Lavinia's memory the sick-sweet tang of death and decay, like the smell of a newly opened trunk full of old, mildewed clothing.

Her frown grew darker. "I am here," she said, raising the lamp. She saw a figure standing at the end of the hallway. "Who are you?" she demanded as it moved toward her.

The lamplight flowed up the folds of a wide blue skirt, passing a trim, belted waist, a white lawn collar and smoothly netted hair to touch features that had the half-forgotten quality of a memory willfully suppressed.

Lavinia had been present at an exhumation fifteen years before, during her journey to Saratoga. Her uncle, Alexander Wheeler, had died in New York during one long, hot summer, a year before that. He had been embalmed and hastily buried in the Episcopal churchyard near Broadway. Lavinia's family had decided to request his exhumation, and had made arrangements to have his body shipped back to Georgia, where it would be interred in the family plot in Savannah. As the only Wheeler in New York, Lavinia had been required to identify the corpse and sign the necessary papers.

It had not been an experience she cared to repeat, though she had not been forced to have recourse to the vial of smelling salts she had brought with her. But the memory of her uncle's softened, blurred and discolored features was still vivid after fifteen years, and she found it somehow rising up again in her mind as she gazed upon the carefully sweet face of her brother Gaylord's fiancée, advancing to kiss her cheek.

The persistent feelings of disaster came into focus all at once. The four years that had flown past had torn Lavinia's world apart, but they seemed to have left no mark on the shadow before her. Face, form, even the cloying scent of the gardenia pinned above the woman's smooth chignon had remained unchanged from that terrible summer of 1860 when Lavinia's mother lay dying and Lavinia's world was falling around her.

"Why, Louise Hamiter," Lavinia said through a rising wave of remembered nausea. "What are you doing here?"'

CHAPTER TWENTY-NINE

"This lady's cool now, and that fellow looks like what he wants is a long drink and a longer roll in the grass."

"Doesn't sound too bad to me, I'll admit," Toby said with a grin as he smoothed Beau's glossy neck. He unfastened the bridle's buckles and then, keeping a loop of rein about the gelding's neck, knotted a rope halter. "There you are," he said, sliding the reins over the horse's neck and taking hold of the halter. "Eat up. You've earned it."

"Hard to believe that fellow's broken to harness," Sheppard said thoughtfully, watching the gelding amble into the field. He swung his right leg over the cantle of his saddle, his booted feet hitting the ground with a thump a moment later. "I'd have pegged him as a lady's hunter. He can certainly jump."

"Probably was at one point, Sarge," Toby said. "Thing is, the government came through here and took everything on four legs without cloven hooves, no matter what it was used for. Miss Lavinia gave up her entire stable except for old Absalom, from her hunter right down to the fat old blind pony she used to drive as a little girl. What would those Rebs have used those monsters of carriage horses for? For cavalry? They were pacers, for God's sake!"

"I guess if you're desperate, you'll make do with anything," Sheppard said as he flipped up the saddle skirts and unbuckled Dixie's girth. "It sure was odd to see harness galls on that gelding, though. He's obviously a lady's mount. Someone's heart was broken."

"Well, if Miss Vinnie's heart was eased by having him, I can't be too worried," Toby said. "You ready to turn the mare out? I'll keep the gate open for her."

"Right you are," Sheppard said. Dixie was wearing a halter now. He gave her a slap on the rump and watched her trot into the pasture. "It's a good thing you were around when I came in," he said to Toby. "I'd still be cooling them down."

Toby shrugged. "I was coming to see you any rate," he said. "I talked with the boys and they'll be doing everything we talked about, and they'll be practicing it regularly, too. You said to drill, and drill's what we'll do if it'll make us good."

Sheppard nodded. His expression was distant for a moment before he turned to smile at Toby. "You're already good, Toby," he said. "Best lot I've had to train. Heck, you needed little training. The rest now is just honing."

Toby smiled at him. "I'll pass the word on," he said. "It'll make everyone glad." He added, "And I'll take that tack from you. Go on up to the house. After today you're probably hungry, and you're probably want a good wash, too. Whew! It felt pretty rough for a while there!"

Sheppard clapped Toby on the shoulder and headed toward the house.

Pretty rough was a good way to describe it. And the roughest moment had come when, as he was facing down that company of foragers, he had heard Lavinia's buggy rattling down the street toward him, blocking the aims of half the townsfolk.

Well, it was over, night was falling softly across the land, and his evening walk with Lavinia was perhaps forty minutes away. He had come to treasure the time alone with her, filled with the laughter that had grown with their blossoming friendship. Her sometimes tart, matter-of-fact utterances had been delighting him from the first time he had heard her speak her mind.

The sound of her soft voice and the way her consonants shaded off into vowels in the cultured drawl that his New York-bred ears found charming, was doubly delicious when wedded to the dry irony that she was capable of dispensing. To cap it all, she had a most devastating way of throwing him off-balance with yet another instance of the whole-hearted generosity and kindness that had sparked his admiration the first time they had met, just as he was innocently enjoying the beguiling combination of her voice, her manner and her words.

He was beginning to wonder how he could manage to live without her, and the thought was strange to him. He had been fortunate in his marriage to Sarah, and he mourned her sincerely. He had accepted widowhood as the price of having loved her in his life, and had resigned himself to a solitary old age. Now he was not so sure that solitude was to be his fate.

He paused to listen to the mockingbird, trilling in the garden. He had almost spoken his thoughts to Lavinia that afternoon. He suspected that she, too, had been about to say something along the same lines, though the delighted confusion in her expression made him think that maybe she had not realized it until that moment.

He listened a moment longer, smiling. Sunset had been falling and mockingbirds greeting the deepening nights for centuries before people had started writing about it. They would be singing long after the last person alive at the exact moment he was occupying died. There was no reason to hurry, and every reason to savor each moment as it unfolded.

He was singing, himself, as he strode toward the brightly lit kitchen. He could see Callie's white head through the window, bent over something, probably a pot. She was speaking, but Sheppard could not catch the words.

Dear God, he was hungry! He paused to fill a bucket at the pump, doffed his jacket, rolled up his shirtsleeves, and washed his face and hands. A spotlessly clean flour sack towel hung at the nail by the door; he dried, ran his fingers through his damp hair, and then rolled his sleeves down again and buttoned the cuffs.

A moment later, fastening the last button of his jacket, he stepped into the kitchen and nodded to Callie, who was rolling out pastry on a floured cloth. Meg, standing beside her and watching with her head to one side, looked up, saw him, and went flying to him with her arms outstretched.

"That's my little princess!" Sheppard laughed, swinging her up into his arms and soundly kissing her round cheek while she squealed and giggled and kissed him back. "Were you good today, sweetheart?"

Callie turned an ashen face to him, but her voice was composed and almost flat. "Good as gold, the darling," she said between short, brisk strokes of the rolling pin.

Sheppard's brows drew together at her expression. "Why Callie, what's wrong?" he said.

"Sorrow and disaster, Sergeant Asa," Callie said. "And a time of trial. Correction is grievous unto him that forsaketh the way, and he that hateth reproof shall die, that's what the Book says. We have sinned, I see that we have. The Book says, too, Hell and destruction are before the Lord: how much more then the hearts of the children of men? It is our time of testing, Sergeant Asa, and we mustn't shun the burden, but must lay it upon the Lord."

"You aren't making any sense," Sheppard said, one eye on Meg, who was staring from him to Callie with round eyes. "You make it sound as though we're all doomed."

Callie lifted her eyebrows as she took up a biscuit cutter and pressed neat little rounds into the batter. "You'll see," she said. "You'll see."

"Uncle George says she's got the roo— the room— roomatiz," Meg said.

"That'll upset anyone," Sheppard told Meg as he set her down.

"You'll see," Callie said again. "Well, go on in. Miss Lavinia's waiting for you. She needs you, Sergeant."

"I'm on my way," Sheppard said.

"And you, lamb," Callie said as Meg tucked her hand into Sheppard's. "Stay here with me. There's no need for you to go back to that wicked woman."

"What wicked woman?" Sheppard asked.

Callie cocked an eye at him. "I thought the lord had granted that we had seen the last of her," she said. "But the Lord's ways are unsearchable."

Meg, who had been listening wide-eyed to this dissertation, drew closer to Sheppard and said that she wanted to stay with Daddy.

"The scriptures warn us to shun evil!" Callie intoned.

"I won't let it come near her," Sheppard said, opening the door to the hallway. "She'll be fine with me. Come along, little chick."

Meg followed him willingly enough into the dark hallway, though she was holding his hand tightly. As they reached the door to the dining room, though, she held her arms up to him and said, "Pick up!"

Sheppard was lifting her as he crossed the threshold. He looked up from her wide eyes to meet Lavinia's gaze, and nearly recoiled from the tightly leashed wrath he saw there.

Two other women were in the room with Lavinia. One of them was an older woman with a face that seemed a worn, slightly softened reflection of Lavinia's above a wide lace collar and genteelly subdued gown. She was watching Sheppard's entrance with an odd mixture of fear and welcome. A pale-haired woman, perhaps ten years younger than Lavinia, stood beside her, tall and slender in blue taffeta with a carefully sweet face that was at that moment schooled to chill indifference. The woman's dark eyes rose from the yellow braid on Sheppard's sleeves to rake across his face.

Meg drew closer to Sheppard. "Papa," she whispered in his ear as she stared at the younger woman. "What's white trash?"

** ** **

The question, voiced in innocent bewilderment, echoed. Sheppard's eyes, suddenly wide, went from Meg's trustfully upturned face to Lavinia's.

Lavinia stepped forward in a whisper of sage green muslin. "White trash, darling," she said with dulcet clarity, "is a term we use to describe people who are rude and call other people names. If you don't do that sort of thing, then you aren't 'white trash'. Do you understand, poppet?"

Meg nodded.

Lavinia turned to the two women and indicated Sheppard with a graceful motion of her hand. "Aunt Amabel, Miss Louise Hamiter, allow me to present Sergeant Major Asa Sheppard of the Federal Cavalry. Sergeant Sheppard is assigned by General Stanley to protect my property, which he has done admirably thus far. Sergeant Sheppard, this is my aunt, Amabel Wheeler Swithin." She nodded to the older woman, who smiled and inclined her head. "And this—" motioning toward the younger, pale-haired woman, "—is Louise Hamiter."

Sheppard managed a bow while holding Meg. "It's a pleasure to meet Miss Wheeler's family and friends," he said.

"Miss Hamiter is not family, strictly speaking, Sergeant," Lavinia said, smilingly precise. "Nor is she a friend. She was my late brother's fiancée. Our dealings have been at a remove since Gaylord's death in late 1861." She turned smiling eyes on Louise Hamiter. "Indeed," she said, "This is the first I have seen or heard from Miss Hamiter since my brother's funeral."

A well-timed squirm on Meg's part coupled with an urgent request that he put her down and take her back to Aunt Callie so that she could help with baking the biscuits saved Sheppard the necessity of thinking up a suitable reply. He excused himself, stepped into the hallway, nearly colliding with an unusually sepulchral George, handed Meg over, and went back into the dining room.

"Really, sister," Louise Hamiter was saying, "Should you speak so before a lackey?" She fell silent as Sheppard entered, but her faint half-smile did not alter.

Mrs. Swithin made a distressed motion with her hands. "Louise, dear!" she fluted.

Sheppard looked from Lavinia to Louise Hamiter. He had no trouble understanding Miss Hamiter's meaning. He felt his color rise.

Lavinia's eyes were glittering behind their spectacles, and she was making no move toward the table. "Sergeant Sheppard, who is not a lackey, is too much of a gentleman to object to the flat truth," she said.

Sheppard turned to Mrs. Swithin, who was still cooing distressedly. "May I have the pleasure, Ma'am?" he asked, offering his arm. And was nearly bowled over by the naked gratitude of her expression.

** ** **

"I was in Marietta when the Federal troops approached," Mrs. Swithin said. "I thought, since they had been west and were headed east, I'd be best advised to head west. So I did."

"And you brought Louise Hamiter with you," Lavinia said.

Mrs. Swithin's hands fluttered to her lap and gripped tightly. "She came to me and asked where I was planning to go," she said. "I couldn't very well say 'Away from here—and without you,' now could I?"

Lavinia let the question pass without response. "She has plenty of kin," she said. "She could have gone to them."

Aunt Amabel's plump hands, busy with her knitting, stilled for a moment. "Her father had fled," she said. "How could I leave her defenseless in the face of the advancing Federals?"

"There are the Savannah Hamiters," Lavinia said. "Why didn't she go to them? Why inflict herself on Fairlawn?"

"Lavinia!"

"I mean it with all my heart," Lavinia said.

"But she spoke of the months she spent with you the year before the war," Amabel said.

Lavinia did not look at her. "The summer my mother died," she said softly. Her gaze was fixed on the stars rising in the slightly brighter sky beyond Horn Mountain's distant bulk. "Have you ever lived through a time," she said slowly, "so strong and so unrelenting in its pain that when it was through you half feared that mentioning it, even in the silence of your own thoughts, would only serve to bring it back?"

Aunt Amabel raised her head and turned to look full at her.

"That entire summer," Lavinia said. "My mother was dying by slow degrees and I was the only one of her family to understand what was happening. My father spent his days riding, my brother dallied through the summer days with Louise, and I tended my mother as she faded away in pain. And Louise was there every time I turned around. 'Lavinia dear, the water this morning was chilly: perhaps it would ease you if I had the ordering of the house niggers.' 'Dear Sister, drawn and peaked as you are, you should be sitting in this chair and resting rather walking through the garden. Things can wait: we don't mind the delay.' 'Vinnie dearest, is it quite proper to be riding a horse when your dear mother is so ill and needs you so badly?' 'Why Lavinia it surprises me that you should be putting up those preserves. Really, the task is far beyond your strength now that you are no longer young.' And, of course, 'Dear Lavinia, that pink gown doesn't become you. I've laid out some black gowns for you to choose. They will be so becoming to your age and station. Try them, do: and try these caps, as well.' "

Aunt Amabel's hands fluttered to a stop as she looked up at Lavinia. She slowly pushed the knitting up toward the base of the needles, wound a turn of yarn around them, and then thrust them into the ball of yarn. "I didn't know," she said.

Lavinia speared her with a direct gaze. "You might have known if you had stayed here, as I had asked after you had come to see my mother," she said. "Then you wouldn't have been so shocked to hear darling, sweet Louise calling an orphaned three year old white trash, and you wouldn't have so much as turned a hair to see Louise apply the term 'lackey' to a man who has almost single-handedly saved this town from harm. Only think what you missed, Aunt Amabel."

Amabel took up her knitting again, drew the needles from the ball of yarn, and smoothed the fabric. "It was shameful of me to leave," she said. "If I had it to do again I wouldn't have stayed away. I—tend to take the coward's part." She added with a slightly shaking voice, "I am—often afraid of pain. It is easier to ignore pain than to fight it. James was like that, Gaylord was like that, and so am I. But you, now..."

Lavinia lifted her eyebrows.

"I think you're a throwback," Amabel said. "I've heard tales of old Abijah Wheeler when he came down from Boston to open a shipping office in Savannah in 1740. Determined and courageous, that's how he was described."

Lavinia drew a long breath. "That was an entirely different time from this," she said. "People were building a new life in a new land. Nothing was set, nothing was safe. Like the settlers at Roanoke colony, thinking of their homes in England, wishing their world was safe and simple again—"

"And don't you think folk feel that way now, Lavinia?" Aunt Amabel asked. "Don't you think a hundred years from now people will look back at these days and wonder how we all survived? I wonder it right this moment: how have we survived with our decency intact when all around us has turned to ruin and destruction?"

"Some of us have not," Lavinia said. "That much have I learned, to my cost."

A mockingbird sang softly in the deepening twilight. The sound made the grimness of Lavinia's expression ease a little. She looked over at Mrs. Swithin and quickly leaned forward to kiss her cheek. "You, dear Aunt, may stay here as long as you wish," she said. "This was your home, as well, and you're welcome here."

"But what will you do about Louise?" Aunt Amabel asked as Lavinia got to her feet and shook out her skirts.

"I am not sure," Lavinia replied. "There's no hurry to decide. Aunt, dear, I'm going to stroll in the gardens. I'll be back later with Sergeant Sheppard. I think you'll enjoy making his better acquaintance." She gathered her skirts and descended the steps. She turned. "And as for Louise," she said, "She'd best mind her p's and q's."

CHAPTER THIRTY

"It was 1860," Lavinia said. "That was the summer my mother died. We had removed to Wheelerville for the summer a little earlier than usual, since the doctors thought the cooler mountain air would be beneficial to her. Gay had remained in Savannah to help with some of Papa's business concerns. He met Louise at her uncle's summer house at White Bluff and offered marriage three weeks later."

They had paused at the near paddock to pet the horses and look over the stables. Lavinia had brought some scraps of sugared bread from dinner, and Dixie, always quick to scent a treat, had planted herself squarely before Lavinia. Now she nudged Lavinia's shoulder and then, seeing that no more was forthcoming, turned her attention on Sheppard.

Now that the way was clear, Beau came up to beg a treat. Lavinia, quiet for a moment, stroked the gelding's soft muzzle and then gave him some bread.

"Three weeks," said Sheppard.

The bread was all gone. The horses, despairing of any further treats, turned away to crop the thick grass.

Lavinia tucked her hand into Sheppard's arm and walked beside him along the path to the gardens. She looked down at the fingertips of her right hand, just visible within the crook of Sheppard's left arm. "She came to visit shortly after," she said. "I was busy with the household concerns, as I had been since my mother's health began to fail. I suppose I wasn't the best hostess I might have been, but I kept wishing that Louise would just go home and leave me alone."

"Did your mother like her?" Sheppard asked.

Lavinia frowned as she tucked the flowers into the brooch at her shoulder. "I don't know," she said after a moment. "She was weak and in pain, but looking back I think she was often trying to make me smile... You'd have liked her, Sergeant."

"She was a great lady, from all I've heard," Sheppard said, gazing along the path toward the soft, pale blur in the twilight that was the house.

"She'd have liked you, too," Lavinia said.

"A Yankee?" Sheppard teased.

"My great-grandfather came to Savannah from Massachusetts," Lavinia said with dignity. "So it'd be a little like the pot calling the kettle black." She tightened her fingers for a moment. "Well," she said. "Mother died, the summer ended, autumn came and went, and Louise finally went back to Macon. Gay and Louise were set to marry in June of 1861. That never happened. The war came and Gaylord joined the armies. He died in Richmond late in 1861."

"I saw your brother's grave in the cemetery beyond the house," Sheppard said. "I'm sorry."

"He was only one of many throughout this continent," Lavinia said. "He contracted typhus in camp. And then he came down with pneumonia, which killed him. His gravestone names him a hero of the Confederacy, but he never got within sound of a battle."

"I'm sorry," Sheppard said again.

Lavinia was frowning before her as though she had just seen something unpleasant and was trying to understand it. She raised her eyes to his after a moment. "What?" she said.

"I said I was sorry."

She shook her head. "Don't be," she said. "Not for Gaylord. For all that he was a bruising rider over a fence, he was...a little tender-hearted when it came to danger. I think his death from disease was a kinder fate than anything else might have been."

She smiled a little at Sheppard's expression. "I mean it, Sergeant," she said. "You told Abner that you hunt in New York. I'm sure you've seen a gun-shy dog driven mad by the sound of firing."

"My children's spaniel," Sheppard said. "I'd meant him to hunt with me, but it was a disaster."

"Well, Gaylord was like that. He was caught alone in a thunderstorm when he was just a toddler, and I think it marked him," Lavinia said. "He was terrified of gunfire if it weren't within the confines of a shooting gallery. That's why he never joined the militia in Savannah, even though it was practically a requirement for every gentleman who wished to have a place on the social register. He said he didn't care for bandbox soldiers. I think he would have died if he had known that someone else had discovered the petted, perfect son's one secret flaw. He'd have bolted at the first sign of cannon. He would have deserted and then been cashiered at best and shot as a coward at worst."

""You're being too harsh," Sheppard said. "He would have come around. A lot of men come to their first fight afraid. They go through it and get over it."

"Maybe in time," Lavinia conceded. "But he had no time, and that sort of fear runs in my family."

"You stayed at Fairlawn during the fighting," Sheppard pointed out.

Lavinia leveled a look at him. "I stayed in the root cellar with my shawl over my ears," she said.

"Yes," Sheppard persisted. "And you came out afterward. And," he added, "you drove into town today when you knew very well there might be firing."

"That was different," Lavinia said. "A friend was in danger."

Sheppard turned to face her and took her hands in his. "A friend?" he queried.

She tried half-heartedly to pull away and then raised her eyes to his and returned the pressure of his fingers. "Come on, Sergeant," she said. "It's getting late and Aunt Amabel is anxious to make your acquaintance. I suspect Callie's made us some cold tea. We can sip it and look at the stars from the veranda."

He nodded and started to release her hands. She held him a moment longer and then tucked her hand into his arm and strolled beside him back toward the softly lit house.

"Sergeant," she said as they reached the steps.

"Miss Lavinia?"

"Louise Hamiter sent my brother into the army."

The intent quality of her voice made Sheppard look quickly down at her as Aunt Amabel rose from her chair and came forward, smiling.

"She made it so that he had to go. And now she's back," Lavinia said. "I thought you should know." She ascended the steps to greet Amabel, leaving Sheppard standing at the foot of the steps, gazing up at her with thoughtfully narrowed eyes.

** ** **

Lavinia tilted her head to the side, shifted the jug slightly, frowned at it, and then adjusted it again, turning it until it caught the light full on its salt-glazed surface. The morning sun, warm from crossing the green lawn, made the old brown glaze glow almost golden.

She looked away from the jug and around the room. This was where it had sat in state until the guns roared against Fort Sumter, shattering the United States of America and threatening to shatter the jug as well. Lavinia had hustled it, and the rest of the collection, up the stairs to be locked away in her armoire where it had stayed until, with the war right on her doorstep, she had carried the entire collection to the root cellar.

Now, she thought, maybe it was safe to bring it out again. Just the one piece, her favorite, to sit in the good parlor where it had always sat, and remind her of the strength of other people during other terrible times.

You've seen the loneliness and the terror, she thought, smiling at the jug. *And you survived it. I think I can, too.*

She stood back and let her gaze travel around the room, seeing the changes. Before the bluecoats' arrival half a lifetime ago, the house had seemed somehow darker. There had been a sense of weariness, of remembering and mourning. The drapes had seemed a little faded, the rich-colored carpets threadbare against the oak floors, the shadows lingering at the windows, the silver that sat on the table in the evenings just a little duller. And she-had she truly been the gray-faced woman who had moved about the house, barely able to lift her head when she was alone?

And had the bright, blessed change somehow been brought about by the strife and slaughter that had left rows of graves on the west lawn and rows of beds in Fairlawn's ballroom? Was it even, perhaps, tied to that tonic mixed by Major Haskell? She paused, gazing at the jug with wide, wondering eyes and thought, Why not? There was no evil so stark, so terrible that it could not somehow, somewhere, whatever the cost, be turned to good.

Her commonsense asserted itself. "You've got to break a few eggs to make an omelet!" she said aloud. She smiled at the jug again, her hands clasped before her in a gesture of joy from her childhood. It would be safe where it was, and so would she, God willing, and so would all those she loved. She could feel it with every fiber of her being!

"Lavinia."

The bleakness of the voice, in such complete contrast to the joy and peace she had felt so profoundly a moment before, was like a blow between the shoulder blades. She turned and saw Dr. Meacham standing in the doorway.

He was grieved, a damp towel in his hand, his sleeves pushed up to his elbows and his hair tousled.

Lavinia wanted nothing to do with grief. She smiled at him, willing him to share her happiness. "Look, Dr. Meacham," she said. "I've put Sir Walter Raleigh's jug out again! Isn't it wonderful? Do you know, I think we'll be seeing the end of all of this soon—"

"Lavinia," Dr. Meacham said. "I must speak with you right away."

Lavinia looked more closely at him and saw that he was barely suppressing fury and somehow, oddly, fear. "Why, what's wrong, Doctor?" she demanded.

"It's Pierce," Meacham said on a long, shaken sigh. "Oh, God help us, Vinnie!" he said. "May I sit down?"

Lavinia frowned at him with sudden alarm and then motioned to a chair. "What is wrong?" she repeated. "His fever hasn't returned, has it?"

"It's back with a vengeance," Dr. Meacham said grimly.

Lavinia sat down, herself. That was very bad news. Pierce, lung-shot and with a perforated bowel, was in the most precarious of conditions. A wasting fever had threatened to consume him only a month ago. It had been brought under control, but the danger was not past yet.

"Do we have enough quinine to treat him?" she asked, thinking of the stores that the Union army had left back in May. "Major Haskell warned me that something like this might happen."

"It's more than a question of quinine, Vinnie," Dr. Meacham said.

Lavinia stared at him. "What do you mean?" she asked. Her eyes were snapping by the time he had finished telling her.

She rose and went to the hallway, turning at the doorway to nod to Dr. Meacham. "I will have Miss Hamiter brought here," she said, deadly intent. "I intend to learn what she has to say about this."

** ** **

"Really, Lavinia," Louise said with a calm smile. "I don't understand the reason for all this fuss. There was nothing to it, after all. I listened to the fellow—for far longer than I wanted to, I promise you!—and I answered him. That's all. I can hardly be blamed for his taking what I said amiss, can I?"

"Tell Miss Wheeler the nature of your answer," Dr. Meacham said. "I only supplied her with a general outline."

Louise's eyes lowered to her hands, folded placidly in her lap and then raised to Dr. Meacham's with an intent innocence that struck Lavinia oddly. "What was there to tell?" she asked. She looked at Lavinia with a warmer smile. "Really, Sister," she said. "Much is being made of some jesting banter that I gather the man was in no state to comprehend."

"Maybe you would like to tell me what the jesting banter was?" Sergeant Sheppard said, stepping so suddenly into the room that Aunt Amabel, sitting nervously in the corner and fingering her knitting, gave a muffled shriek and dropped her ball of yarn. Sheppard cast her a quick glance, swept his gaze across Lavinia and Dr. Meacham, and then turned on Louise with a narrow intentness that made even Lavinia catch her breath.

"I don't know what you're talking about, Sergeant," Louise said with cold composure.

Sheppard moved to the center of the room with Corporal Higgins following him on his crutches. "I would like an explanation, from your own lips, for the fact that one of my men, left in my care and recovering nicely when I saw him last, is at this moment prostrate with a brain-fever," he said.

Louise stared at him and then turned on Lavinia. "This ruffian is daring to browbeat me," she said. "Are you going to stand for this treatment of me by an enemy?"

"I don't think the 'ruffian' is being unreasonable, Louise," Lavinia said. "In point of fact, he is saving me some effort. Whatever you said has upset both Dr. Meacham and Sergeant Sheppard, neither of whom are excitable men. I will have to hold off making any judgment until I know just what was said, and how. Perhaps you'd best tell me without any further delay."

"I made a joke," Louise said. And then was silent.

"Tell Miss Wheeler the 'joke,' " Sheppard said.

Louise fronted Sheppard. "I find your manners execrable, sir!" she said through her teeth. "Is it the custom of northerners to browbeat ladies in this fashion?"

"A lady doesn't go to a wounded, delirious man and tell him that his wife is cuckolding him!" Sheppard returned.

Aunt Amabel sat forward, staring.

Lavinia looked from Sheppard to Louise. "Cuckolding, Sergeant?" she said. She looked at Dr. Meacham, who lowered his eyes.

"Then, Miss Wheeler, you haven't heard what she said to Private Pierce?" Sheppard said.

Lavinia smoothed the chains of her chatelaine and raised her eyes to his. "No, Sergeant," she said. "I haven't yet had that pleasure. Please tell me."

"I think I'll let Corporal Higgins," Sheppard said, "He's the one who told me." He turned to the corporal, who was balancing on his crutches and looking unhappily from Sheppard to Lavinia.

Lavinia nodded to Higgins. "Please sit down, do," she said, sweeping a thoughtful glance at Louise. "Tell me what was said."

Higgins cleared his throat unhappily, his usual jauntiness gone. "Well, Miss Lavinia, it's like this," he said. "Miss Hamiter came to see us fellows this morning. I thought at first it was very kind of her. People don't like sickrooms as a rule, and there are still a few of us who look like death warmed over. Pierce is the worst, though he is—was—coming along nicely. Anyhow, she came in, looking cool as a cucumber and pretty to boot, and everyone perked right up. It's nice to have a pretty girl to talk with when you aren't quite feeling the thing. Makes you feel like more of a man."

Lavinia looked up at him, her color deepening.

Higgins smiled at her. "It's true," he said. "Begging your pardon, but you yourself have done wonders coming in like you have, smelling of lavender and verbena, smiling like the sweet lady you are—well, it's the truth, I swear it! Anyhow, she—" he said the word with awful emphasis, "—came in and walked up and down and looked at everyone. It was like we were exhibits in a raree show. Pierce was feeling a twinge of the fever, and he had his wife's picture out and was holding it to his heart like he does at times—"

Louise started to sit down. Lavinia silently lifted her eyebrows at her; she rose again.

"Anyhow, she saw the picture," Higgins continued, looking from Sheppard to Lavinia. "She took it and looked at it, and she smiled. It was the oddest smile, now I remember it. Made me think of a rattle-snake reared back to strike. And when he, smiling like his heart was like to burst, said he was just married and she was expecting their first baby, what does she do but say that she'd read in a reputable journal that army wives have-have—" He stopped and looked helplessly at Sheppard.

"Go on," said Dr. Meacham. "Tell her all of it. I was standing right there, Lavinia. He's true as gospel so far."

"Taken lovers," Higgins said unhappily. "He stammered out some-thing about what did she mean, and she stood there as calm as death and told Pierce that his wife was cuckolding him—"

"Really, the language I am hearing!" Louise began.

"You're the one who used that word initially," Dr. Meacham said with awful, leashed fury. "Do you have a better word for it now? Something to suit the delicacy of your sentiments, maybe?"

"Fiddle-dee-dee!" Louise sniffed. "It was a joke, and if the poor man didn't have the humor to understand—"

"Humor!" Higgins gasped in disbelief. "I heard what she said and how she said it. That was meant to hurt and it did! Hell, the doctor can tell you how she said it! Teasing him along, making him relax, then jumping in with that comment like a blow from a sledge-hammer."

"He's right, Lavinia," Dr. Meacham said. "There was no joking in-volved. She spoke the words to hurt him, and she rejoiced to see that she had succeeded."

"Louise!" Aunt Amabel gasped.

"It was a joke," Louise said again. "Those Yankees don't have the sense of humor to understand it—"

"Some of us 'Rebs' don't, either!" Dr. Meacham said.

"There are jokes that shouldn't be told," Lavinia said. "Dr. Meacham, is Private Pierce's condition dangerous?"

"Yes," Meacham answered. "His emotions have upset him and he's out of his mind. His fever is back and it is raging."

"He had to be tied down, Miss Wheeler," Sheppard said. "I just came from seeing him. God alone knows if he'll recover, but at this moment it's as though he was kicked in the abdomen and all Dr. Meacham's work has been undone. He keeps saying that he wants to die. He might just get his wish, if this keeps up."

"But why should anyone pay attention to something obviously

meant to hurt?" Lavinia demanded.

"Who can understand the thoughts in a fevered brain?" Dr. Meacham said. "We can deal with the symptoms, but if his reason's been overset—I don't know, Lavinia. I don't know."

"It was a joke," Louise said again.

Aunt Amabel was sitting forward, her eyes flashing. "It was a wicked, heartless joke, then!" she said. "I am ashamed of you, Louise! Of all the unmaidenly, unladylike things even to think of doing to a healthy man, much less a wounded one—! What would your mother say to such a thing? And your father!"

"I can't say I'm surprised at it," Sheppard said. He took a step toward Louise. "I am beginning to understand what I have seen and what I have heard. A mind that can come out with such a comment and take the sort of pleasure you have in saying what you did is unhealthy for all it touches. I had an inkling from what I heard last night. If I hadn't been too hesitant to believe evil of someone, I might have been able to keep this from happening. It won't happen again—"

"I find your speech offensive," Louise began.

Sheppard spoke over her. "And so that we understand each other, Miss Hamiter," he said, "You had best listen carefully. I don't want you anywhere near any of my men ever again. Stay away from my men from this moment on! I don't want to see you in the hospital, in the walks with any of my men, or anywhere near any of them at all. Do you understand me? That's an order!"

Lavinia drew a slow breath and started to speak, but before she could say anything, another voice spoke into the silence.

"Papa?"

Meg was standing in the doorway and looking around, wide-eyed, at the people gathered in the parlor. She faltered, frightened by the frowns and the tension, but then she saw Sheppard and went skipping over to him.

No one spoke; she threw a nervous look at Louise and half-hid behind Sheppard. "Papa?" she said again, slipping her hand in his.

Sheppard's blazing, intent glare had been fixed on Louise's face all that time. It softened, faded, and he looked down at Meg. "What is it, Peanut?" he asked.

Meg craned her head back to look up at him. "It's afternoon, Papa," she said. "Can we go riding now? You promised."

Sheppard bent to lift Meg and kiss her on the cheek. "Of course we can, Sweetheart," he said. "You go on to the stables and wait at the door for me. I'll you meet you there in just a moment." He set her down and smiled as she went skipping out the door. His smile was gone when he turned back toward Louise. "Now, Miss Hamiter," he said. "You heard what I said: did you understand it?"

Louise was watching him with a thoughtful light in her eyes that Lavinia mistrusted. "You made yourself offensively clear," she said.

Sheppard nodded. "Then see that you do as I say," he said. He left. A moment later Lavinia saw him through the window, making his way toward the paddock.

Louise watched him leave and then tossed her head and turned back to Lavinia. "Is there anything else you need of me?" she asked. "Or may I return to my sitting room and my book?"

"No," Lavinia said after a moment's thought. "I think everything's been said that needed saying."

"There's been too much made of a simple jest," Louise said.

"If it was a jest, then it is one that should never have been made," Lavinia said, rising. "It did you no credit. Well. The matter is closed. It won't happen again, for if it does I will see that you are blackballed from polite society in Atlanta, Savannah and Richmond for the rest of your life. And you know that I am able to do it, Louise. Dr. Meacham, I'll come with you and see if I can speak with Private Pierce. Maybe I can undo some of the harm Miss Hamiter has done."

CHAPTER THIRTY-ONE

Meg wriggled her shoulders more firmly into the soft grass of the lawn and gazed up into the sky. She could see a flock of rounded, puffy cloud-sheep moving slowly from east to west. She had always liked to watch the clouds. She could just remember a pretty, blue-clad lady lying beside her, holding her in her arms and laughing up into the sky with her. They often would find bunnies and lambs, and sometimes the lady would point to what looked like strands of wind-whipped silk.

'Those are mares'-tails, Meg,' the lady would say, hugging her tighter. 'Colder weather's coming!'

Meg would always ask about the mares. She wanted to know who rode them. Angels? What color were they? Could she ride them? The lady would tickle her and say that she, Meg, might someday, if she were a good little girl.

Meg knew that the lady had been her mother, and that she was no longer where Meg could see her, but that she still loved her very much. She thought she could remember being kissed and held by the lady just before she went away, and she remembered that the lady had looked weary even as she had smiled.

But now things were beginning to blur a little. When Meg thought of 'mother' she pictured another lady who wore spectacles, smelled deliciously of lemon verbena, and had long, silken, red-brown hair that she let Meg brush and braid. This 'mother' was soft-voiced like the mother she could barely remember, and she had a pleasant way of making a nice, wide lap to sit on, and cuddling her when they read stories together.

Sometimes Meg's father would sit with them, though Meg usually saw him in the stables, or else at bedtime when he always came in to kiss her good night. There was no question that he was her father. The pretty lady—her mother who was gone now-had told her that her fa-

ther was a soldier, and she had said he rode a horse. Meg could remember her mother, wearing her pretty blue dress, telling her long ago
that when her father came back he would let her sit on the horse with
him, and everything would be happy and bright.

Although the pretty lady had started wearing black and had
stopped speaking of Meg's father, what she had said had certainly
happened. Meg remembered being lost, frightened and cold, hiding in
the spongy darkness of a rotting, hollow log and whimpering with fear
and hunger. And then her father had come to her. She had known him
right away: he was a soldier and he was leading a brown horse. He
had said her name and smiled at her, and when she had crawled out
from that log he had held her and rocked her until she stopped crying,
and everything had been warm and safe and happy from then on.

She always watched for him in the afternoons, and if he came in
early enough from what her newer mama described as his 'duties', he
would sometimes take her up before him on his big horse and they
would gallop. She hoped he might do that this afternoon, but it wasn't
late enough yet for him to come, and so she watched the clouds and
daydreamed.

A cloud the exact shape of a gourd scudded overhead. Meg
watched it move behind a tracery of live oak leaves. A butterfly, minc-
ing across her field of vision, made her forget the gourd and sit up.
Butterflies were made to be chased: Meg ran after it, almost dancing
in her efforts to catch it.

Her hair streamed behind her, its ribbon half-untied and straggling
over one shoulder. Her grass-stained calico dress was caught up in two
chubby hands, and old George, watching from the window as he polished Mrs. Louisa Wheeler's heavy old Georgian silver tray, caught an
entrancing glimpse of two twinkling legs clad in glisteningly white
pantalettes.

He smiled indulgently. Dear little peanut! He had his own share of
grandchildren, but this little one had managed to wriggle her way right
into his heart. She often followed him around the house, chattering
and getting into things. Callie sometimes said the child would be the
death of her, but George had seen how Callie beamed when she said
this.

"That little monkey's stolen your heart, sissy," he said.

He remembered the words now as he watched Meg skipping along.

She was heading toward the burying ground, which was a good thing. Sergeant Sheppard, whom George had judged to be a wise father, had said it was all right to let her go there. It was pretty and peaceful, and the graves would not frighten her. It was best that she know the truth, he had said.

George took a swipe at the tray with the polishing cloth and then looked out the window again. He could see Meg's blue dress flickering in the grass—

He stiffened and swore an oath that would have earned him a pair of ringing ears if his sister had been anywhere near him. Miss Hamiter was crossing the lawn toward the burying ground, her high-held head turned on its length of neck like that of a rattlesnake rearing back to strike.

Now what was that she-snake doing following Meg? She had done enough harm calling the child white trash two days before and then snapping at her this morning when Meg, with a three-year-old's love for finery, had gotten into her trunks and handled her gowns, smudging some of them. A child can be hurt as deeply as an adult: Meg had followed George and Callie around the house, clinging more than usual and asking questions about trash. And now that woman was following Meg to the cemetery.

"Sweet Jesus!" George exclaimed. He set the tray down and hurried toward the stairs. That she-serpent was up to no good! He cupped his hands around his mouth. "Callie!" he called. "Where's the Sergeant and Vinnie?"

Callie, who was getting deaf, hadn't quite heard him. "What did you want?" she called back.

"Where's the Sergeant and Miss Lavinia?"

Callie appeared at the foot of the steps and cupped her hand about her ear. "What?" she repeated.

"Sweet Lord preserve us, Woman!" George exploded. "One would think you're a post! Get an ear-trumpet for God's sake, and—"

"You hold off taking the Lord's name in vain, Brother!" Callie snapped. "The Bible says—"

"God love us all, Sister, how can I speak at all with your jawing?" George demanded. "Now you listen to me! I need to know where the Sergeant is—"

"He's on his patrol, of course, as usual!" Callie shouted. "Whyever do you ask?"

"I need to speak with him," George replied. "Where's Miss Vinnie?"

Callie stared quizzically up at him. "With the wounded, the lamb!" she said. "Now why do you need her?"

"I'm glad you aren't my wife!" George said. "Listen: Meg's gone to the boneyard, like she likes to do—"

"What is wrong with that?" Callie demanded. "She puts flowers on her mother's grave. Sergeant Asa says it's good for her and I agree—"

"Well, that yellow-haired, whited sepulcher is going right after her!" George said. "I saw them!"

"What?"

"Louise Hamiter was following Meg to the boneyard with that look in her eye."

"Jesus save us all!" Callie gasped. "And her shrieking like a fishwife just this morning when she caught the poor little mite going through her pretty dresses! Thank goodness Miss Vinnie stopped her before she could give the child a shaking!" She looked around and gathered her skirts. "She means evil, you mark my words! I'm going after her and telling her to leave Meg alone!"

"What'll that accomplish?" George demanded. "She'll just call you a nigger-wench and me a buck, and where'll that leave our little girl, in Jesus' name?"

"You just watch your language, George Wheeler, and let me think!" Callie said. "We've got to stop her!"

"How could anyone be so hateful and still live?" George demanded.

"Go on with you!" Callie said. "I'll go after Miss Vinnie and you send Isaiah after the Sergeant, and then we can all go after little Meg. God willing, there's no harm being done!"

** ** **

"We found more tracks, Sarge!"

Abner Wigfall had been wondering, during his canter to Wheelerville from the southeast with the news burning inside him, what effect his words would have. Now, having voiced them, he still was not sure.

Silence had crashed in at the end of the sentence. Caesar, leaning on the pommel of his saddle and gazing at him with mild interest, lifted his eyebrows and slowly sat back. Four of the plantation hands, afoot before him, turned and stared.

And Sergeant Sheppard raised eyes that seemed suddenly sightless. "More tracks," he said.

"Yes, sir. Lots of them."

Sheppard's eyes shifted, fixed on the jagged backbone of Horn Mountain. "How far?" he asked. "Toward Allatoona?"

"Yes, sir," Abner replied. "A couple miles from where we found Meg's folks."

Sheppard's brows contracted. He blinked and lowered his gaze to frown back toward Wheelerville. "I was afraid of that," he said. "Did you find anything else?"

"I could smell burned wood, sir," Abner said. "And there were tracks, like people coming and going a lot. I didn't get to see anything else. The point riders went ahead. They came back and spoke to Captain Townsend. He called me over right then and told me to go after you, so I didn't get to see what it was. I did go through that clearing where Meg's family was found." He shivered at the memory. "I wouldn't go there by night, not if you paid me!" he said.

Sheppard's long, thoughtful gaze shortened. "You keep thinking that way, son, and you'll never set foot outside your own bedroom," he said. "Everywhere you turn, you'll find that someone died there. Well, I guess you'd best take me to Captain Townsend."

"Yes, sir," Abner said.

"Right," said Sheppard, turning Dixie. "Lead the way. Caesar, you'll continue the circle as you planned while Toby looks over the houses around here. I'm not comfortable with what Abner here's told me. I'll get back to you with what I've seen this evening."

"Isaiah's coming this way," Toby observed laconically as the young man came pelting toward them.

Sheppard frowned and closed his eyes against a spray of fine red dust as Isaiah reined his horse to a skidding halt. "If you're trying to ruin that brute, son," he said, "you're going about it the right way."

Isaiah was shouting. "—to the house at once!"

"What?" Sheppard demanded.

"Miss Callie needs you at the boneyard right away!"

"What's wrong?"

"It's Meg!"

Sheppard looked blank. His expression suddenly darkened to a scowl. "It's that Hamiter woman!" he said.

"I don't know for sure, Sarge," Isaiah said. "But you're needed in a hurry!"

Sheppard turned Dixie toward the town. "Tell Townsend I'll talk to him tonight!" he said to Abner, and then clapped his heels to Dixie's sides and was away at a gallop with Isaiah right behind him.

** ** **

"—and the Yankees killed her dead and left you an orphan without a penny in the world and no one to care for you," Louise Hamiter said. She watched the color drain from Meg's face with an odd smile. "You poor little vagabond," she said.

"No!" Meg gasped. "Mama's in Heaven!"

Louise smiled down at her. "She is dead," she said.

"B-but she's in Heaven!" Meg whimpered. She stared up at Louise with tear-filled eyes. Suddenly she was filled with a terrible need to be held. The lady was so pretty in the blue dress that was the exact color of her mother's. She stretched out her hands to the lady. "Is—isn't she in Heaven?"

Louise drew her skirts away with the abrupt motion that Meg's mother had used to avoid their dog's muddy paws. "Your mother is dead," she said.

The cold finality of the words and the icy stiffness of the smile chilled Meg to the bone. She understood somehow that this pretty lady whose silk dresses had so entranced her, hated her and wanted her to hurt. Meg looked down from her face to the grave before her, and it seemed as though the brightness and warmth had gone from the sun and not even butterflies could make her laugh again. "B-but she—" she began.

A warm, smiling voice spoke above her head. "You have to die, poppet, before you go to Heaven. You know that: you heard it in church with me just this last Sunday. Don't you remember? When you die, God takes your hand and leads you to Heaven."

Meg gasped and looked up to see her new mother smiling down at her. The other lady, somewhat disheveled, with a grass stain down the side of her skirt, was pushing herself to her feet a few paces farther back from where she had been just a moment ago.

"Now come here, dearest," her new mother said, holding out her arms. "And listen to me. You have to die to go to Heaven, and then you're with God and you're just like an angel. You can still love those people you left behind when you went to Heaven, just as your mama loves you right now."

Meg looked fearfully at the other lady and then went into her new mother's arms, so shaken and frightened and glad for her warmth and her sweet scent that she did not turn around when she heard hooves pounding toward her. She only looked up in time to see her father's big brown horse clear the fence around the burying ground with an effortless leap that landed it right beside them in a flurry of hooves and flickering tail. The next moment her father was holding her and Meg knew that everything was going to be all right.

** ** **"

What happened?" Sheppard demanded over Meg's head. "Isaiah came galloping to me, yelling that I had to get to the cemetery right away."

Louise' mouth thinned. She turned and started back toward the house.

Lavinia seized her by the arm and swung her around. "Oh no, Louise," she said in a voice of ice. "You're going to stay right here until we sort this out. Do you hear me?" She turned back to Sheppard. "Louise told Meg that her mother was murdered by Yankees, and that she is a worthless, unwanted vagabond."

Meg shivered and burrowed against Sheppard's shoulder.

Sheppard's eyes fastened on Louise and narrowed. The sudden, white rigidity of his jaw made her shriek and try to pull away. "What did you say?" he asked gently.

Lavinia tightened her grip. "Miss Hamiter told Meg that her mother had been murdered," she repeated. "By Yankees."

Meg looked up at him with huge eyes. "That's what she s-said," she faltered.

Sheppard took Meg by the shoulders and held her a little away from him. "Why were you talking with her in the first place?" he asked.

"I w-went to see M-mama's grave," she said. "I picked some flowers for her."

Sheppard looked at the grave and saw the handful of buttercups. "I see," he said. "But how did Miss-How did this woman come to be here?"

"I d-don't know," Meg said. "I was here, and she came up and started talking to me. I t-told her I th-thought she was so p-pretty, and her dresses were pretty, and then she... Papa, is it true? Was Mama killed?"

"Listen, sweetheart," Sheppard said. "Terrible things happen. You know that, don't you?"

"No," she said.

Sheppard's teeth showed briefly in an honestly amused grin. "Now think about it, Peanut: you remember how it hurts when you skin your knee, don't you? Or when you bump your head? Remember how you pinched your finger in the door yesterday? That sort of thing happens all the time."

"But she said m-my mother was killed by— By Yankees—" She pulled away and looked up at Sheppard. "Was she?" she asked.

"No, darling," Sheppard said. "She wasn't. Don't you remember? I took you in to see your mother, just before she went to Heaven. She was tired, and she was very sick, and she had been frightened very badly, but no one killed her."

"Why was she frightened?" Meg asked.

"She was frightened because some bad people had scared her. She was frightened because you were lost and alone in the woods. She was frightened because she was sick, and because her baby had died. But she stopped being frightened. Don't you remember how she saw you and smiled, and how she kissed you and called you her little angel?" When Meg was quiet he repeated, "Can you remember?"

Meg finally raised her troubled eyes to his and nodded slowly. "But *she* said Mama was killed by Yankees," she repeated.

Sheppard set a gentle finger under her chin and tilted her face up toward his. "Look at me, Meg," he said. "No Yankee hurt your mother. I'm a Yankee. I found you for your mother and brought you safe to her so she could see you and kiss you before she went to Heaven. Do you believe me?"

"Are—are Yankees bad?" she asked.

"No, dearest," Lavinia said. "They aren't bad any more than anyone else."

Meg stared up at him and then turned to peer fearfully over her shoulder at Louise Hamiter, who was standing quietly beside Lavinia. Suddenly she threw her arms about Sheppard's neck and buried her face against his high, yellow-braided collar. "But she said—" she wept.

Lavinia, watching the tenderness with which Sheppard gathered the child to him, almost recoiled at the pure rage in his eyes as he looked straight at Louise.

Sheppard spoke clearly. "She is a liar. You must never again listen to anything she says."

Louise took a step forward. "Now of all the rude—"

"Be quiet!" Lavinia hissed.

Meg hadn't heard her. "But why did she say it?" she sobbed. "Was I bad?"

The rage was still there, coupled now with a terrible, intent smile as Sheppard stroked Meg's tumbled hair and smoothed her back. "No, Sweetheart," he said. "She said what she did because she's a wicked, sinful woman who is filled with hate. She tells her lies so that she can hurt people, and because she is evil, it makes her happy when she does it. And she only hurts people who can't hurt her back, so she's a coward, too, which is just as bad as being a liar. She's evil, and you had better stay away from her. That's all."

Meg was still whimpering a little, but her terror was gone. Her father was holding her and fussing over her, and the world was almost as bright as it had been before.

"Come on, Louise," Lavinia said. "We're going back into the house. You've done enough harm for the day."

"Did you hear what he said about me?" Louise demanded furiously as they headed toward the house. "Am I expected to stand for that sort of language from him?"

"Tell truth and shame the Devil," Lavinia said. She nodded at Louise's shocked expression. "Now listen carefully, Louise. You're here on sufferance, and I'm not inclined to be patient with you. If I catch you anywhere near Meg from here on, I'll send you away from Wheelerville so fast you'll wonder what happened."

"Why, Sister—!"

"You're not my sister," Lavinia said. "And after seeing this afternoon's work I couldn't be happier about it! I saw your expression yesterday, when she came to ask Sergeant Sheppard to go riding with her, and I thought you might mean her harm. I decided that I had to be mistaken. It's a pity I didn't follow my instincts. What could that poor, orphaned little innocent possibly have done to merit your viciousness? You called her 'white trash' to her face and then told her, when she came trustingly to you, that her mother was murdered by Federal troops! Do you know, Louise, she told me just this morning that you were the prettiest lady she had seen?"

Louise's lip curled.

Lavinia nodded. "I thought you might have that reaction," she said. "What can I expect of someone who would send a petticoat to her fiancé when he is agonizing over the question of whether to risk his life in the army? Oh, you thought I didn't know about that, did you? Well, I did! Now get in the house and go to your room for the rest of the night. I haven't yet decided what to do about you. At the moment I want to send you to your kinfolk in Macon, but I want to talk it over with Sergeant Sheppard."

She watched Louise step over the threshold and make for the stairs. "And Louise," she said softly as the woman gathered her skirts and set her foot on the first step.

Louise turned.

"If Meg has a single nightmare from this day's work, you'll be taking up residence in the henhouse. Do you hear me? Now get out of my sight!"

CHAPTER THIRTY-TWO

The still evening air was ringing with the sound of crickets. The day had turned into twilight; the sky's deep, intense blue shaded down from its zenith to a golden tinge outlining Horn Mountain to the west. The house at Fairlawn glowed softly in the dusk, and the wide front door stood open, revealing the upward, spiraling sweep of the staircase. Off to the western side of the house, the double doors opening from the main parlor had been flung wide, spilling lamplight across the veranda.

One of the horses, pastured on the other side of the house, whinnied, drawing an answering neigh from another of the new arrivals, stabled in the barn. One of the hounds kept for rabbit hunting was baying in the distance near the town, in pursuit of a hare. The distant noises almost covered the sound of quiet speech.

"She's sleeping just fine, the poor little angel," Callie said from her rocking chair, positioned beside the French doors. She looked across at Sergeant Sheppard with a half-smile. "Though she asked me a lot of questions about dying."

Sheppard, sitting side-saddle on the wide porch railing, where he had an unobstructed view of the lawn approaching the house, folded his arms with a frown and leaned back against one of the pillars. "You didn't tell her it was like falling asleep, did you?" he asked. "My middle one, Lydia, was afraid to fall asleep for about a month after hearing that!"

"Do you take me for a fool?" Callie demanded disgustedly. "Lord bless you, no! No, I said it was like being born all over again, or like starting out on a long journey. She understood me, I think."

"Thank goodness!" Lavinia said. She was sitting beside Callie, her chair angled in such a way that she had a good view of the parlor. "It doesn't appear that any harm was done to Meg at least. What about Private Pierce?"

Corporal Higgins, perched on a chaise longue with his sound knee drawn up, looked down at his hands, linked about his knee. "He's coming along a little," he said. "Mrs. Swithin's visits have done him a power of good, but he was thrown for a loop, and it's going hard with him. Mrs. Swithin's calmed him down, though. She reminds me of my mother, and the other men look forward to seeing her. Pierce told her what was troubling him the second time she came to visit, and she had the good sense to laugh at it and tell him that no one heeds liars. He showed her his wife's photograph and she exclaimed and said what an honest, open soul she seemed to be. I think it got through, a little. Gave him something to chew on. Anyhow, she's an angel!"

"And speaking of the devil," Sheppard said, "Where's the Hamiter woman?"

"She's in the house," Lavinia said. "I left her in the smaller sitting room with a book. Don't worry, she can't come near us without being observed, and sound doesn't carry well from here."

"All right, then," Sheppard said. "Who's with Meg?"

"I left Bathsheba with her," Callie said. "Meg took a shine to her, and Bathsheba's agreed to sleep in with her at least until things get straightened out. The little lamb is enjoying it: she brushes Bathsheba's hair and helps her to arrange it."

Sheppard nodded. "Meg's in good hands," he said.

"Which leads us to the reason I asked all of you to come here," Lavinia said. "For well or ill, we have all of us dealt with Louise Hamiter. I don't think any of us will disagree when I say that things would be a lot more comfortable if she weren't here. The question is, what should we do about her?"

Sheppard was silent.

Callie, her hands folded before her, said, "She's spread grief and sorrow, certainly."

Higgins muttered something about a 'pain in the ass' and then blushed.

Lavinia smiled at him. "Don't be embarrassed, Corporal," she said. "Louise Hamiter has done a great deal of harm in the short time she's been here. It's my judgment that we would be best advised to have her leave at once."

Sheppard turned back from frowning down the drive and looked at her.

"At once," Lavinia repeated. "I can see no reason to put up with her after the havoc she has wreaked in this household, and I hardly think anyone would blame me for showing her the door. She has kinfolk in Macon; let her go there." She saw that Sheppard's expression was still reserved. "Well, Sergeant?" she said. "You don't appear to agree with me. Have you any objections?"

Sheppard frowned and shook his head. "I do," he said. "It's too dangerous."

"It might be dangerous for you, perhaps," Lavinia said after a moment's thought. "You would be crossing a part of Georgia that is held by Confederate troops, but if we consider that Louise is a citizen of Georgia, surely that objection would no longer exist."

"I didn't mean that," Sheppard said. "My men have been performing sweep patrols along with Al Townsend and his people, and they've found signs of guerilla activity."

"'Guerilla' activity?" Lavinia repeated.

"Marauders," Sheppard said. "The sort of irregulars who murdered Meg's family. Al Townsend saw tracks just this morning: he says they're nearby. It would be too dangerous for her."

"I can't find it in my heart to be terribly disquieted by any threat to Louise Hamiter," Lavinia said. She lifted her chin at Sheppard, who was eyeing her with a frown. "It occurs to me, Sergeant, that marauders might recognize in her a kindred spirit and accord her the courtesy they would give one of their own kind."

Higgins grinned and even Callie's stern features softened with amusement.

Sheppard did not smile. "That sentiment does no one any credit," he said. "I remember all that happened to Meg's family if you do not."

Lavinia pushed her spectacles back on her nose and opened her eyes at him. "I have no trouble remembering it, Sergeant," she said. "I repeat my comment."

"You remember—and you still speak this way?" Sheppard said. He looked around at the group. "Shame on you all!" he said.

"I can't get upset when someone kills a cottonmouth moccasin," Higgins said. "In this case, though, Sarge, seeing how she looked and what she said to poor Pierce, who never hurt anyone—or not since he was here, at any rate— I'd be more worried about someone tromping a moccasin than doing the same to that yellow-haired piece of bad news."

"'...It shall bruise thy head...,' " Callie quoted. "'...And the God of peace shall bruise Satan under your feet shortly.' "

Sheppard lifted an eyebrow at Callie. "'But I say unto you, Love your enemies, bless them that curse you, do good to them that hate you, and pray for them which despitefully use you, and persecute you, that you may be the children of your Father which is in heaven, for He maketh his sun to rise on the evil and on the good, and sendeth rain on the just and on the unjust.' "

Callie lowered her head.

"I am sorry, Miss Callie," Sheppard said, "but I haven't changed my mind. We can't send her away, much though I'd like to."

"Maybe we could have Al Townsend's group escort her away," Higgins said with the air of one who has found the answer to a terrible puzzle.

"It would be dangerous for them as well," Sheppard said. "The group we've been tracking numbers about thirty, that they can see, all mounted. I can't spare that many men from defending this town, and I won't risk any less escorting a worthless piece of baggage like that woman."

"Oh, so you do concede her worth, Sergeant!" Lavinia said.

Sheppard looked at her. "Let's not spar like this, Miss Wheeler," he said. "I don't like to harm anything when it isn't necessary, and in this case exposing a human being, however nasty, to the sort of danger I've witnessed is unthinkable— What did you say, Corporal Higgins?"

Higgins, who had muttered something curt and pithy about the doubtful nature of Miss Hamiter's humanity, was silenced.

"We have a term for people with Louise Hamiter's propensities, Sergeant," Lavinia said. "It is 'trash.' "

"I have a term for what you need to use in dealing with trash," Sheppard said. "It is 'charity.' " He looked back at Higgins. "At any rate, all our men are needed here."

"So it would appear that we're stuck with her, if you're to have your way," Lavinia observed with disgust.

"God give me strength!" Callie muttered.

"There must be other options," Sheppard said.

"The stables, perhaps?" Callie suggested.

"Naw," said Higgins. "She'd spook the horses into a colic. We can't have that."

"Perhaps Miss Dixie would kick her," Lavinia suggested. "That would settle matters."

"She'd sprain a hock," Sheppard said. "And she's a valuable horse. Stop it! Shame on you all!"

"Perhaps you have another suggestion, Sergeant?" Lavinia said. "No? Then it appears we must put up with Louise."

"But surely Mr. Townsend can take her somewhere else!" Callie exclaimed.

"It's too dangerous," Sheppard said. "I would advise against it." He added calmly, "And I think he would listen to me."

"Very well, then, Sergeant," Lavinia said. "It seems, from what you have said, that we must do nothing about this viper we're nursing at our bosom."

"Not 'nothing,' " Sheppard said. "I suggest everyone keep a careful watch on her. Be aware of her movements and take steps to keep her from harming anyone."

"How can we do that unless we lock her up?" Higgins wondered.

"Never mind," Lavinia said. "I will put the word out that Louise Hamiter is to be watched, and that she isn't to be allowed near the wounded or Meg."

"We're on to her," Sheppard said, rising.

"That's correct," Lavinia said. She looked up at him and rose to her feet.

Sheppard offered his arm. "And let us be honest for a moment," he said.

"How much more harm can she do now that we're aware of her?" Lavinia set her fingertips lightly on his arm and smiled at him. "Very little, indeed," she said, and descended the steps to the garden path with him.

** ** **

"Did you enjoy your tête-à-tête on the veranda?" Louise asked an hour later. She was seated in Lavinia's mother's favorite chair with her feet set elegantly on the hassock before her. A book was open on her lap, but since it had been face down since Lavinia had entered, it was doubtful how much she had read.

"My 'tête-à-tête,' " Louise?" Lavinia repeated. "Whatever do you mean?"

"I heard you there on the veranda," Louise said.

"You couldn't have heard much, Louise, if you thought only two were there," Lavinia said. She went to the shelves, selected *Waverly*, and turned, her fingertip lightly tracing the book's ribbed spine.

"More than two?" Louise said. "It must have been quite a gathering! I hope the festive occasion didn't go to waste!"

"There were no festivities," Lavinia said. "We were, in fact, discussing some rather somber matters, although I found the conversation enjoyable." She opened the book, smoothed the length of cherry-red ribbon that served as place marker, and then closed it again.

"Really?" Louise pursued. "What were you discussing?"

Lavinia smiled at the book. "We were talking about snakes, Louise," she said. "We discussed them at great length."

"I can't credit it!"

"Oh, we all found the subject fascinating," Lavinia said with a dark smile. "I daresay you would have, as well."

"I am astonished at you!"

Lavinia lightly balanced the book on her fingertips. "You would be putting your astonishment to better use, Louise, if you directed it at the impertinence of nearly every comment you have made to me since we met," she said. "You never got to know me very well. You were too busy passing your time with Gaylord to learn about me. All you knew of me, in fact, was that I was Gaylord's older sister, tired and weighted down with the cares of nursing a dying mother. I was someone to patronize and bully. If you had married Gaylord and come here, I daresay you still wouldn't have made any more push to make my acquaintance." She eyed Louise's expression and added gently, "It isn't sound strategy, you know: thorough acquaintance with the enemy is a very powerful weapon."

Louise was finding the conversation baffling. "Do you think I view you as an enemy, then?" she demanded.

"Your view of anything is a matter of complete indifference to me," Lavinia said. "But as to this evening's conversation, I think you would have found it fascinating, as I did."

Louise had closed her book and was staring at her.

Lavinia tucked *Waverly* into her pocket and smiled across at Louise. "I was a singular child," she said. "Callie said I wasn't feminine enough, for all that I didn't climb trees. I could ride and shoot with the best of them. I imagine I still can."

"I declare, I can't conceive—"

"I daresay," Lavinia said. "Why, do you know I once came upon a big timber rattler sunning himself on a rock. He made no move to harm me, so I let him alone—until he coiled tightly, sounded his rattle, and commenced to frighten Jupiter—remember him? My hunter?"

Louise looked up at Lavinia.

"I dismounted and let Jupiter go a pace or two away," Lavinia said. "And then I caught that rattler's neck in a cleft stick, set my foot on his head, and ground it into the rock, leaving the body coiling and uncoiling on that rock like a twist of wire."

"Lavinia!"

"I might have known you'd feel sorry for the snake, Louise," Lavinia said. "Don't look so pale. Much though I dislike distressing anyone, I should warn you that I do that sort of thing to all snakes I encounter, one way or another. It's something to keep in mind, isn't it?"

CHAPTER THIRTY-THREE

"Here are the tracks, Sarge," Al Townsend said, frowning down at some marks in the dirt. "They're pretty clear: shod horses, moving at a fair clip, and they were hugging the downside of the ridge." He touched one of the prints with a fingertip.

"I think you're right," Sheppard said. "I make them thirty at least, and not recently shod." He looked southeast at the uneven backbone of Pine Log Mountain. Allatoona lay south of the mountain and beyond it, even farther to the south, was Atlanta, currently playing unwilling host to Sherman's armies. "How far to Allatoona?" he asked at last. "Two days' ride?"

Townsend straightened and looked up at Sheppard. "If that much," he said. "Maybe a little less." He settled the reins over his mount's neck, set a foot in the stirrup, and swung back into his saddle.

Sheppard looked at the tracks again. "They look a lot like the ones I found where Meg's family was killed," he said slowly. "You didn't see any others between then and now. Maybe they followed the armies south. In which case—" He stopped.

"In which case, why're they here?" Townsend supplied. "I was wondering, myself. Slim pickings south of here? Too many armies there?"

Sheppard looked away from the tracks and up into the sky. Clouds were blowing from the west and piling along the eastern horizon. "Settling in for the winter," he said. "I hear tell it's supposed to be a cold one."

"Could be," said Townsend, squinting at the clouds himself. He blinked and looked back at Sheppard. "We found a burned-out house a few miles south of here," he said. "Recently burned."

Sheppard directed a bleak look at him. "Any sign of murdered people?" he asked.

Townsend nodded.

"Treated like the others," Wallins said behind them. "We buried 'em."

"I knew them," said Haller Reeves. His voice had fallen from its usual pomposity. He had gone to Townsend the week before and quietly asked to join the militia. Townsend had nodded, assigned him to Sam Wallins' group, and kept an eye on him. He had told Sheppard privately that the man was shaping up surprisingly well.

Reeves took out his handkerchief and mopped his forehead. "I knew them," he said again. "The Pike family. They were good folk, hard-working folk with two sons in the army... She was Ed Pickens' sister. It made me sick!"

"It was yesterday we found them," Townsend told Sheppard. "I sent Abner to you just before. I figured he didn't need to see those bastards' handiwork too soon. Time enough for him to get used to the pretty corpses."

"It was terrible!" Reeves said. "And poor Ed was in a state!"

"Meg's family was worse," Townsend said. "At least these people were shot."

Sheppard had been squinting down along the line of tracks. He looked up. "The point is that we're going to keep that from happening at Wheelerville," he said, gathering his reins in his left hand. "The first thing to do is make certain they can't come across us and surprise us."

"We've set sentries," Townsend said. "And they're changed often."

"The same's being done at Fairlawn," Sheppard said. "Is it enough?"

Looks were traded all around.

"Maybe not," Townsend said at last.

"Maybe we should get all outlying families into town," Wallins said. "You did that with Fairlawn's people. I hear there was some grumbling."

"There was enough," Sheppard agreed. "I reminded them of Meg's folks, though, and it stopped pretty quickly. What do you plan to do?"

Townsend looked over at the Wheelerville Militia, ranged below the crest of the hill, then turned and frowned back along the line of the hillside. "I'd say we follow the tracks back to where they started, or as far as we can," he said. "You want to come along with us?"

Sheppard considered for a moment and then nodded. "If anyone asks, I'm your prisoner," he said.

Wallins snorted. "It won't get that far," he said. "We'll just hustle you into the trees. What d'you say, Al? Three point riders? I'll be glad to go."

"Sounds good," Townsend said. He picked out two others and sent them ahead.

Sheppard watched them assemble. "Keep an eye open," he said. "I have a feeling this group's big enough not to care how much of a mess they make."

Al Townsend was frowning thoughtfully. "You thinking of going in and wiping them out, Sarge?" he asked.

"I wish we could," Sheppard replied. "If we had a big enough group..."

"Heck, Sarge," John Toombs said, reining his mount around. "We can muster fifty anyhow with both our groups! If we could clean 'em out—!"

Townsend was shaking his head. "Point is we don't know if we can," he said before Sheppard could say anything. "If we were killed, who would protect the town?"

"I never thought you'd be a coward!" Reeves exclaimed.

"He isn't being a coward," Sheppard said. "He's being smart. We don't know what we're facing, and until we do, it's pretty bad sense to pick a fight."

"And what if they bring the fight to us?" Reeves demanded.

Sheppard smiled at him. "Why, we'll just make them regret it!" he said.

✻✻   ✻✻   ✻✻

Lavinia looked up from her embroidery frame. "They're back?" she said faintly. "But how can that be? I thought they were gone!"

Sheppard had been watching her. "I told you about them last night," he said, pulling off his gloves and setting them on the table beside his cap. "I'm afraid they're very much with us."

Lavinia looked blindly down at the jumble of colored threads in her basket. "The guerrillas," she said. "I heard you use that term, but I didn't think you could be serious. Why, the armies left us behind months ago. They're at Atlanta, and we're far to the north."

"That's the point," Sheppard said. "These riff-raff don't get fat preying on people who can fight. The last place they want to be is near a large, well-organized force of fighting men."

"So they've come north," Lavinia said. She pushed herself to her feet without her usual grace and made her way to the jug, sitting in state on the marble-topped side table. She took it between her shaking hands and lifted it. "I...I thought it was over," she said, staring down into the amused eyes of the jug's face. "I thought we were safe. That is why I brought this out." She lifted her head. "I thought we were safe and I could relax and breathe easily once more. But the nightmare just keeps going on, with no hope of us awakening."

Sheppard came closer to her. "Lavinia," he said.

Lavinia turned the jug, staring down at its rough glaze. "Tell me all of it,"

"The group numbers more than thirty," Sheppard said at last. "They're armed."

"There is more," she said, raising her eyes to his. When he hesitated, she said, "Tell me, Sergeant!" '

"They are mounted, and they can ride fast. Townsend's group followed them for several miles, and I went with them. From what we could see, they had army weapons and plenty of ammunition."

When he fell silent she said, "There's more that you aren't telling me, isn't there, Sergeant? They killed people." She saw his expression and gave a muffled cry. "Oh I was right! Oh, dear heaven! Just like Meg's family—wasn't it?"

"Al Townsend found one family," Sheppard said.

Lavinia tightened her grip on the jug until her fingertips were white. "Tell me," she said again.

"Haller Reeves knew them," Sheppard said. "An older couple named Pike, husband and wife."

Lavinia closed her eyes and opened them again. "Hanson and Verena Pike," she said. "I knew them, too. She was Mr. Pickens' sister. He came south from Connecticut to teach school here, and they met and married. They were such a kindly pair, far older than their children. Their sons—their sons are in the armies. I remember how they came to Fairlawn last year seeking help with the harvest." She looked around the room. "We sat right here and she told me of her first grandchild— Toby sent five men back with her to help reap— Dear heaven! They weren't— Oh Sergeant, they couldn't have been abused like Meg's family!"

Some hells are made worse by being hidden. Sheppard spoke

quickly and to the point. "They were shot," he said. "In the head. It was over almost immediately. The lady was not molested beforehand: Dr. Meacham confirmed that this morning. They left her alone. From what Meacham says, they didn't suffer at all."

Lavinia carefully set the jug down. "I would never have thought I'd be grateful to learn the details of a murder," she said. Her voice shook. "Merciful heaven! What must their sons be thinking? And poor Mr. Pickens! He must be distraught!"

"We can't let that happen here," Sheppard said. "I've spoken to Townsend and the rest, and if we gather the people close to this town, where they can assemble quickly—" He broke off at Lavinia's expression. "Are you all right?" he asked.

Lavinia set her teeth against the rising pressure in her throat. "I will be fine," she said. "I wasn't murdered. My home wasn't burned. Not yet. You and Mr. Townsend will handle it as you best see fit, with Judge Prescott's guidance. And now, if you will excuse me..."

Sheppard rose as she passed him and went toward the stairs.

"Miss Wheeler," he said, following her.

She turned at the first step. "Thank you for your report, Sergeant," she said. "All that you have said sounds most well-advised. Thank you. And now, if you will excuse me..." She did not look down as she climbed the stairs.

✷✷   ✷✷   ✷✷

Lavinia's arrival at the top landing came as a jolt. She had not even been aware of climbing the stairs. It was almost as though she had dreamed it all. Or maybe the war with all its want and heartache was the dream.

It was just possible, she thought, opening her bedroom door, that if she closed her eyes tight, took a deep breath and then opened them, she would find that the past four years were the dream and the unruffled, serene life she had known would be the reality. She would look out her bedroom window and see her horses grazing in the fields beyond the house and frisking up to the fence to beg a treat. Her mother would come sweeping into the room wreathed in smiles, with talk of her latest charitable project that promised to be great fun during the winter in Savannah.

Her father would be riding past the house, and he would rein in and lift a negligent hand to wave to her and her mother. Lavinia would smile down at him, ignorant of the shameful truth of his dealing with the female slaves at Fairlawn.

Lavinia opened her eyes and looked around. Her bedroom was a little plainer, her dress a little more worn, and she was very tired. Dreams were pleasant for a time, but their enjoyment tended to falter after a while, and it was best not to chase them. She sat down opposite the large cherry wood armoire with a sigh and arranged her skirts around her.

Another day past, and she was exhausted. And yet, she had done so little: fed the chickens, tended the wounded, tolerated Louise, made an inventory of the mending, supervised the laundry...

And learned of the death of two you knew and respected, she thought.

She turned away from the thought and saw the pottery ranged on the shelves. They were neatly arranged, perfectly dusted, and the pieces with faces seemed to be gazing at her with wry amusement.

As well they might, she thought with another sigh. She lifted one of the cups with careful hands and fingered its rough edge. Its owner had lived through fear, desertion, hardship and danger. How reassuring to remember that when sometimes she felt as though no one had ever done so but her. Holding this, touching it, reminded her that it could be, and had been, done triumphantly, if she could somehow find the strength as they had.

They had bade farewell to so much that they had held dear, just as she had. Surely they, too, had sat and remembered better days and happier times. She closed her eyes and let the scraps of memory flow over and around her. Memories, sometimes surprising in their substance, emerged, grew sharp, and then faded.

There was that sage moiré dress given her when she was sent to that finishing school in Richmond. How its silken folds had whispered at her movements! Her hunter, Jupiter, now gone far away on some battlefield. Where was he now? Or was he even alive?

She remembered the surge and the feel of flight as he took a jump during a hunt. She remembered the glossy-coated mounts, the beautifully garbed riders sharing their stirrup cups... And then another picture rose to her mind: all the horses lying dismembered on her lawn after the battle, torn to pieces by bombs, bloated and rotting. Jupiter could well be one of them, taken on some distant field by a death he had never been bred to endure—

She wrenched her thoughts aside and faced a picture of her father sitting beside the fire with the pots around him, smiling at her and telling her— Telling her—

But he was dead now, too, and dishonored. All that remained of him was in the ground, pinned beneath a granite tombstone. All that she had loved, gone irretrievably on the tide of that faraway summer when her mother had languished and died, bringing the safe, happy world of the Wheelers down around them. Her mother, her father, Gaylord her little brother, all gone in a tide of death, and now it was surging back toward her in a dark flood, claiming all around her.

Suddenly Lavinia was consumed with the sort of tearing, convulsive sobs that she hadn't felt since she was a child, wrenching, gasping sobs that left her doubled over and helpless with the pain.

The people who had owned the pots had survived: how had they done it? There had to be a way that she could learn. How to keep courage and sanity in a world gone mad? How to recapture the dream? How to—

She heard a tapping on the door. "Miss Wheeler?"

She knew the voice; it was not a part of the dreams. She looked up, wildly brushing at her eyes. "W—what is it?" she said in a wavering voice.

"Miss Wheeler? It's Asa Sheppard. There's some good, hot tea waiting for you downstairs, when you're ready. I've put it by the fire to keep it warm."

"Thank you," she said, thinking inconsequentially that if she were somehow able to step back into her memories and cancel the present, she would never again hear that voice saying her name, or walk through the warm summer twilight with the voice's owner. That thought was as painful as the others.

Silence fell. Lavinia could see him hesitating, one hand on the door knob, his brows creased, as clearly as though he were standing there before her. She could see him open his mouth, take a breath

"Miss Wheeler, Callie asked me to tell you there's fresh biscuits coming from the oven at any moment, and she'll have a few of them set aside for you, along with some hot soup."

She heard his voice trailing off, but there was still no sound of his feet moving away down the hall. She moved slowly toward the door and stopped, her hand resting on the knob, her head bent as she listened.

"Miss Wheeler? It'll come out all right. I promise: it just takes time. All you can do till then is keep going, and you know you never have to keep going alone. You've got some allies now. Together we can whip whatever comes against us.

"It's no use crying over what is past, especially when it never existed in the first place.," he said through the door after a moment. "You know better. How is this time now different from any other time that this world's seen? You talk of Sir Walter Raleigh's jug—don't you think the folk who had that pottery saw conditions just as bad as these? If it wasn't the Indians, it was outlaws, and if it wasn't any of them, it was the British or the Continentals. They had to fight every day of their lives, and so have you, though I suspect you don't know it for that. We can fight those guerrillas, Lavinia. We can fight them and we can whip them, just as those settlers fought catamounts, bandits and thieves."

Lavinia felt the fear easing. He was right: she could fight, and so could Wheelerville. Not only would they survive, they would triumph. It was amazing, she thought, how much better she felt now that she was armed with a plan and allies. She swallowed and leaned her forehead against the door as hope came flooding in with the words. "Thank you, Sergeant," she said. Her voice sounded almost normal.

In the pause that followed, she could almost see Sergeant Sheppard tilt his head, considering.

"Well, I'll put the tea by the fire," he said at last. "And I'm going to put some sugar in it for you, too. Things need sweetening from time to time, no matter what the cost. Just enough to take the edge off when it gets too rough."

"Thank you," she said again. "I'll be right down." She added, "I— haven't forgotten our walk this evening, if it is still convenient for you."

She could hear a smile in the reply. "It's always convenient, Miss Wheeler." And then she heard his steps moving away down the hall.

CHAPTER THIRTY-FOUR

"I spent most of the day with Private Pierce," Lavinia said later during their walk that evening. "He keeps talking of his wife as though she were before him and on trial for a crime."

"Maybe she is," Sheppard said. "In his mind."

Lavinia lifted her face into the freshening night wind and looked over at him. The rising moon's faint light traced the lines of his face, turning his light brown hair to a cap of silver, softening the glare of yellow braid at collar and sleeves to pale gold.

She could feel the lines of the braid beneath her fingers; she brought her other hand up to clasp the one tucked into his arm. "In what way is she standing trial?" she asked.

"He probably keeps thinking of what the Hamiter woman said about his wife," Sheppard replied. "He's continually remembering the accusation, defending her in his mind-and then demolishing the defense. He's probably see-sawing between conviction and acquittal."

"But that's so foolish!"

"He's a man in love," Sheppard said. "And love can be pretty foolish at times, especially if the one you love is far away from you. And it sure can hurt. Pierce is sick just now, and he can't think straight. Believe me, I know. He just doesn't have the strength to think, 'You're being stupid!', even though he probably knows deep down that that's the case. He needs strength, and he just doesn't have it."

"No," Lavinia said. "I can see that it's taking all he has just to keep alive."

Looking down at her, Sheppard could see the marks of strain in her expression and feel the unaccustomed clutch of her hand on his arm. He held her hand more firmly in the crook of his arm and spoke calmly, "Your aunt said he's better and so did Dr. Meacham."

Lavinia sighed and shook her head. "If only it could be true," she said. "But I just don't see how... I had so hoped there'd be no more graves."

"Wait and see," Sheppard said. "You've had no word from God either way, and you'd be foolish, yourself, to try and second-guess Him."

Lavinia did not reply. She drew her hands away and took a couple of steps forward. She said, "I thought, walking up the stairs this afternoon—it was after I learned about the Pikes—how it might be if I could close my eyes, open them and find that I had dreamed all of this. All the death, all the grieving..."

Sheppard was silent.

Lavinia lifted her face into the stars. "It was a pleasant notion for a while," she said. "I remembered Jupiter, my old hunter, I remembered how happy my family had been, how serene everything had seemed, how bright and blessed compared to now."

"If I could somehow make it that way for you again, Lavinia, I would," Sheppard said quietly behind her.

Lavinia turned back to him and tucked her hand in his arm once more. "It occurred to me that if I could go back to those days, if this war were to melt away like last night's dream and all be as it was before—why then you would melt away, as well, and I would never be able to know you."

She drew a deep breath and took his hand lightly in hers. "Asa," she said.

His hand curved to hold hers, and she saw that he was looking down at her, his expression still and attentive.

"You don't know how much you have come to mean to our peace and happiness here at Fairlawn," she said. "Or how very grateful I am for all that you have done to make—to make things easier for me, and prettier. If closing my eyes would make this world vanish, and I could open them and step back into that stifling, serene past, why I would never close my eyes again."

She could feel him watching her. She lowered her eyes and turned away as she spoke. Her voice quivered and steadied through the tightness in her throat. "You've been so good a friend, Asa," she said. "I don't ever want to lose you."

His hand came quietly down upon her shoulder, warm and firm through the thickness of her shawl. She turned to see him smiling at her.

"You never will, Lavinia," he said. "As long as I'm alive."

He hesitated, then spoke. "I guess I can tell you that you saved my life," he said. "I was wounded and the pain and darkness just wouldn't go away. Sarah had been dead for two years, my children were far from me, and there was no one I could look to for joy and laughter. And then I saw you standing in the sun that morning, and you gave me a reason to go on living."

"You came riding out of the sun that morning," Lavinia said. "I turned east to see the sun rising—and there you were." She squinted at her smudged glasses and polished them on a corner of her handkerchief, "Though I was tempted, from time to time, to give you a good shaking! You can be a very vexatious man!"

"I'll return the compliment," Sheppard said on the hint of a smile. "You're a formidable and sometimes infuriating woman."

They smiled, turned and continued strolling.

"We'll be conducting our first drill tomorrow morning," Sheppard said in a different voice. "Townsend is talking with the people in town, and I've been speaking with the Fairlawn folk. Regular drills, talks…It'll be best if we get them in place quickly."

Lavinia nodded. "I'm glad you came," she said again. She frowned at a sudden thought and said, "Louise didn't know about the militia until today. She was talking about it this morning. You would think she had discovered something shameful! Has she said anything to you about it?"

"I haven't talked with the Hamiter woman," Sheppard said. "I don't want to, either. I'll let someone among the household who can stomach her deal with her. Mrs. Swithin, maybe."

Lavinia sighed and shook her head. "She complicates everything," she said. "She comes from a difficult family. How Aunt Amabel has stood that tribe for so long is beyond me to understand! We were all surprised that Gaylord had fallen for a Hamiter."

"Well known for their disposition?" Sheppard asked.

"Notorious," Lavinia said.

Sheppard looked grim for a moment. "Her reputation doesn't lie," he said. "And I hear from you that Private Pierce is still fevered. Is there no end to that woman's wickedness?" Lavinia turned to look back at the house. "Oh Asa," she said, "Whatever are we to do for Private Pierce?"

"We could pray for a miracle," he said.

** ** **

Asa Sheppard took out his pipe, inserted a finger into his tobacco pouch, frowned, and peered into the leather sack. After a moment he sighed, took out a good-sized pinch of tobacco and proceeded to pack it into the bowl of his pipe. When the pipe was filled to his satisfaction he cocked an eye at the man lying on the cot before him. "Well, then, By," he said. "How's it going with you?"

Byron Pierce watched Sheppard take out a match from the brass cylinder in his pocket and strike it against the side of his trousers. He closed his eyes as the match flared, and turned his cheek against the pillow, sparing a quick glance at the dark window beside the bed. "I'm fair to middlin', Sarge," he said.

Sheppard frowned at the glowing bowl of his pipe, withdrew the match, and extinguished it with a flick of his wrist, sending the burnt match arcing into a nearby chamber pot a moment later. "That's all?" he said. "You were doing just fine last week. Now you look like death twice warmed over. What happened to you?"

"Nothing," Pierce said, looking away from him.

"You've got an odd way of showing nothing, then," Sheppard said. "All this time you've been mooning over that ambrotype of your wife, and now nothing. Out with it: what's gotten into you?"

Pierce took his lower lip between his teeth. "It's nothing," he jerked out.

Sheppard drew in a mouthful of smoke, held it, and then let it slowly trail out the corner of his mouth. "Well," he said in a gentler voice, "You know best." He eyed the pipe. "So you're doing fairly," he said. "Doc Meacham thinks you were making good progress—until recently, that is. He was saying he thought you could go to a sweetened mash pretty soon. Get you away from that everlasting toast tea and barley—water. He said he thought you could have fried hominy, and maybe some bacon."

"Bacon?" Pierce said, his pale face brightening.

"That's what he said," Sheppard said. "It'd have to be minced fine so it wouldn't rough up your innards, but you'd get the taste of it in your mouth. And they make good bacon here, I can tell you! Best I've had since I last saw my wife!"

Pierce's eyes had been shining. The glow died and he looked down at his hands, folded across his stomach.

"Another two or three weeks, Doc says, and you'll be up and about for a spell, too," Sheppard said.

"Did he really say that?" Pierce demanded.

Sheppard, eyeing the man's fever-flushed cheeks, said, "That's what he said just about a week ago. That was before 'nothing' bothered you and sent you flat on your back again, mind. Now he's not so sure."

Pierce wiped at his eyes as Sheppard leaned across and set his wrist against his forehead and then his throat.

"But we'll give it our best shot," Sheppard said with a sudden, genuine smile as he took his hand away. "Actually, you don't feel terribly warm, which is a blessing."

He drew thoughtfully on his pipe again. After a moment he reached into the breast of his jacket and took out a photograph. "Did I ever show you this, By?" he asked. "It's my children. I don't have one of my wife with me, sorry to say. Maybe you can loan me that one of yours. She's a sweet-souled little thing, from the picture you have."

Pierce was staring wide-eyed at the photograph.

"They're a lively crew," Sheppard said. "Or the first two are, at any rate. I don't know the youngest very well—he was born while I was away, and I saw him for the first time last Christmas, though I try to write all of them regularly."

He set the pipe down and busied himself with putting away his tobacco pouch. "By rights I should have one of little Meg, as well," he said. "She calls me 'Papa' now. I've a mind to take her back to New York with me when all this is over, if they don't find any of her kinfolk. She's not much older than my youngest, and they'd think of her as a sister. I say the more the merrier, when it comes to children."

He bent an intent look at Pierce, who was still staring at the photograph, his face white and drawn.

"I w-wanted children," Pierce said. "Once I did, anyhow."

"Of course you did, a strapping fellow like you with that sweet, pretty young wife of yours," Sheppard said. "You'd be a born father, and by her photograph, she's true and kind."

Pierce's eyes were filling with tears.

"I do wish I had a photograph of Meg to carry," Sheppard said again. "One of her wearing that blue calico dress Miss Lavinia made for her. I've seen her time and again chasing butterflies in that dress or another Miss Lavinia made up for her. Or else she's waiting by the pillars when I come back from patrol, hoping I'll take her riding. Have you seen her since she came here?"

"I've seen her off and on," Pierce said. He had taken something from beneath his pillow and was holding it clenched in his hand. "She comes in to visit with us all. She likes Higgins' new wooden leg, and she sits on my bed and tells me stories sometimes. She likes to play nurse, just like Miss Lavinia. She was in just yesterday with Aunt Amabel..." He fell silent for a moment. "She surely is a little darling."

Sheppard frowned. "That she is," he said slowly. "But she wasn't smiling much a couple days ago. The Hamiter creature went to her with a mouthful of lies a while back that had her crying fit to break her heart."

Pierce looked up at him, wide-eyed. "W-what did she say?" he asked.

"Just that her mother was murdered by Yankees like me," Sheppard said. "Just that she was alone in the world and everyone was laughing at her for a pauper and a vagabond. Can you imagine? Saying that sort of hurtful lie to a babe like her!"

"That's terrible!" Pierce said, levering himself up on his elbows with a grimace of pain.

"Lie back," Sheppard said, and waited until he was obeyed. "It was terrible," he agreed after a moment. "And it was more so because the poor little chick didn't have the sense to know a hurtful lie when she heard one. She looked as though someone had cut the heart out of her world."

"Oh God!" Pierce said. "How could she do it?"

Sheppard looked thoughtful. "I tell you, By," he said. "There's a breed of evil creature that's filled with hate. It gets its pleasure by causing pain. And yet for all that, it shuns its own pain like a curse. It's cowardly: it avoids those who can fight and preys on the weak and helpless, instead. A trusting, innocent child, a sick man..." He took the pipe from his mouth and eyed the glowing tobacco in the bowl.

"Is she all right?" Private Pierce asked. He was still gazing at the photograph of Sheppard's children. His breathing was coming unsteadily, as though he were trying to hold strong emotion in.

"She is now," Sheppard replied with a touch of grimness. "Though it was touch and go for a few minutes. I won't let the Hamiter creature near her now. That much at least I can do, even if I can't have her jailed for slander, as I'd like. Meg trusts me enough to believe what I tell her—"

"I know I'm being a fool, Sarge," Pierce interrupted in a rush of words. "They tell me over and over, but I can't—I can't help it! I keep hearing those awful words and I keep thinking they're wrong, and I keep trying to think of Emily and how good it was between us. Just when I've got a good picture in my mind, it changes and it's like I'm watching her turn from something beautiful to a monster. Everyone says she lied, but I can't forget how she sat right there, where you are, smiling at me, so calm and so ladylike, and it was like she put a hex on Emily so that I saw a devil where I thought there was an angel."

"That's just what she wanted to do," Sheppard said.

"Maybe so," Pierce said desperately. "But I can't seem to get it out of my head, Sarge! I keep thinking if only Emily were here—If I could only see her, talk to her—just for a moment!" He finished almost in a whisper, "I miss her so badly..."

Sheppard smiled down at him. "You'll be all right," he said. "Don't forget, you've been sick. Things you would laugh at when you're hale and healthy—knock you over. I can see you're getting better, and it'll all come right in the end, trust me, no matter what that evil liar said. The Hamiter creature's slanders are just slanders: they haven't changed the truth. The Book says the tongue 'is an unruly evil, full of deadly poison'. It takes a while to get over the poison, I know. But the truth will out."

Pierce closed his eyes. He looked white and pinched against the sheets. "I'm so afraid of it, Sarge," he said.

"Nonsense!" said Sheppard. "No one should fear the truth! Didn't you go to Sabbath school? 'Ye shall know the truth, and the truth shall make you free'. You just have to wait and see." He got to his feet and stowed his pipe away after touching the bowl to see if it was out.

"I'll talk to Doc Meacham about that bacon," he said. He smiled at the sudden brightening in Pierce's eyes. "I'll see if you can have it tomorrow noon," he said.

CHAPTER THIRTY-FIVE

Al Townsend reined his horse to a halt and looked around. "We've gone far enough for now," he said. "Let's take a breather." Harness creaked and jingled behind him and he could hear the rustle of dry leaves and the stamp of shod hooves upon the hard ground of late autumn.

"Why are we stopping here, Al?" John Toombs asked. "We've got a ways to go yet."

"That's right," Townsend said, looking back over his shoulder at the rest of the group and weighing them in his mind. They were a likely lot, in his opinion, though most of them fell outside the ages of conscription, between eighteen and thirty-five. John Toombs, a strapping twenty-two-year-old, and Sam Wallins, who had just turned thirty-four, were exempted because of their professions of wheelwright and blacksmith while Haller Reeves, who was turning 35 in the spring, was exempted because he published a newspaper.

If you're not too particular about your definition of a newspaper, Townsend thought to himself, looking back at the group. Several of them were just not up to long, strenuous activity. Like Haller Reeves, ambling forward on his gray mare with his brows drawn together.

"Did you see something, Al?" Reeves demanded. He was puffing a little with the effort of keeping up a sitting trot over uneven ground. Townsend was willing to lay a bet that his backside was giving him problems. And it had taken Reeves a week of losing various hats in the course of patrols to realize that he needed to put his hat on a lanyard.

Townsend eyed him and considered telling Reeves that he was the reason for the decision to give the group a breather. He judged that the potential for amusement did not outweigh the potential for damage to morale. Besides, despite his apparent change of heart, Haller Reeves could still be pretty savage with his pen when he put his mind to it.

"Didn't see a thing," Townsend said. "And if it's all the same to you, Reeves, I'd just as soon it stayed that way for a time. Not seeing any burned houses or butchered folk suits me just fine."

"But we've got a ways to go!" Toombs objected again. "I don't know why you're stopping here!"

"You're right, Jack," Townsend said. "We've a far piece to go, but it's early yet and we aren't going to die if we don't get there in the next five minutes. You got a reason for being in a rush? Maybe you want to practice riding point? Go right ahead: you can take Reeves along with you: be good practice for him."

"A rush?" Toombs repeated, realizing what Townsend was saying. "Not me!"

Reeves' face brightened. "You'll let me ride point?" he said. "Why, surely! I need to learn—"

"There's nothing to it but keeping your eyes peeled, Haller," Sam Wallins said. "And it's not that great an honor!"

Reeves shot him a look and turned back to Townsend. "I could go, Captain Townsend," he said again. "I need to learn!"

Townsend, looking into his eyes, thought they looked just about as pleading as his hound dog's. "We're taking a stop here," he said. "But you and Jack can ride on a pace, southeast toward Atlanta. No more than a mile should do it, then you can circle back this way. Keep a good lookout and come back and tell me what you see. The rest of you, loosen your girths and let your horses stretch their necks."

He turned away from the group and watched Toombs and Reeves ride away. He had a pretty good idea what they were likely to find. He had been looking at it in his own mind for over a month now.

He loosened his mount's reins and frowned southeast, the eyes of his mind skimming the hills like a swift-flying hawk, passing over the turns of the Oostanaula River where it drained from the Chattahoo-chee, crossing over Dykes creek and the Etowah River before circling Cartersville and Acworth. The beautiful green meadows below Kennesaw Mountain were still riddled with earthworks. Marietta lay beyond it and, south and east of them, Atlanta sprawled wrecked and smoking beneath the sky, at the mercy of the bluecoats.

He frowned at the picture in his mind and turned northward again, straining his inner vision toward Richmond and the very heart of the Confederacy.

He sighed after a moment. It was no use. Try as he might, he could not summon Virginia to his mind again, for all that he had spent a year and a half marching up and down through the Old Dominion State and Maryland with a gun on his shoulder and a pack on his back, covered with the 'sacred soil' and not as appreciative of the honor as everyone had said he would be.

Like many other healthy, active young men his age, he had wanted to 'see the elephant' when the war came along. He and three of his best buddies from the town had rushed to enlist, all of them nervous about the required medical examination and even more nervous about the smallpox vaccination Doc Meacham had insisted on giving all of them before they left for the armies, saying they stood a greater chance of being killed by the disease than by the bullets of the Yankees.

Well, Al Townsend had seen the elephant, all right. He had seen it at Manassas, at Chantilly, at Antietam and so many other places filled with the whine of bullets, the smell of blood and the graves of his friends. He had been wounded twice and mentioned in several reports of the battles. Once he had been formally commended. By the end of his first year with the armies he had decided he had seen more of the elephant than anyone in his right mind would ever want to see. Even now he could hear the whistle of shot overhead, feel the showers of dirt stinging his face, the tremble of the ground as charges exploded all around him.

It had happened when he had found himself in one of the nameless towns in the eastern part of Virginia, clutching his regiment's standard, waving it over his head and screeching like a gut-shot catamount. He had charged to the edge of a heartbreakingly steep parapet, and gazed into a forest of steel muzzles that all were pointed at him. The threatened breakthrough had been averted, and he had stood aghast, his breath fluttering in his throat, his mouth suddenly metallic with the taste of his own mortality.

The war had roared on around him, the bullets had whined, the campfires had smoked and he had helped to dig many and many a grave, and filled them with people who could easily have been his brothers but for inconsequential details of accent and uniform.

It had all come to have the feel and taste of a continuous nightmare, and the stripes marching up his sleeves did not compensate for the pain, exhaustion and privation that had helped win them. He had straightened one day, a hand to the small of his aching back, scowled down at his worn shoes, and decided that he had had enough. His term of enlistment had expired months before, he had not been paid since before its expiration, and it was time to go home and let someone else have a turn gaping at the elephant.

Joseph Brown, the white-bearded governor of Georgia, was denouncing the newest conscription measure passed by the Confederate government, the one that extended Townsend's term of enlistment another two years, or until the end of the war. Townsend, who had trouble understanding how someone could change something he had agreed to without talking to him about it first, had decided that he was in complete sympathy with the old gentleman, and it was time to do something about it. He had given his musket to someone who needed it, and set off for home.

It was wintertime, Ambrose Burnside's bluecoats were trying to get comfortable for the winter after having been stuck in the mud, and he was plain tired out. No one had tried to stop him except for a dapper young shavetail, serving as Officer of the Day, who had tried to place Townsend under arrest. Townsend, who had always been a strong, strapping man and handy with his fists, had taken exception to the measure. The shavetail had retired, staggering, with a black eye and a couple of cracked ribs. Townsend could still remember the man's name: George Benton.

It had taken Al Townsend two months to get back home to Wheelerville, and by that time the battle of Gettysburg had been fought and lost, and the town had changed. The cemeteries were crowded with new occupants, and his reception among the living had not been quite as cordial as he could have wished. He had spent months, until the arrival of Sergeant Sheppard, fighting an odd, shameful notion that he had not done well. He had begun to realize that while he might have left the war, the war had come to Georgia and he was fighting in it all over again. He had lately found himself wondering whether he would do well to fight it in uniform once more.

He sighed and looked south again. Richmond could take care of its own problems. For the moment he was helping to take care of the problems of Wheelerville, Georgia.

"Al!"

Townsend frowned and turned his horse, thinking of old battles and old graves. From the look of the sky, he had been sitting there and drifting for a long time. Toombs and Reeves were sitting their horses behind him, flanking another man who was mounted on a heavily laden mule. "That was quick, boys," he said. "What did you find?"

"Intruder," said John Toombs.

Haller Reeves was beaming. "We ran across him half a mile off, coming northwest. I was the one who saw him!"

"It didn't take much seeing," Toombs said. "He was in clear view and coming across a bare stretch of land."

Townsend frowned at John Toombs. "You did a good job, Haller," he said. He looked the prisoner over, noticing the full saddle bags that nearly obscured the cantle of the saddle. "All right, then, friend," he said. "You better have a good explanation for being here!"

The man grinned at him. "Well, I'm looking for a place called Fairlawn, for starters," he said. "It's in a town called Wheelerville. I've got letters to deliver. Can you point me that direction?"

"Maybe," Townsend said. He looked beyond the man to Toombs. "Did you check to see if he had any papers on him, Jack?" he asked.

"I've got a safe-conduct," the man said. "A pass through the lines signed by General Stanley and counter-signed by General Sherman. And I got another from General Hood in with them."

"I'll just bet General Hood was pleased," Sam Wallins said.

"He didn't say a whole lot about it," the man replied. "But he gave me the pass and let me by."

Townsend took the papers from him. "You're not in uniform," he said. "You could be hanged for a spy, you know."

"I'm not a soldier," the man replied. "And I'm haven't made any secret of what I am."

"Then maybe you can tell us just what you are," Haller Reeves said as Townsend held the papers at arm's length and scanned them with a scowl.

The man directed a distant look at him. "I'm a courier," he said. "I told you already. I got letters for people at Wheelerville."

"Hm," said Townsend, handing the papers back. "Where are you heading after that?"

"Gainesville, first," the man replied. "Then I've got to go into South Carolina, towards Spartanburg. Look, are you going to tell me how to get to Wheelerville?"

"We'll do better than that," Townsend said. "We'll take you there."

He nodded to Sam Wallins. "Blindfold him," he said. "And see you do a good job of it. You'll be bringing him to Fairlawn. Take Reeves with you."

**   **   **

Lavinia took a deep breath and gazed west toward the distant mountains. Callie spoke of it as 'lifting up the eyes toward the hills', and said that strength and blessings came to those who did so. She had spent most of the day tending the wounded, soothing Private Pierce's worries, and dealing with Louise's complaints, which showed no sign of abating in volume or impertinence. She had followed all that by trying to cope with a rare, and annoying, temper tantrum from Meg that had resulted in the child being sent to her room. She had descended the stairs and plunged herself into writing up and reviewing a list of supplies she thought her household would need for the winter. And all of this had been done to a backdrop of Callie moaning about her rheumatism. Now she felt as though she needed strength, and the sooner the better.

Geese were crying far overhead; she looked up to see a long skein of them raveling against the lowering sun. The mountains were knife-edged against the sky; the year was drawing to a cold close. She drew her shawl closer about herself and spared a quick thought for her list of supplies.

She had laid by yams and sweet potatoes, had preserved the summer's fruits and vegetables, had potted meats and cooked hard bread against the want that might come. She thought she had enough to care for her household and the wounded, but was she protected against the sort of disaster that she had seen coming from this terrible war?

The geese were growing more distant. Lavinia watched them with a touch of envy. At least they could flee the want and privation while she and hers had to remain where they were and face what came. Others might call it cowardice, but she thought 'common sense' was a better word.

She shook her head and turned her thoughts to more profitable channels. She had enough: unless an army corps descended upon her, there would be no want. She began to smile. For that matter, even if an army corps were to descend upon her, it would find nothing, unless it knew where to find her hiding places, scattered throughout the woods.

They wouldn't know, she thought. The rows of glistening glass jars would remain right where they were, untouched except at Lavinia's direction. There was game in the woods and corn in the barns and hidden throughout the property. With the grace of God they would get by, as people had done for generations before her.

Her smile faded. No, she might as well face things, she thought. She was not afraid of privation. She was afraid of those guerrillas. She drew a deep breath, willing herself to recall the sense of assurance she had felt when she had discussed it with Sergeant Sheppard. The fear receded after a moment. She had allies, after all, and people were ready to fight. She knew how to shoot a pistol, and Sergeant Sheppard had said he was going to take her out behind the house and show her how to load and fire a musket. She would learn, and while she was learning, she would pretend that she was firing at the men who had raped and murdered Meg's kinfolk. Who knew? She might even find learning enjoyable.

In the mean time, she had best get indoors again. Private Pierce was to be fed bacon for his evening meal, the first really solid food he had been allowed since he was wounded. She had selected a side of bacon and would slice four good pieces from it, fry them, drain them well and mince them fine. She thought she could serve them along with some spoon bread: it should perk him right up.

She sighed. Maybe it would take his mind off Louise's lies. She prayed it would, at any rate. She smoothed her apron with a sigh, lifted the keys from their ring at her waist, and started toward the door. If only the Sergeant would allow her to send Louise away! But no, he would not hear of it, saying that it was unchristian and cruel. She sniffed at the thought. Cutting Louise's head off with a dull knife would be cruel. Sending her away at once was commonsense.

Motion across the lawn halted her; she pushed her spectacles back up her nose and frowned. Four mounted men were coming toward her. She recognized Haller Reeves at once by the utterly graceless way he sat his horse. Sam Wallins was behind him, following another man she had never seen before. Abner Wigfall was bringing up the rear.

She went to the head of the porch steps and awaited them. Now that the men were closer, she could see that the unknown man was blindfolded and riding a mule that was piled high with sacks of some kind.

"Afternoon, Miss Lavinia," Sam Wallins called, lifting his hat to her as he reined his horse in beside the blindfolded man. "There's a fellow here wants to see you."

"Why is this man blindfolded?" Lavinia demanded.

"Pure caution," Wallins replied. He was working at the knot of the blindfold as he spoke. "This fellow was carrying a safe-conduct signed by General Sherman, among others. He was asking about Fairlawn. Al Townsend sent us to escort him here, but he thought it best to secure him." He had the blindfold in his hand now, and the man beside him was blinking in the waning light. "There you are, friend," said Wallins. "Make your curtsey to Miss Wheeler.

The man, seeing Lavinia, lifted his hat. "Pleasure, Ma'am," he said. "My name is Lucius Adams, from Spartanburg. I'm peaceable: I've got some messages here to deliver."

"Messages?" Lavinia repeated.

"Letters from home," the man replied. "I was staying around Atlanta till now, and I'll be heading toward Gainesville and then Spartanburg after I leave here."

"He came through Yankee lines, Miss Lavinia," Reeves said. "He's got a pass signed by Sherman, and by General Stanley, too—the fellow who came through here back in May. There's one from General Hood, too."

"It seems, sir, as though you are well vouched for," Lavinia said.

The man had been unknotting one of the sacks at his right thigh. He looked up with a grin. "I guess you could say that, Ma'am," he said. "Yankee or Reb, no one minds letting a messenger through, once they're sure he's on the up-and-up. I've a message from General Stanley for you—" He offered it to Lavinia with a bow. "The general was anxious that I deliver it to you right away, and he said to send his kindest personal regards."

Lavinia scanned the address and began to smile; the handwriting was the same as that on the Order. She looked up to see the man rummaging in his saddlebags.

He took out a thick packet of papers as she watched, and scanned the superscript. "Say, ma'am," he said. "Do you have a fellow named Byron Pierce here? I've surely got a bushel of news for him!"

CHAPTER THIRTY-SIX

Asa Sheppard halted Dixie in sight of the house and, against his usual practice, dismounted, loosened her girth and ran the stirrups up the leathers. For all his brave talk to Lavinia the night before, he was tired and disheartened. The guerrillas' depredations were continuing, from what he had seen on this day's patrol. Caesar's people had brought word of other establishments being despoiled and molested, and it was obvious to him that Wheelerville, as the most prosperous settlement in the area, was certainly in danger.

He reached the stable and paused to lift Dixie's saddle from her back and set it on the fence rail just outside the door. Thanks to Sheppard's habit of taking the last mile home at an easy amble, the mare was completely cool and only needed a quick brushing. Her winter coat was beginning to come in full and thick, a good sign that the winter would be a harsh one.

He led Dixie into her stall, measured out her grain, and cleaned her feet while she ate. That done, he retrieved the saddle, took it and the bridle into the tackroom, and sat down to inspect the bridle.

"Sergeant? Is that you?"

Sheppard looked up from polishing the bit. Something in the tone of voice didn't sound quite right. "It's me all right, George," he called. "Did you need me?"

"Miss 'Vinnie does," George replied, coming into the tackroom. "She's been asking for you!"

"I'll be right with her, then," Sheppard said, frowning at the buckles on the bridle and fingering a worn spot on the reins. "Just as soon as I finish this."

George took the bridle from him. "It's urgent," he said. "I'll take care of this for you. I ran old Mr. Wheeler's stables here and in Savannah for years until the arthritis got me."

"Then you're a better horseman than me," Sheppard said with a grin. His expression grew a little more serious after a minute. "Is everything all right?"

"Fair to middlin,' " George replied, scraping with his fingertip at a piece of dried saliva on the bit ring. "But you'd best see her quick!"

"But what's wrong?" Sheppard asked. "It's not some new deviltry of that Hamiter woman, is it?"

"I can't say," George replied, his head bent over the bridle. "Best let her tell you." He looked up and added, "Hurry up, now!"

"I'll do that," Sheppard said.

The time it took to go between the stable and the house was occupied with speculation on what new emergency might have arisen to call for the summons. Was it some new mischief of that vicious pale-haired witch? Was Meg sick, maybe? Or Private Pierce having a relapse? He hoped not. He thought he could more easily deal with an attack by bushwhackers than any fresh tragedy among his friends.

He stopped before the front door and looked up at the brightly lit windows. The evening wind was rattling the dry leaves on the alley of oak trees; it died as he listened, and he heard the sound of singing coming from the house.

He quietly opened the door and stood in silence. Singing, indeed, a rich, melodious mezzo-soprano trilling a swift-changing medley of tunes, running from 'Annie Laurie' through to 'Jeannie with the Light Brown Hair'. And the voice itself was so familiar— "Callie?" Sheppard breathed.

"Her full name is Calliope, you know," Lavinia said behind him on the breath of a chuckle. "She was named for the muse of melody—and you can see the name is quite apt!"

Sheppard turned to see Lavinia coming through the doorway to the formal parlor. The lamplight lay warm on her hair, but the glow in her eyes cast the mahogany and gold highlights into the shade. She came to him with her hands outstretched, and drew him back into the parlor.

"Lavinia?" he said as she led him to a chair by the fire. He spoke in a hush, almost afraid to break whatever enchantment had banished the exhaustion, care and grief from her expression and had brought back the pert, laughing girl that he had glimpsed from time to time.

Her eyes were shining, her cheeks flushed. She was all but dancing where she stood, her hands clasping and unclasping before her. "It's happened!" she said. "Oh, Asa! It happened!"

The sight of her in transports was new and beguiling, and Sheppard allowed himself to enjoy the view before calling her to order. "What's happened?" he asked with a smile.

"The miracle, Asa!" she said on a note of breathless laughter. "The miracle we were praying for: it came today!"

"The miracle?" he repeated as her hands tightened on his. "What do you— Do you mean Pierce?"

"Yes! Oh Asa, only imagine! He heard from his wife! A long, lovely letter fit to make anyone weep for joy! And his family, too! The spell is broken and Louise is utterly undone! Oh I could dance for joy!"

** ** **

"So between the letter from his wife— Asa, it was so meltingly romantic, I wanted to cry—with the photograph she had enclosed, showing her looking so plump and wistful, with her wedding ring held in plain view, and the letters from his mother, his three sisters, his neighbors and everyone else from his home town, there was no room for even the tiniest sliver of doubt. Someone—I think it was his brother; at any rate, the note was just the sort of nonsense a brother would write—anyhow, he wrote that Mr. Pierce's wife was missing him so badly, all she could do was talk of him, and everyone was getting sick of hearing his name."

Sheppard sat back with a grin. "That must have eased him a lot," he said.

"Oh it did, I promise!" Lavinia said. "And then his mother wrote that she had taken the girl into her house so she could be properly cared for while she was awaiting the baby. She—Private Pierce's wife, Asa—she sent him a locket with flowers made from her hair and a portrait in watercolors painted by a friend."

"I'll have to see it," Sheppard said.

"You won't be able to avoid it," Lavinia said. "He's been showing it to everyone." She looked down to hide a smile.

Sheppard watched her, entranced by the glow in her cheeks. "Now what are you laughing at?" he demanded.

Lavinia dimpled and pushed her spectacles up her nose. "Well..." she said. "That portrait doesn't really favor her, unless the photographs I've seen are unbelievably flattering, which I can't believe. In fact, the portrait is wretched, but don't tell him that. He's besotted. Everyone's seen the locket and exclaimed over it, so you will, too. And you'd better not laugh when you see it, either, or I'll—Well, I'll give you a scolding, anyhow! He's keeping her letter under his pillow."

Sheppard sighed, sat back and closed his eyes. "Thank God," he said.

"Amen," said Lavinia.

Sheppard tilted his head against the chair back. "Now tell me," he said, still smiling. "Where did this miraculous letter spring from?"

Lavinia was watching his expression. "General Stanley sent them," she said. She nodded as he opened his eyes. "Yes," she said. "That day he came to visit me and view the cemetery, we sat and spoke at some length. He told me he would notify the families of the convalescents here, and he said he would try to send on any letters that came, if it were in his power. That is what he did, and Private Pierce is happy again."

Her voice had dropped slightly. "Asa," she said.

He opened his eyes.

"Now that everything is going well," she said slowly, "Don't you think it's a good time to send Louise away from here? She could pack tonight and leave at first light tomorrow."

Sheppard sat forward. "Absolutely not," he said.

"But now that we have some good news, we don't want her around any more."

"That's the truest word anyone's spoken," Sheppard said. "But it's out of the question."

"Oh Asa! Then I must put up with her constant sneaking and lying and malice? And Meg must be in danger from her venom? In Heaven's name, why?"

"There's a large group of bushwhackers operating around here," Sheppard said. "You know it very well! I can't spare the men to escort her, and anyone who is traveling alone is in danger. Do I have to remind you of the Pike family? Or of Meg's family, come to that?"

"No, you do not," Lavinia said, annoyed. "But you're being unreasonable! She's not in any danger!"

Sheppard stared at her. "You don't believe that," he said. "And I'll tell you something else: if she were to leave here and be molested by those brutes, you would never forgive yourself."

"I would probably cheer them on," Lavinia said. She eyed his expression. "Oh very well," she said in disgust. "You're right, as usual. But if only there were some way to send her away from here. She'll give me a fit of the vapors yet! You should have heard her complaining all day!"

"I am sorry," Sheppard said. "Believe me, I don't want her here any more than you do." He sighed and closed his eyes again. When he spoke again, it was to change the subject. "I can hardly believe that letter came for Pierce," he said.

"There were quite a few," Lavinia said. "Some came for the men who've died."

"I'll write their families," Sheppard said. "I don't know how to send the word, but we'll find a way."

"I should be the one to write," Lavinia said. "I was with so many of them in their last moments. I kept an account, in case their families came after the war."

Sheppard had opened one hazel eye and was smiling at her. "You are priceless, Lavinia," he said.

"The men are all so happy tonight," Lavinia said. "No one here was forgotten..." She watched Sheppard. "Asa..." she said. "Aren't you even going to ask if you got a packet?"

Both eyes snapped open. "I did?" he said.

She took a well-stuffed envelope from the table beside her. "It's about time you asked!" she said, offering it to him with a suppressed smile. "From the feel of it, there are some photographic cards in there."

He took it from her and looked at the writing. "My sister wrote this," he said.

"Indeed? Is she taking care of your concerns, then?" Lavinia asked, folding her hands neatly in her lap.

Sheppard took out his pocket knife and cut the envelope open. "She's taking care of my children," he said. "She and her husband are childless, and she's been a mother to mine since Sarah died." He looked thoughtful for a moment. "I don't know what she'll do when I return. If I return..."

"Dear Heaven!" Lavinia gasped. "Don't say that!"

He unfolded the letter and scanned it with a spreading smile, then looked up at her. "I'm sorry," he said. He handed her a small packet of photographs after a moment. "Here," he said. "Look at these while I read."

Lavinia took them from him and eyed the images set on their pasteboard backers. Three children looked solemnly up at her from between her fingers. She offered them back to him. "Shouldn't you see them first?" she asked.

He looked up from the letter and shook his head with a smile. "I'll spend the night gloating over them, most likely," he said. "Go on ahead. I'll take them when you're done."

Lavinia looked down at the photographs. The top one showed Sheppard's children looking noticeably more grown than the one she had seen in May. The daughter, Lydia, was shaping up to be a little beauty, while Jesse, the oldest, was a younger version of his father. She could see the pearl-handled penknife tucked into a pocket.

She smiled and set the photograph aside. The next one showed a woman who looked to be about ten years younger than Sheppard, with the same eyes and mouth. It was odd to see that those features that were appealing on a man could also be pretty on a woman. She was wearing a velvet cloak with an ermine capelet, tippet and muff. She was standing beside a draped column, one hand tucked into the arm of a tall man who appeared to have been forced to stand too long at the photographer's brace, which was visible just beyond his feet.

Lavinia turned the photograph over and read the back. 'Rebecca and Charles Ruland. December, 1863.' A recent photograph, then. She looked more closely at the faces. Rebecca—Sheppard's sister?—had the hint of a smile in her eyes and a faintly quirky mouth that spoke of a lively sense of humor. She could be a friend, perhaps, if they ever met.

Lavinia looked down and slid the last photograph from beneath the one of Rebecca. Her mouth was suddenly dry, and she could feel a quiver in her fingertips.

Asa Sheppard, in the uniform of an ordnance sergeant, was smiling down at a woman dressed in dark, shiny taffeta with a lace shawl about her shoulders. Her waving hair framed her face in wings, and Lavinia could see a very fine brooch at her throat, and what looked to be gold drops in her ears. She was looking straight at the camera with the hint of a smile. She had a pleasant, calm face, but there was a hint of fatigue about the mouth. Sheppard's arm was about her waist, and the woman's hand lay atop his with easy affection.

Lavinia lifted the photograph of the children and eyed their faces and then the woman's before turning the woman's photograph over and reading the back. 'Asa and Sarah Sheppard. January, 1862.'

Asa and Sarah Sheppard.

Lavinia gently set the photograph down and looked over at Sheppard, who was reading his letter with a wide, happy smile.

"S-Sergeant," she said. He looked up at her.

"Is... Is this your wife?" she asked, offering the photograph.

He took the photograph from her and gazed at it, his smile fading to something at once deeper and more sad. "Yes," he said. "That was Sarah. I had forgotten that we'd had this taken. My sister had been begging us for years to have our portrait taken, so we finally did. Sarah hated cameras and said they made her ugly."

"She wasn't ugly from that picture," Lavinia said.

"No," said Sheppard. "She wasn't ugly at all. She was carrying Caleb then."

"She died bearing him, didn't she?" Lavinia asked.

"Yes." Sheppard's voice was quiet and the smile had faded a little. "I was fighting at Pittsburgh Landing while she lay dying, and I didn't know it. I didn't get the word for a month." His voice quivered on the edge of a break and then steadied.

"I'm sorry," Lavinia said.

The corners of his eyes were taut with remembered grief as he looked beyond her. His gaze shortened to her after a moment. "Why should you be?" he asked, handing the photograph back. "Peacetime has its casualties as well as war. It's something we all must learn to live with."

CHAPTER THIRTY-SEVEN

Lavinia set the enameled silver hairbrush down with a happy sigh and gathered her hair at the nape of her neck. She divided it into three parts with nimble fingertips and plaited it into a thick braid that hung to her hips. Years of familiarity had inured her to the beauty of the glossy, red-brown cord; she pushed her spectacles down her nose with a fingertip, frowned at its end, tied a length of ribbon around it, and flipped it back over her shoulder.

She was almost ready for bed. The dress she had worn that day lay neatly folded on the chair beside the door, her nightcap, carefully starched and pressed, was waiting to be donned and tied under her chin, and Waverly lay half-finished on the stand beside her bed, a slip of paper marking her place. A lamp, filled with cottonseed oil, sat beside the bed, which had been smoothed and turned down. There were some matters to tend to before she slid between the cool, smooth sheets and piled the pillows behind her shoulders.

She removed her spectacles, folded them, and set them on her dressing table, then took up the small Bible that her great-grandfather Wheeler had taken with him to Savannah from Massachusetts. She smoothed the worn leather with a fingertip, then opened it and read her evening's passage from the second epistle to the Corinthians, smiling at the final verse as she closed it and set it aside.

Thanks be to God for His unspeakable gift.

Unspeakable, indeed! she thought as she smoothed the cuffs of her nightgown. Who could have thought that that smiling, nondescript messenger with his battered slouch hat and dejected mule would bring such joy with him that Fairlawn fairly rang with it?

It had been like a fair, a festival and a grand fête rolled into one. Callie had been singing right up until the very moment she extinguished her candle for the night. Meg and Bathsheba had joined hands and danced down the hallways to the laughter and applause of those wounded who were able to get around. Corporal Higgins had joined them in a jig, his wooden leg clumping on the golden pine floors, while George limbered up his fiddle and played reels and jigs, quite forgetting his arthritis. Aunt Amabel, pink-cheeked and laughing, had hurried to the piano and played along.

There were only two somber notes in the entire evening. Louise had retired to her rooms pleading a headache. She had not had to plead very hard to be excused. And Sergeant Sheppard had arisen after reading his letter, folded it and put it into his jacket, and then excused himself, saying that he had some urgent business to attend to in town. Sheppard had spent most of the evening in town with Al Townsend and the messenger, discussing various things. The disposition of troops, most likely, or what the messenger had observed on his way from Atlanta to Wheelerville. His absence had cast something of a shadow over Lavinia's enjoyment.

The messenger had said that he would be departing the next day, or the one after, heading for Gainesville. He had offered to carry any letters anyone cared to send with him, and Lavinia had prepared a nice, thick packet for him.

She looked at General Stanley's note, lying on the dresser, and smiled again, remembering some of its elegantly turned phrases and the sense of sincerity and concern that she had received from it.

I take this opportunity to redeem the promise I made to you, Dear Madam, during my last visit to Fairlawn, and I regret that the exigencies of the current situation prevent me from performing that glad duty in person. For better of for worse, when this conflict has reached an end, I pledge to do myself and my wife, Eleanor, the honor of calling upon you in friendship, and in behalf of my lady, who asks that I convey her kindest regards to one she terms 'a lady of true Christian charity and beauty', I extend to you her invitation to visit us in Boston, should circumstances ever permit you making such a journey. Your welcome, and that of anyone who has the honor of your friendship, is assured.

She was smiling as she set the letter down. Such a gentleman, and such a fine man, to remember his wounded and make provisions to send their letters from home on to them. When this war was over, if Fairlawn was in a condition to allow it, she certainly would invite the general and his lady to come and visit her. The journey from Savannah to Wheelerville could be accomplished in under a week, and she would enjoy playing hostess again.

She let her mind toy with the idea. It would be so good to entertain at Fairlawn once more. Or perhaps, if the General and his lady came in December, she could have them stay at her home in Savannah. From what was said in this letter and the previous communications from the general's headquarters, Sergeant Sheppard obviously held a high place in General Stanley's regard; he would be there, as well, along with his children.

Lavinia turned her thoughts away from Miles and Eleanor Stanley, and thought instead of Jesse, Lydia and Caleb Sheppard. She would enjoy showing the eldest, Jesse, all the spots along the creek where she had found nice, fat trout. She would sit little Caleb and Meg on her lap together and tell them stories. And Lydia would probably enjoy learning embroidery, if Sergeant Sheppard's sister, Rebecca, had not already started teaching her. Rebecca and her husband could visit as well...

She faltered a little. Would Rebecca like her? Or would she view Lavinia as an enemy who sought to steal her foster-children's affections away? Daunting thought! But she brightened after a moment. It was too happy a day to spend any time worrying, and she refused to believe that a blood relation of Asa Sheppard could be petty and suspicious. They would be friends, the Stanleys would come to be friends as well, and the children would romp through fields and along streams from which the threat of death and destruction had been banished. The thought was deliciously warming, and it was not so implausible as she might once have thought.

Blessed, blessed day to have brought such hope back to her!

She paused, eyeing her bed, then squared her shoulders and reached for the apple-green brocade dressing-gown that hung on its peg on the wall. She had some visits to make before she settled down for the night.

** ** **

"She looks so pretty and happy in that photograph!" Lavinia said, handing the photograph back to Private Pierce and taking up her candle. "Now all that remains for you to do is make certain you get back home so you can be happy along with her."

Private Pierce's expression was a little somber as he took the photograph from her and gazed at it. "There's so much that could still go wrong..." he said. "Doc Meacham tells me I maybe won't be able to do a lot of the things I used to. Like ride, or even maybe swim..."

"Oh boo-hoo," growled the man in the bed next to him, who had lost a leg and one hand.

"Well, I mean it," Pierce said. "I used to go through the woods all the time—"

Corporal Higgins sat up. "You were doing that right up to the time you stopped a bullet," he said through a grin. "Don't tell me you're longing for the bad old days! I always thought you were soft in your head!"

The sally was greeted with laughter.

Lavinia shook her head at them. "You're talking like a child," she told Pierce. "Of course you'll have to slow down as you get older, no matter what happens. How many people do you know that can do at forty what they did at fifteen?" She saw that he, at twenty-three did not quite understand her; she shook her head. "Never mind," she said. "I've spoken with Dr. Meacham, myself. You may not be able to do strenuous things—though he's not certain yet—and you'll have to be careful what you eat. But a lot of people who haven't been wounded have those restrictions and live comfortably with them. I don't think you'll find them as irksome as you fear."

Hope was very new to him. He looked down at the photograph, his fingers smoothing his wife's cheek. "Maybe not," he said.

"Certainly not," she returned. She smiled down the line of beds at the men who were watching her and returning her smile. She leaned closer to Pierce and said firmly, "And I have a prediction to make about all of you: you will be happy for many years! I feel it in my soul!"

She straightened and took up her candle. "Rest and recover and make your families' happiness complete," she said. "You'll be making me happy, too!"

Private Pierce set the photograph in its hiding place under his pillow. He was relaxed and smiling now, the hectic color gone from his cheeks, the glazed, restless expression from his eyes. "Miss Lavinia?"

he said.

"Hush!" she said. "What is it?"

"I was stupid to-to take on like I did. I didn't mean to be any trouble, but I know I caused you worry. You've been such an angel, I'd have died rather than trouble you, but I— But I wasn't thinking very well, I guess."

"You were ill," she said. "You aren't any more. Stop worrying about things."

He smiled at her. "I guess I will now," he said.

"See that you do," Lavinia said. "Now try to get some sleep. There'll be time to rejoice in the morning."

Pierce was blushing. "If..." he began. He swallowed, took a breath, and started again. "If I had to get wounded, it's a blessing from God I was wounded so I could have met you. I... I wish I hadn't been so much trouble."

"Hush now," she said again. "And this time I mean it! None of you have been any trouble, except that I want each of you to recover. And so I still do. It's been a joyous day for all of you, and it'll be a happy night, as well. Now all of you: close your eyes and get the sleep you need to get strong! That's an order: Do you hear me?"

She was rewarded by a growl of laughter and several surprisingly snappy salutes. She returned the smiles of the men around her, and left the ballroom, carrying her candle with her.

** ** **

She paused in the hallway and looked around. The house was dark and quiet now; the sigh of the night wind through the trees lining the alley was the only sound disturbing the silence. She lifted the small watch that hung at her waist and peered at its face by the light of her candle: 10:30. Long past her time to be in bed, but she was not even the slightest bit sleepy.

A faint hint of tobacco, tingeing the wind that pushed its way through the cracks about the door, made her smile suddenly, gather the skirts of her dressing-gown, and step onto the veranda.

Sergeant Sheppard was sitting in one of the porch rockers, as motionless in the night as one of the pillars. The glow of his pipe was a tiny bright spot in the darkness and starlight. He rose, the pipe in his hand, as she came toward him.

"I wondered where you had got to," Lavinia said.

"I was talking with Al Townsend's group," he said. "I took the messenger into Wheelerville and we spent the evening going over some things he had seen. He had a lot to tell us."

Lavinia smiled and sat down in the chair beside him. "'Asa, Asa,' " she paraphrased. "Thou art troubled with many things.' "

"You're a fine one to preach—Martha!" he retorted with the touch of a grin. "And I'm not sure 'troubled' is the right word. It's just that I've been given a lot to think about."

Lavinia decided that he was probably thinking about those guerrillas. She shied away from the thought and raised her eyes to his. "Is your family well?" she asked.

Sheppard smiled around the stem of his pipe. "Very well," he said, taking the pipe from his mouth and setting it on the railing of the balustrade. "You can read the letter yourself tomorrow."

"I'm glad," she said. She looked down at her hands. "I'm sorry you had an old grief come calling unexpectedly," she said in a small voice.

He looked thoughtful. "If you mean Sarah's photograph," he said slowly, "that was not a grief. There's nothing to regret: we were happy together, and though she died before me, I'll always love her, as she'll always love me. You can't lose something you've loved, even though it may have died. It's always a part of you, as close to you as your own heart. I didn't realize that at the time Sarah died: it's not something you can understand until you've gone through it. I think Meg has some inkling of it, though. It's odd: she's so young, but I sense that she'll be a remarkable woman when she's grown." His eyes raised to hers and crinkled a little at the corners. "Like you, a little, Lavinia," he said.

Something warm and alive in his voice, the hint of things set in motion long ago and now approaching fruition, of conclusions, hinted at when she had not been paying attention, becoming indisputable and concrete no matter what she might now say or do, made her shiver with an emotion strangely like dread.

He rose and held out his hand to her. "You shouldn't be outside like this," he said. "You'll catch cold without a coat, and then where would we all be without you?"

To her unspectacled eyes the outline of his face was slightly blurred, but she could see his hand outstretched toward her. She reached for it and felt it close around her fingers.

The strange, half-breathless sense of dread eased. "I thought you could bring your children here after the war," she said as he bent to retrieve his pipe. "You could come visit, and your sister and her husband could come as well." She tried to laugh. "I guess I was daydreaming," she said. "But the pictures in my mind were so clear, so distinct, I could not deny them. would so love meeting Jesse and Lydia and Caleb, and we could continue friends as before..."

"'When this cruel war is over,' " Sheppard quoted. "'Pray that we meet again."

"Oh we will," Lavinia said. "How could we not? I said I didn't want to lose you."

"And I said you wouldn't lose me," he replied. "Ever."

The intent quality of the words could not be denied, nor could the hint of a question in the way they were spoken.

Having no answer, Lavinia remained silent, her heart thundering so loudly she thought he must surely be able to hear it.

He had stopped speaking for the moment, but Lavinia seemed to hear an echo of the timbre of his voice in the sigh of the breeze through the dry leaves along the alley of oaks. When he spoke again, it was as softly as the wind, so that she did not at once realize that it was him speaking.

"Lavinia..."

She looked up at him, her eyes, without their spectacles, wide and unfocussed. "Asa?" she said.

"Meg will be as remarkable as you are, Lavinia," he said. "And if God is good to those who love her, she will be as warm and as beautiful as you have been to me from the moment I saw you that morning in May."

Her hand was still in his. He looked down at her for a long moment, then gently drew her to him, bent and kissed her forehead.

Her right hand closed about his. "We'd best go inside now, Sergeant," she said as her left hand freed itself despite her words and rose to smooth his cheek and the thick, soft hair that curved along his temple. She regretted the fact that the lack of her spectacles, lying atop her dresser, prevented her from reading his expression as he released her and stepped back.

"It's been such a long day, Asa," she said, "and you need your rest if you're going to be a guardian and a stronghold for everyone who needs you." She paused for a moment, weighing her words, and then added carefully, "As you have been for me since I first met you that lovely May morning."

CHAPTER THIRTY-EIGHT

Lavinia opened her eyes to the glow of sunlight streaming in through her window. From the angle of the sun she must have slept later than usual. She could hear Callie's supple voice trilling hymns away down the hall. The singing was approaching her door: Callie bearing a breakfast tray, no doubt. She was hungry; she hoped there would be hot chocolate with cinnamon for her.

Lavinia stretched, her hands high above her head, and then lay back, smoothing the coverlet and trying to remember what it was that had made her so happy the night before. She stopped trying after a moment. It did not matter, she thought, she would remember it presently, and in the mean time she had a day to plan.

She gazed at the bright window. If it were as fine outside as the sunlight seemed to show, she would have Jupiter saddled and ride toward the hills. She might be able to persuade her father to accompany her; she could ask Callie to have Cook pack a picnic lunch. They could engage in an impromptu steeplechase; Jupiter loved to jump.

She reviewed her wardrobe in her mind, her eyes half-closed. The habit of moss-colored serge would be best, she thought. It was such a becoming shade and cut, and she always felt pretty when she wore it.

She yawned again and pulled herself more upright, sparing a moment to wonder why she was in her parents' bedroom rather than her own. She smiled after a moment. Of course. They were in Savannah already, getting things settled for the winter, and she was lingering within sight of the mountains here. She always hated to leave Wheelerville: it held all her happiest memories.

The thought brought the question once again: what had made her so happy the night before?

She heard a tap at the door and sat up, beaming. "Come on in!" she called, and watched as the door swung open, seemingly of its own accord, to show Callie coming toward her with a covered tray.

Lavinia's smile grew gentler. Dear Callie! She was growing more frail, she could see. In fact, she was getting too old for the sort of work she was being asked to do. Lavinia had been talking with her father about Callie, intending to bring him around to the point where he would allow her to purchase the woman-and then make some long-needed changes to make her life easier.

He had been unexpectedly resistant, even evasive to the point of stubbornness, if such an uncomplicated and not overly intelligent man could be described as evasive. It was a little puzzling, but Lavinia had never found her father's occasional obstinacy much of a challenge. She had brought him to heel on far more serious questions of business; she would bring him around without too much trouble.

Callie had paused just inside the door. "How are you this morning, Lamb?" she asked.

"I've never been better, Callie," Lavinia said, eyeing the tray. "I'm so hungry I could eat Jupiter, saddle and all! And I'm all set for some of your chocolate!"

Callie stared. "Chocolate?" she demanded. "We haven't had chocolate since the war began!"

The beautiful, sun-drenched morning seemed to grow dark for a moment as Lavinia's lips framed the words: the war.

She stared from Callie, who had suddenly grown grayer and more bent, to the little girl who stood beside her.

"Morning, Mama!" the girl chirped as Callie bent to give her the tray.

Lavinia sat back against her pillows, gazing blankly at the window as the beautiful memories slipped away one by one. There would be no steeplechase with Jupiter, and her father would never again ride beside her. All gone never to return in this life.

Lavinia looked back to watch the child make her way across the carpeted floor with Callie moving behind her. A name came to her as the girl turned a flushed and beaming face up toward her. "Good morning...Meg," she said.

"You be careful with that tray now, hear?" Callie said, watching her with a smile. She looked at Lavinia. "You were dreaming, Vinnie," she said.

"I was," Lavinia said, piling her pillows behind her. She knew where she was, and when she was, but she had the sense that a very important piece of information was missing. "I dreamed this war never happened, Papa was alive, and I still had Jupiter." She took the tray from Meg. "Thank you, Poppet," she said, lifting the cover. A plate of biscuits, fried ham and gravy sat before her, with a bowl of preserved fruits to the side and a small porcelain pot of coffee beyond it.

She looked up to see Callie watching her.

"I wish it were true for you, Vinnie," Callie said.

"If it were true," Lavinia said slowly, "I wouldn't have Meg, here. And I would still be trying to talk my father into letting you go. Some memories are best left as memories. Callie, what happened yesterday?"

Callie stared. "Yesterday?" she repeated. "Why, you're dreaming still! Letters came, a whole bushel of them! That poor Private Pierce is happy again—"

"Papa showed me a picture of my brothers and my sister," Meg said, taking out a photograph with grubby fingers and offering it to Lavinia.

The final piece of the puzzle fell into place as Lavinia took the photograph and smiled down at the solemn, chubby faces. That was why she was happy. She gave the photograph back. "Thank you for my breakfast," she said, lifting her fork and spearing a chunk of fried ham.

"Can I sit with you?" Meg asked.

"Certainly," Lavinia said, bringing the fork to her lips. "And you can help finish what I can't eat."

"Don't let her eat too much," Callie said. "She had more than her share today." Her color heightened slightly. "I thought to celebrate, so I made the men hominy, bacon and flapjacks."

The ham was smoky and dry. Lavinia took a swallow of coffee. "You're growing strong, darling," she said, "to carry this all by yourself."

"Papa says I'm getting to be an armful," Meg said as she looked down at the photograph. "He says I'm littler than Lydia, but bigger than Caleb. Does that make me Lydia's little sister?"

Lavinia cut off another piece of ham and offered it to Meg. "Why, I think it does," she said as Meg obediently opened her mouth.

"Can I help you brush your hair?" Meg asked around the ham.

"Finish chewing before you speak," Callie said.

Lavinia smiled at Callie and broke open a biscuit. "You can brush my hair after I'm dressed, Darling," she told Meg. "If you come back in ten minutes I'll be ready for you."

Meg nodded and slid from the bed. "You can watch my picture," she said. Her face grew a little sad. "My mama in heaven had a picture of her and me," she said. "It was in a shiny black box with curlicues and flowers on the outside and a gold thing on the inside around the picture. Mama looked pretty in it. She was wearing a pretty dress, before she started just wearing black. I sure wish I had that here."

"Well, you have this one," Lavinia said, accepting the photograph from her. "And I have a gutta-percha box we can put it in."

"What's gutty percha?" Meg asked.

Lavinia patted Meg's cheek. "Gutta-percha," she repeated. "It's the shiny, black material they make photograph cases from. I'll get one for you after breakfast. Ten minutes now, mind. I'll be waiting!"

She smiled as Meg and Callie left the room, then looked down the photograph of the Sheppard children and turned it over in her hand. Her smile faded slightly as she saw the stain of blood on the back. It was the one taken the year before, that he had been carrying when he was wounded.

She turned it again and looked down at the three faces gazing back at her. Lydia, Caleb and Jesse, who was proudly holding his pearl-handled knife.

"Maybe someday," she said to them, and set them down on the counterpane while she finished her breakfast.

** ** **

"General Stanley said he'd give me a pass that would take me through his lines and let me head toward Gainesville, but only if I would agree to go to Wheelerville first," the messenger, Lucius Adams, said. "I told him I would, and he gave me the pass and asked General Sherman to do the same." He nodded to Sergeant Sheppard and addressed himself to the plate of breakfast before him.

"Some people would wonder why you didn't take the messages and burn them, once free of the Yankees, and head where you pleased," Sheppard said with a smile.

The messenger shot him a disgusted look and ate another forkful of hominy. "I gave my word," he said with dignity. "And broken promises come back to haunt you. Besides that, I'd heard from General

Stanley that the people at Wheelerville were especially fine—
specifically Miss Wheeler."

Sheppard smiled and sipped at his coffee. It was eight o'clock and
he had already been up and about for over three hours, taking care of
concerns involving provisions and the placing of guards. From what
Adams had told him the night before, the renegades were not far away
at all, and it was time to be doubly vigilant.

That to the side, he had not been sleepy. The night had been a time
to remember and reflect, to look back at the past with gratitude and the
future with hope.

"Speaking of Miss Wheeler," Adams said, "I hope she'll be here
soon. I don't like to leave without saying my farewells. From what
General Stanley said, I wouldn't have expected her to be a slugabed."

"She isn't one," Sheppard said with a wry smile. "She's up with the
sun most days. That's not a good thing, either: she takes a lot upon
herself as the mistress of this plantation and town, and she isn't strong.
If she's sleeping late today, it's a good thing, and she's earned it."

Adams looked at him and shook his head. "She's quite a lady from
what I hear," he said.

"She's an angel," Sheppard said. "I can testify to that. She took in
some severely wounded men right after the fighting here: seventy of
them, no less. Not only that, but she took them into her house and
nursed them herself without any sort of rest. It's thanks to her charity
and self-sacrifice that those of us who survived are all doing so well."

Adams looked at him and then smiled and looked away toward the
door. A second later he was on his feet as Miss Wheeler came into the
room accompanied by Meg. To his sharp eyes it seemed that Miss
Wheeler's color was a little heightened, and she was avoiding looking
at Sergeant Sheppard, who had poured a half cup of coffee and was
busy stirring milk into it.

"Please sit down, Mr. Adams," she said with a smile. When he was
seated once again she said, "I regret my lateness. I assure you I am not
lazy by nature."

"That was explained to me, Ma'am," Adams said. "Not that I had
any doubts about it, to be sure."

Lavinia lifted her eyebrows at Sergeant Sheppard, who handed her
the cup with a warm smile. "I see," she said.

Meg elbowed herself up into Sheppard's lap. "Do you like her hair,

Papa?" she asked. "I brushed it myself!"

Sheppard eyed the braided chignon with a smile. "It's beautiful, Sweetheart," he said. "But then it always is."

"I like it best when she takes the pins out and lets it down," Meg said. "Don't you?"

"I wouldn't know," Sheppard replied.

Lavinia ignored them with some difficulty. "You told me that you are leaving today, Mr. Adams," she said. "You are welcome to remain here and rest before you continue."

Meg was watching with wide eyes. "Maybe you can brush her hair for her, Papa," she said. "I'll bet she'll let you if you say please."

The table fell silent. Lavinia, looking everywhere but at Sergeant Sheppard, felt her color rising. To make matters worse, Aunt Amabel came through the door followed by Callie and Bathsheba. By their expressions, they had heard the entire exchange.

"Good morning, Aunt Amabel," Lavinia said as Sheppard and Adams rose to their feet.

"Why don't you ask her, Papa?" Meg pursued.

Sheppard sat down again, settled Meg on his knee, and said, with the trace of a quiver in his voice. "No, Peanut. Grownup men don't brush grownup ladies' hair unless they're married. Since I'm not married to Miss Lavinia, I can't brush her hair, even if it is pretty, so it's no use for me to ask her. Do you understand me?"

"Oh," Meg said. She digested things in silence and then brightened. "Can I try some coffee?" she asked.

Bathsheba dimpled and poured her a thimbleful in a cup, and then added three thimblefuls of milk.

Aunt Amabel took the chair offered by Adams and smiled up at him. "It would be a pleasure to have you stay here, Mr. Adams," she said. "I add my voice to Miss Wheeler's."

Adams was seated again. "Thank you kindly for the invite," he said, scooping up a forkful of hominy and eggs, "But I'd best move on today. I have kin in Gainesville and in Spartanburg, South Carolina, and I've had some news that requires that I go to them."

"Dear Heavens!" Aunt Amabel said. "I surely hope it isn't bad news!"

"Not at all," Adams said. "Everyone's safe and well, from what I hear. No, it's my sister's family. Her man's in Virginia and she needs someone to take care of some business for her, so I said I'd go. I never thought I'd tangle with the Federals outside Atlanta. It delayed me a couple weeks: it's fortunate I encountered General Stanley when I did, or I'd still be there!"

"Then of course you must leave today," Lavinia said. "I'll send some provisions with you, and the people of this town can see you safely on your way."

"I take that very kindly, Ma'am," Adams said. "And I'll surely be happy to carry any messages your people care to send that way!"

** ** **

By the time Lucius Adams left for Gainesville he had his saddle-bags stuffed full of letters, a generous-sized haversack full of supplies, and three of Al Townsend's men as an escort as far as North Canton. His departure had been slightly delayed; Aunt Amabel kept remembering people she wanted to send messages to, and Bathsheba was called back to the house twice to bring them out.

She came running light-footedly to Adams the last time with two envelopes in her hands and a wide smile warming her face. "That's it from the house!" she panted, offering the envelopes. The top one had a spot on it that caught Lavinia's attention for a moment until Bathsheba spoke again. "I'm sorry I took so long, but Miss Louise called me at the last minute and said she had a message too!"

Louise. Lavinia had not thought of her all that day, and she felt a twinge of remorse for the omission. For all her faults, Louise was far from home and had friends and family to write to just like anyone else. It was just as well she had gotten the word and been given the chance to write. She turned from watching Adams take the envelopes to see Sheppard frowning at the packets. "What is it?" she asked.

He blinked and looked down at her. "Nothing," he said. "I noticed a spot on one of the letters, but it just means someone's pen blotted the paper. Say, Adams," he said, raising his voice, "Good luck and God-speed! You've given me some good information."

"I just hope you don't have to use it," Adams said, setting his heels to his mount. "Ma'am, your servant!" he said, and was away.

He was whistling as he rode off with his escort, trailing a group of Fairlawn's children, who laughed and chattered behind him. Lavinia, standing beside Sergeant Sheppard, watched him go; he turned to wave at them, and she watched him diminish along the line of oaks edging the approach to the town.

He waved once more and then spurred his horse to a trot. The next moment he was lost to their sight in the grove of beeches, as though he had been suddenly cut off.

Just as though he had been killed, Lavinia thought, gazing at the flickering leaves. The thought chilled her; it seemed all at once that the sun had lost its warmth. She drew her shawl more closely around herself and looked up, shivering, to see that the sun still hung, round and bright, in the blue October sky.

Sheppard looked down at her with a touch of worry. "Are you all right?" he asked. "You're shivering."

The feeling of cold was still there. "I felt a chill," Lavinia said, smoothing her shawl about her shoulders. She slipped her hand into the crook of his proffered arm and leaned gratefully on it. "It was as though I might hear of a death, or of some terrible news."

"A goose walked across your grave," he said with the touch of a smile.

She stared up at him. "What does that mean?" she demanded.

"It's what Sarah used to say when she got a sudden chill," Sheppard said. "She'd say 'I guess a goose just walked across my grave!' We always laughed, it sounded so silly." He gazed thoughtfully after Adams and then looked up at the sky, where the west wind was pushing the clouds toward the eastern horizon. "It looks as though we're in for some sort of a change," he said.

Lavinia, clinging to his arm and still feeling the lingering traces of the chill that had shaken her, looked at the clouds and wondered what form the change would take.

CHAPTER THIRTY-NINE

Sam Wallins looked around at the wind-stripped trees two days later. "Looks like it'll be an early winter," he said. "The leaves are all gone now. Sky's getting dark earlier, too."

Al Townsend nodded. "You're right," he said. "It's getting cold, too. An early winter for sure." He looked over at Sergeant Sheppard, sitting at ease in his saddle and frowning southeast toward Atlanta. "What do you think, Asa?"

Sheppard looked back over his shoulder and lifted his eyebrows. "God pity you if you ever come to New York, Al," he said with the hint of a grin, "if you think this is cold." He turned back, settled his reins and said in a different tone of voice, "What did your men find?"

"We left Adams at North Canton with a group heading toward Gainesville," Wallins said. "After that we circled south and west before swinging back this way. We found signs that an army went by— not too big a surprise, considering that we knew General Thomas and his force were heading that way—but there were other signs as well."

"Like what?" Townsend asked.

"Property destroyed, for one," Sam Wallins said. "Houses burned, barns pulled down. Citizens robbed. Everything taken was small, portable and valuable."

"I gather you didn't think it was the 'curst, thieving Yankees' who did it," Sheppard said.

Wallins cocked a sardonic eye at him. "Save it for Haller Reeves," he said. "You might even be able to make him blush now: he's changed. I was going to say that we found all this well away from the route General Thomas took. As though whoever was doing this were afraid to run into his outriders."

"Hm," Sheppard said. "Were they taking any particular direction?"

"Not that we could tell," Wallins replied. "Though we didn't have enough time to do a thorough scout."

"I told them not to leave themselves open to attack," Townsend interjected. "I didn't want anyone killed, and I didn't want them to draw those bastards back this way if they ran into them."

Sheppard nodded.

"They hit here and there," Wallins said. "It seemed to me like they might be trying to cover their tracks, but Haller told me later that he thought it looked as though they were being pretty haphazard, going wherever the urge struck them."

"What worried me," Townsend interjected, "was what they said about the pickings betting pretty slim. Wheelerville is pretty much untouched."

"I see," Sheppard said. "Forewarned is forearmed, as they say. I'd be happier if I knew what we were dealing with, though."

"What's there to know?" Townsend asked. "They're a pack of bastards, that's what we know."

Sheppard shook his head at Townsend. "Besides that," he said. "Where are they holed up? How will they hit?"

"I'd say we know already," Sam Wallins said. "We've seen their work, and we can guess the rest. We surely know how they'll attack and we almost know when."

Sheppard looked thoughtful. "I've an idea it'll be soon," he said.

Townsend lifted his face into the October wind. "Yes, soon," he said. "And I think it'll all be ending soon. Everywhere."

Wallins and Sheppard looked at him.

"I've had a feeling for a while..." Townsend said. His face was uncharacteristically grim. "The dying is happening all over," he said. "I could almost taste it, like something at the back of my throat, when I was with the armies. You can see it every time you turn around. Things are coming to a close, shutting down. Whether for me or this war, I can't say."

Wallins was frowning. "Do you mean people?" he asked.

Townsend gave a brief smile. "Oh, them, certainly. I sure dug my share of graves before they put stripes on my sleeves and said I didn't have to any more... No, I mean things we've known all along, things that were part of our lives."

Wallins' frown deepened. "God Almighty, Al!" he complained. "You're giving me the willies! I don't know what you mean!"

"It's hard to explain," Townsend said. "But... Did you stop to think that however this fight turns out, the big farms like Fairlawn will be gone? There won't be any slaves to run them. Why should they stay here when freedom lies just across the Ohio? Abolition will come, all right. It can't be stopped now, not since they fired on Fort Sumter. Why, just look what Miss Lavinia did. And after all the killing ends, there won't be the manpower to keep the big farms running. There won't be any freemen to work them—the graves are swallowing them all. They'll all be gone, even if the South wins this war."

Townsend looked over at Sheppard, who was nodding thoughtfully. He shook his head. "I don't mean to misuse the Good Book," he said, "but you could say that even victory will be swallowed up in death..."

Sheppard did not comment, but Wallins seemed shaken. "Even the Wheeler's farm?" he asked.

Townsend looked thoughtful. "Well, maybe not that one," he said. "Miss Lavinia had the right idea, freeing her people and having them share the crops. She'll do all right. Her pa or her brother'd be doomed if they had lived and this had been up to them."

"I get the feeling they weren't the smartest," Sheppard said.

"Those fools?" Townsend said. "They couldn't find their butts with both hands and written instructions! My family's known them from way back. My pa was the blacksmith in town. Wallins, here, was his apprentice. They weren't the smartest, nor were they nice. Miss Lavinia had all the brains and the heart for the past two generations. If she'd been born a man, the Wheelers would've given the army a general worth fighting for and worth listening to instead of that gun-shy fool of a brother of hers who died before he even saw a battlefield, and who joined because he didn't want to be a laughingstock."

Wallins saw Sheppard's startled look. "Oh hell," he said. "We all knew about it: we couldn't help seeing it. He'd flinch if someone so much as dropped a saucepan! Or all but climb a tree if someone shot off a gun! And he was so coddled and cosseted, no one ever made him get some sense!"

"I'm not sure that's something you get over," Sheppard said.

Townsend looked scornful. "Hell yes!" he said. "If you weren't being loyal to Miss Lavinia, who loved that ne'er-do-well beyond any sense I can see, you'd agree with me. I've seen it done. So have you. You do it with anything you want to teach: start out slow and work up. Don't tell me you never got a gun-shy dog used to firing. That mare of yours wasn't born liking explosions either, I'd bet.

"Gaylord Wheeler just peacocked around and chased skirts that couldn't rightly run from him and acted like he was God's gift to the South. And more than that, the summer before the war broke out, he and his pale-haired icicle of a fiancée came here and acted like Miss Lavinia, who was worn to a frazzle taking care of her dying ma, was some sort of antidote. For sheer gumption she's worth six of them! I tell you, it almost tickled me pink to hear that the fool's fiancée sent him a petticoat!"

"You knew of that, then," Sheppard said. "Miss Lavinia told me, and I got the feeling that it was a secret."

"Secret!" Townsend said. "We all knew. That yellow-haired bitch made sure we all would."

"She sure is a prize," Wallins said through his teeth. "No blinking it: what a wife she'd make a man!"

The thought required no response. Sheppard was silent for a long time. He finally turned Dixie back toward Wheelerville and nudged her to a walk with the others following him. "From what I hear, the armies are going to be moving shortly," he said at last. "That'll make those guerrillas restless. I think any attack will come within the next week."

Townsend had drawn in beside him. He nodded. "I agree," he said. "We've both seen the signs. Question is what to do about them."

"We'd best move everyone to the town," Sheppard said, quickening the pace to a trot. "There's no use trying to deny it: I'll tell Miss Lavinia now."

Wallins drew abreast of them. "It's the best thing to do," he agreed. "But I don't envy you. She's a sensible woman, but she sure hates bother and while she'll give her all if she thinks it's necessary, from what I've seen she doesn't like to be put out without reason."

** ** **

Sheppard had a lot to think about as he rode back to Fairlawn from Wheelerville. He had discussed evacuation plans with Townsend and Wallins on the way back to the town. That was the easy part of the problem. Lavinia's fear of the guerrillas, which Sheppard admitted was very well-founded, was a deeper, more difficult one. Sheppard's return to Fairlawn was occupied with ways to bring up the subject of the guerrillas with Lavinia in a manner that would not upset her unnecessarily. He had some ideas by the time he reached the stable, and it only remained to find a way to open the subject. As he dismounted, though, the question was taken out of his hands.

One of the plantation's children had been waiting by the door of the stable as he rode up. The child grinned at him and took Dixie's bridle while he dismounted, then went running off toward the house without a word.

Ten minutes later, as Sheppard bestowed a valedictory pat on Dixie's shaggy neck and watched her trot off across the field, Lavinia arrived breathless and smiling with her shawl thrown about her shoulders and her hat slightly askew.

Sheppard cocked an eye at the child, who was peeking out from behind Lavinia's skirt, and then smiled at her. "I gather you've been waiting for me," he said. "Your scout was pretty helpful before he disappeared."

"He always is," Lavinia said with a smile at the boy. "Thank you, Gabriel," she said to the child. "Run to the house now and ask Miss Callie to give you a cookie." She straightened as the child hurried off. "I have been waiting to talk to you since noontime," she said, beaming. She cocked her head at him. "You must have found out some interesting things on your patrol," she said. "We did," Sheppard said.

Lavinia paled. "Not—not bad news, I hope?" she said.

"Not at all," Sheppard replied. "I'll tell you about it while I clean up the tack. But your news first. What is it? Good news, by the look of it."

Lavinia's color had returned. "It's the best of news!" she said as they went back into the tackroom. She waited while he pulled the one chair forward for her and then sat down on a nearby stool with Dixie's bridle across his lap. "Asa, you'll never guess," she said. "Louise came to me and said she wanted to leave right away!"

Sheppard looked up from buffing the bit with a clean square of cloth. "What?" he demanded.

"She wants to go! And just as soon as possible! Tomorrow, if we can do it! Isn't it marvelous? It was all I could do to keep my composure and act sorry! I told her to go ahead and pack her things and I'd send her off in the morning with my blessing!" She saw that Sheppard had lowered his head and was working on the bridle's buckles. "Asa?" she said. "What is the problem? Don't tell me you aren't happy!"

Sheppard shook the bridle and looked up. "I wonder what mischief she's caused to make her want to clear out so quickly," he mused.

Lavinia tsked impatiently. "No more mischief than before, I'm sure," she said. "This is an answer to everyone's prayers: and haven't you heard that it's foolish to doubt God's gifts? Let her go, and good riddance to her!"

"I can't do that," Sheppard said. He looked up and caught her wide, puzzled gaze. "I can't send her away, Lavinia. Not now. Not when we have to evacuate Fairlawn at once or else remain in terrible danger."

He watched the wide, puzzled gaze become blank, almost blind. "I can't do it, Lavinia," he said. "I'm sorry."

** ** **

"Evacuate?" Lavinia repeated through lips that felt stiff. "But why?"

"It is the only thing we can do," Sheppard said. "The guerrillas are back. We've had a glimpse at them, and we've seen what we're up against with them. They're a large, vicious group, and we have a great many helpless people to protect here."

Lavinia looked over Sheppard's shoulder through the window and back toward the house, rising against the sky beyond them like a fortress, resplendent in its white pillars and verandas. "Helpless?" she said. "I can't imagine who you mean!"

"Can't you?" Sheppard asked. "Think of it: there's Callie and George, the plantation families—"

"They're in the Fairlawn Free Militia!" Lavinia objected.

"Their children and wives aren't," Sheppard said. "Gabriel, Bathsheba, the little children. How many does that make, Lavinia? Add to that Meg, your Aunt Amabel, and the wounded."

Lavinia was still gazing up at Fairlawn's bulk. "But the wounded are all soldiers!" she objected. "They all know how to fight!"

"They're sick men," Sheppard pointed out. "Some are missing arms and legs, and others are so weak they still have trouble sitting up. Many have lost all heart for fighting. And even if they hadn't, how well do you think they can fight now? What do you think the recoil from a musket would do to Private Pierce's abdomen? You are an intelligent woman, Lavinia. You know I'm right."

Lavinia was still gazing at the house through the window. "But to move them—to move the entire household—! Don't be ridiculous! We could protect them as well within the house! They'd be safe there!"

"No, they wouldn't," Sheppard said. "That group of renegades attacks like a striking rattlesnake. Your house would be an easy target. Those wide, tall windows, those galleries that run the length of the house on all sides. What is to stop someone from breaking any window he pleases and walking inside? We don't have enough people to protect the house against that sort of attack: we'd need at least one person to guard each window."

"But why would they even come to Wheelerville? They haven't yet: maybe they'll pass us by and we won't have to worry about them!"

Sheppard set his hands on her shoulders and shook her. "Look at me, Lavinia," he said. "Pickings are getting pretty slim now. My patrols have seen how the fighting around Atlanta wrecked things, and so have Townsend's. Wheelerville is still untouched, and people around here know it. The town's known to be prosperous, it's supported the armies throughout the war, and its militia groups are still a secret. Why do you keep saying it's not in danger?"

Her eyes searched his face for a long moment before lowering. "Because I want to think it," she said at last. "I... I guess I am a coward." She took a deep breath and lifted her chin. "But still," she said. "Fairlawn is a large, well-built place. We could defend it, I know we could! We could be safe!"

Sheppard shook his head. "You know we can't," he said. "I've explained it to you and I know you understand the strategic problem, but there is more to it than that. No, listen to me: I was assigned to guard you. I can't do that if you stay at that house while those raiders are abroad."

Lavinia lowered her eyes.

Sheppard was watching her expression. He said quietly, "If you insist on putting yourself in danger here, then you are endangering me as well. I must protect you or die trying. If you stay here, then that's exactly what I'll be forced to do."

She looked at the bridle, lying in his hands. "Are you quite serious, Sergeant?" she asked.

"Serious as death, Miss Wheeler," he replied.

She took the bridle from him and set it on its brass hook on the wall. "I won't have anyone hurt because of my stubbornness," she said, looking unseeingly up at the gleaming leather and brass. "You least of all. Once was enough." She turned away from the bridle and moved past him toward the tackroom door.

"Lavinia," Sheppard said.

"We'll move the Fairlawn people into Wheelerville, as you suggested," Lavinia said from the doorway. "I'll tell Callie, and she can pass the word along through the household. And I'll tell Louise she can't leave now."

"It is for the best," Sheppard said.

"I believe you," Lavinia said with an attempt at a smile. She abandoned the effort. "I don't know where everyone will stay when we go to the town," she said.

"That's the least of your worries," Sheppard said, offering his arm.

They walked quietly toward the house. Sheppard, looking down at her, saw that she had dropped all thought of her objections to the move and was grappling with the logistics of it with her usual briskness. He firmly suppressed a smile; a moment later he was meeting her calculating gaze with a credibly calm expression.

"Dear Heaven," Lavinia said. "Not only must I tell Louise she must stay, but I must tell everyone we're still to have her with us!"

Sheppard's eyes began to dance. "You can refer everyone to me," he said. "I'll handle any abuse they care to dish out. But we'd best hurry: we should be moving by tomorrow morning at the latest."

"Tomorrow morning!" Lavinia looked at him, appalled, then whirled to stare at the house, her mind filled with questions of bedding, supplies and transport. She turned back to see that Sheppard was, unaccountably, smiling warmly down at her. "Of all the annoying things—!" she exclaimed. "You might at least have given me some notice, with all the times you've been coming back looking grave! Have you any thoughts on how to do all that in about twelve hours?"

Sheppard took her hand between his. "Slow down, Lavinia," he said. "It'll get done: we'll do it together and you won't be under any strain at all. I'll be here to help you. It's no trouble for me. No trouble at all." He hesitated, watching her as she drew her hand away and ascended the porch steps. After a moment's swift, half-shaken draw of breath he said, "Lavinia. If only you knew—"

Lavinia had ascended the porch steps. Something in his voice made her turn toward him again. She saw his expression, his hand half-outstretched toward her. "If only I knew—what, Asa?" she asked, moving to the top porch step.

Sheppard smiled up at her. "—how very much I love you," he said.

She took his hand and descended the four steps to the walkway, her eyes never leaving his face. "Why, Asa—" she said through a dawning smile.

The sound of the door opening behind her made them drop their hands and turn toward the house. "I see our warden is back," Louise Hamiter said. "I will be packed shortly. I trust everything can be properly arranged."

CHAPTER FORTY

Louise Hamiter had stared icily at Lavinia and Sheppard as they entered the house. By the time Sheppard had told her, without unnecessary gentleness, that she would be staying in Wheelerville for some time, her expression had been almost incandescent with fury. She had started to protest with more than her usual venom; he had cut through her invective with the comment that he had a lot to do and little time in which to do it, and he would send for her when it was convenient.

The hours between that moment and the present had been occupied in writing: directions for the various parties looking to him for leadership in case of an attack by guerrillas, a list of supplies, his daily report.

Sheppard frowned down at his journal. It had been empty when he had first arrived at Fairlawn in the middle of May. Now it was nearly full. How odd to think that the activities of the past five months could be chronicled in so few pages!

He opened the journal at random and read with a growing smile. Mid July: an account of one of the Fairlawn Free Militia's first patrols. Isaiah, usually a nimble rider, had been neatly dumped by his mount, a wily old cavalry beast scavenged from an abandoned skirmish field in early June and brought back to condition under George's watchful eyes.

Sheppard firmly suppressed the urge to page through the journal and instead wiped the tip of his pen and reviewed what he had just written. His account had flowed easily: where he rode, what was seen, what discussed, what steps resolved upon. Facts were easy to capture, but the important things eluded his pen: Meg's welcoming beam as he stepped into the house after the day's patrol, the taste of warmed cider presented by Callie, the sound of voices around him speaking of the unimportant, day to day things that formed the fabric of his life and made this brief assignment of his a taste of heaven.

He could not record the sheen of candlelight upon Lavinia's hair at supper, or the warmth of her hand in the crook of his arm, felt through the layers of cotton shirt and wool sleeve during their customary, though hurried and strangely silent, evening walk.

Lavinia's hand had seemed to quiver on his arm during that walk, and she had kept her eyes downcast and hardly spoken, though he had caught a smile on her lips. Had he spoken too suddenly? It did not occur to him that his quiet, almost matter-of-fact statement had upset or angered her. His love for Lavinia Wheeler, complete and mature, left no room for the see-sawing emotions of an adolescent crush.

He sighed and sat back to think, his mind ranging over countless quick moments, nuances of speech, her expressions during their exchanges. Once she had almost touched him, that evening after the foraging party had passed through the town. The night before Adams' departure he had kissed her, and she had not pushed him away.

Kissed her forehead, he corrected himself, and then smiled at the memory of her hand curving along his temple. She loved him, he was certain of it. It was only a matter of time before they could straighten things out between them. Unfortunately, time was the one commodity that he lacked.

He knew his time at Wheelerville was coming to an end. Sherman's armies had taken Atlanta after John Hood's forces withdrew. There was nothing to occupy Sherman's interests to the south and west, and the rich port of Savannah lay southeast of them, with South Carolina to the north. Sherman would be moving, and Sheppard doubted that he would be leaving a garrison behind in Atlanta. The southern forces would be following him, and Wheelerville would once again be in Confederate hands. He would have to go to their commanders, present his credentials and request safe conduct to his lines, which they might or might not grant. His time was measured in weeks at the very most, and there were things to be done immediately.

Some of them might be downright fun. He smiled at Isaiah, who was sitting quietly beside him. "All right," he said. "Bring the Hamiter woman in and I'll talk to her now."

He set down his pen and watched Isaiah nod and then leave the study. Four minutes at the most lay between him and an interview that promised to be interesting and even enjoyable. In the meantime...

He smoothed the journal's page with his fingertip. It had no account of that afternoon's conversation with Lavinia, but he would never forget it. And if his time was short, what of it? There were ways of expeditiously smoothing things out. He would take Lavinia in his arms and kiss her the next time they were alone and untroubled. That should clarify matters very nicely, and he had an idea as to the reception such an action might receive.

He looked up, smiling, to see Louise Hamiter standing before him and looking him wrathfully up and down.

Sheppard caught himself as he started to rise, sat back, and subjected her to the same sort of appraisal she was giving him. The slight movement had not gone unnoticed; her expression grew colder than ever.

"I believe it is the custom to stand when a lady enters a room," Louise said. "But perhaps that is not generally done in Yankeedom?"

"The custom, north and south, is to rise when a lady enters the room," Sheppard said gently, but with a dark smile.

Isaiah, standing beside the door, began to grin.

** ** **

"Then she said, stiff and uppity, 'I am unused both to being summoned and to being kept waiting, sir. Nor am I accustomed to gratuitous insults!'"

"Whoo!" said George, who was seated at his ease at the kitchen table. "What'd he say to that?"

"He was mending his pen," said Isaiah. "He put it down and said, 'A statement of fact is never an insult.'

"She started chewing on her lip. She said she guessed he had a good reason for refusing to talk to her till just then, and he said he had. She looked at him funny, and he said, bland as you please, that he'd been busy.

"That's when she wanted to know if she hadn't, and he said she hadn't been busy in any useful way."

"That's telling her, the whited sepulcher!" Callie crowed. "Then what?"

"She wanted to know if she could sit down and he said she sure could. She waited, and when he continued doing what he was doing, she finally got her own chair and sat down, looking like a martyr.

"He'd taken up his pen again and was fiddling with the tip. When she said he was refusing to allow her to leave he said she was right, and when she wanted to know why he said because at the moment it wasn't convenient or safe for him to do so."

"That's the way to treat her!" Bathsheba said.

Corporal Higgins looked thoughtful. "I don't know," he said. "It doesn't pay to rile a rattlesnake. They can surprise you. Did he act a little nicer after that?"

"Well, he said he couldn't spare the men he'd need to escort her, and when she said she would be perfectly safe, he said she was probably right, but his men would not."

Callie and George traded looks.

"That's the Sarge for you," Higgins said. "I'm sure she had some more to say.

"Oh yes," Isaiah said. "She stared at him. 'I shall go by myself, then,' she said.

"'I won't allow it,' he said. 'If you go, you go with an escort. At the moment it's too dangerous, and I won't expose my men to danger needlessly.' "

Isaiah's expression grew somber. "That's when she said, 'You're very tender about the safety of a passel of niggers!,' " he said.

The faces around the kitchen table were glowing with laughter. George folded his arms and sat back in his chair. "All right, then, Isaiah," he said. "What'd he say?"

"He looked her up and down, said her manners surprised him, and then took up some papers. She was supposed to leave after that, I guess, but she didn't get the hint. I guess she didn't want to, and she just kept on railin' at him like a shrew. Said she wanted to know what right he had to tell her what to do.

"He said, 'I've been given the job of seeing that the people of Fairlawn and Wheelerville are kept safe, and that assignment gives me the right.'

"You'd think that would shut her up, but it didn't. She said, 'Well, I'm not from Wheelerville or Fairlawn, so I can come and go just as I please.'

"He says, 'No you can't. You're going to stay here until I say you can go!'

"She tells him he's being a tyrant and says she wants to know why he's keeping her here.

"He says, 'Your coming and going endangers the town right now, and you're staying put until it doesn't.'

Higgins had been listening with his eyebrows raised. "She probably had something sharp to say to that," he remarked.

"She wasn't doing very well just about then," Isaiah said. "I think she was really upset about having to stay, too upset to be as nasty as she was capable. She said, 'I can't believe you actually want me to be here!'"

"He looked at her and smiled the nastiest smile I've seen him give. He said, 'You're right on target. I don't want you here. But no matter how I feel about you, I've got others to consider and I'm not going to let any of them go into danger for you. Now you'd best get out and occupy yourself with something useful. This household is moving to Wheelerville tomorrow and you'll be with them.' "

Higgins looked thoughtful. "I'll bet she didn't like that," he said slowly. "For that matter, I don't, myself. I wonder if he was wise to say it like that."

** ** **

"Starlight, star bright, first star I see tonight, I wish I may, I wish I might have the wish I wish tonight." Lavinia smiled at Meg, sitting snugly in her arms. "Can you say that?" she asked.

Meg looked up at her and smiled back, then looked solemnly out the window at the evening star. She repeated the words, then sat back against Lavinia's velvet bodice. "Now what do I do?" she asked.

"You make your wish, darling," Lavinia said.

"Oh," Meg said, staring at the star.

"Quickly now, before the other stars come out," Lavinia said.

"What should I wish for, Mama?"

"Whatever you want that's good," Lavinia answered.

Meg thought things over. Her hand stole to her pocket and emerged with the picture of Sheppard's children. She had been carrying it around since he had given it to her, and now that it was ensconced in state in a gutta-percha case that Lavinia had provided, she kept taking it out and staring at it.

She opened it and looked at the faces gazing up at her. "Maybe I'll wish to see Caleb and Lydia and Jesse," she said. She directed a wide look up at Lavinia. "Would that be all right, Mama?"

"Of course, darling," Lavinia said. She stopped at the staccato sound of feet on the stairs.

Louise erupted into the room, moving with vehemently restrained force. Her hair was disheveled, as though she had been running, and her bosom was rising and falling with suppressed emotion.

She saw Lavinia and Meg and stopped where she stood. Her teeth bared; "Odious, selfish man!" she hissed. "This war will end just like everything else, Lavinia, and so will he!" She drew herself up with a semblance of her former dignity. "And you just think on this: one day he, too, will be just a mound under a tree-just like the rest of them!- and I pray it'll be soon!"

She was gone in a whirl and rustle of taffeta.

Lavinia's lips felt stiff and her heart was thudding. She looked down at Meg, who was sitting very still and staring after Louise.

"Well, Poppet," Lavinia said with an effort. "Did you make your wish?"

Meg nodded. "I wished she'd be happier," she said solemnly. "She's never been happy. Maybe if she is, we can all be happy, too."

Lavinia held her tighter. Callie had bathed the child and washed her hair; Lavinia could catch a faint lavender scent against her lips as she dropped a kiss on Meg's head.

There was so much to do in so little time, she thought. And so much to fear and to mourn. Her thoughts turned to Sheppard's face upturned toward her just that afternoon as she was ascending the porch steps. If you only knew how very much I love you... So much to fear, and so much to lose.

"I hope so, darling," she said, drawing the child to her and kissing her again. As her lips touched Meg's smooth cheek and she felt the warm little arms close about her neck, she found herself visualizing another, older face and the warm strength of other arms around her.

CHAPTER FORTY-ONE

Meg came out onto the porch and sat down on the top step, her lower lip protruding just a touch. It was getting cold, the sky was gray, and a rising wind was carrying the smell of rain to her. The wind was bringing another sort of smell as well, a musty, rank, somehow frightening one that no one else seemed able to sense. She had tried to tell the grownups of it, and had been greeted with preoccupied smiles.

Meg decided that it had something to do with what had happened the morning before. Her father had awakened her while it was still dark outside and had told her that they were going to stay in the town with friends. When she had wailed a protest and tried to go back to sleep, he had lifted her in his arms and carried her, blankets and all, to her mama's waiting buggy.

Meg could remember the buggy jolting and swaying with Uncle George grim and silent at the reins. His presence had reassured her a little, though she would have been happier if her mama or her father had been there. She had finally fallen asleep.

She had awakened in an unfamiliar room amid strange scents. Aunt Callie had been strangely silent in the morning when she washed and dressed Meg.

Things had grown worse. Meg found that she was staying in a house she had never seen before. The food had been odd-tasting, as though the person who made it did not know how to cook. The people there talked in whispers, and whenever she came near them they stopped talking and smiled a little too brightly at her. And when some of them did talk to her, it was to ask her questions about where her father slept and where her mama slept.

They had seemed surprised and even a little disappointed to learn that her father slept on the top floor of the east wing of the house with the other men like Uncle George and Isaiah, while her mother slept in the other wing, in a large room on the second floor near Aunt Callie, Bathsheba and her. They were even more disappointed to learn that her mama had a lock on her door and turned the key every night.

She missed her father, who was nowhere to be seen. Aunt Callie, who came over during the day, told her that he was out on patrol with the other men. Her mama was busy much of the day over at Dr. Meacham's house. Aunt Callie told her that the sick men who were staying in the large room in her mama's house had gone there, and some of them needed care.

Meg was sorry for them: to her, 'sickness' meant 'stomach-ache', and she had a very lively memory of one suffered at the last church outing. She hoped they were feeling better. She pitied them, but she was beginning to pity herself more. Her cup was running over: she had been left in the care of strangers, away from the home she loved, and herded in with other children from the town, whom she did not know.

She looked down at the steps, plumped herself down on the top step, and reached into her pocket to get out the photograph of her new brothers and sister. Her hand came away empty.

The discovery that she had left the photograph back at Mama's big white house was the final drop in Meg's cup of misery. She whimpered experimentally and then decided that it was not worth the effort. No one that she cared for would hear her, and they were all too busy to pay attention at any rate.

Her father always told her that if she didn't think something was right, she should change it. She decided that she would go and fetch that photograph.

She stood up, brushing her hands against her neatly washed and ironed frock and went down the steps. The big white house was somewhere down the road, she knew; she started walking.

She did not even stop when she caught sight of a big, smooth rock that was sure to have a flourishing colony of doodlebugs beneath it.

** ** **

"They're getting closer," Caesar said. "Isaiah and Toby got a look at them." He nodded at Sheppard. "Large group, just like everyone thought."

Sheppard frowned and exhaled slowly. He had not been aware that he had been holding his breath until that moment. Too much had happened to preoccupy him, beginning with the fact that not all of the Fairlawn people were accounted for in the town. He suspected the count had been inaccurate, but he had judged it wise to ride to the house and look around for himself. He had conducted a quick circuit of Fairlawn and found nothing. He had been ready to return to the town when Caesar had found him. "Townsend's folks told me yesterday he thinks they're definitely heading this way," he said.

Caesar shifted his massive shoulders and lifted his eyes to the house's silhouette. "No doubt of it," he agreed. "You saw it coming. They heard of the place and think we're easy pickin's."

"They'll find out otherwise," Sheppard said. "I'm sort of looking forward to teaching them."

"Me, too," Caesar said. "It'll even the score for little Meg's family."

"It'll even a lot of scores," Sheppard said, nudging Dixie in a half-circle with a touch of his heel and setting her head toward the town. "And cut down on the ones that'll need to be evened in the future," he added over his shoulder. Caesar, riding stirrup to stirrup with him, nodded. They spurred to a trot and caught up with the rest of the Fairlawn Free Militia patrol two miles outside of town.

Isaiah was very subdued. He kept looking over his shoulder, fingering his reins, listening while the others were busily bringing Sheppard and Caesar up to date on their patrol.

Caesar noticed him and rode closer. "Any more sign of those guerrillas?" he asked.

Isaiah shook his head. "Nor do I want to see any," he said. "One look was enough to show me they're evil! And you don't just have to look." He frowned and reined his horse in a tight circle to face the sound of approaching hooves.

Al Townsend, winded and disheveled, came up at a canter on a lathered horse. "They told me you saw them!" he panted, dragging his sleeve across his forehead. "How close were they?"

"A few miles, maybe," Caesar said.

"What about your fellows?" Sheppard asked.

"The same," Townsend said. "We didn't catch a look at them, but we've seen fresh tracks. I'd say it's time to pull our patrols closer to town. If we can draw 'em in and ambush 'em, so much the better."

"I won't argue with that," Sheppard said. He looked over at the Fairlawn people. "Come on," he said. "I've got to go back and tell the Judge what we've found. We need to talk, Al. Why don't you finish what you were doing and meet me back in town there or at Pickens' place?"

Townsend nodded and watched them ride off before turning his horse and frowning southward again. He raised his head and sniffed at the wind. Something was making him very uneasy: it would be happening soon, and he did not think it would be pleasant. "Come on," he said to the others. "One more circuit and we'll go in. Haller, you ride with me and tell me what you see. It'll be good training."

** ** **

"I found her three miles out from town, cutting across the fields," Sam Wallins said, adjusting his hold on Meg, who was sitting on the pommel of his saddle and staring around with her thumb in her mouth. "She told me she was going home to get something."

"It's a good thing you found her, Sam," Townsend said.

Reeves, beside him, was staring white-faced from Wallins to Meg. He had been a little self-conscious while patrolling with Townsend, but he had eased a little and done a good job. Townsend had just been telling him that he had improved greatly when they came across Sam Wallins and Meg. "She shouldn't be abroad now!" he exclaimed. "It's dangerous!"

"That's why I picked her up and brought her back, Haller," Wallins said. He smiled down at Meg. "What was it you were going to get, Miss Meg?" he asked.

Meg removed her thumb and studied it briefly. "My picture," she said, pushing away from him a little to return Al Townsend's astonished stare with a heart-meltingly wide-eyed smile that she usually reserved for Sheppard. "I left my picture and I wanted to get it."

Townsend, not expecting such an attack from so young a lady with whom he had previously exchanged nothing more than the commonplace civilities proper between adult and child, was an immediate conquest. He forced himself to lift his eyes from Meg to Wallins. "Where did you find her?" he asked.

"Pickens' cornfield," Wallins said. "He finished harvesting the field corn late last week and hasn't put the stalks in shooks yet. It was a wonder I saw her: that dried stubble's twice her height. Good thing she had that pretty blue ribbon in her hair."

"Picture?" Haller Reeves said. "What's she talking about?"

Meg gave him an intent, speculative look. "Does he really keep bales of hay in his house to eat?" she asked Townsend.

Wallins, trying to smother a laugh, gave vent to an explosive snort that made Meg giggle.

"Could be," Townsend said with the straight face that had won him a fair amount of money in various poker games over the years. "Now why were you running away, little girl?"

"I wasn't running away," Meg said with commendable patience. "I left it, and I wanted it because everyone's miserable and things smell bad."

"First she's says she wants a picture and next she's talking about hay and bad smells," Reeves complained. "Best take her back to Miss Lavinia.

"I'll be doing that right away," Townsend said. "Give her over, Sam. I've got to meet the Sarge at Judge Prescott's for a pow-wow, and I can drop her off along the way, or afterward."

Wallins nodded and lifted Meg as Townsend came alongside. "Careful with her, Al," he said. "She's such a little mite, she's likely to blow off your saddle like thistledown."

"None of you are making any sense," Reeves said.

"Maybe we're not making sense because you aren't listening right, Haller," Townsend suggested. He looked down at Meg and his voice gentled. "What did you mean about the smell?" he asked.

Meg leaned back against Townsend's chest and tilted her head back to stare up at him. "It just smells funny," she said, wrinkling her nose. "Like when people are scared." She cocked her head and added, "Or when they're mad." She saw that Mr. Townsend was nodding thoughtfully. "It's sour," she said.

Townsend frowned southward once more, then looked at her. "That isn't a good thing," he said. "We're going to take you back to your mama. You'll have to stay there until it's clear to go back to the house. I don't want you leaving your mama, do you understand?"

"But I want my picture!"

"We'll see what we can do about getting it for you soon," Townsend said. "But for right now, little Missy, you've got to stay with your mama. Understand?"

Meg pushed her lip out.

Townsend was looking over at Wallins and Reeves. "I'm off to the judge's," he said, "She can talk to Sheppard. Maybe he can make her see some sense. Then I'll take her to Miss Lavinia."

Meg's pout turned to a smile at the name 'Sheppard'. "Can we gallop?" she asked.

** ** **

Townsend handed Meg down to Aunt Amabel and then straightened. "There she is, Ma'am," he said. "Safe and sound and well. She'd best stay with you from now on. We don't want her running off again." He looked up and saw Louise Hamiter standing in the doorway and nodded politely.

Aunt Amabel set Meg on the ground and kept hold of one hand. "Why, where was she, Captain Townsend?" she asked. "No one missed her until just a few minutes ago! It threw us into an uproar!"

"She'd left her photograph in the house when you all were rousted out of there yesterday morn, Ma'am," Townsend said. "She decided she'd go back to fetch it. Sam Wallins found her crossing the cornfields. I took her to the Sergeant, over at Judge Prescott's, soon as I heard about it. He gave her a talking to and another picture to take its place, so she's all set." He smiled at Meg. "Aren't you, sweetheart?" he asked.

"Yes, sir, and thank you kindly," Meg said. She added a bobbing curtsey, as her mama had taught her, and beamed up at him.

Aunt Amabel went to the edge of the porch and gazed fearfully at Townsend. "Is it safe now?" she asked.

Townsend spoke as gently as he could. "No," he said. "It isn't. They're coming. Tell everyone to go to safety: you know what to do. We'll come around soon to tell you all what's happening, but for now, lay low."

Aunt Amabel nodded and tried to thank him. Her voice failed her; she went into the house, leading Meg by the hand. Meg lingered at the door to smile again at Townsend and wave.

Louise stayed where she was, staring at him.

"Will you see the word is spread in this house, Miss?" Townsend asked, touching the brim of his hat to her. Louise nodded and went inside. He remained, frowning after her, then shook his head and turned his horse.

** ** **

Meg lay down on the pile of ironed, folded sheets and drew several more over her. She needed a pillow: another sheet, nicely crumpled, served very well. She ducked her head beneath the sheets and inhaled their fresh, flower-like scent. They smelled almost as good as her mama's sheets.

She raised her head and listened. Everything was quiet downstairs, and just as well. The half hour between her return with Mr. Townsend and the present had been a very uncomfortable one. Everyone was creeping about, wide-eyed and silent. That wicked Miss Hamiter had shushed her in a particularly nasty way when she sat down on the front porch to sing to herself. She had salved her wounded feelings by inserting a finger at each corner of her mouth, pulling them apart and thrusting out her tongue as far as it would go while crossing her eyes.

Having shown the Hamiter woman what she thought of her, Meg decided to see what she could to make things more bearable for herself. She was a sensible little girl: the grownups were giving her the fidgets so she had withdrawn out of their sight. Mr. Townsend had said to go to safety, and the armoire filled with sheets seemed the safest, best hiding place Meg had seen. She remembered her father telling her that it was smart to get inside or under things, and the sheets were almost as good as a hollow log, she thought.

She reached into her pocket and took out the photograph. It was too dim to see it well, but she could feel the cardboard backer and know that the photograph was there, the solemn faces of her sister and her two brothers gazing out at her. She closed her eyes and pictured herself standing with them, smiling at them, posing for a photograph with them.

Her eyes felt heavy; she closed them and held the photograph against her. A moment later she was asleep.

That was unfortunate. If she had only kept her eyes open a moment she might have heard her mama come in, and she could have run down the stairs to throw herself into her mother's arms and show her the new photograph. As it was, she did not even hear her mother saying, on a note of panic, "Where's Meg?" Nor did she hear the subsequent commotion that rang through the house.

CHAPTER FORTY-TWO

Asa Sheppard sat back in his saddle, his eyes narrowing on the distant plume of smoke coiling upward through the brightening sky in the near distance. The men around him drew together. Widened eyes followed his gaze. Hands tightened on weapons, smoothed tangled manes, circled thick hide belts and gripped.

"Sighted by Caxton's mill," Sheppard said. He slowly drew the reins through his hands and frowned into the glare of the sky and then looked over at Townsend. "You were right, Al," he said with the edge of a grim smile. "They're coming from the southeast, just as you said. That explains the smoke."

Townsend, as impassive as Sheppard, swept a glance around the circle of faces and nodded.

"The southeast," Reeves said. "Well, then, what do we do? Do we go after them?"

The silence stretched out for twenty seconds, a minute, almost two minutes before Sheppard looked away from the smoke toward Reeves. Even then he only traded a long, thoughtful stare with Townsend.

"They're coming," Townsend said. "I'd hoped—" He did not finish his sentence.

Sheppard nodded.

Caesar nudged his horse forward. "Sarge?" he said. "Shall we gather the people at the town hall?"

Sheppard looked up and said, "Yes. Gather them. The sooner the better. Toby, you and Isaiah go back to Judge Prescott's and tell them what we've seen and decided. Al, you send whoever you want to talk to the people in town, and I'll send one of my men along to back him up. We can gather them at the town hall, as we decided. It's too dangerous to do anything else. They'll be safer together." He added grimly, "And it'll be easier to kill those monsters if we don't have to worry about innocent people getting hurt."

** ** **

Lavinia frowned at Aunt Amabel and took a quick turn around the room. "Didn't I hear that Sergeant Sheppard gave her another photograph?" she demanded.

"That's what Mr. Townsend said," Aunt Amabel said unhappily. "But they didn't get the one she'd left behind in the first place."

"That was careless of her," Louise said.

Aunt Amabel's voice was downright chilly as she said, "She's barely four years old, Louise. And she was sleepy and pulled from her bed in the middle of the night."

"Excuses," said Louise. "The brat's been a bother since she first came."

"That's nothing you would know of," Lavinia said. "You came well after she did."

She frowned and took a turn around the room. She had spent most of the day with Corporal Higgins and the wounded. The men were relaxed and ready to fight, even looking forward to it. She had returned to this place prepared to put up her feet and do some embroidery, but that had fallen by the way with this new fright. "I still don't see," she began.

"No, listen," Aunt Amabel said, twisting her hands together before her. "She was heading toward Fairlawn when they found her. They never did get the photograph she left behind."

"That doesn't make any sense, Aunt Amabel," Lavinia said. "If she has a new photograph, what would she want with the old one?"

"Children her age have little to do with sense, 'Vinnie," Aunt Amabel said. "She left her photograph and she wants it. If nothing else, she'd think it could bear the newer one company."

Lavinia had paused to consider. She finally nodded. "Very well, then," she said. "When did you last see her?"

"It was when Mr. Townsend brought her back," Aunt Amabel said. "Maybe an hour ago, all told, counting the time we've been looking high and low."

"We've looked everywhere we could think of," Eleanor Wigfall said. "She's gone for certain."

Lavinia frowned. "We'll have to remedy that," she said.

"I'll tell my Abner and the others that they must go find her," Mrs. Wigfall said.

Lavinia was frowning again. "No," she said, smoothing the chains of her chatelaine. "That'll take too long. I'll go get her myself. You can tell them when they get back."

"You can't be serious," Callie began as Lavinia took up her cloak and swung it around her shoulders. And then, watching as she fastened the buttons at the throat, "Lavinia! You mustn't! It isn't safe!"

Lavinia took up her hat. "No, listen, Callie," she said. "We've had no word from the men, and it'll only take a minute. Beau's fresh and fast, and I'm a good rider. I'll go to the house, find Meg and the photograph and bring them back here. I'll go straight there by the road—that's the way Meg would take—and go back over the fields."

"You're not being wise, Lavinia!" Callie exclaimed.

"And how wise would you be if you knew a child was in danger?" Lavinia asked. She smiled at Callie and said more gently, "Don't worry, Callie. I'll be fine."

** ** **

Fifteen minutes later, gazing up in relief at Fairlawn, Lavinia smiled. The place was whole and unharmed, and no one was in sight, though the column of smoke some distance off had caused her some worry. In and out: it would not take long at all. She knew where Meg would go, and it would only take a few minutes to make certain the child was there.

She trotted Beau to the stableyard behind the house, dismounted at the block, and looped the stirrup up over the fixed head of the sidesaddle. She would not be long; she left his bridle on, patted his neck, and hurried into the house by the unlocked kitchen door.

The kitchen was as spotless as she had expected, right down to the rows of freshly scrubbed and buffed copper pots hanging in a line above the large fireplace. Lavinia found herself fighting a most undignified grin at the thought of Callie leaving a messy kitchen.

The rest of the house was every bit as neat and every bit as echoingly empty. Lavinia could not shake the odd, uneasy sense that she was an intruder. Gazing down the hallway at the row of doors opening to right and left, she felt an unaccustomed tingle between her shoulder blades. She gathered her skirts and hurried toward the servants' stairway, opening midway down the hall. It took barely twenty steps to ascend from the main floor to the second floor. Within three minutes she was in the west wing and standing in Meg's room with no sign that the child had been there recently.

** ** **

"What do you mean she's gone to the house?" Sam Wallins demanded.

"She's gone after Meg," Mrs. Wigfall said. "The child wanted her photograph!"

"Wanted her—" Wallins repeated. "But we brought the little girl back here once already!"

"Well, once doesn't seem to be enough," Callie said. "She's gone again!" She watched the color drain from Wallins' face. "Now what is wrong?" she said.

"We've seen 'em," Wallins said. "They're coming fast."

** ** **

The three faces, quivering on the edge of smiles, gazed solemnly up at Lavinia from the small square of pasteboard half-hidden beneath some brightly printed handkerchiefs in Meg's top drawer. She smiled down at them and touched Caleb's apple cheek with a fingertip. "Some day," she said.

She tucked the photograph into the pocket of her skirt and looked around the room. Meg was probably nowhere in the house, Lavinia decided. That was plain enough from the presence of the photograph. If she was not in the house, she must be upon the way. All the more reason to get a strong, bold rider to the child at once before any harm could be done. Lavinia could be that rider, but she'd best hurry.

She went to the head of the stairs and then paused. It was just possible that Meg had gone to Sergeant Sheppard's rooms. He had told her that Meg liked to watch him shave on Sundays, and she enjoyed setting his few belongings in order. She decided she'd best go and make sure Meg wasn't there. The easiest way to get to the east wing and the men's quarters was to ascend the enclosed servants' stairway once more, leave it at the third story and go down the main hallway to Sergeant Sheppard's room.

Lavinia sighed and went into the dim, stuffy stairway, begrudging every minute that kept her from finding Meg. The dim, close walls, muffling all but the loudest sounds within the house, completely hid the drum of approaching hooves.

** ** **

"Gone to Fairlawn?" Sheppard repeated. "But she was told to stay here!"

"She thought it best to go," Callie said.

"In God's name!" Sheppard exclaimed. "Why, when she was told to stay where she was?"

"Meg's turned up missing," Callie said.

** ** **

Lavinia descended the steps to the ground floor and hesitated in the hallway, looking around at the silent furnishings, drinking in the faint scent of oil soap and wool rugs. It was all so neat, orderly and dead, the rich furnishings seeming to glitter in the dim light, the air sluggish and still.

There was no hint of Meg's presence. A quick inspection of Sergeant Sheppard's rooms confirmed the impression. Wherever Meg might be, she was certainly not at Fairlawn, and it was best that Lavinia leave there, as well.

The grand parlor was to her left. Out of habit, she turned and went in there. Sir Walter Raleigh's jug was sitting in solitary state in the middle of the marble-topped table. Lavinia gazed for a moment and then went to it. There was time to move it out of harm's way.

The glaze was warm and rough between her palms, the colors earthy and reassuring, the face's smile almost mellow.

She lifted it—

The smash and tinkle of broken glass made her turn, her breath quivering in her throat. Another crash set her heart to pounding heavily. Her ears caught rough voices and the clump and clatter of heavily shod feet on the porch floorboards.

That group of renegades attacks like a striking rattlesnake. She could hear Sheppard's voice in her head. *Your house would be an easy target. Those wide, tall windows, those galleries that run the length of the house on all sides. What's to stop someone from breaking any window he pleases and walking inside?* Lavinia drew a long, shaking breath, and hurried into the hallway, the jug held before her like a shield.

The chaotic world of Lavinia's fears had forced a way into her waking world, knocking its order awry and leaving one of its nightmare denizens bestriding the Chinese carpet in Lavinia's front foyer.

He stood just inside the front door with a musket in his two hands, watching Lavinia with a silent intentness that turned her mouth to sand. A trail of splintered glass led from the smaller parlor; Lavinia could see specks glistening in the folds of his boot toes. A stray finger of sunlight, falling across his eyes, made them seem to glint with the tawny ferocity of a catamount.

Lavinia lifted her chin and held the jug more tightly before her, her thoughts circling, sick with horror and growing anger, about the memory of the mutilated, burned bodies of Meg's family.

"What are you doing here, sir?" she demanded.

CHAPTER FORTY-THREE

"Good God!" Townsend said, staring at Sheppard as the rest of his group mounted and gathered their reins. "I was careful that word would get to her! Didn't she get my warning?"

"It seems she didn't," Sheppard said.

"But I swear— I made sure she'd be told!"

"I don't doubt you, Al," Sheppard said. "The question is whether your word actually reached her."

Townsend spared a glance over his shoulder at the rest and then turned back to Sheppard. "No, I can't believe it!" he exclaimed. "I said it was important!"

"Who'd you tell?" Caesar asked.

Townsend motioned his men into line. "I gave Meg to Miss Amabel," he said. "She took her away—"

"Mrs. Swithin got the message, then?" Caesar pursued.

The group was ready. Townsend's eyes narrowed as he motioned them forward. "No," he said after a slight pause. "Miss Amabel left with Meg. Miss Hamiter was in the room, so I told her."

"The word didn't get any farther than her," Sheppard said, turning Dixie toward Fairlawn. "She didn't pass it on, Miss Lavinia went out into danger, and Meg's missing, too."

** ** **

The guerilla took a step toward Lavinia as she pivoted and backed toward the stairs with the jug held before her. "Get away from me, you villain!" she snapped. "Intruding in my home! Think shame on yourself and get out at once!"

He laughed deep in the back of his throat, and took another step toward her. His movements were like those of a boy playing dodge-ball; she realized that he was toying with her.

Lavinia raised the jug in both hands and hurled it with all her force. In later years, remembering through the motions that were engraved in her mind, oddly slowed and stylized, she would recall feeling as though the movement of her arms, up and then forward, had the force of an avalanche. The rough glaze of the jug rasped across her fingertips; she heard the hum of the air moving across the mouth of the jug, followed closely by an echoing thud as it struck the man's parrying forearm.

She saw the jug seeming to hover in the air, spinning slowly, slowly as it began to arc gently downward, gaining speed and momentum. She saw the jug glance from the arm of the settee and come to rest upon with a final thump upon the settee's horsehair-stuffed cushions. The face smiled upward at the ceiling, mirroring the smile on the intruder's face as time and movement crashed back into normal speed and Lavinia whirled and leaped for the main staircase.

The man dropped his musket with a yell of triumph and lunged after her. His reaching hands were inches from the hem of Lavinia's skirt; he clutched at it with a snarl of triumph.

Lavinia gasped and caught up her skirts just as he jammed the toe of his boot against the steps and sprawled forward, bruising his knees on the sharp-edged risers.

The moment's pause gave Lavinia time and impetus to gain the top of the stairs. She ran, light-footed as the girl she had once been, down the hall, past the bedrooms, past the upstairs sitting room, past the music room to the doorway of the servants' staircase. She opened it, gathered her skirts in her fists and plunged down the dark steps. She had left the downstairs door unsecured; she slammed it behind her and shot the three brass bolts that fastened it, then dropped the thick walnut bar across the door.

Thought moves swifter than lightning, diving cormorant-like down through the murky depths of a lifetime of memories to seize the one crucial thought and bring it to the surface. As Lavinia rammed the last heavy brass bolt home and collapsed against the wall, the memory flashed into her mind of a September day when she and Gaylord had kept a despised, and soon departed, governess locked in that unlit, dusty stairway for most of the long afternoon.

Action followed swiftly on the heels of thought. She was still alone in the house except for the one intruder: she had time. She raced back up the stairs, her breath burning in her lungs, sped down the hallway again, and reached the upper door just as the man's feet came crashing upon the bare steps upward toward the landing.

Lavinia slammed the door shut, bolted it, and then stopped, her hand clenched against her throat.

Bang!

A long splinter of wood ripped away from the small, jagged hole that appeared below it.

** ** ** **

"Abner said we were to meet you," Toby said.

"That's right," Sheppard said. "Miss Wheeler's back at Fairlawn and Meg may be there as well."

"God Almighty!" Isaiah gasped.

"You watch your language, boy!" Toby snapped at his son. "Everyone else from Fairlawn's accounted for, Sarge: we checked."

"All right, then," Sheppard said. "There's no time to waste. You and Caesar pick half your group to stay here with Townsend's gang—and be quick! The rest come along and be ready to fight!"

** ** ** **

The man was firing through the door. Lavinia recoiled as another hole opened beside it, and then another. The door was solid walnut, chosen for strength. Sergeant Sheppard had said it was good and sturdy, and Lavinia knew that it would hold. She flattened herself against the wall and edged away until she could turn and run.

A glance out the window on the landing showed her that the others had come up and were just outside. Their horses, heaped with plunder, were tethered to the railing. As she watched, two of them, still mounted, circled toward the front of the house while another headed for the henhouses.

She froze; she could hear other voices inside, near the parlor, along with the sound of tearing cloth and breaking glass. They had heard the commotion, but the plunder in the house was delaying them.

Lavinia gnawed her lip, thinking furiously. The raiders would be out for sport and for revenge, and a lone woman would afford them plenty to keep them occupied. There was nowhere to hide in the house, even if she did not know that the raiders would be trying to find her. They would be thorough in their search, and she could look for no mercy. She remembered the pillar of smoke coiling upward in the distance and knew that she could not remain in the house. Even if she could somehow hide in the attic, she knew that they would set Fairlawn ablaze and she would die nonetheless.

An uproar downstairs made her jump. The captured raider was yelling and banging on the downstairs door now. Much good it would do him, she thought, hearing two more shots, the thudding of heavy boots upon the hardwood floor, and then rough laughter.

Lavinia, leaning cautiously around the corner, watched them all move toward the servants' stairs. She remembered the man's musket, left at the foot of the stairs. She might be able to take it.

She thrust all memory of Meg's family from her mind. Something had to be done quickly, and it was useless to hang back for fear of what might happen. She was still alive; she had a chance to get away with her life. She went silently down the steps, her hand holding the jingling chatelaine still in the folds of her skirt, and took up the gun. It felt like the heaviest thing she had lifted in years, and it was unloaded with no ammunition nearby. No matter: Sergeant Sheppard had said guns were almost as useful as clubs as they were as firearms.

She carried it with her and made her silent way away from the voices. The crash of crockery indicated that they were too busy stealing and destroying to trouble her. She went silently through to the kitchen and out the pantry door, continuing until she had reached the herb garden, where she stopped to get her bearings.

The stable and its paddock were close by, and she could see Beau from where she stood. If she could make it to the stable without being seen, she could mount the gelding without any trouble. Once in the saddle, it would be only a few minutes' work to gallop to the town. Beau was a born jumper with a good, mile-eating stride, and Lavinia had hunted across her land for years. Once safely back at Wheelerville she could warn the town. It was worth a try.

She thought that Sergeant Sheppard was probably heading toward Fairlawn even as she hesitated. The thought warmed her: she could get safely away to him if she only had the courage to go forward.

She heard laughter coming from the other side of the house. The sound made her mouth thin. Whatever was occupying their attention, it would keep them from seeing her. She stepped out briskly, holding the musket before her, rounded the corner of the stable, and slammed full into a tall, bearded man who was carrying her father's best saddle slung over his shoulder and a repeating carbine like Sheppard's held easily in his right hand.

His teeth glinted in a grin as his eyes raked her. "Well, I'll be damned!" he said. "A toothsome little piece come to pay a call!"

The nightmare was upon her. She recoiled, gasping, "Asa!"

"'Asa' will have to wait!" the man crowed as he dropped the saddle and carbine and stepped forward.

** ** **

Judge Prescott checked his rifle, shook his powder horn, and opened his pouch of musket balls. "Here come the rest," he said. They had checked just beyond sight of Fairlawn in order to give Caesar's group time to catch up and join the Wheelerville Militia. He squinted down the road and added, "We're most likely in time: I don't see any sign of smoke."

"Good," Sheppard said through his teeth. "Blast that Hamiter creature! What could she have meant by it? Nothing good, I'll bet! By God, if anything's happened to Lavinia or Meg, I'll have the law on her for murder!"

He stiffened suddenly, his head rearing upward like one who had just heard someone calling his name. His voice was almost icy as he spoke. "We're going in at a trot right now! There's no time to lose!" The line of horsemen swept forward.

** ** **

Lavinia heaved the musket upward and swung it like a club. The man arched backward and laughed as the butt went whistling harmlessly past his head, pulling her off-balance. Her hair half-slipped from its pins and fell across her eyes.

"Now—!" he exulted.

Lavinia reversed her grip on the stock and jabbed with the muzzle of the gun, wishing a bayonet had been fixed to its end as the piece's weight added force to the blow.

The guerilla seized the gun's barrel and swung it aside, throwing her sideways. "A spitfire!" he laughed. The next moment he had flung the musket to one side and dragged her to him.

Lavinia tried to twist away as he brought his face closer to hers. Her vision was filled with pale, black-lashed eyes. A quick snatch tore her spectacles from her face. He threw them aside and shifted his grip to her throat.

Lavinia was too frightened to scream as he bent her backwards and bore her down to the ground, his face inches from hers. His knee drove between her legs, pinning her against the ground as his full weight came down on her chest and shoulders. She felt his hand grasping at her skirt, reaching for the hem. He shifted his weight for a moment, trying to pull her skirt clear of his knee with one hand while the other, circling her throat, shifted to the neck of her dress, gripped and tore her collar aside.

Now she did take breath to scream, but he slammed her, hard, on the side of the head. The next moment his mouth came down on hers, smothering sound and breath, as her ringing ears filled with the shriek of tearing cloth. Her clawing hands could get no purchase: pinned beneath him with no hope of rescue or relief, she arched against the crushing weight of his body, frantic with the memory of the rope-burned, mutilated bodies of Meg's womenfolk.

He was shaking with laughter as his mouth remained locked stiflingly on hers. He shifted and tried to tear at her skirt again. The repetitive clumsiness of the motion caught a cold, aware corner of her consciousness, drawing her attention away from her panic and toward him with the scornful, measuring gaze of a fighter sizing up his opponent.

At the moment there was only one of him against her: if she was to be saved, she would have to be the one to do it and it was now or never. He was too heavy for her to thrust aside; she cast about for anything she could use as a weapon.

Her right hand encountered a length of fine, cold chain: the pendants of her chatelaine. Her groping fingers found the needle-pointed scissors that hung from it.

She thought she heard hoofbeats, but her eyes and her attention were fixed on the guerilla, whose hot hands were at her waistband.

He pulled away a little and fumbled at his belt, laughing down into her eyes. "I've got you!" he gloated.

The scissors were securely in Lavinia's fist. "You've got a pass to perdition, you hell-hound!" she snarled through her teeth, and swung her arm upward with all her strength.

She saw his expression change to horror and nausea as the scissors' point broke through the cloth of his jacket, tore through his skin and plunged into his abdomen, spilling blood over her hands in a sticky tide.

He recoiled backward, and she was out from beneath him and scrabbling in the grass for his carbine as the hoofbeats grew louder. She snapped the loading lever forward and back, jerked the piece up and pulled the trigger with a cry of triumph as he lunged to his feet and grabbed for her.

The bullet tore upward and sideways through his breastbone, lifting him for a split second and then hurling him backward to land flat on the ground as a second and then a third bullet ripped into him.

He lay motionless for the space of time it took Lavinia to drag a deep, shuddering breath into her lungs, then he arced backward and crashed to the ground again, gasping for air like a beached fish.

Lavinia leaned on the carbine, breathing in shuddering gasps as she fumbled the tatters of her bodice back into place and tried to spit out the taste of his mouth. The man's gasps became shrieks that half-obscured the sound of shouting coming toward Lavinia from the direction of the house.

The realization of what was happening made Lavinia draw a shaking breath and stiffen her quivering knees. The others, alerted by the three shots, were coming out to investigate. She had to get on Beau and ride off. She turned toward the gelding just as a group horses and riders burst into the paddock. Someone shouted her name; she looked up to see Asa Sheppard at their head, white-faced with shock. Dixie, sharply reined, skidded to her haunches and all but sat in the dust.

Sheppard kicked his feet from the stirrups and leaped from the saddle. "Dear God, Lavinia!" he gasped. "There's blood on you! Did he hurt you?"

Lavinia dropped the smoking musket and reached blindly for him. "Asa!" she cried. "Oh Asa, I did it!" She caught hold of his shoulders, her fingers tightening as though somehow she could make him a part of her and be safe from danger. "I did it!" she sobbed. "Did you see me? I didn't let him get me! I killed him!"

Sheppard held her against him for a moment. "I saw you," he said, looking over at Townsend, who was staring from her to the dying guerrilla. "You were very brave! None of us could have done better." He gave her a slight shake. "But did he hurt you?"

The question cut through the rising shock and made Lavinia grow still. "I s-shot him before he could," she said. "He t-tore my c-clothes.

That's all. Oh, and he hit me. B-but it wasn't too bad."

She could feel him reel, as though all the stiffness had melted from his bones for the moment, then he held her more closely and looked over her head at the others. "Dr. Meacham, you'd best stay here with her," he said. "She needs to be looked at right away. The rest of you go carefully: there may be others about—"

"They're in the house and out back—" Lavinia sobbed.

"What?" Sheppard demanded.

"I l-locked one of them in the s-servants' stairway. There are others in the house-I don't know how m-many-I had to get away before they saw me."

Sheppard blinked. "Get 'em," he said to the others.

"He u-used five shots," Lavinia sobbed against his shoulder. "I c-counted... S-sergeant, I'm s-sorry. I c-can't s-seem to s-speak properly..."

"Hush, love," Sheppard said. "It's all right. You've fought a battle and now it's over you're having a reaction. That's all, and it's normal. Any soldier can tell you that."

She had to speak. "T-there were m-more in the y-yard," she said, shivering. "Th-they didn't see me. I th-think they w-went to the smokehouse. Th-there are more."

"We'll find 'em," Sheppard said. "And now we'd best get you to safety." He had been unbuttoning his jacket one-handed as he spoke. He set it about Lavinia's shoulders and looked over at Dr. Meacham, who was bending over the raider and frowning terribly. "Is that piece of trash dead yet?" he demanded, his hands busy buttoning the jacket around Lavinia.

Meacham straightened. "He is now," he said. "You do good work, Vinnie."

Lavinia lifted her chin as Sheppard fastened the collar of his jacket. "M-my spectacles!" she said. "He threw them away in the bushes, just before he knocked me down."

Sheppard growled something short and contemptuous.

"We'll look for them after we've settled with these bastards," Dr. Meacham said. "Sergeant, you can go after the others."

Sheppard blinked and drew a breath. "Right," he said. "Find a place to put her safely where she can have some quiet—the barn, maybe. Take—let me see—" He scanned the militia that had remained with him. "You, Abner," he said. "You stay with Miss Wheeler. Isaiah too. I'll be back once we're finished. For now she needs to sit quietly. I wish we could get her to her bed."

"No, w-wait," Lavinia said.

Sheppard looked at her. She was white with the onset of shock, her hair was falling from its pins in untidy festoons, her eyes were wide and unfocussed without their spectacles. Dirt and grass smudged her skirt and the side of her face, blood was soaking her dress, and the over-large cavalry jacket with its brass buttons, service stripes and chevrons sat upon her with as much grace and elegance as a gunny sack. And yet, in the moment that she raised her eyes to his face and tried to smile at him, she was the most beautiful woman he had ever seen.

"You've got to find Meg," Lavinia said. "She was missing when I left Wheelerville and I wasn't able to find her here, either."

CHAPTER FORTY-FOUR

Asa Sheppard drew a long breath and gazed down into the jug's laughing eyes. If he did so, he could almost shut out the sight of torn upholstery, smashed china, splintered furniture and powdered plaster around him. But only almost; the sun, lowering toward the west, glinted upon shards of window glass too small to be caught, sending the reflections flashing upward into his eyes.

He looked up again, frowned at the broken windows, and went slowly into the grand parlor, holding the jug in his hands.

The parlor was the first room the raiders had attacked, and it had borne the brunt of their destruction. They had slashed the portraits of Lavinia's parents again and again until the canvas hung in rags. They had hurled the pink Chinese vases against the walls and stomped the fragments into powder. Someone had slashed at the heavy velvet curtains with a knife and then, finding the work too slow, had hooked a double-fistful of velvet and with one stout wrench had brought the heavy curtain rods down in a shower of dust and plaster.

Sheppard set the jug back in its place of honor and frowned around at the wreckage with a distasteful twist to his mouth. Horsehair had been pulled from the settee in great, untidy tufts and scattered around the room. The tall pier glass had been splintered, by the looks of it, with a musket butt. Destruction had had its moment there in the parlor, but the wreckage could have been five times worse, to Sheppard's mind, and he still would not complain so long as the one item missing from the scene remained missing: there was no stain or stench of blood. That was all outside, well away from the house.

He had gone straight from Lavinia's side to the house only to find that the raiders had fled. Al Townsend and his men had pursued them across Fairlawn's lands, fighting them from building to building. Judge Prescott had killed two as they ran toward the stables. Toby and four of his men had ambushed three more by the smokehouse. Eight more had gone down in a hail of bullets in the meadow beyond the stable, and Sheppard had personally ridden down two of them near the springhouse.

The rest had dropped their weapons and raised their hands. Sheppard, remembering the expressions on the faces of Wheelerville's citizens, thought they would be regretting their surrender shortly, especially if Haller Reeves, shot in the fighting by the stable, died. He would be going outside in a moment to inspect the bodies, but first he wanted to see what had been done with the house so that he would know what to tell Lavinia and what to keep from her.

He drew another long breath, expelled it, and went into the formal dining room. The table, cushioned by one of the fallen curtains from the parlor, was heaped with the plunder taken from the raiders' saddlebags. He could see scraps of brightly colored cloth tied in bundles, small books, elaborate photograph cases, sewing scissors, hand mirrors, ribbons, baby shoes, all jumbled together without reason or sense, and everywhere the glint of gold: watches, earrings, rings, some of it tarnished and rust-stained, all waiting to be sorted and listed the next day. For now, it would remain in the house, guarded by Sam Wallins and Caesar, who had volunteered to stay at Fairlawn along with a contingent of men.

Sheppard frowned at a tangle of gold chains and then turned on his heel. He had to return to Wheelerville and see how Lavinia was doing, and whether Meg had been found.

He went through the house and out the front door to where one of Caesar's men was holding Dixie. He paused, though, nodded to the man, and hurried back into the parlor. He was outside again in under a minute with Sir Walter Raleigh's jug wrapped in a scrap of cloth. It would cheer up Lavinia.

Judge Prescott, sitting his horse beside Dixie, watched him emerge from the house. "We've laid out the carrion over there," he said, and then, nodding toward the jug, asked, "Are you taking that to Miss Lavinia?"

Sheppard handed the bundle to him and swung up into the saddle. "I thought it might make her feel better about things," he said, taking the jug back and setting it into a saddlebag. "She told me it makes her feel better to think that other people who owned the pottery lived through times as hard as these and survived."

"That's true," Prescott said. "But she's done all the surviving she needs to today."

Sheppard cocked an eye at him. "I don't know," he said, turning Dixie away from Wheelerville toward the stable. "I think the hardest part is yet to come."

"How so?" asked Prescott. "She's won!"

Sheppard frowned at the line of bodies stretched out just beyond the stable. "She's met what she feared and she's won against it, but that doesn't cancel the fact that her fears actually came true. Each time she remembers that, she has to make herself remember that she beat it. She can do it, and in the end it'll be for the best, but she's not strong, Judge: she needs help."

"She's strong enough for three men," Prescott said. "You've seen what a will she has. She gets her way without having to raise her voice."

"I should have said 'robust,' " Sheppard said. "And you know I'm right about that. She's plucky and gallant, but she's been carrying a heavy load for the past few years and it's beginning to tell on her."

Prescott frowned over at him and then nodded his head. "You've known her less time than I have, but you're right," he said. "The jug will be a help and a comfort to her." He turned his horse toward the line of bodies and nudged it to a reluctant amble. He dug with his heels when the animal balked at the smell of blood and tried to shy. "Whoa, horse!" he said through his teeth. "Good God, Sergeant! You'd think with all the fighting over the past few months this beast would be used to the smell!"

"It's a hard thing to get used to," Sheppard said. Dixie's shoes were nearly touching the shoulder of the man Lavinia had killed. "Some of us wish we hadn't." He frowned down at the row of dead. "They're all pretty young," he said after a moment. "What do you make it? Twenties at the most?"

"Twenties," Judge Prescott agreed. "They're very well equipped."

"They've had dozens of battlefields to scavenge from in the past months," Sheppard said. "And hundreds of homes to raid."

"They've done that," Prescott said. He leaned forward to stare. He finally sat back with a rueful half-laugh. "It's odd," he said. "I'd thought I'd be able to tell if they were north or south."

Sheppard nodded toward the closest corpse. "That one's wearing a Georgia belt buckle," he said. "I see other Confederate insignia, as well." He added softly, "The leader was wearing a uniform."

"Then these men were southerners," Judge Prescott said. "I am ashamed to be one, myself, now."

Sheppard sat back and eased his stiff left shoulder. "Some were born and raised in the south," he said. "And some in the north too, I'll wager. The point you've got to remember is, they weren't with any army. No army would have them. They were scavengers and murderers banded together to get as much loot as they could with as little effort as possible."

** ** **

Lavinia sighed and closed her eyes for a moment, reveling in the lassitude that seemed to engulf her. She remembered that she had faced her greatest fear and come away victorious. The triumph had all but undone her. She had sat for a lifetime in the barn with Isaiah and Abner, listening to the sound of firing, her teeth clenched upon the shudders that had threatened to engulf her.

Isaiah had stirred and gone outside when silence had fallen. He was smiling when he came back in, and he had announced that the raiders were all taken care of and it was all right for Miss Vinnie to go back to town. He had ridden with her and Abner, and when they had reached Abner's house, he had told Mrs. Wigfall and Callie to give Lavinia some morphia and put her to bed: Sarge's orders. She was to get some sleep and let the others worry about Meg.

Callie had given her a cup of something sweet and sticky that had driven away her shudders, had tucked her into bed, spoken soothingly about Meg—where was the child?—and drawn the blinds.

Time had drifted, skeins of memory weaving a web that was half-dream and half-imagination, filled with remembered snatches of conversation, faces almost recognized.

The door opened as she drifted along, the faint click of the latch falling into silence. A woman came into the room and stood at the foot of the bed.

Things were blurred for Lavinia without her glasses, but she could see that the woman was dressed in dark, shiny taffeta with a lace shawl about her shoulders. Her waving hair framed her face in wings, and Lavinia thought she could see a very fine brooch at her throat, and what looked to be gold drops in her ears.

She seemed somehow familiar, though Lavinia could not see her face clearly. She remembered vaguely that she was a friend. "Who are you?" she asked drowsily.

The woman smiled but was silent. Lavinia could catch the faint scent of mimosa.

"Have you found Meg?" Lavinia asked as the woman came closer and smoothed her pillow.

The woman smiled more warmly and set a finger to her lips.

"She's all right, then?" Lavinia said. "Oh thank goodness! I was so worried." She blinked back tears of relief and fatigue and looked full into the woman's face. What she saw made her falter for a moment.

"Sarah?" she said.

Sarah Sheppard smiled at her and sat down beside the bed.

"You're here, then? Asa will be so happy! He thinks you're dead!"

Sarah Sheppard's smile bordered on laughter. She shook her head and took Lavinia's hand. Her fingers felt warm and firm, and Lavinia felt the last lingering traces of the afternoon's shock and fear melting away.

"He'll be happy," she said again,. "He's missed you."

Sarah shook her head again. Her head tilted slightly, as though she were listening.

Lavinia, listening too, heard footsteps in the hallway.

Sarah flashed a laughing glance at her and then turned toward the door as it swung open.

Sheppard came into the room, followed by Callie. As Lavinia watched, Sarah gazed up at him, turned to smile once more at Lavinia, and was gone. Just for a moment it looked as though Sheppard had walked through her.

"Lavinia?" Callie said. "Wake up, child! We've got some good news for you: we've found Meg, and Sergeant Sheppard's just come back from Fairlawn. Everything's just fine!"

Lavinia opened her eyes and found everything as she had seen. Sheppard was standing near her bed with a bundle in his arms and an expression in his eyes that she wanted to see more closely. Callie was standing beyond him, her eyes suspiciously reddened, but she was smiling.

"Was I sleeping?" Lavinia asked.

"Yes, thank the Lord and morphia!" Callie said.

Lavinia looked over at the chair and then closed her eyes again.

"No wonder, then," she said. "But it seemed so real..."

"Miss Lavinia," Sheppard said.

She opened her eyes again and smiled up at him. "What is it, Asa?" she asked.

Callie cleared her throat and sat down near the door.

Sheppard looked at her and then turned back to Lavinia.

"Did Callie say they found Meg?" Lavinia asked as he sat down beside her bed. "Where was she all this time?"

"She was curled up and sleeping in the linen chest," Sheppard said. "She came wandering out just ten minutes ago, knuckling her eyes and yawning. Mrs. Swithin saw her and raised the cry."

"I'm so glad she's safe," Lavinia said. "What happened with everyone else?"

"The raiders were beaten," Sheppard said.

"Was anyone hurt?" Lavinia asked.

"Several of them were killed," Sheppard answered.

Lavinia looked at him. "I meant any of our people," she said.

Sheppard looked down at the bundle in his hands. "One man was hurt," he said. "Haller Reeves. He hasn't died, but they don't know yet... He's hurt badly."

"Poor man," Lavinia sighed. "After all his trouble and bluster he joined the militia and came to this. Tell him I'm thinking of him and praying for him."

Sheppard nodded. "It'll do him good to hear it," he said.

Lavinia folded her hands before her and leaned her head back against her pillows. Someone had braided her hair: Callie, no doubt. She looked up from the braid to Sheppard's face. A hint of suppressed tension in his position made her lift her eyebrows at him. "Was there anything else?" she asked.

"They did some damage to the house, too," he said.

Lavinia nodded. "I heard them breaking and smashing things," she said. "It kept them from hearing me, so I was glad for it. Was it very bad?"

"They did a lot of damage," Sheppard said. "Portraits slashed, vases broken, the curtains pulled down—"

"It's good they didn't get into my house in Savannah, then," Lavinia said. "All my most valuable things are there."

Sheppard stared at her.

"Don't look at me like that," she said. She frowned. "Or don't look at me like I think you're looking at me. I wish I had my spectacles. Were they found?"

"Yes, they were," Sheppard said, reaching into his pocket. "The more fool me for forgetting! Here: Al Townsend had his group crawling around through the bushes on their hands and knees looking for them."

Lavinia put the spectacles on her nose and looked around. They were bent; she took them off and adjusted them, then donned them again. "That's much better," she said. "He tore these from my face—" An involuntary movement from him made her break off and look at him.

He was smiling at her but the smile seemed strained. "You beat him," he said. "Never forget that."

"Yes," she said. "I beat him. I wanted to keep shooting him again and again, but I didn't know how many bullets were in his gun."

Sheppard unwrapped the bundle. "I brought you this," he said. "To remind you that others have gone through hard times and lived."

"Oh, Asa!" Lavinia said, taking the jug from him.

"You've added some history to it," Sheppard said. "People will see it in centuries to come and take comfort to think that this jug lived through an attack by bandits."

Lavinia's expression was thoughtful as she turned the jug in her hands. "I wonder if any of them wanted to shoot and shoot and keep shooting until their attackers were a pile of rags," she said.

"I don't know about them," Sheppard said, reaching out to touch the glaze. "But I know I have." His hand began to shake. He lowered it.

"Asa?" Lavinia watched as he turned away from her, pushed to his feet, and went to the window. "Asa?"

"When I came riding into the stableyard in time to see that man—" he began, speaking with difficulty. He fell silent and lowered his head.

Lavinia spoke gently. "But it's all right now, Asa," she said. "Meg's safe, you're alive, and I'm fine, though I'm a little tired. But that will pass. There's nothing to fret over. Asa, won't you turn around and look at me?"

He turned, wet-eyed and helpless.

The sight made her heart turn over. She held out her hands to him.

"Come sit down," she said, taking his hands as he went to her and holding them warmly for a moment. "You're all in, yourself, and no wonder, trying to think and fight for everyone! Here, hold the demijohn and think for a moment about all the people who've had it and lived through terrible times to emerge triumphant. Just think of it, Asa: you're one of them now, and so am I."

He tried to smile at her as she took one of her lace handkerchiefs from the table beside her bed and handed it to him. "I'm ashamed of myself," he said, wiping at his eyes. "I wanted to cheer you up."

"You already have," Lavinia said. "Do you know what you did for me? When I was trying to get away, I kept thinking of you. It gave me the strength to fight. If you hadn't been here, at Wheelerville, I wouldn't have had that to hold to, and then where would I have been?" She looked over at Callie, sitting quietly beside the door. "I needed you," she said softly. "And you came just as I needed you most."

CHAPTER FORTY-FIVE

Al Townsend looked up at the facade of Haller Reeves' house and reflected on appearances and prejudices. The building was white-washed clapboard, built of Georgia pine harvested, cut and milled at the Wheelers' sawmill. It had been framed and constructed in the third decade of the current century; Townsend could just remember watching the framework going up as a boy of six. It had been a plain building, well-built but with nothing singular to recommend itself to visitors.

Haller Reeves' father had started the Wheelerville Gazette shortly after that, and by the time Haller had stepped into the family's publishing business, the paper was the largest in western Georgia, with a following as far north and east as Charleston, chiefly because of its columns devoted to livestock.

The paper's success had encouraged Haller to turn his attention to political matters, and he had had the opportunity, over the ten years leading up to the war, to rub shoulders with some of the more fiery politicians in Georgia. He had gone to Milledgeville and watched the legislature in action, and had spent part of several years in Savannah as well. He had returned with a taste for good living and a desire for splendor that was, unfortunately, thwarted by his house.

Al Townsend looked at the columned portico that sat on the front of the Georgia pine clapboard house with as much congruity as a false nose upon a baby's face and shook his head. Haller Reeves, wishing for Fairlawn's grandeur, had transformed his house into a monstrosity. And Al Townsend, at once contemptuous of Reeves' particular brand of pretention and envious of his prosperity, had watched and laughed himself sick behind the man's back.

Now, gazing up at the facade through the shadows of night, Townsend saw the house for what it was, the attempted realization of a dream that was harmless and even a little pathetic. And now it was too late for him to say so, although he had tried just then. Maybe Reeves had understood him.

He looked down at the hat that he was clenching in his hands, turned it over, and finally settled it on his head, pulling it low over one eye. His horse, tethered by the door, lifted his head and stretched an inquisitive nose toward him. Townsend had too much to think of; he wanted to walk. He patted the beast absently, unhitched the reins, and led the horse down the street toward the Wigfall house, where the faint glow of light in the windows showed that people were still wakeful.

** ** **

John Meacham sat down with a sigh. The night threatened never to end, and the long, fearful day had already exhausted him. He often wondered what would happen if his strength ran out when people needed him. It had not happened yet nor, he supposed wryly, was it likely to do so soon. Or not very soon. And yet, of all the days of his life, this day had come closest to that realization.

He knew he should be getting back to Haller Reeves' house. Whatever was to happen would happen better if he were present.

He sighed and closed his eyes. In a moment he would gather himself and rise, collect his medicines, and go back to Reeves and his anxious-eyed wife. In a moment.

He heard the clop of hooves coming toward him along the street and opened his eyes to see Al Townsend leading his horse. The soft, reflected light from the house traced his features and seemed to emphasize the silence and exhaustion of his expression.

Years pass very unevenly Meacham reflected, his mind casting back to the arrogant young man who had hurried off to war at the first call for troops early in 1861 and contrasting that memory with the man who now faced him, trying to smile up at him. He was far more than only three and a half years older than the youngster who had joined the army.

Dr. Meacham returned his smile. "Evening, Al," he said.

"Evening, Doc," Townsend said. He looked down at the reins in his hands as though he was not sure why they were there.

"Can you sit down a moment?" Meacham asked.

Townsend flexed the reins and finally nodded. "I can pause a spell," he said. "I just came from Reeves' place."

"I'll be getting back there soon," Meacham sighed. "Is he worse?"

"Doesn't look too good," Townsend said. He caught Meacham's annoyed expression. "I mean it," he said. "But I can't say how he'll go. Gut-shot's not good news, no matter what."

"I think it's not as bad as it might be," Meacham said.

"It isn't?" Sheppard asked, coming onto the porch. He nodded to Townsend and sat down beside Meacham. "That's good news!"

"Maybe," Meacham said. "It depends on how he does over the next twenty-four hours. The next day will decide."

"I left him in pretty good spirits, I guess," Townsend said. "For someone who's gut-shot, that is. I think he wanted to recover."

"The problem," Sheppard said, "is that he's gut-shot."

"That's not necessarily a death sentence," Meacham said. "Private Pierce has done well."

"We can hope and pray," Sheppard said. He turned at the sound of the door opening and closing behind him, saw Louise Hamiter emerging from the house in a hiss and murmur of taffeta, and turned away.

Dr. Meacham rose and Townsend touched his hat to her. Sheppard folded his arms and was silent.

"How is Miss Lavinia?" Townsend asked.

"She's doing well," Sheppard said with a smile. "She's a lady with a lot of firmness of mind. She seems to be recovering surprisingly well."

Louise Hamiter strolled to one of the chairs and sat, disposing her skirts about herself in a blue froth and directing a calculating smile at Al Townsend. "Oh pooh!" she said. "All this talk of recovering! What did she get but just a little fright?"

Sheppard's voice was dry. "She was attacked by renegades," he pointed out.

"She wasn't in any danger," Louise said. "Why, I'd be inclined to think that it is all an act. And it is not a particularly convincing act to those of us who know her."

Sheppard's eyes narrowed, but he kept silent.

Dr. Meacham slowly put his feet up on the porch railing. His expression was distant for a moment; it shortened and he scanned Louise much a researcher might scan a colony of especially puzzling particles under a microscope. "Do you think so?" he asked. "Interesting."

"She only suffered a fright," Louise repeated.

The conversation was making Sheppard scowl. "She was hit, hard, several times," he said. His voice was slightly altered, as though he were trying to keep it level. "And her attacker made it pretty clear he meant to rape her."

"A fright," Louise said, directing a glance of aloof dislike at him. "And she is doing fine now. Tucked in and fussed over by everyone. It pains me to put things so bluntly, but dear Lavinia is faking matters or I am much mistaken."

Townsend was listening with complete, annoyed disbelief. "You know," he said, clearing his throat, "it occurs to me that she'd not be in this state, faking or not, if you'd passed on the message I gave you today."

Louise turned and looked him slowly up and down, her gaze lingering on his smoke-begrimed hands and his less-than-clean jacket. She turned back to Dr. Meacham without speaking.

Sheppard's color was darkening. Townsend had the impression that he was holding his tongue because he did not think he could control it.

Dr. Meacham eyed the two men with a touch of amusement, drew a long, considering breath and looked at Louise. "Well, Miss Hamiter," he said. "Miss Lavinia certainly had a fright. The question we face is what sort of fright she had and what she was afraid of. The fright came from a group of renegades that has been terrorizing this part of the state for some months and that killed little Meg's family as well as some other families, all known to people in this area. Am I correct so far?"

Louise looked at him.

Sheppard was relaxing a little. He lifted his eyebrows and sat back.

"But of course I am," Dr. Meacham continued. "That being the case, I think it's safe to say that Miss Wheeler was afraid of this group, especially in view of all they had done, starting with Meg's family. Which begs the question, Miss Hamiter: did you see Meg's family when they were brought to Wheelerville?"

Townsend, listening with a puzzled frown, said, "She didn't. She showed up the same day that Sheppard here stood off that Yank foraging party."

"I thought as much," Dr. Meacham said. "It appears, then, that you didn't see the burns, Miss Hamiter. Among other things."

Louise stared at him. "I did not, sir," she said. "I do not see how that changes matters."

"-or the butchery," Meacham continued as though Louise had not spoken. "The burns were almost the worst, perhaps because there were so many types. Flame burns on the hands and feet of that feeble old man, and all over the body of a man so badly burned and hacked that I could not even guess at his age."

Sheppard pushed himself to his feet with a grimace of disgust. "Excuse me, Dr. Meacham," he said. "I must check on the guards, and report to Judge Prescott."

Dr. Meacham smiled and waved him away. "Go on, then, Sergeant," he said. "Go on. You lived through this once and there's no need to go over it again. Send my regards to the judge. Now where was I? Ah yes, Miss Hamiter: such a variety of burns, too! The one man was hanged—I hope it was before he was burned—and the one woman had rope burns about her ankles, for what purpose one can only guess. It must have been terrible for her, though, for she seems to have fought the ropes: the abrasions and rope burns gouged deep into the flesh, especially on the inner ankles. They cut through to the bone, in fact. And what they did to that newborn baby surpassed anything I have ever seen."

Dr. Meacham continued speaking, the words falling upon Townsend's numbed ears almost without form. Louise appeared to be listening very reluctantly, for at one moment Townsend saw Dr. Meacham reach out and grip her elbow and hold her in her chair as he continued to talk.

At least, Townsend thought he was talking, for Louise Hamiter's expression of disgust and horror continued to grow. Dr. Meacham seemed to be waxing clinical, steepling his fingertips, with his head slightly to the side as was his habit when discussing a particularly vexing case. But Townsend could not hear him, and just as well, for the memory of the murder of Meg's family needed no refreshing. He pushed to his feet and made his farewells through lips that felt stiff.

"Must you be going, then, Captain Townsend?" Meacham asked. "Well, go on then, go on. Duty calls, I daresay, and you have various claims on your attention. No, no, Miss Hamiter. You need not leave. I know for a fact that you have no useful occupation to claim your attention, at least for the moment, and it is a pleasure to discuss this fascinating case with one who is not troubled by it. Now where was I? Ah yes: the question of whether the attackers had any sort of medical training, since the type and location of the incisions on the corpses led me to conclude..."

His voice seemed to fade away as Townsend led his horse away from the place.

He came to the mounting block before one of the houses and gazed at it for a moment before gathering the reins, setting his foot in the stirrup and stepping into the saddle. He wiped his forehead after a moment and turned the horse toward Fairlawn.

** ** **

"Is all safe and well in the town now?" Judge Prescott asked Sheppard at the same moment that Al Townsend was riding off down the street. He was frowning down at some papers and making notations. As Sheppard watched, he tapped them into alignment and set them aside.

"Safe and well for the most part," Sheppard said. "I hear from Townsend and the doctor that Haller Reeves may not be as badly off as they had feared.

"That would be a boon," Prescott said. "Odd to think that he of all people might die a hero."

"I've seen less likely ones," Sheppard said. "But I'd rather he didn't die."

"He may not. He comes from a line of ornery folk. Well, all's safe then," Prescott said. "We must be thankful for our deliverance." He smiled at Sheppard and added, "And do not think, my dear Mr. Sheppard, that I am ignorant of who is responsible for that deliverance."

"You may want to thank Al Townsend, too," Sheppard said.

Prescott frowned toward the window as a rider went clattering by. "Too late," he said. "He's heading for Fairlawn, from what I can see. Well."

"And your own excellent aim," Sheppard said with the edge of a smile."

Prescott inclined his head. "I knew my years of squirreling would not go to waste," he said. "And tell me, how is Miss Vinnie?"

"She's recovering," Sheppard said. "Callie's dosed her with laudanum from our store, so she's sleepy, but I think she'll be all right. Thank God she had the gumption to fight those monsters off as she did!"

"Oh, she's never lacked for gumption in the years I've known her," Prescott said. "Even as a little girl, coming here summers and running along the creeks with a fishing rod and a supply of worms. And later, as a grown woman, riding to hounds and taking the most bruising fences without so much as a blink!"

"She has courage," Sheppard said. His smile had faded a little.

"Did she need the jug?" Prescott asked.

Sheppard looked over at him. "I needed it," he said. "She let me hold it." Prescott's long-fingered hand slid the pile of papers toward him. He began to shuffle the pages without looking at them. "It's taking a toll of everyone," he said with a quizzical lift to his eyebrows. "Even you."

"I never claimed to be made of stone," Sheppard sighed.

"It's hard when the woman you love is in danger," Prescott said. He did not follow that comment with anything related. Instead he said, "How is Louise Hamiter doing?"

Sheppard's smile was back and knife-edged. "Not well," he said. "I left Dr. Meacham giving her a detailed description of the bodies of Meg's family."

Prescott frowned. "Is that kind?" he asked.

"I don't care," Sheppard said. "So long as she stays away from me, I won't complain."

"Maybe it'll give her nightmares," Prescott said.

"We can only hope," Sheppard said. "And in the meantime, we can go through what those scum left and see if we can figure out who they are and if there are any more of them that we missed."

CHAPTER FORTY-SIX

"I don't understand why they took half this stuff," Abner said, sorting through the pile of jumbled scraps of metal and wood before him. "Heck, if I'd found it lying by the roadside, I'd have left it lay!"

Corporal Higgins grimaced at the debris and poked at a broken daguerreotype case. "They're looking for gold," he said.

"In a picture case?"

"There's shiny yellow metal there," Higgins said. "They probably thought it was gold."

"Where?" Abner demanded, opening the case. He scowled at the metal matting. "Hell," he said, "I can't see anyone thinking this was gold!"

"No one said those creeps were smart," Higgins remarked.

Abner pushed the cracked case away and sifted his fingers through the yellowed scraps of ivory before him. They clattered and rattled like china. "And all these teeth!" he said. "Look at them! They were crazy as loons!"

Higgins made a notation on a sheet of paper and traded grins with Sam Wallins, who said, "Look at the teeth again, Abner, and see what you see."

Abner bent his gaze to the teeth. "Gold," he said.

"That's right," Wallins said. "Throw a handful of those in a good, hot fire, kindled atop an iron plate, and when it cools you'll end up with enough gold to buy a good horse."

"But there's no skin sticking to the teeth!" Abner objected.

"Probably got them from cemeteries," Higgins said. "Or maybe an old battlefield that wasn't cleaned up."

Abner stared.

"That's right, son," Higgins said. "There's a pretty brisk trade in teeth after a battle. I hear barrels of them are being sent overseas to England right now."

"Th-that's horrible!"

"Well, they don't need 'em any more," Wallins said comfortably. He eyed the pile of loot and then looked over at Higgins. "You getting all the count?" he asked.

"Sure am," Higgins said, picking up the pencil again and eyeing the tip. "Those fellows made quite a haul."

Abner's eyes were still wide. "Do you think they got anything else from a graveyard?" he asked shakily.

"All these wedding rings, probably," Higgins said. "And any gold buttons you see. They must have left a rare mess between where they started and here."

"They sure left a mess here," Abner said.

Wallins pushed a pile of hair jewelry to the side and nodded. "Just wait 'till Miss Lavinia sees it," he said.

"Or Callie, come to that," said Higgins.

"Till they see what?" Sheppard asked, coming in the door. He nodded to Wallins and Higgins, smiled at Toby, and lifted an eyebrow at Abner.

"The wreck those bastards made of the house," Abner said.

Sheppard looked around the room with a thoughtful twist to his mouth. "It can be cleaned up," he said. "I was going to ask you, Toby, if you had the makings of plaster here: the holes in the wall could be replastered, and when it's dry the curtains could go up again. I guess the only thing to do with the china is to sweep it up, but the rest of the damage can be taken away. It beats me why they didn't smash those huge mirrors when they had the chance."

"Maybe they didn't want the bad luck," Wallins suggested.

Toby looked up from the sack of coins he had been counting. That doesn't make any sense," he said "Seeing that they already dug up graves!"

"No one said those creeps were smart," Higgins said again. "I've got some figures for you, Sarge, if you want to look at them. Toby's not finished counting the coins yet, and there's a wad of greenbacks and Reb shinplasters, too, that needs counting, but it'll give you an idea what they were toting with them."

Sheppard strolled over to Higgins and read over his shoulder. He whistled thoughtfully. "That much gold!" he said.

"That isn't counting the teeth," Wallins said.

Sheppard lifted his eyebrows at the teeth. "Lots of dug-up cemeteries around, I guess," he said.

"Or toothless Georgians," Higgins added. "Though I think we'd have noticed that."

"Very funny," Wallins growled.

"They must have raided a few cemeteries," Higgins said. He cocked an eye at Abner and added, "Those teeth are too old and too dry for anything else. You can't even smell the embalming."

Abner shuddered.

Sheppard saw the motion and aimed a stern look at Higgins, who looked down, grinning. He turned to Abner and said mildly, "Are you going through that pile of photographs, Abner? Good idea: keep an eye out for any writing on them that'll give us a clue as to who they robbed." He added, "One thing's sure: they weren't likely to have taken those pictures from a graveyard."

"They—they weren't?" Abner asked. His hands were beginning to unclench.

"It's too damp in a coffin, son," Sheppard said. "Anything paper or wood would be spoiled in just a few weeks. These fellows want things that are easily reached: teeth, rings, watches, maybe. They're not inclined to go pawing around a coffin after soggy papers and rotted wood and gutta-percha that isn't worth anything, so you don't have to worry about it. Do you understand me?"

Some color was coming back into Abner's face and he was beginning to relax. "Yes, sir," he said.

"Good," said Sheppard. "Now keep a good eye on what you see with those pictures. If you notice anyone you even think you recognize, give a yell."

"Yes, sir!" Abner said with a grin.

Sheppard turned to the others. "I'll be around the grounds," he said. "I want to see what they did around the place. Let me know if you find anything." He frowned at the others, "And the rest of you lighten up!"

Wallins watched him go and then turned back to Higgins. "I'll bet he'd rather be in town," he said thoughtfully.

"Maybe," Higgins agreed. "But it'd be awkward for him being there while they questioned those scum."

"Yeah, I guess he's smart to stay here," Wallins said. "They were wearing some Confederate equipment."

A muffled noise from Abner made both men look over at him. He was staring, wide-eyed and pale-faced, at an opened daguerreotype case.

"All right, boy," Toby said from across the table. "What's eating you now?"

Abner pushed himself to his feet, still staring at the case. He set it down with an oddly groping motion, turned away, stepped off the rug, and vomited on Miss Lavinia's polished hardwood floor.

** ** **

"So you maintain that you went from Alabama to Georgia chasing after Yankee cavalry," Judge Prescott said. The prisoner, manacled and seated at the heavy oak table in Wheelerville's jail and courthouse, inclined his head. "That is correct," he replied.

"Why were you here instead of out with the rest of the army, fighting Sherman and his Yankees?" Townsend demanded. He had been sitting more or less quietly for the past hour while Judge Prescott conducted a very thorough questioning, but it was apparent that his patience was wearing thin.

The man looked up at him from under half-closed eyes and then flicked a half-contemptuous glance around at his questioners, who were ranged in a circle around him. "Orders," he said. "Do you argue with your officers?"

"Depends on what they order me to do," Townsend said. "Burning houses and torturing old folk and raping women might just give me pause."

The man lifted an eyebrow. "I didn't touch any woman yesterday," he said. He stretched his legs out before him and crossed them at the ankles. "Does someone say I did?"

"Someone says your group did," Townsend said.

The man looked from him to Judge Prescott, who was conducting the questioning while seated behind his desk with a pen in his hand. His bearing was calm and even a little amused, and he was surprisingly spruce for a man who had spent the day before riding hard and fighting, and had passed the night in a crowded jail with the rest of his group.

"He has stated the case accurately," Judge Prescott said, toying with the cord of his pince-nez spectacles. "One of your men certainly did try to molest a lady of this town. She fought him off, fortunately for your group."

"An Amazon, I take it," the man said. "Good for her! Look: I had nothing to do with attacking her, and most of the rest of my group would sooner die than do anything of the sort. Let us be reasonable: you're Confederate and so am I. The attacker is gone. Why don't you just let us go?"

"Releasing you does not seem advisable at the moment," Prescott said. "Your group is suspected of having done some things that do not sit well with law-abiding and right-thinking folk. That is why you're being detained for questioning by this committee." He looked at the man over his spectacles and said, "None of your answers have served to reassure me as to your actions past or future. In fact, you seem to have forgotten that you and your men were taken in the act of robbing and molesting one of our townsfolk."

"There's a war on," the man said. "Mistakes happen. The man who attacked that woman will pay the price, which is only fair. There is no need to detain us when we would be better occupied fighting the Yankees."

Al Townsend folded his arms and frowned at the man. "I guess you mistook Fairlawn plantation for a fort," he said. "And you mistook the lady for a general!"

The man looked him up and down and turned back to Prescott. "I haven't objected to these manacles," he said, holding up his wrists. "And I haven't objected to this forum, which is irregular, to say the least,"

"You can set you mind to rest on that point," Judge Prescott said. "I am the chief magistrate for this county, and cases of murder, vandalism, robbery and rape are within my authority. This is, as you have pointed out, war. You would be best advised to answer my questions directly. And as to Captain Townsend—" frowning at him over his spectacles, "If you will sit down, Al, and hold your peace, things will be handled better and more smoothly."

Townsend pulled a chair forward and sat, straddling it. Prescott nodded to him, looked back at the man and sat back in his chair. "Now, sir," he said. "We have been watching your group for some days. Your actions do not match our idea of the activities followed by an army."

"Watching us?" the man said. "Odd: we didn't see anyone shadowing us."

"That's because you were too busy wrecking things and murdering people to keep a good lookout!" Townsend flashed.

Judge Prescott looked at him. "Alan," he said. He sat back and folded his hands before him. After a moment he removed his pince-nez spectacles from the bridge of his nose and polished them on his handkerchief. "There is something in what Captain Townsend says," he said at last. "You are certainly careless that way. And you're destructive, which we don't like. And you attacked civilians. You spoke of orders a moment ago. Very well, then: why were you here and what were you doing?"

The man, whom Judge Prescott had singled out as the probable leader of the group because of his uniform and bearing, sat back and steepled his fingertips before him in a gesture whose elegance and culture seemed somehow discordant. He was smiling slightly to himself when he replied. "Under the circumstances, I judge that I can tell you," he said. "Though I must request that you not allow the word to go beyond this room. We were directed to forage for the armies fighting Sherman. Food is very scarce and the good people of the Confederacy are not inclined to give it when it's needed. As to the damage, why we had made a good haul and my boys were whooping it up a little. I would have chastised them severely if I had caught them before you caught us." His eyes narrowed and he added, "And I haven't yet brought up the question of you arming niggers and firing on your own men!—but that's all it was. Look, let us go and I'll forget to write up a complaint to the military authorities."

Prescott slowly drew the pen through his fingertips as he looked the man up and down. He seemed well-bred, with elegantly formed, long-fingered hands. "That's very generous of you," he said. "You're a man of breeding, by the look of you, with some schooling after college: the law, perhaps?"

"Medicine," the man said with a thin smile.

Townsend stared.

"I see," Prescott said. "Our town physician would be most interested to hear that. Well, sir, as to your offer: I am tempted to take you up on it, except for some problems that can probably be straightened out if we look into them properly."

"Are you dealing with this bastard, Judge?" John Toombs demanded.

"Sit down, Jack, and shut up," Townsend said.

The prisoner directed a distant look at them and then turned back to Judge Prescott and lifted his eyebrows. "Such as—?" he said.

"Your men killed a citizen, for one," Prescott said. "The man died this morning."

"So? Your people killed quite a few of mine," The man returned. "You haven't heard me saying anything."

"That is because it isn't a crime to kill vermin!" Townsend gritted. "You were attacking us! We were defending ourselves!"

"Al," Judge Prescott said. He put his glasses back on and scanned the prisoner for a long moment. "He does make a point," he said at last. "There is, as well, a question of attempted rape. One might possibly mistake our townsfolk, who were defending themselves in good faith, for the enemy. But I cannot imagine that anyone would mistake a lady, dressed appropriately for a woman and seeking to get away from your group without attracting notice, for an enemy soldier." His eyes narrowed slightly and he added, "I recall, in fact, that the lady was wearing a dress of green plaid taffeta and a straw hat with silk roses at the brim. That apparel is, I need hardly say, nothing at all like the uniforms I have seen on the federal troops that have come through here in the past several months."

"I was given no chance to discipline the man, myself," the man said.

"That might have been interesting to see," Prescott said. "Well. The lady was fleeing another man who menaced her, and whom she had just succeeded in locking in the back stairway when her attacker came upon her. It would appear, thus, that you had two would-be rapists in your group. Would you have disciplined him as well?"

The room was silent. The prisoner moistened his lips and took breath to speak just as a knock sounded at the door.

Judge Prescott turned toward the sound. "Come in," he said.

Sam Wallins entered the room. He looked paler than usual, but he took a folded paper from his pocket and handed it to the judge. "They've finished the inventory, more or less," he said. "Here's the write-up. Higgins says the numbers are pretty much on target."

Prescott scanned the paper. "I see," he said. "This is all very interesting." He folded the paper and set it aside. "Well, sir," he said to the prisoner. "For a foraging party working in an area peopled mostly by civilians, you had very little luck. All you seem to have been able to gather since Atlanta fell is two hams, a bushel of corn and a sack of flour. Hm." He opened the paper again. "All that is edible, that is," he said. "I can see that you did get quite a haul of some other items. Rings, other jewelry, cloth... Interesting."

"You'll be interested in this, too," Wallins said, offering two photograph cases. "Abner tossed his lunch and the last five meals before it when he found those." He watched as Judge Prescott took them and opened them.

Prescott's hands shook slightly as he put the cases down and looked up at the prisoner. "It would appear, sir," he said, "that you did considerably more than to simply take forage."

He pushed the cases toward Al Townsend, who opened them and gazed, then drew a shaken breath and set them down.

Caesar picked up the cases and opened the top one.

Sam Wallins opened the sack and took out a small silver bowl, which he set upon the table without comment.

Without the slightest warning, Ed Pickens hurled himself across the heavy oak table and bore the prisoner to the floor, his hands clenched about the man's throat. "You murderer!" he snarled, and then, the others upon him, wasted no further breath in speech.

It took the combined efforts of Sam Wallins, Judge Prescott, Al Townsend and Caesar to pull him off the man and subdue him. Even then, pinioned and panting with his fists bunched and white-knuckled, he tried to wrench himself out of Caesar's grip, his eyes blazing fire.

"Let me at him!" he said through his teeth. "He's a dead man!"

Judge Prescott nodded to Wallins, who led the prisoner out of the room and back to his cell ahead of the muzzle of a drawn and cocked pistol.

"I don't understand!" Caesar said.

"Take a look at the photographs," Judge Prescott said. "Meg and her mother are in the one on top. And Meg's mother and an officer are in the other." He looked at Pickens with some puzzlement. "Although the bowl—"

Pickens was struggling again. "It was my sister's!" he said through his teeth. "He's one of the scum who killed her and her man! He's the leader! God help us all, he tortured and killed the others too and he almost killed Miss Lavinia! God *damn* you, Al Townsend, let me go!"

"Release him," Judge Prescott said. He looked at the photograph while Pickens rubbed his shoulders and glared. "Well," he said, "It puts a far different face on things."

Wallins came back. "He's a cold son of a bitch," he said. "He didn't even turn a hair, though he must know he's dead now."

"He knows he's dead," Caesar said. "From what I saw of that list, they've been robbing and looting."

"And killing," Wallins said. "Some of that gold had blood on it. And that bowl there ties them in to Ed's sister's murder. Toby says Miss Lavinia, too, can identify it as being taken from Mr. and Mrs. Pike."

Al Townsend had lifted the photograph cases and was gazing at them with an unreadable expression. "Benton," he said.

"What?" Caesar said.

"George Benton," Townsend said. "He was the adjutant of the regiment I left when my enlistment was up. He tried to stop me: he was Officer of the Day. I broke a rib and some teeth for him. He bought it at Bristoe Station in the fall after Gettysburg."

"What more do we need to see?" Pickens demanded. "They're murderers! Torturing, thieving, raping monsters! How can we let them live?"

CHAPTER FORTY-SEVEN

Murderers, Sheppard thought with a sigh, taking the chair at the foot of Lavinia's chaise and pulling it forward. Callie, standing by the door, smiled at him, nodded, and went out, leaving the door ajar.

Sheppard waited until her footsteps had faded down the short hallway before turning to look at Lavinia, who was sleeping quietly. Her spectacles were neatly folded on the table beside the chaise. She seemed somehow younger and less guarded without them.

A day had passed since the attack, and Lavinia was still resting on Dr. Meacham's orders. She had been tired and quiet, but she had also smiled at Sheppard and had Meg in with her, reading stories and napping with her.

Sheppard sat back and looked at her. Slumber became her, undoing the havoc wrought by three years of war and its sacrifices, and leaving her smiling and relaxed. The lines of her pointed face were softened by the loosened hair that trailed over one shoulder in a braid.

Sheppard had lost too many loves during the past three years to face the thought of losing another easily. Lavinia's escape from harm had shaken him badly, and the turmoil in Wheelerville that had come on the heels of the capture of the raiders was making him feel slightly ill. He was content to sit quietly and wait until Lavinia woke up, away from the noise and the hatred that he could almost taste.

In view of all that had happened and all that he believed was about to happen, he had decided that it was time to say what needed to be said, if Lavinia seemed ready to hear it. He spared a half-rueful smile at the sudden flutter of butterflies in his stomach.

The patch of sun, lying across Lavinia's knees like a spill of gold, had awakened her with its warmth. She lifted her face toward the light and yawned. She yawned again, stretched, and opened her eyes, gazing up at the ceiling for a moment before pushing herself upright against the pillows that were mounded behind her.

She saw him the next moment, her face lighting up in welcome as she groped for her spectacles. "Why, Sergeant!" she said. "You should have awakened me!"

"And risk annoying Callie?" Sheppard asked. "I don't think so." He nodded at the open door. "She's down the hallway if you need her."

"I'm fine and she needs some rest," Lavinia said. "Have you been sitting there long?"

"Not long," Sheppard said with an answering smile as he rose, retrieved her glasses for her, and sat again while she put them on. "You needed to sleep and I needed to sit still for a moment. It worked out well for both of us." he said.

"Well, I'm awake now," she said. "And all the better for seeing you. I assume you're rested up, yourself, from watching me sleep." She smiled and added, "If not downright bored."

"I'll admit it was restful," Sheppard said. "But now I have something important to discuss with you."

She looked up at him and lifted her eyebrows.

He took the handkerchief from the bedside table, unfolded it and smoothed the embroidery with a fingertip. "Are you feeling better?" he asked.

She laughed at him and folded her hands before her. "How can you ask, Asa?" she demanded. "They say ill temper is a sign of good health, don't they? Here I am, ordered to lie abed, pampered and cosseted until all I want is just to get up and do something and tell everyone to stop hovering!"

"It's just as well they're doing it, even if it does make you cross," Sheppard said. "You haven't given yourself much chance to lie quietly and gather your strength over the past few years."

"I might have known I'd get a lecture from you," Lavinia said in disgust. "You've been talking to Callie. To hear her, I'm about to succumb to consumption and die a pallid, lingering death like the tiresome heroine of one of those appalling French novels!"

"You might at that," Sheppard said. "You've been bearing a heavy load all alone for a long time. It's taken a toll."

"A toll indeed!" Lavinia sniffed. She pushed her spectacles back on the bridge of her nose with her fingertip and scanned him with annoyance. "I declare, Sergeant, next you will be singing 'Believe me, if all those endearing young charms'!" she said. "I've had plenty of help since May. Let us have no more of this line of talk, sir! It is making me tired!"

"You certainly are getting better," Sheppard said with the hint of a smile. "I can tell."

"Meaning that I'm ill-tempered," Lavinia said. "That was not very kind of you, sir!" She started to laugh. "Mrs. Wigfall is probably sick to death of me, and I'm growing sick of lying down, I admit! When can we return to Fairlawn?"

"Tomorrow, if you like," Sheppard said. "The sooner I'm away from this town the happier I'll be."

Lavinia looked at him, alerted by an odd tone to his voice. He almost sounded as though he were holding on to a relatively trivial subject in order to steel himself to discuss something more important.

She heard shouting in the street, sounds rather than words. She listened a moment, puzzled, then turned back to him. "Why not this evening?" she suggested.

He had paused to listen too, his head slightly to one side. He drew a breath and then shook his head. "We're cleaning up the place. It'll be ready for you tomorrow," he said. "You don't need to come in to broken china and ripped cushions."

"I knew those scoundrels were doing it when I was trying to escape," Lavinia said stoutly. "I didn't get a chance to see what it was they were doing, but I was glad it was keeping them occupied. Is—is it very bad?"

"Very bad," Sheppard said gently. "They smashed things, tore down the curtains–damaged the walls where they did that—cut up paintings."

"Oh," Lavinia said. She looked over at the jug that sat within view on the dresser. "At least that wasn't damaged," she said.

"No," Sheppard said. "It was spared." The unspoken, but still audible, part of the thought hung in the air, making Lavinia frown slightly. "How did it get to be on that settee?" Sheppard asked.

"The one fellow was standing in the doorway," Lavinia said. "I didn't like his looks so I threw it at him. I missed." She sighed and then looked up at him with a half-jaunty smile. "Well, at least they didn't go to my house in Savannah and wreck things there," she said. "That would have been tragic. Fairlawn is lovely, but there's nothing valuable there."

She caught his expression and said, "No, sir, you have already made me a fine speech about being a cabinet maker and appreciating fine old furniture the first full day you were at Fairlawn, so you can save your breath."

She saw that he was smiling, which was the effect she had intended. "Now, Asa," she said. "You can tell me what's been troubling you since I awoke."

"I didn't say—" he began.

A strident voice, shouting across the street, silenced him. "Monsters, I tell you! Demons from the pit!"

Lavinia ignored the words. "You didn't have to," she returned. "You've been sitting there like someone about to break some news that is important and probably bad. From all this noise, I'm probably right. It's almost worse than when those raiders were attacking. What's wrong?"

He drew a long breath. "We captured those guerrillas," he said.

"That's excellent news," she said. "I hope you killed a few, too!"

Sheppard directed a long, thoughtful look at her. "We did," he said finally. "And we've found out something else. Our men were going through the loot those people had with them. There were two photographs. . . We now know Meg's family's name. There were other things among their saddlebags, so there was no doubt. Some of those people were the murderers."

Lavinia stared at him. "Meg's family..." she said blankly, caught by the thought of Fairlawn without the child's chatter and mischief. "Oh, dear. I must write and see..." She drew a long breath and relaxed against the pillows. "If that is so," she said after a moment, "then I am glad for Meg's sake, if not my own. What will happen to those men?"

"I think they'll be tried for murder, and executed," Sheppard said. He shot an uneasy look toward the window. "Ed Pickens wants them hanged at once."

"Mr. Pickens?" Lavinia said. "But why? He's always so gentle... What's happened?"

"He says they killed kin of his. That old couple south of here. He says hanging's too good for them, and I think some of the people here are beginning to agree with him."

She looked at him. "The Fiskes," she sighed. "Oh, Asa, I'm so sorry about all this."

"They're getting nothing more than justice for what they've done, I suppose," Sheppard said slowly.

"I am sorry for everyone here," Lavinia said. "You most of all. You've seen so much trouble and pain. You were getting some rest here. I imagine that's why General Stanley assigned you, since you were wounded. It must be hard for you to encounter this horror and ugliness where you thought it was safe and peaceful."

He looked down at his hands for a moment. "No matter how much trouble or pain I may see here, Lavinia," he said, "the fact is that you're here, as well, and that makes it bearable."

She smiled into his eyes as her hand came to rest atop his. "I was fortunate that you came here," she said softly as he bent his head and kissed her hand. "Heaven knows I wasn't expecting you."

He looked up at her, smiling.

"Now," she said with a return to briskness. "You didn't come here to talk about those renegades or those folks howling in the street like—like savages. Tell me what was troubling you when I first awoke."

Sheppard pushed himself to his feet and went to the window.

She stared at his back, puzzled and a little apprehensive. "Asa?" she said. "What is it?"

He traced the outline of a pane of glass with a fingertip and said, "I probably won't be here in another month."

Lavinia sat back with the breathless feeling that someone had just punched her in the stomach. She brought her voice under control and said, "Why do you say that? Have you received new orders?"

He was still staring out the window at the street, which sounded as though it was filling with murmuring people. "Only old ones," he said. "My orders are to stay with you until I am relieved by my forces, or until your armies come through. When that happens I must go to them and request safe conduct to my own lines."

"But the armies are nowhere near here!"

"Listen to me, Lavinia. The armies are on the move. Those guerrillas were riding ahead of General Thomas' divisions. From what we've seen, he's coming back this way and your people will most likely be following him, hoping to draw the rest of my army away."

"Menace the one force in the hope that the other will come to its rescue," Lavinia said slowly.

"That's what I think they want," Sheppard said. "Whatever happens, I'm pretty sure your people will come this way, and when that happens, when they're here..." He stopped and looked down at Lavinia.

"What?" she said.

He continued with a half-grimace. "According to my orders, when they're here, I must go to them–"

"–Show them your papers, and say 'If you please, sirs, won't you let me rejoin my army and fight you some more," Lavinia interrupted without ceremony. "Don't be foolish! Do you think they will let you go? They'll send you to a prison camp, and I've heard of them if you haven't! Terrible rumors I didn't want to believe: men like skeletons, filthy, muddy fields, and no hope of exchange because both our governments have forbidden it! You'll have to hide!"

"I can't do that," he said over his shoulder. "I must take my orders to them and ask for a safe conduct." He lifted an eyebrow at her. "You're an intelligent woman, Lavinia. You're known to have a Safeguard posted here. If I do otherwise, they'll accuse you of being a spy."

"We'll just see about that!" Lavinia said hotly. "I'll write to my friends in Milledgeville and in Richmond! How could they think such a thing?"

Sheppard turned away from the window and came back to her chaise. "It's been done," he said, taking her hands in his. "At any rate, I have no choice. Let's not argue about it any more. Time is short and I have a lot to do."

Lavinia's eyes had a wide, almost blind expression for a moment before she turned them on him. "How soon will this be?" she asked.

"Within the month, probably," he said again. "My guess is that it'll be within two weeks."

"Two weeks!" Lavinia exclaimed. "But that's so little time!"

He held her hands more firmly. "I don't think it'll be any more than that," he said. "I'm sorry. It's a wonder I was here so long."

"So long!" she repeated. "But it was hardly any time at all. Just enough time for me to realize..."

Lowering her head to gaze at his hands, brown, callused and square, as they held hers, she let the sentence die away. The wedding ring on his left hand was worn and scratched from years of wear, and there was a long, thin graze along the back of his left hand, probably received during the fighting She looked up to see him smiling at her in an odd, arrested sort of way that made her feel shaken and breathless, herself, and somehow afraid.

"You won't be defenseless when I'm gone," he said, releasing her. "I've seen to that. Wheelerville and Fairlawn have their militias–"

She lifted her chin at him and pretended not to notice that he was bending closer to her and his hands had come to rest, warm and strong, on her shoulders.

"What do I care for that?" she asked above the quickening beat of her heart. "I can take care of myself! It's you I'm thinking of! Even if you escape the prison, you'll be going back to the war, riding and fighting with the armies, in danger— Oh Asa, whatever will I do without you?"

He drew her even closer. She could feel the flutter of a pulse in his fingertips as he tilted her face toward his. "You started to say, 'Just enough time...,' " he said.

She looked up into his eyes as the slow ticking of the clock on the mantel seemed to falter. She could feel the rough, horsehair stuffing of the chaise behind her, she could smell a touch of soap coming from the handkerchiefs on the bedside table.

The memories came crowding back, a tall chestnut mare and her rider looming out of the sun on a bright May morning... The reassuring feel of rough wool and braid against her cheek one terrible October afternoon when her nightmares had broken into her waking world and been defeated... His voice in the starlight, talking of grief and memory and love.

He was smiling at her. "Lavinia," he said.

"Kill them all!"

"Hang them, I say!"

She wanted to step into the warmth of his smile, but she was tired and the ugly words mocked and shattered the dawning sense of joy that she had felt only moments before.

She recognized voices almost against her will. People she knew, whose gentleness and honor she had always trusted. What had happened to them? All at once it seemed to her that everything she had once treasured was in terrible danger, and she was too weary and too heartsick still to do anything to stop it.

Sheppard, looking down into her eyes and reading the emotions there, lowered his head and smiled a little sadly.

"Break down the jail and haul them out!"

One voice snarled, "Hang 'em up and let 'em strangle for an hour!"

Lavinia shrank against Sheppard. "That was Mr. Pickens!" she breathed. "I knew his voice!"

"Let them see how it feels!"

Lavinia gasped. "And that was John Toombs! Why, they're leading a mob! In Wheelerville!"

The voices rose, grew louder, harsher. Lavinia could feel the rage and hate almost like a sickness at the back of her throat. "God help us, Asa," she breathed, staring toward the window. "What's happening to this town? Can't you stop this?"

Sheppard turned away from the window. "I can't," he said. "All I can do is protect you and your household."

"But—"

"I'm not the law here," he said grimly. "If the law here allows this–"

One voice sounded above the rest, strained and almost hoarse with vehemence. "Go home, all of you, and stop acting like animals! You'll have your hanging tomorrow, don't worry! Whether you like it when you do is another question!"

The noise subsided, and they could hear the sound of people moving in the street.

Sheppard drew a long, shaking breath. "God bless Judge Prescott," he said. "But will his word it hold?"

"That was appalling," Lavinia said.

Sheppard shook his head. "Those renegades have to be punished," he said. "You said so yourself."

His words shook her. "I never meant that they were to be—to be lynched without a trial!" she said.

The door opened and Callie came into the room. She looked at the two of them and then cast a grim glance at the window. "It's coming," she said. "'Without are dogs, and sorcerers, and whoremongers, and murderers, and idolaters, and whosoever loveth and maketh a lie.' "

Lavinia flinched. "Oh Callie!" she whispered.

Sheppard directed a frown at Callie that made her blink. "There is a time and a place for everything, Miss Callie," he said. "And this is not the time for that sort of sentiment."

Callie's expression softened, grew rueful. "Hush now, Lamb," she said to Lavinia. "They can't hurt you."

"They won't if I can help it," Sheppard said. He pushed Lavinia away slightly. "Listen to me," he said. "I'm taking you home to Fair-lawn this evening, along with Meg and Callie and Mrs. Swithin. And I suppose we'd best bring the Hamiter woman, as well. You won't have to stay a moment longer here and you won't have to listen to this filth. You'll be safe there."

Lavinia buried her face against his shoulder and wept.

CHAPTER FORTY-EIGHT

The coverlet had sifted softly down, leaf by leaf, red, yellow, brown, dry and curling or still supple with the last traces of summer's sap. Maple, oak, beech bound together with red-brown pine needles, tinged with the scent of pine sap released by the warmth of the sun. The coverlet was constantly in motion, quivering slightly, rustling with the wind and growing still again so that the quiet, burdened groan of the mill wheel could be heard above the wind.

The soft motion of the leaves split into a second of chaotic movement. Leaves swirled aside, baring dark, deep waters roiled by the passage of a heavy object, and then swept back over the disturbance, quivered and were still again.

Al Townsend rubbed his palms against the rough fabric of his trousers and watched the leaves move back to cover the water. He lifted his eyes after a moment and let them move along the edge of the trees bordering the millpond.

He had gone there so often as a boy, swimming with his friends, casting fishing lines into the water and bringing out fish, all the time peering over his shoulder, watching for the miller. He remembered the thrill of bringing in a good-sized fish. The yelling and fist-shaking of the miller had only served to make the fish more delicious when it was rolled in milk and cornmeal and fried in butter.

His dawning smile grew wry. Showed how much he knew then as a smart-aleck kid, he thought. He knew now that the man had stocked the pond expressly for little boys with fishing poles and worms, but he had also understood the spice of the forbidden. None of the boys had caught on until years later.

Townsend sighed and looked back down at the leaves on the pond's surface. In better times they would have been cleared out before they had a chance to build up, rot and choke the wheel. But the miller's four sons had gone into the armies and three of them had been killed, that Townsend knew about.

Between the immense tragedies of the war and the more usual, but no less devastating, tragedies of daily life with its hazards, the man had little heart for living, much less clearing out his millpond. And that, Townsend thought, was a pity to match all the other griefs he had observed over the past year.

He frowned at the pond and then at the wheel, turning sluggishly with its burden of rotting leaves. It could be fixed. With the mill working once more, people could bring their grain to be ground just like before. Townsend could get some of the men from the town out there with a pontoon of logs and scoop the leaves in. It would give the man something to live for, and give the townsfolk something worthwhile to do.

Townsend's face twisted with disgust after a moment. If, that was, they were over their blood-lust.

The scene kept repeating and repeating in his mind. The ugly words and uglier gestures, the writhing, strangling men, the shouting townsfolk as red-faced as the men they were killing. It had made him wonder who were the men and who the monsters, and whether they all should maybe be killed for humanity's sake. Were those people from Wheelerville? He couldn't believe it!

The wind rose a little, sharp-edged with cold. He shivered, blew on his hands and drew his coat closer around himself. It was going to be a rough winter. This damned war! He thought back to another winter, with the Federals stuck in the mud and his own wet, freezing, ill-clad men no better.

He frowned down at his hands and sighed, rubbing the tip of his left ring finger. It was still numb, a souvenir of a long night on guard duty two years before. He had been glad to leave a war whose romance and gallantry had been far outweighed by its pain and squalor, but the war had come to him in all its ugliness and horror. He had done what he could to stop it, but this day's work had shown him that it wasn't enough. There was one thing more for him to do.

He looked back at the leaves. They were still again, showing no sign of the recent disturbance. But the rock that he had thrown lay at the bottom of that pond, beneath the tapestry of gold and crimson leaves, and nothing he or anyone could say or think would return it to the state it was in before the rock had been thrown. Just in the same way had the war struck deep into everyone's soul, changing things, changing people. It was time he understood that and did the thing that he had known he must do all those long months ago.

The decision was made; he suddenly felt as though he were able to draw a deep breath for the first time in over a year. It would be hard, but it was the only thing he could do.

But first he had some business to attend to.

He went to his horse, mounted and turned the animal's head south. And then he paused to look at the millpond. It could be cleared once the insanity had subsided a little. He could try. It might make the ugliness recede, and there were generations of future fishermen to consider.

He clucked to his horse and headed toward Fairlawn at a canter.

** ** **

Lavinia contemplated the splinters of glass still embedded in the hardwood floor of the hall. The floor had been sanded and oiled, but the fragments were still there, serving as a reminder. Looking at them, she seemed to hear the shattering glass, the thump of booted feet upon the floor and hear her own heart racing in her ears.

She blinked the memories away. If victory was so hard to bear, how much more terrible would defeat have been! Better to see the triumph and rejoice in it.

And there was so much to see. The wall had been replastered where the curtain rods had been torn away. The wrecked furniture had been sent to the workshops until such time as Sergeant Sheppard could look at it and see if it could be repaired. The broken china had been swept up and dumped into the refuse pits, the slashed portraits of Lavinia's parents stored in the attic, and other paintings hung in their places.

"It's a judgment upon us, Vinnie," Callie said behind her.

Lavinia turned to look at her. "What are you talking about, Callie?" she asked. "A judgment? On what?"

"On our wickedness," Callie said glumly, nodding toward the contrast between the faded paint on the walls and the darker, more vibrant colors that had been sheltered by the portraits. "Cleanliness is next to godliness, and the Lord has shown up our laziness!"

"Not my laziness!" Lavinia said with the hint of a chuckle. "Nor yours, either, Callie dear. Let it be: paint fades, no matter how often you scrub it." She added, "And maybe it's a judgment on your house-pride, since you insisted on scrubbing those walls out of all conscience and likely made them fade!"

Callie sniffed. "Don't be foolish!" she said, but her voice was happier, and it made Lavinia smile.

There was a great deal to smile at: things were calm again, the wounded were back at Fairlawn and so was she, and so was Sergeant Sheppard. And Louise had elected to stay in Wheelerville, glory be to Heaven! If everyone managed to forget that there was a hanging going on in town this day, everyone was happier.

Lavinia looked across at Callie again and smoothed her skirts. "I'm going to look in on the men," she said. "You can frown at the walls while I do so. Though you could also check on Meg and see if she's up from her nap yet. The Sergeant is napping in the parlor: we'd best let him sleep. Poor man, he's exhausted."

"It's all that horror in town," Callie said. "Praise God we're away from there!"

"Amen," Lavinia said with feeling and thankfulness.

Ten minutes later, having left Private Pierce's bedside, she stepped onto the porch for a moment and saw Bathsheba staring, transfixed, as most of the townsfolk of Wheelerville, armed and furious, came marching across the lawn toward her with Ed Pickens at their head.

** ** **

"Gentlemen, I must protest!" Lavinia said again. "This is an outrage!"

"The outrage happened in town, Miss Lavinia," Ed Pickens said grimly from the bottom step. He had led his crowd right across the lawn and up to the steps of the house. They had stopped there only because Lavinia had planted herself at the very top of the steps and was watching them with a frown that they had never seen before. That had made them mill around a bit, murmuring and shouting, before Pickens had stepped forward demanding to see Sergeant Sheppard and threatening all sorts of mayhem when he came outside.

"You're not making any sense!" she exclaimed, casting an urgent look at Bathsheba and praying the girl would understand.

It worked. Bathsheba, wide-eyed, caught the look, nodded, and went silently into the house. Ed Pickens folded his arms with a scowl. "I don't expect womenfolk to understand what's at issue here," he said. "This is a matter for men to sort out, and the sooner the better! Where is he? He's got a lot to answer for!" He started up the steps once more.

Lavinia stepped in front of him again. "I do not recall inviting you into my house, sir," she said with the edge of a smile. "I certainly would not do so while you are behaving in this fashion, and let me tell you, Edward Pickens and the rest of you—it has been a long time since anyone has behaved so rudely to me! 'Womenfolk' indeed!"

"Where is who?" Sheppard asked, stepping onto the porch. He was buttoning his jacket and his hair showed signs of having been hurriedly smoothed. He saw Lavinia's dismayed expression. "Miss Bathsheba told me you wanted me," he said with a smile. "I was napping, or I'd have come out sooner." He looked out at the crowd and lifted his eyebrows. "Hello," he said. "What's this?"

"Get him!" Pickens said through his teeth.

Several men started up the steps.

"Stop it, all of you!" Lavinia cried. "Don't you come a single step nearer! What is the matter with you?"

Sheppard cast an eye over the group and folded his arms. "Stand aside, Miss Wheeler," he said. "I don't know what this is about, but I've no doubt they'll explain. In the mean time they don't have to 'get' me: I'll come to them."

He suited action to words. "All right, Ed," he said when he was in front of them. "What's gotten into all of you? I see Sam Wallins here, too—all the Wheelerville Militia, in fact. What's wrong?"

"We thought you were a friend to this town," Pickens said. "We thought you were one of us. We thought you were helping us, but we know differently now!"

"What are you talking about?" Sheppard demanded.

The tone of the crowd was changing. "You Yankee bastard!" shouted John Toombs. "We might have known you'd stand by your own!"

Sheppard's smile had not altered. "You're not making any sense," he said.

Bathsheba stepped from the house, touched Lavinia's arm and nodded toward the window. Corporal Higgins was standing there and watching. His arms were folded, but Lavinia caught the blue-gray glint of gun metal beneath his left arm. She could see Toby behind him with a knot of blue uniforms. She turned her head and saw Caesar standing just beyond the end of the porch.

Sheppard's hands were nowhere near his pistol. "Calm down and let's talk," he said. "I've been here all day—"

"Tell that to the marines!"

"—and I don't know what's got you all so riled. Haven't I stood by you when those monsters attacked? Didn't I help train you into a crack unit I'd be proud of?"

Sheppard looked around at the crowd of men. "Listen to me, whatever happened, I had no part of it. I've been here all day— I just awoke from a nap, come to that!"

The commonsense words were having some effect. People were relaxing now, listening. All except for one man, who had stooped and picked up a rock. He hefted it in his hand, eyed Sheppard, and let fly.

"We're not enemies here—" Sheppard began, and then flinched sideways, one arm up to shield his face as he saw the flung stone and tried to dodge it. The rock caromed from his upper arm and smashed into the window behind him, shattering the glass.

The sound made the days roll back like a dark tide, leaving Lavinia facing her nightmare once more with the choice of stepping into it or leaving it behind her. She set her teeth and wrenched herself from the grip of memory, speaking coldly above the thunder of her heart.

"Put your weapons away!" she said. "All of you! Shame on you all, acting like this! Corporal Higgins, come away from the window, and you, too, Toby. Send the others back to the parlor. Sergeant Sheppard, go into the house, but stay within call. And now you, Edward Pickens, can tell me what has happened to make you all behave no better than beasts!"

"They were cheated of their spectacle," a voice said quietly from the edge of the yard. "And now they're mad."

** ** **

Al Townsend had come silently up to the edge of the crowd, unnoticed in the flurry of activity. Now he rode forward through the throng of men and stopped before the steps. He touched his hat to Lavinia and to Bathsheba, peeking through the doorway, and then dismounted.

Lavinia's voice shook slightly. "What do you mean, Mr. Townsend?" she demanded.

"There was supposed to be a hanging today," he said. "Those bastar— Sorry, Miss Lavinia. Those monsters. That was well and good: they robbed and murdered, and some of the folk they hurt were close kin to people here."

He looked at Pickens and then back at Lavinia. "You reap what you sow," he said. "But these fellows wanted to take it a little farther and make them suffer."

Lavinia's gaze grew blank.

"They decided that hanging was too quick, so they just strung them up and left them twisting and choking there while they sat and watched, happy as you please, men and women both, cheering, clapping, whistling, shouting things." Townsend's voice was flat as he nodded toward one of the large windows and added, "Anyone who cared to look around would've seen some children at the windows, craning their necks to see, just as little Miss Meg, there, is doing this minute."

Sheppard looked, saw Meg's face framed between the curtains, opened his mouth to speak, shook his head, and fell silent.

"And then somebody shot them," Townsend said. "All fourteen of them." He looked back at the others. "Spoiled all the fun," he said. "At least, they seemed to think it was fun, though I'd have called it something different. And now they're hopping mad."

Pickens was still glaring at Sheppard. "He's a meddling–"

"You can stop looking at him and start looking at me, Ed," Townsend said scornfully. "I'm the meddler, and I'd gladly do it again!"

"Well you sure have your nerve! We had leave to kill them!"

"You had leave to hang 'em!" Townsend said. "You didn't have any right to torture them! And you know, Ed," he said, "I don't think Verena would have liked what you tried to do, either."

"Now listen—!"

"No, *you* listen!" Townsend snarled. "I've known all of you all my life, and I thought you a nice enough bunch, even if you were a little dull and goody-goody and called me a hooligan and a bully. I thought you were a good lot to grow up with, and I thought you were doing pretty good all this time. I was the worst of the lot, thinking about the fighting I had seen and mad at the world. This bluecoat here had to wipe the street with me before I got any sense, but I got it at last. Hell, do you know what we almost did? We almost survived a *war* without getting twisted. We almost worked together, Yank and Reb, freedmen and freeborn, without griping about the color of our uniforms or the color of our skins! God help us all, we almost did it, but we just missed."

He looked around. "And you know what else you did just now? You almost let yourselves become monsters like those others! I don't believe in coddling killers like those bastards. But how do you know they all were those torturing rapists? And even if they were, how could you take the law into your hands like you did? Look at you! Making noises like you're going to lynch these men in blue who have acted as our guests and our friends!"

Someone audibly shuffled his feet. People were looking aside, avoiding his stare.

Townsend hooked his thumbs at his belt. "Well, I did it, just like you thought Sarge did. I shot them all so they could die quickly, and I did a good job of it. I meant it as a kindness: God will forgive me, and I don't care a damn how the rest of you view it. I'm just sorry the children had to see it, but it's better than them watching those fellows dangling and choking to death."

He jerked his chin toward his horse. "If you want proof beyond what I've told you, you can look at my packs. Those two repeaters I scrounged from that battlefield are there and so are the used ammunition tubes that went with them. Go take a look!"

No one moved.

"Go on!" said Townsend. "You came here ready to make Sarge pay for this 'outrage', but your sense of direction is about as sharp as your sense of decency. If you're bound to lynch anyone for this 'outrage', then I guess it'll have to be me. Which of you's going to try to put the rope around my neck?"

He looked around when everyone was silent. "I didn't think so," he said. "You're dumb as posts and mean as snakes, but you're teachable. Or you used to be, anyhow: I'm not so sure now. Maybe you're just too yellow to give it a try. I'm not going to stick around and find out, either. I'm giving you notice right now: I'm through with leading this militia unit. You can take care of yourselves. Militia! You're just a rabble! I'm leaving you in a week's time and going where people know right from wrong. Go home, all of you, and think shame on yourselves!"

He turned to Lavinia as the crowd began to break up. "I'm sorry for my language, Miss Lavinia," he said. "But it was the only way to get through to them. And I'm sorry you and your people had to be troubled. I don't think it'll happen again."

CHAPTER FORTY-NINE

Meg took a sturdy grip of the cross bar of the gate, set a foot on the bottom bar, gripped her tongue between her teeth, and pushed off with her other foot. She held on as the gate swung open in a slow arc. She picked up speed, giggling, and when the gate finally thumped up against its post, she pushed off and swung the other way.

"All right, Mistress Meg, what are you doing here?"

She looked over her shoulder and saw her father's friend, Mr. Townsend, sitting astride his horse and watching her with a smile.

Meg favored him with one of her best smiles. She liked Mr. Townsend: he wasn't her father, but he was an acceptable substitute, having a horse and a disinclination to preach, unlike many of the grownups Meg knew. He had twice taken her for rides in the days since the bad people had tried to scare and hurt her mama. She had seen him the day before, too, when the grownups from the town had come to the house.

That had been a strange day: Meg had watched from the window, and she had not been able to understand all that had happened. The grownups had been frowning, and Meg could tell that her mama and her father had been worried and upset. Although they had both smiled and spoken the way they did when they were being friendly, the others had been very rude, and someone had thrown a stone and broken one of her mama's windows.

Meg had found that very interesting: when she broke something on purpose, her skirts were pulled up and someone, usually Aunt Callie or Mama, gave her bottom a good spanking. And yet although it had been clear to Meg that the grownup who had thrown the stone had meant to do it, no one had made a move to spank him.

This was a fascinating discovery: Meg decided that she wanted to be a grownup, too, and the sooner the better, although she had not liked the awkward feel of the two days that had passed since then, with everyone being so carefully quiet and polite and no one from the town seeming to want to talk straight to anyone at her mother's house.

Grownups were odd.

But Meg happened to like this particular grownup. She grinned at Mr. Townsend and pushed away from the upright. "I'm swinging!" she said over her shoulder. "It's fun!"

"I noticed," he said. "But bad people are still about: shouldn't you be at the house where your folks can keep an eye on you?"

Meg pursed her lips and blew some strands of hair away from her face. "Mama can see me," she said.

Townsend looked over his shoulder at the house. Miss Lavinia could see Meg if she happened to be standing at the corner window on the very top floor of the house, leaning far out and squinting.

"I guess she can, if you push a point," he said. "I'm not sure I'd let you if I were her."

Meg widened her eyes at him and pushed away again.

Townsend watched her swing past him in a blur of pink calico and eyelet lace and tried another tack. "Did she say you could swing on the gate?" he asked.

"She didn't say I mustn't," Meg said serenely. She dragged her toe in the dust and brought the gate to a halt. "Can I ride your horse?" she asked. When he did not answer right away she said, "I jumped off the gate!"

"All right," he said. "Where's your pa?"

Meg shook her hair in the wind and considered. "He's gone riding," she said. "He was with Uncle Caesar."

"Right, then," Townsend said. He dismounted, lifted Meg to the saddle, and swung back up, himself. "I'll tell your mama we're going out," he said, heading toward the house.

Meg sat quietly, her hand playing in Mr. Townsend's horse's salt-and pepper mane while Mr. Townsend spoke to her mama.

Once they were away from the house, she cocked her head up at him and said, "I think some soldiers are coming."

Townsend looked around. "Where?" he said.

"You can't see them," she replied. "But they're coming."

"Who told you about them?" Townsend demanded, turning his head to peer over his shoulder.

"Nobody did. I just know," she said with the calm serenity of a seer. "Can we go into town and watch for them?"

** ** **

374 · DIANA WILDER

They rode into Wheelerville twenty men strong in a river of butter-nut and gray, glittering with the casual glamour of polished gun stocks and oiled leather. Sun-toughened and windblown, they had the arro-gant assurance of tried strength in their frayed and faded uniforms. Their horses were as lean as they were, mounts and men moving to-gether with the wild grace of centaurs. Four mule-drawn wagons rumbled behind them.

The leader, a narrow-eyed, rangy young man with an imperial, a long mustache and the twin collar pips of a captain, swept a consider-ing gaze down the street and then spurred over to Abner Wigfall, who had stopped and was watching them with widened eyes.

"I need to speak with the law here, son," the captain said. "It's a se-rious matter."

Abner glanced speculatively at the man's collar, assessed his rank and probable age, and suppressed his objections to being described as "son" by someone barely ten years his senior. "You'll want Judge Prescott. He's in the big brown stucco house, back along that street," he said, pointing. He looked up at the man and added, "I'll take you there and see you in, if you'd like."

** ** **

"I'm Captain Andrew Fullam, Judge," said the man, swinging down from his saddle. "I'm with Delacroix' command. I've been sent to check out reports of enemy troops quartered in this town. Where are they?"

He paused to toss his reins over to Isaiah, who had just left the house and was heading down the steps. "Here, boy," he said, "Hold my horse for me."

Isaiah caught the reins, wooden-faced, and stood like a statue, though his expression was thoughtful for a moment.

Judge Prescott lifted his eyebrows. "'Quartered' here?" he repeated. "I'm afraid you were misinformed, Captain. This town saw a battle back in mid-May, and there were casualties on both sides. Some of the Federal wounded were left behind when the armies moved on. They're still disabled, and while they're bluecoats, you can hardly call them 'troops' any more."

Captain Fullam twirled one end of his long mustache around his fingertip. "I'd like to see them, nevertheless," he said. "Can you tell me where they are?"

Judge Prescott smiled. "I'll do better than that, Captain," he said. "I'll escort you, myself. It isn't far: just outside town, the better to keep an eye on them. Just give me a few minutes to get ready, and I'll be right with you. In the meantime, have your men dismount and stretch their legs."

"Massa Prescott," Isaiah said.

Judge Prescott hid his surprise at Isaiah's accent and schooled his features to indifferent tolerance. "What is it, Isaiah?"

"I'se got to git back t'Miz Vinnie or she'll tan my hide fo' sho'."

"Go on, then," Judge Prescott said.

"Yassuh," Isaiah said. He moved through the throng of horsemen, pulling his forelock. Once he was out of sight he straightened with a thoughtful grimace. A few minutes might just be enough time to take the warning to Miss Wheeler. He moved carefully away.

** ** **

"How many men, Isaiah?" Lavinia asked, aghast.

"There were twenty of them, Miss Lavinia," Isaiah said. "Armed and mounted, and they look like they've seen a lot of action!"

Lavinia traded looks with Corporal Higgins. "Twenty men," she said.

Higgins nodded. "Were they regular cavalry?" he asked.

"Hard to say," Isaiah replied. "They were mounted, anyhow, and they had what looked like yellow collars to their uniforms, but the armies look so ragtag now, it's hard to tell. I saw some buckles with Georgia's coat of arms on them."

"Hm," said Higgins, "Militia, maybe. Or maybe some of Morgan's boys, survivors of his old command."

"He said he was part of Delacroix' command," Isaiah said.

"Morgan's boys, then," Higgins said. He looked back toward the house. "Well, we're sitting ducks here," he said after a moment. "They know we're here, and there isn't anything we can do to deny it. Wounded men, unable to fight." His mouth twitched into a smile. "Or not much, at any rate. And they think we're so dangerous they need to send a company of graybacks after us. No use trying to hide us. Isaiah, where's the Sergeant?"

"He was out along the creek with me," Isaiah replied. "We'd returned from sweep patrol. We stopped at Judge Prescott's for a moment, then he—"

The rapid thudding of hooves made everyone turn with varying expressions of dismay. The expressions relaxed a little when they saw Al Townsend coming up at a gallop with Meg before him.

Townsend brought his horse to a halt. "There's the devil to pay!" he panted, handing Meg down to Caesar. "A squad or so of cavalry heading toward town. They're armed and they look like they mean business!"

"They're in town right now, talking with the Judge," Higgins said.

"What?"

"They got a report of bluecoats quartered in the town and they want to check it out," Higgins said.

"Quartered in the town—?" Townsend began. "How did they—?" He stopped and shook his head impatiently. "Where's Sheppard?"

"I was with him at Judge Prescott's just before the fellows arrived," Isaiah said. "He left soon after we came. He said he was going to patrol the woods and then head here. He seemed uneasy..." He looked over at Townsend. "We have at least a half hour," he said.

"Shoot," said Toby. "He must have ridden out the opposite way they were riding in."

Lavinia traded a long look with Higgins. "We can't let them find him," she said. "He'll want to come here and talk with those men. He told me as much. He said he has to show them the order and request a safe conduct."

Higgins frowned. "He can't be that stupid," he said.

"He's that honest," Townsend said unexpectedly. "That's what a Safeguard is supposed to do."

"And he thinks he won't be sent to a prison?" Higgins asked disgustedly.

Townsend was looking thoughtful. "He might not be, at that," he said, but before Lavinia or Higgins could say anything, he added, "Depends who he talks to. But I don't think these fellows are the ones. I can find him and hold him up a little, but I don't think I can keep him very long. I'll bet he senses something."

Lavinia nodded and turned to Callie. "The sergeant usually comes in by way of the kitchen when he's through with his patrol," she said. "Can you detain him?"

"I'll try," Callie said. "But I'll have to do some thinking: that man's not going to want to hide!"

"He's stubborn," Isaiah said. He frowned at Higgins and then looked over at Lavinia. "I'd better get out of everyone's sight Miss Lavinia," he said after a moment. "Those fellows don't know I live here, and maybe it's best we don't tell them. They'll figure out I carried a warning. I'll go out toward Caesar's. I know the Sergeant heads in by way of the stable. I can head him off if Al can't find him."

"That's an excellent thought, Isaiah," Lavinia said. "Take the horses and hide somewhere safe."

Higgins was frowning and unconsciously rubbing his knee. "If these are Morgan's boys—or Joe Wheeler's, for that matter—they won't be impressed with the Order," he said slowly. "Can we intercept him?"

"We'll have to," Lavinia said grimly. She fingered her hair and considered for a moment. "I can keep them occupied, I think," she said. "I'll make myself presentable and act as though they're paying a morning call. It may throw them off balance while something is done."

"You're going to talk to them?" Higgins said.

"I am the lady of this house and the mistress of this plantation," Lavinia said. "Or course I will speak with them. And I will escort them throughout the house, and take as long as I possibly can and show them as little as I possibly can. Mr. Townsend, would you please see if you can find the Sergeant?"

"If he's in the woods, I'll find him," Townsend said, taking a good grip of his reins.

Callie suddenly smiled. "I think I can handle him," she said. "Mr. Townsend can hold him up a little, and then Isaiah will have to take his horse away out of sight. And he might as well take your Beau, while he's at it, or they'll be confiscating the both of them after they finish going through every hayrick and peeking under the beds. I'll handle Sergeant Asa. There'll be no trouble at all. Just make sure that intruder is taken through the cellar first."

CHAPTER FIFTY

Captain Fullam frowned at Corporal Higgins. "Where's the rest of you?" he demanded.

"In the graveyard behind the house, Captain," Higgins replied, settling his crutches more securely. "That's where they buried my leg and the other pieces of us that were cut off." He added, "The ones who died are there, too. There were about eighty of us, Union and Reb, to begin with, and you see what's left."

"Come along, Captain," Lavinia said. "I have tea for you in the parlor."

The captain followed her to the larger parlor. Once seated—he did not wait for Lavinia, which caused some raised eyebrows—he took out a folded slip of paper from his pocket and frowned at it. "I understand there's a sergeant of cavalry staying here," he said, folding the paper again. "Where is he?"

Something about the paper, a mark of some sort, looked odd to Lavinia. She adjusted her spectacles. "Captain—" she began, then stopped as Bathsheba wheeled in the tea cart.

"There was a sergeant major assigned as a Safeguard to protect the hospital and Miss Wheeler's property," Corporal Higgins said. "Last I knew, he was riding a sweep patrol, like he usually does, looking for bummers or raiders. He's led the town in fighting off quite a few attacks in the past months. And come to that, he stood off a Union foraging party, too, at gunpoint, a while back. He's a good tracker: I'd not be surprised if he caught a glimpse of you and took off."

"A fine Safeguard!" the captain said with a touch of scorn.

"A savvy one," Higgins countered accepting a cup of tea from Lavinia with a smile. "Whatever the cause, I'm senior of the men here, and if you have anything to say about these boys, you can say it to me."

"Captain," Lavinia said again. "Do take your tea and see if it is to your satisfaction." She gave him her best smile, and then, setting down the teapot with a rustle of sage moiré silk sleeves, said, "And won't you have a biscuit?"

"I don't mind if I do, Ma'am," he said, sipping the tea and then looking around again. He had seemed surprised to be received by a lady in a silk afternoon dress, adorned with pearl earrings, brooch and necklace. The sight of the invalids had seemed to surprise him, as well, and his expression had eased slightly as he set the paper back in his pocket.

"Was there something you needed, Captain?" Lavinia asked, passing a teacup to Judge Prescott.

"It is a question of looking into something," Fullam said, drinking some tea and then taking a biscuit. "Not a question of needing."

"Oh?' Lavinia said. "What did you wish to look into?"

"There was mention of troops quartered on this town," Fullam said. "And some other concerns, as well."

"We have the Wheelerville Guards, if that's what you mean," Judge Prescott said.

"Do you now?" Fullam asked.

"We certainly do," Prescott said. "We've rendered assistance to our armies with this group and have done a good job standing off marauders and bummers."

Fullam frowned. "Standing off marauders?" he repeated.

"That is correct, sir," Lavinia said. "They were following the armies, scavenging. It was dreadful. They came here, looking for plunder: you can see the marks on the plaster yonder, where they tore down the drapes, in fact. The Guards came in and defeated them."

"I see," Fullam said. "And where were the bluecoats during this time?"

Lavinia smiled and sipped her tea. "Why, the wounded were safely in the town," she said. "It was suggested they be given guns, in case the marauders came into town. But it wasn't necessary."

"I see," Fullam said. He drained the tea in his cup without any apparent relish, finished his biscuit, and rose.

Lavinia looked up at him. "Was there something else that you needed, Captain?" she asked.

Fullam ignored the stares of Judge Prescott and Corporal Higgins, took a couple steps toward the ballroom, and turned. "I need nothing, Miss Wheeler," he said. "I came to look into things and report back and I have done so and will be finishing here."

Lavinia got to her feet and went to him. "And...what dispositions will you be making, sir?" she asked.

Captain Fullam was at the door to the ballroom. He turned, looked at Higgins and then beyond him to the other soldiers ranged along the room. He paused as Pierce tried to lever himself up on his elbows, then released his breath. "I regret to say, Ma'am, that these men will have to be taken away from here," he said. "I've some wagons brought along for the purpose—"

"Taken away?" Lavinia repeated. "Where do you propose to take them? Certainly not to a prison!"

"I have no choice, Miss Wheeler," Captain Fullam said. "They are enemy troops." He frowned at the wounded men and added, "I've seen enough of what their kind have done within this state to keep me from feeling sorry for them."

"But these men have not done anything," Lavinia said. "If anything, they have helped to protect the people of this town."

"I am sorry, Miss Wheeler," Fullam said. "But I can't believe that."

His tone was surprising. "I beg your pardon?" Lavinia said.

"Let me be honest, Miss Wheeler," Fullam said. "I was told to check out a report that this town was harboring Yankee troops. Now, I can see that those fellows back there aren't fighting men, but that still leaves the question of a healthy fellow who was staying here by all reports, carrying weapons and actually fighting. And this town tolerated him!"

Corporal Higgins started and drew himself up to his full height. Lavinia laid a cautioning hand on his arm.

Judge Prescott spoke quickly. "Are you taking these invalids to a prison in their condition? Do you wish to kill them, then?"

"My orders are clear," Fullam said. "I am sorry if they trouble you."

Lavinia lifted her eyebrows. "Sorry?" she repeated. "I should think you would be ashamed, rather! Look at them! Wounded, convalescent, none of them would remain in the armies if they were behind their own lines. Why, Private Pierce here would be discharged at once. They all would. What harm can they do here?"

"Most of them can fire guns, Ma'am," Captain Fullam said.

"They certainly can do that," Lavinia agreed. "They have done so in defense of this town, as any of the townsfolk can attest. The Sergeant assigned to be our Safeguard did not act alone. But it is pure folly to think them capable of marching or fighting in a battle! By that token, sir, the dead buried in the meadow beyond this house—which you can see through the window, if you wish to look—should be taken up and carted away. They afford scarcely less threat than the collection of one-armed, one-legged, fevered men collected by those mounted ruffians and hustled out of here!"

She saw that he was looking down and decided to press her advantage. "You know that I am right, Captain. In the name of common sense if not humanity—"

Captain Fullam interrupted wearily. "Miss Wheeler, I don't see any reason to go on wasting everyone's time in this fashion. I have my orders. The men are to be moved out without delay. I will obtain their names and home directions so that their families can be notified—"

"You would do as well to line them up before a wall and shoot them!" Judge Prescott flashed.

"I am sorry, sir, but I have my orders," Fullam said again.

"But they can't travel like this!" Lavinia exclaimed. "And even if they could survive the journey, they will die in a prison! If you could only wait a week, Captain—two weeks at the most! I have friends in the armies; they can arrange to parole these men, and your command need not worry about them."

The word 'worry' seemed to grate on Fullam's pride. "You are mistaken, Miss Wheeler," he said. "We are not at all worried. I am obeying my orders to take all steps to find that sergeant and these men and take them away. Be glad that I am not doing more: there was a question of the loyalty of this town. I had thought the report was mistaken, but your very tender concern for these men, and your lack of concern for the whereabouts of this mysterious sergeant you have living with you, makes me wonder if it was right after all."

Corporal Higgins shifted on his crutches and fixed Captain Fullam with a glare. The other soldiers murmured, and Bathsheba, who had been staring wide-eyed at the pocket where Fullam had placed the folded note, drew closer to Lavinia.

Judge Prescott took breath to speak, but Lavinia silenced him with a hand on his arm. She turned to Bathsheba and said, "Go get the Order, child. It's in my escritoire. Bring it to me." She turned then and faced Captain Fullam.

"If by your last comment, sir," she said, icy and gentle, "you mean to add to your rudeness in giving a lady the lie direct by implying that you suspect me and this town of treason, then allow me to assure you that the tax records for this county will show that Fairlawn and Wheelerville have paid their share of taxes promptly, and have exceeded it by more than 50 percent. More than that, I can show you graves in the cemeteries of this town that will amply illustrate that our nearest and dearest have freely given their lives in defense of this cause. And if you are seeking still further proof, then I will gladly refer you to General Johnston, who was defending Atlanta until recently, and to General John B. Gordon, a personal friend of my family, who is serving with General Lee.

"Both of these gentlemen can attest to the assistance that Wheelerville and Fairlawn plantation have sent to them in the form of horses, men and supplies, all freely given despite our want. More than that, my family, and I as its representative in Savannah, have extended credit to the government of Georgia and to the Confederacy that runs into a sum that would make your head spin. If it is necessary to produce witnesses to my loyalty and character, I can provide an array of them of a stature and prominence that should satisfy even the most stringent of critics! I see that Bathsheba is back with the Order. Give it to the good captain, child. There, sir, is the order written out by General Miles Stanley. Read it, and see if there was any threat from this lone non-commissioned officer in the middle of this fair-sized town."

She watched Bathsheba hand the Order to Captain Fullam and said, "As you will see, not only did this Safeguard bear arms, he was ordered-by the Federal Commander-to do all within his power to protect me and my property, which, you will recall, is this entire town and plantation, from all threat. He took his duties very seriously. He cooperated fully with the government of this town, assisted in patrols, and served as an advisor on questions of practice. Judge Prescott, Dr. Meacham, and any of the other town leaders will be glad to clarify his duties and his performance. "

She paused while Fullam scanned the writing and then said, "And now tell me, sir: does that answer you to your satisfaction, or do you intend to insult me and this town further?"

Captain Fullam's color heightened. "I did not mean to offend you,

Miss Wheeler," he said. "I have my orders, and I must carry them out. The orders are to clear all Union troops out of here. Be glad that I am not following the rest of my orders."

"Are you threatening us?" Lavinia demanded. "'Following the rest of your orders', indeed! They were based on a gross misunderstanding of the situation here, and I have shown you how matters really stand. There is no question of the loyalty of this town! The presence of these invalids here reflects only on the kindness of this town, and to insist on taking them into danger is the height of unnecessary cruelty."

"I have my orders," Captain Fullam repeated.

Lavinia gazed at him for a long, silent moment and then nodded. "Very well, then, Captain," she said. "Obey your orders. I will not stop you." She smiled faintly at the sudden surprise in his expression and continued.

"But this matter is not closed by any means. I will be pursuing it through official channels, and I will not rest until this insult to my honor and my hospitality has been righted, and everyone—everyone!—responsible, from least to greatest, from civilian to military, has been disciplined to my personal satisfaction!"

Corporal Higgins blinked. Judge Prescott cleared his throat.

Captain Fullam moistened his lips. "I do not tolerate threats, Miss Wheeler," he said.

"It is a simple statement of fact and intent, Captain," Lavinia said crisply. "You just go right ahead and do what you call your job, and be assured that I shall not hesitate to do my Christian duty, as well. Do you understand me, sir?"

Captain Fullam lowered his eyes. "I understand, Miss Wheeler," he said. He turned to Corporal Higgins. "I need an assurance from you that your men will not run away before we bring the wagons."

"We are all missing arms or legs, Captain," Higgins said mildly above the storm of jeers and laughter that greeted this. His lip curled and he added, "But if it will make all you heroes feel better, I'll say that for the sake of the kindness we've received at the hands of Miss Wheeler and the rest of this town, we won't endanger them by fighting you."

Lavinia looked back at the men and then turned to Captain Fullam. "You have heard Corporal Higgins, Captain," she said. "You can bring up your wagons while my people see to feeding and provisioning these men. The Lord alone knows when they'll get another square meal where you're taking them."

Fullam was frowning. "They will be well cared for, Ma'am," he said.

"That had better be the case, sir," Lavinia said. She nodded to the two teamsters and then frowned over at the group of mounted men. "And now, since you are very concerned about bringing these dangerous invalids away without mishap, Captain," she said, "I suggest that you position your men all around the windows and doors of this room. You all seem like strapping, healthy fellows who have had a chance to recover from the rigors at the front. I am sure you can capture any of these invalids who tries to hobble out of the house."

"Now Miss Wheeler—" Fullam began.

"No, Captain," she said. "I insist. Bathsheba, dear, would you take the captain to Miss Callie and ask her to show him and any other of his escort through the cellar? Let him look on all the shelves and make sure no one is hiding behind the jars of lard. He may also wish to look inside the kettles we use for boiling soap. Once he is through in the cellar, you can take him around the rest of the house."

Fullam's face was growing red. "Now really, Miss Wheeler—" he tried again.

"It is no trouble, I assure you," Lavinia said with relentless cordiality. "You will not be forced to take my word for anything, since you have made it very clear that you view it as worthless. Bathsheba will show you into every room in the house. Be thorough, Bathsheba: be sure to open every wardrobe and have him and his men check under every bed and in every kneehole desk. And don't forget the dumbwaiter or the privies, either. I would not have him neglect his orders or waste a moment in unnecessary thought."

** ** **

Sheppard came springing up the back steps to the kitchen, whistling 'Annie Laurie" through his teeth. He loved late October's brisk, windy days, the trees flaming and flickering in the sun and the wind, the increasing coolness. He was singing as he opened the kitchen door and stepped inside to the heady smell of baking biscuits and cider mulling on the stove.

He saw Callie and smiled at her. "Have you been out?" he asked. "It's a splendid day! Sun and wind and the beeches turning yellow—I love autumn!" When she was silent he looked closer. "Callie?" he said, "Are you all right?"

Callie moistened her lips. "I-I'm fine," she said as she set a bowl of dough aside and went to take his pistol from him. "I just need to catch my breath. I'm fine."

"No, you're not," he said, coming forward to peer at her. "You're pale, and you look like you've had a fright! What's wrong?"

"It's nothing, Sergeant Asa," she said. "I'll be fine. I just need to c-catch my breath."

"Right," he said as he led her to a chair. "Your eyes are as round as an owl's! Sit down and tell me what's scared you."

"I feel such a fool," Callie said as he led her to a chair. "Please don't let's talk of it. I'll give you a biscuit—"

"If something's bothering you, Callie, then tell me! Maybe I can take care of it. You look like you've had quite a turn."

Callie looked down at her hands. "It was a rat, Sergeant," she said.

Sheppard sat opposite her and propped his elbows on the table. "A rat?" he repeated skeptically.

"A huge one. The biggest I've seen! He looked at least five feet long, had the ugliest whiskers and eyes like coals—"

"Oh come now! A rat in this house? I don't believe it! Where was this monster?"

"Downstairs, by the racks of watermelon pickle," Callie said. "I was going down to get some jars—I thought the wounded would like them—and I heard a sound. I turned and saw that rat! He came out from behind the rack of preserves, and he sort of twiddled his whiskers and—and chattered at me!"

"In the cellar?" Sheppard said.

"Yes, Sergeant!" She raised a trembling hand to her chest. "Oh Lord, I daren't tell Miss Lavinia; She'll have a fit of the vapors!"

"Lavinia Wheeler having the vapors," Sheppard said meditatively. "I'd love to see that!"

"Oh no, Sergeant," Callie said. "She hates rats! They send her into palpitations."

"Palpitations?" Sheppard said. "Interesting. Well, all right, then. I'll go find him—"

Callie seized his arm. "No, don't!" she cried. "I don't want you to get hurt!"

"Hurt? By a rat? What's he doing? Carrying a pistol?"

"It's not a joking matter, Sergeant. He was huge! I'll call in the ratter tomorrow."

Sheppard shook his head at her. "Callie——" he began.

She got to her feet and picked up a wash rag. "I-I should go back downstairs and clean up, though..." she said. Sheppard stared at her. "What are you cleaning up?"

"The pickle jars I dropped," Callie said, twisting her apron in her hands.

"In the cellar?" Sheppard asked

Callie nodded.

"Now wait a minute, Callie," Sheppard said through the edge of a grin. "You're forgetting that the terrible, pistol-toting rat is down there."

Callie looked at her apron. "Well..." she faltered. "If I were to take a broom or a shovel..."

"You're not making a lot of sense," Sheppard said. "First you're scared of a man-eating rat, then you want to go after him with a broom?" A sudden thought struck him and he leaned forward. "Open your eyes wide, Miss Callie," he said. "I want to look at them."

She obeyed; he peered at her for a long moment and then shook his head. "Your pupils match," he said. He got to his feet and headed toward the hallway to the cellar door. "All right, I'm going down there. I'll kill that rat for you. Heaven's sake, Callie, don't look so frightened! There's no need to be scared by a rat! I'll kill him and clean up the mess, and you can be comfortable again. Miss Wheeler can get the vapors from something else. Get a lantern and follow me."

Callie took the lantern from its hook and trailed behind him. She stood well back as he opened the door and then smiled weakly as he tuned to look at her.

"I don't dare come down," she said. "What if that rat runs over my foot?"

"Maybe I should look at your eyes again," Sheppard said grimly.

"What do you mean?"

"First you're terrified of this rat, then you want to chase him with a broom, then you don't want to go down the steps because you're afraid he might run over your foot. Well, he'll have to run over mine first, and I'll stop him before he does. Now come on!"

"No, I daren't!"

Sheppard looked at her and then shook his head. "Don't, then," he said, descending the stairs. "What a chicken! Just stand on the steps and hold that lantern up so I can get the light." He turned and smiled up at her. "That's good," he said, drawing his saber. "Now where are those pickle jars?"

"Over there in the corner," she said. "Can you see there, by the shadows?"

He turned and frowned where she pointed, then moved past a long work table piled with the ends of tallow candles. "Good lord, what a jumble!" he said. "There's enough junk down here to stuff a normal-sized house. Are you sure you didn't see a pack rat named Wheeler?"

"Miss Vinnie wouldn't be amused," Callie said.

"The truth hurts sometimes," he said, moving through the narrow aisle cleared amid the debris. "Hold the lantern higher, Callie. I can't see—"

He turned as the light went out simultaneous with the thud of the door closing.

"Callie!" he shouted.

Tumblers creaked and clicked once and then again, followed by the rasp of a bolt being driven home.

"What are you doing?" he yelled, groping his way back in the direction he had come. He came up against a wall that seemed to be alive with spiders.

He recoiled and fell over what felt like a tangle of chairs. "This isn't funny, Callie! Open the door at once!"

"You stay right there, Sergeant," Callie said through the door. "It'll come out right. Just stay there and relax."

Sheppard, on his feet again and gingerly feeling along the wall, knocked over what appeared to be a stepladder. He cursed. "God damn it, Callie!" he said again, "it's not funny!"

CHAPTER FIFTY-ONE

Bathsheba stared unseeingly down at the hem of her apron as she drew it through her fingertips. The war had burst into her world, taking away with it all that had been safe and secure. Captain Fullam and his company of Confederates had departed around late afternoon, taking Fairlawn's soldiers with them. They had waited only long enough to allow Miss Lavinia to give the soldiers a good, solid meal and pack provisions for them.

Miss Lavinia's voice had not been raised once from its customarily genteel tones, but she had been white-faced and bright-eyed with tightly controlled wrath; Captain Fullam had made himself scarce during that time. Bathsheba had helped Miss Lavinia tuck blankets in around the most seriously injured of the men, and when the wagons turned out of the driveway, they had stood at the gatepost with the rest of Fairlawn's people, waving farewell.

Fairlawn had seemed almost to explode into action once the soldiers were out of sight. The Fairlawn Free Militia, composed of her family and her friends, had assembled hurriedly, seen to the condition of their weapons, gathered provisions, and then gone back to their homes to say their farewells before heading silently into the woods. Bathsheba's father had been unusually grim-faced; Bathsheba, watching him ride off, thought that he and the rest of the militia had seemed as insubstantial as shadows riding off into darkness. She had sat in a dark corner and cried, and then, remembering what she had seen earlier, and what it had meant to her, she went off in search of Miss Lavinia.

She found Lavinia moving purposefully through the house, a closely written sheet of paper in her hand. Her movements were unhurried as ever, but the hem of her dress churned and billowed in silent witness to the vehemence of her mood.

Bathsheba cleared her throat. "Miss Lavinia," she said, "I've got to talk to you. It's important."

Lavinia turned and looked at Bathsheba. What she saw made her stop and stretch out her hand. "You look sick, child," she said. "What is it?"

Bathsheba's message was urgent, but she faltered a little. "I'm scared, Miss Vinnie," she said through shaking lips. "I saw Pa ride away, and I thought— They all might die—"

Lavinia's eyes were fixed on hers. They softened as she drew Bathsheba into a quick, comforting embrace. "You're not alone, 'Sheba," she said. "All over this land there are so many hoping and praying. Wives, mothers, lovers, fathers, children, all fearing and hoping that their loved ones will be spared. All wishing that they had said more, praying for a chance to say what was left unsaid... All we can do is hope and trust. I know it's hard, but take comfort: we're doing all that we can to be safe and careful."

Bathsheba dabbed at her eyes with her handkerchief. "I don't mean to be foolish, Miss Vinnie," she said. "I-I'll be fine."

"You're not foolish," Lavinia said. "Or if you are, then so is everyone else in this country."

Bathsheba looked up at Lavinia and smiled hesitantly. It was a moment she would remember in later years, the first time that she was acknowledged as a grown woman. She looked down again, a little confused and oddly elated.

"Now what did you need to tell me?" Lavinia asked.

Bathsheba had rehearsed the ways she planned to deliver her news, but the various tactful wordings seemed wrong. She raised her head, took a deep breath, and said, "Louise Hamiter sent those soldiers after our wounded men. I know it for sure."

Lavinia's eyes seemed somehow blank, just for a moment. "Tell me how you know," she said.

"Did you see that note the captain had?"

Lavinia frowned. "Yes?" she said. "I got a glimpse of it."

"It had an ink spot on it. Did you see that?"

"I caught sight of something," Lavinia said. "But I couldn't see it clearly. Now that you speak of it, it's clear that it was an ink spot. Why?"

"I've seen that spot before, and on the same piece of paper," Bathsheba said. "I remember it: it was shaped like a butterfly, with a spot on the lower wing. I think the ink pot was jostled when the person was writing, and the ink splashed on it. I saw writing around the spot, like the writer wanted to avoid it and use the paper. That was good paper, Miss Vinnie, too good to be wasted."

Bathsheba folded her arms and looked straight at Lavinia. "That was the letter that Miss Louise Hamiter gave me to take to that messenger the day he left. Do you remember? He was the one who brought the letter for Mr. Pierce, the one that made him smile again."

"The miracle-bearer," Lavinia said quietly. "I remember."

"I had that paper in my hands," Bathsheba said. "I took it into town and gave it over to that fellow who came riding through, who had offered to carry letters."

Lavinia's expression grew thoughtful. "There were several letters sent out that day from Fairlawn, she said. "I remember I wrote to Cousin Sally in Charleston." She paused, frowning. "Think carefully, Bathsheba," she said. "Are you certain it was Louise Hamiter's letter?"

"I'm as sure as death, Miss Vinnie," said Bathsheba. "She gave it to me to carry, and it had that spot on it."

Lavinia was frowning. "But the blot was on the inside, where the writing was," she objected.

"I could see it through the paper," Bathsheba said. "It had soaked through, and I looked at it pretty hard, 'cause it was an odd shape. I could make out some of the writing through it, too."

"Did you read the writing?" Lavinia asked.

"I wanted to, Miss Vinnie," Bathsheba said. "But I was taught better."

"Now that is a terrible pity," said Lavinia. She was frowning; Bathsheba couldn't tell if she was joking.

"Anyhow, I remember it also because Miss Louise yelled to me from the house and called me 'pickaninny' and said I was to hurry and make sure the note went out or she'd see my hide was tanned but good."

"She said what?" Lavinia demanded.

"Oh, I didn't pay her any mind," said Bathsheba with a teenager's expansive, scornful tolerance. "I took the note, and since it was the last one I got, I looked at it really well on my way."

"And you remember the spot," Lavinia said thoughtfully.

"Yes, Ma'am. I did make out a line about 'troops', too. And it was addressed to a colonel. I couldn't read the name very well 'cause Miss

Louise had written funny, like her hand wasn't working right."

Lavinia was standing quietly, drawing the chains of her chatelaine through her fingers. "That scheming strumpet," she said softly. "To be so hateful and so stupid—" She saw Bathsheba and broke off. "Thank you, Sheba," she said. "You have been most helpful. Go take an hour or two and relax: I think you have earned it, both for this day and for all the others during the course of this terrible war. But before you go, ask Isaiah to run to the town and fetch Mr. Townsend. Tell him it's time."

** ** **

Five minutes later, standing before the mirror in her bedroom, Lavinia reached up and plucked the pins from her hair, one by one, and shook the heavy red-brown coils loose about her shoulders, smoothing it with careful fingers before taking up the scissors from her chatelaine. She selected a long, thick strand, braided it, and snipped it off close to her head. She coiled it quickly and set it aside.

All wishing that they had said more, praying for a chance to say what was left unsaid...

Her jewel box, lifted down from its hiding place behind the corner molding, sat open atop her dresser now, showing an orderly array of hair ornaments, chains, brooches and necklaces of gold, of garnet, of pearl and emerald. She took out a large locket of heavy, plain gold, opened it, and set the coil of hair inside, closing it with a click.

Some minutes later, her hair pinned up again, she waited in the parlor for Al Townsend, tapping the cellar key against her palm.

** ** **

Lavinia set the key in the lock and turned it. The tumblers clicked; she withdrew the key and moved it to the lower lock and turned it there as well. After a moment she slid the bolt back and opened the door.

She took a deep breath. "Sergeant?" she said. There was no answer.

She looked over her shoulder at Al Townsend, then lifted the lantern and descended the stairs.

"Sergeant Sheppard?" Lavinia paused at the foot of the stairs, looked around, and saw the flickering light of a candle set in its own drippings on the large work table.

Sergeant Sheppard was sitting on the table and watching her silently. His arms were folded, his mouth straight and hard. A bruise dis-colored one cheekbone.

The wrath in his expression made Lavinia falter. She had never seen him look so furious in the time she had known him. She took a deep breath, put the lantern down on the table, and faced him. "Are you all right?" she asked.

He shot a scornful glance at Townsend, who was standing on the steps, and then looked back at her. "I'm alive, as you can see," he said, fingering his cheekbone. "And not much the worse for wear. What was all that noise?"

Lavinia was staring at the table. "You found some candles, I see," she said. "How did you light them?"

"I smoke a pipe," Sheppard said. "Except for a jar of watermelon pickle, that pipe is the closest thing to food that I've had for the past—what? Twelve hours? I lost track after a while."

"I'm sorry," Lavinia said. "I didn't have time to do more than I did. But you seem to be all right."

"Oh I'm just fine," Sheppard said, speaking a little more through his teeth than usual. "It's been an exciting time. Sarah, my wife, had the damnedest taste in literature for the daughter of a Methodist minis-ter. She read some very odd stories by a fellow named Poe. They gave me the willies when I read them, but I thought I'd forgotten them, mostly. Well, it seems that I hadn't forgotten them at all. I found my-self remembering every detail of them as I whiled away the hours here in the dark, listening to the noises around me. This cellar only lacked a cask of sherry to make me think I was living one of the worst of them."

Lavinia stared at him. "What are you talking about?" she demand-ed.

He pushed away from the table and faced her, hands on hips. "I didn't believe at first that you were behind this, but the more I thought, the more I knew that you were," he said. "No one else is smart enough or resolute enough. Or maybe it's that I didn't trust anyone else as much. At any rate, I fell for it hook, line and sinker. I assume you had a good reason for getting Callie to trick me into coming down here and then locking me in. What was it?"

CHAPTER FIFTY-TWO

"Then they have a three hour head start!" Sheppard said.

Townsend passed him the plate of Callie's biscuits. "That's right," he said, taking one for himself. "But that's no problem for us: they're heading south and west at the moment, and they have to take the roads, since they're hauling wagons."

Sheppard stared from him to Lavinia. "The wounded," he said. "They took all of them, even Pierce, who can barely sit up?"

"All of them," Townsend agreed, spooning blackberry jam on his biscuit. "Relax, Sarge," he said, and took a bite of the biscuit. He chewed and swallowed. "I think Miss Lavinia scared them with what she said, so they won't be jouncing and bouncing the boys any more than they have to."

"I told them my honor and hospitality were insulted, and I would be watching closely," Lavinia said. "I insinuated that I had friends high in government who would be informed of what had happened, and who would ensure that that captain would suffer the consequences of any brutality."

Townsend smiled a little grimly. "Truth to tell," he said, "Miss Vinnie gave them the idea that the Wheeler family was the only one fighting in this war, and they owned the Confederacy. That mustached popinjay seemed to believe her!"

"The rat that went through the cellar," Sheppard said, looking at Callie, who only smiled.

"Caesar and his troop are tracking the wagons, so they're not out of distance," Townsend said.

Sheppard drew a deep breath and looked around at the kitchen. "Then everything's under control," he said.

"That is right, Sergeant," Lavinia said. She had been sitting quietly, an untouched cup of tea before her. "The only surprise this day was the arrival of those soldiers."

"That was surprise enough," Sheppard said. "I wonder why they thought they had to come and arrest the men."

Lavinia and Townsend traded looks.

"You've got to go after them, Asa," Townsend said. "You've got the papers, you can take them to your lines and you won't be sent to prison for it like I might. It's either that or a prison camp for them."

Sheppard nodded. "You're right," he said. "But my orders..." He did not finish the sentence.

"The Confederate troops came through," Townsend said. "I guess that ends your assignment."

"They came through and left again," Sheppard said.

No one spoke for a moment. Townsend finally got to his feet. "They're gathering outside, Toby and the others," he said. "I'll go see what needs to be done. You'd best eat, Sarge, you'll be going far and fast with a fight at the end."

Sheppard nodded and watched him leave.

Callie quietly set down the frying pan and left the kitchen.

Sheppard looked across the rim of his cup at Lavinia as he took a long swallow of coffee. He set the cup down. "I was sent to guard you, Lavinia," he said quietly.

"But those men are my friends," she said.

"It won't work," Sheppard said. "General Stanley was specific: guard you and keep you from harm. If there was any question of what I was to do, you were to come first."

"But he could not have foreseen this," Lavinia said. "You have no other choice."

Sheppard frowned into the coffee cup. "They'll connect the rescue attempt with you, you know," he said. "That will be putting you in danger."

"No, they won't," she replied. "I have written a very forceful letter of protest, as I said I would. I've sent copies to every official I could think of in Georgia, starting with the governor. I'll be peppering them with letters protesting the action of those soldiers against wounded, helpless men. Why would I be expending so much effort if I were part of a plot to free them?"

"You can't underestimate the minds of fanatics," Sheppard said. "I saw it back in New York when I was on leave. They all but lynched another fellow on furlough for saying that he thought the South had a point about states' rights. You saw how the good citizens of Wheelerville were when they thought I'd shot those prisoners they wanted to hang."

"I refuse to spend my life cowering because I'm afraid someone might do me a mischief," Lavinia said.

Sheppard drained the cup of coffee and reached for another biscuit. "But you shouldn't invite mischief," he said.

Lavinia looked out the dark windows. She caught a glimpse of moving shadows; Toby's people, awaiting Sheppard. "You have to go, Asa," she said.

Sheppard spread jam on the biscuit in silence.

Lavinia turned back toward him. "What else can we do?" she asked. "We both know those men will all die if they're sent to prison. You can save them by going after them. You can't fool me, Sergeant: you know in your heart that this is the only thing we can do."

"Maybe so," Sheppard sighed. He finished the biscuit, rose to his feet and took up his cap. "I just wonder..." He shook his head and did not finish the sentence.

Lavinia carefully set her cup on its saucer, folded her hands before her and looked up at him. "Asa, look at me," she said, "Do you think I want you to leave me now?"

His eyes met hers and warmed in a sudden smile. "I've learned not to guess your thoughts, Lavinia," he said. "I'm content to know that they're always good, if sometimes annoying."

"I could say the same of you, Sergeant," she said with a shadow of her usual tartness.

A sound outside made both of them half-turn toward the door, then look back at each other.

"It's time to leave," she said, rising. "Oh, Asa, I wish..."

"Sarge? We're saddled up now!"

"Lavinia," he said, capturing her hands and holding them between his for a moment before raising them to his lips.

She tried to smile. "I always meant to tell you how much all you have done meant to me."

"You didn't have to," he said. "It meant as much to me."

She looked toward the door and then closed it firmly. Her heart was pounding as she turned back toward him and took his hands in hers. "You told me that you love me, Asa," she said quietly. "I believe you know that I love you. You have known for months, I think." She paused, summoning a smile for him and tightening her hold on his hands. "I wanted to tell you myself before you rode away. If we'd had time—if things had not become so rushed and so jumbled—we could have said it so much better— Oh, Asa!"

The words came in a glad half-gasp as he took her in his arms, smiled down at her, and kissed her as though the future held no fear.

"Lavinia," he said.

"There's no time," she said, clinging even closer. "I took too much time to say this, and it's time for you to go. How I'll miss you!"

"I'll be back," he said.

"There's a war going on, Asa," she said.

"Anything can happen," he said. "If this war brought me to you once, surely it can bring me once again."

She smiled at him. "I'll do my best to believe that," she said. She took out the locket, and watched as he opened it and then looked at her. "I wanted you to have something of me, Asa, so that somehow, some way, I might be with you when you go into danger. If only—"

The next moment she was held tightly in his arms and clinging to him as though she could keep him with her. After what seemed little more than a breath of time, she released him and drew away. "You must go now," she said.

He looked down at her with a world of regret in his expression that changed as she watched into something deeper. He bent and kissed her on the lips, so quickly she wondered later if it had actually happened. Then he released her and went through the door.

She followed him out into the twilight.

Al Townsend was on his horse, frowning down the line of riders. His expression relaxed as Sheppard came through the door and went to Dixie, who was being held by George.

"I'll give you a leg up, Sergeant," George said.

Sheppard accepted the boost into the saddle with a smile, gathered his reins, and looked down at Lavinia.

"Callie is bringing Meg out," Lavinia said. "I thought she should have a chance to say goodbye."

Sheppard smiled as Callie came out with Meg, sleepy and protesting, in her arms.

"She was sound asleep, Sergeant," Callie said.

"We'll be sending her back to bed in a trice," Sheppard said, holding out his arms to Meg.

"Are you going for a ride?" Meg asked through a yawn as he lifted her to his saddle.

"Yes, Peanut," he said. "I've got some things to do and I need to do them right away. I didn't want to go without telling my little girl I was going."

"Will you be back tomorrow?" she asked.

"I'll be back when I can," Sheppard replied. "But I don't know when that'll be. Will you take care of your mama like a good little girl?"

Meg stared at him, round-eyed, and finally nodded.

"That's my girl," Sheppard said. "Now give me a kiss and go back to bed."

She clung to him for a moment, then smiled with a sudden brightness and said, "You'll be back. I know you will. I'll be waiting for you."

"You do that, Peanut," he said, and lifted her down to Callie. "Now go back to bed, and sweet dreams." He watched as Meg was carried into the house. She turned at the door and blew him a kiss over Callie's shoulder.

Lavinia closed her eyes for a moment. "Good bye, Sergeant," she said, aware of the gazes fixed on her. She set her hand on his knee and looked up at him. "Sergeant, if ever you come back to Wheelerville, under whatever circumstances, you will be made welcome."

He raised her hand to his lips and bent to kiss it. "You are a great lady, Miss Wheeler," he said formally. "If I am able to do so, I will certainly come back to Wheelerville."

"God bless you, Sergeant," she said.

He settled his carbine sling across his chest. "Oh, and George!" he said, one eye on Lavinia.

The old man drew himself up. "Sergeant?"

"See those pots are safely guarded! Not a chip! Not a crack! We don't want Miss Wheeler's heart to be broken, do we?"

"No fear of that!" George said. "Miss Vinnie's heart is safe with me!"

"Yes," Sheppard had said, "I suppose it is. See that it stays so. Miss Wheeler: your servant!" he said.

Lavinia met his laughing eyes and smiled, herself, with the difficulty of one who does it only for show. She had realized once again, with a pain completely new, that he was riding out of her life as suddenly as he had ridden into it that May morning. She had seen too many graves open in the churchyard to be able to delude herself as to the likelihood of her ever seeing him again.

"God bless you, Sergeant," she said again. "And keep you safe."

Sheppard flashed a smile down at her. She seemed to see that smile as he turned his mare, raised his hand in salute, and rode away at a trot, taking the moonlight and the promise of sunrise along with him.

Lavinia watched until the group had vanished among the trees, then she turned and went back into the house.

Callie met her at the door with a shawl and cup of hot tea. "God will watch over them," she said.

Lavinia nodded and sipped the tea. "'Woe to those who cause stumbling,' " she said with a pale, ominous smile. "Callie, darling, will you ask George to come to me in the parlor once he's finished with the horses? I've a note for him to deliver to Louise Hamiter in the morning. And then ask him to find some sturdy fellows who can help me move some trunks."

CHAPTER FIFTY-THREE

"When you gape like that, Louise, you look just like a chicken that has had its neck wrung," Lavinia said with contemptuous calmness. She was standing on the veranda, gazing across the eastern lawn at the glitter of morning sun upon what promised to be the last dew of autumn.

She gathered her shawl more closely about her shoulders, cast a quick glance back toward the door, and then faced Louise again. "Your appearance to the side," she said, "I fail to understand the purpose of this visit. My letter was quite clear, and your belongings are in the yard at this moment. There was no need for you to come screeching over here at this ungodly hour. You have awakened Meg, and you have disturbed my people, and you have not succeeded in changing matters."

Louise's pale eyes seemed to grow enormous. "No need— But the letter you sent—"

"—Was quite explicit," Lavinia finished for her, firmly suppressing a thin smile. There was no question of the explicitness of her letter, which had consisted of two sentences. "I don't see what more you need to know. You will leave Wheelerville within the next day. Your belongings are on the front lawn at Fairlawn; those items you do not choose to take with you will be burned.

"But why are you doing this?" Louise cried.

"I think you know," Lavinia returned. "You did, after all, write the letter that brought that troop of cavalry to Fairlawn to take those wounded men away."

Louise paled, but she spoke calmly. "I don't know what you are talking about," she said.

"Yes, you do," Lavinia returned. "The letter you wrote has come back to Fairlawn. I have enough samples of your penmanship to be able to recognize it when I saw it again. Others who saw your note recognized it, as well, and were able to pinpoint when and how it was sent. No wonder you were so anxious to leave on the heels of that messenger."

"Yankees—"

"Wounded, disabled men, Louise. No longer fighting men. But let's set them aside and take a look at your other dealings. You called Meg 'white trash' to her face, and you tried to hurt her by telling her that her mother was murdered. You went to a wounded, half-delirious man and told him that his wife was unfaithful, you called my people 'niggers' and 'pickaninnies, issued orders where you had no right to do so, and generally made yourself obnoxious to any right-thinking man or woman. So, you see, there is nothing more to say. Choose those items you wish to take with you and take them away. The rest will be burned."

"But—"

Lavinia gathered her shawl about her shoulders and took a step toward the door. "That is all, Louise," she said.

The door opened as Lavinia reached for the handle, and Meg came out onto the porch, smiling at Lavinia.

Lavinia had been prepared, that morning, to deal with a sobbing, bewildered child who was looking for her father. She had been surprised to see that Meg's main concern with Sheppard's departure was not the question of why he had to go so much as that of when he would be returning. She was in no doubt that he would return, and she insisted that it would be soon.

Lavinia had decided not to say anything about that, except that soldiers did dangerous things and she might have to wait a long time. Meg had considered that and finally accepted it with no further comment.

Lavinia looked down at her now. "Go back inside, poppet," she said with a smile. "It is too cold out here. I'll join you directly."

"But I want to see the lying bitch," Meg said with the composure of an angel.

"Well, I never!" Louise gasped.

"What did you say, Meg?" Lavinia demanded.

Meg repeated the words. "That's what they used to call her," she said.

"What who used to call her?"

"Some of the men. They didn't know I was there," Meg said. "Mama, what's a bitch?"

"It is a very bad word that ladies don't use," Lavinia said.

"Oh," Meg said. "Like 'white trash'?"

"Exactly like it," Lavinia said.

"But she used it," Meg said.

"I would not use her as an example of a lady," Lavinia said. "Now go on inside. Miss Hamiter is just about to leave."

"If you are throwing me out, Lavinia, at least you can direct the escort–"

"I did not mention an escort," Lavinia said with an odd, brittle smile. Meg looked from her to Louise. "Go inside, Meg," Lavinia repeated.

Meg smiled suddenly. "Yes Ma'am," she said. "I don't want to look at her. She's a nasty, sinful old woman and it de— It def— It defiles anyone to look at her." She paused and looked at Louise. "Now aren't you shamed?" she said.

"Shamed?" Lavinia repeated.

"Yes, Mama," Meg said. "Papa says 'tell truth and shame the devil', and he never lies." That said, she went into the house.

Louise's pale eyes were enormous. "You said you did not mention an escort," she gasped. "B-but you cannot mean to send me out alone!"

"I can and I do," Lavinia said. "You yourself said an escort was not necessary when Sergeant Sheppard brought the subject up as the reason he would not allow you to leave."

"But the marauders—!"

"Marauders, Louise?" Lavinia repeated. "You said that the violence that cost Meg her family and killed the Fiskes was due to Federal troops. And I have it on your own excellent authority that the cowardly Yankee troops are now far from here."

"You mean to kill me!"

"Your fate is a matter of complete indifference to me, Louise," Lavinia said. "And I warned you what I do to snakes when I find them."

Louise's bosom was rising and falling. "It is because that Yankee went away!" she said through her teeth.

Lavinia lifted her eyebrows.

"You're in love with him! How he must have laughed at you, ignoring that ring on his finger! He's gone and you're blaming me."

"But you are to blame," Lavinia said calmly. "Whether or not I happen to love Sergeant Sheppard—he's widowed, by the way—is immaterial. He is a fine man, and I imagine he went after his charges. I don't grudge his departure, except that it comes about as the result of a stain you put on my honor and that of this household. No, don't look at me like that. I have written letters to various of my family's friends in the government of Georgia protesting this action and demanding justice. It may accomplish something, but it won't bring the men back, so you may preen yourself on your success as you ride toward Macon."

She continued, "But don't preen too long: I've also written letters to Savannah, Milledgeville and Richmond. I think you may well be blackballed from society from now on." She smiled and added, "And you may reflect on this: I had wanted you out of this house and this town months ago. Sergeant Sheppard would never give his consent to it. He said it was too dangerous for all concerned. Well, the Sergeant is gone and I am in charge, and I find that the question of the peace and contentment of my household is far more important to me than that of your life. I do not want you here another minute. Now take your belongings and get out of my sight!"

Louise was trembling. "But I can't go alone!" she gasped. "I can't! If Sergeant Sheppard thought it unsafe for me months ago, how would he think it now?"

"You're singing a different tune now that it is a question of your safety," Lavinia said. She paused, her hand on the doorknob, and considered. "Very well," she said at last. "If you can find anyone from this town who has the stomach to tolerate traveling with you, I will allow it. Now begone!"

CHAPTER FIFTY-FOUR

Al Townsend brought his horse to a halt and looked up and down the street. "Right, son," he said to Abner. "Things look to be normal here. So you'd best get home. If your ma needs to know anything, send her to me. I'll just tell her that we were doing some patrolling, and that's the truth."

Abner frowned slightly. "Do you suppose it'll work out?" he asked.

"Oh, I'd imagine it might," Townsend said. "That's a well-trained group of folk, with a lot of gumption, and it's led by a good man. The Sarge's on the side of the angels. He'll do all right."

"Yes, sir," Abner said, looking doubtful.

Townsend looked over at him with a touch of wry sympathy. "You're shaping to be a fine man, son," he said. "Your pa'd be proud of you. But there's something he'd want to tell you, and since he's not here, it's up to me."

Abner looked at him. "What is it?" he asked.

"Just this," said Townsend. "Sometimes, for all your hoping and praying, and for all that you try as hard as you can to get things to happen the way you want them, you don't win. That doesn't mean no one listened to your prayers, or that God abandoned you. It means that what you wanted wasn't meant to be, and you've got to learn to live with it."

Abner's smile dimmed. "You really don't think we're going to win, do you, sir?" he asked.

"No," Townsend said gently. "I don't. The Yanks have the upper hand here in Georgia, and it sounds like they're getting it other places, too. But that doesn't change things for me. I've got to do the right thing, whether or not it'll succeed."

"But what we just did—" Abner began. "Wasn't it wrong, if that's what you're saying?"

Townsend shook his head. "We did our best to stop murder," he said. "That was God's work back there, and it had nothing to do with fighting a war. You keep remembering that."

Abner looked doubtful, but his expression eased as Townsend watched, and he smiled. "Thanks, Mr. Townsend," he said.

"Don't mention it," Townsend said. "Now get on with you. You've had a long day, and you did a good job." He watched Abner ride off and then sat back with a sigh. The past days' activity had only served to confirm the decision he had made the day the raiders had been hanged. He had a few loose ends to tie up in Wheelerville, then he would go. And one of the first things he had to do was go to Sam Wallins to have his horse's feet looked at.

** ** **

"The shoes are still in good shape," Wallins said, releasing the gelding's hind foot and straightening with a grunt. "Considering I'm the one who made them, I'm not surprised. If you want, I can pull them, rasp this fellow's feet, then put them back on. It'll save some trouble down the road."

"Go ahead," Townsend said. "I'm not against dodging a little trouble."

Wallins nodded in a preoccupied sort of way and lifted the gelding's hoof again. "Hand me the clinches, would you?" he asked.

Townsend did so, watching as Wallins cut through the nail ends where they protruded through the hoof. In a moment the shoe had been prized away from the hoof and Townsend was holding it and pulling the old nails out. He watched Wallins set to work on the second shoe. "All right, Sam," he said after a moment. "What's eating you?"

Wallins looked up.

"Your head isn't here," Townsend said. "In fact, you've been in a fog ever since that to-do over at Fairlawn when everyone was up in arms about those renegades." He added with calm deliberation, "Yourself included, which had me surprised."

Wallins smiled wryly as he pulled the second shoe off. "That was a bad day," he said, handing the shoe to Townsend. "And we behaved badly all around. And now things have gone beyond fixing, with everyone gone from Fairlawn like that."

Townsend shrugged. "Were you the one that caused it?" he asked.

Wallins frowned at him. "No," he said, "You know damned well I wasn't, Al!"

"Then forget it," Townsend said. "Mend what you can. The rest will just have to straighten itself out."

"Maybe," Wallins said. "I wasn't happy with myself. I'm still not, for what that's worth."

Townsend shrugged.

"Well, it's over with," Wallins said after a moment.

"Something's not over with," Townsend said. "What is it?"

Wallins hesitated. "The Hamiter woman," he said at last.

Townsend carefully hung the horseshoe on the edge of the anvil. "What about that yellow-haired bitch?" he asked.

Wallins set the gelding's hoof down and handed Townsend the third shoe. "She's over at the church," he said. "I was there, since Reverend Porter wanted me to look at the hinges on the door and see if I thought they needed replacing. I heard voices, and stuck my head in to see what was going on.

There was a group of the ladies of the town, I'd say about ten or so. They were holding that knitting party they have off and on, making blankets and such for the soldiers. The one Miss Lavinia started and usually runs. Well, she's right in the middle of it, and telling lies fit to beat the band."

"And Miss Lavinia was letting her?" Townsend asked, surprised.

"She wasn't there," Wallins said. "That's why the Hamiter woman was doing it. And they were all drinking it in." Townsend's eyes narrowed. "What kind of lies?" he asked.

** ** **

Alan Townsend paused outside the church door and listened. Snatches of conversation came to him, and one voice that he had been listening for especially. Yes, she was in there, and from what he could catch, had not altered her tune any. He squared his shoulders, set his hand on the door latch, pulled the door open, and stepped into the vestibule.

The conversation stopped as the ladies looked up at him. Mrs. Swithin, looking a little distressed, Abner Wigfall's mother with the sort of look that someone might wear who doesn't approve of what she's hearing but is enjoying it nonetheless. The other ladies looked very much the same, and in the middle of them, as Sam Wallins had said, smooth-haired and elegant, Louise Hamiter was looping yarn over a needle and taking a stitch.

Townsend locked gazes with her, watched her slowly set her knitting down. He turned to Mrs. Wigfall. "What's this I hear about people saying that Miss Lavinia and Sergeant Sheppard were carrying on?" he asked without preamble.

Louise sniffed.

Townsend turned back to Louise. "I heard that's what's being said, and I heard you're the one who's been saying it," he said. "It's time you stopped."

"And who are you to speak to me like this?" Louise asked with a lightly contemptuous smile.

"I'm someone who believes in speaking the truth," Townsend said. "And I am one of the few people in this town who seems to remember who and what Lavinia Wheeler is, and a strumpet is something she is not! For that matter, I don't like you saying that about Asa Sheppard, who's a good, Christian gentleman!"

Louise turned her shoulder to him and took up her knitting again. "Why, they've been under the same roof all this time," she said. "Now what do you think happened?"

Townsend stared at her. "You worthless baggage!" he said slowly. "They've been under the same roof with Miss Lavinia's aunt – a good chaperone if ever there was one! – under everyone's eye!"

His expression narrowed. "You're talking like that about a lady who took you in and cared for you when you were in need, and who kept you on in spite of everything you did to make things difficult for her and her household! After all the treachery and heartache you caused!" He looked around at the women listening. "You heard what she said," he said, "And you let her say it! I'm ashamed of all of you! Can't you recognize a liar when you see one?"

"Of all the—!" Louise began.

"Tell me the truth, all of you," Townsend said, "Didn't she come here, all white-faced and tight-lipped, and after a few minutes, looking like she'd simmered down, didn't she start telling things to you in a real sweet, genteel voice?"

Looks were exchanged. Mrs. Wallins cleared her throat. "Well," she said, "I must say that she did."

"Now really," Louise said, "It is too much to expect me to listen to this slander."

"You'd know about slander," Townsend said, looking her up and down, "you lying piece of trash!" Louise slapped her knitting needles and yarn down. "Trash!" she gasped. "If only I were a man!"

"If you were a man you'd have a mouth full of broken teeth right now and I'd have a set of cut knuckles," Townsend said.

Mrs. Wigfall had set her knitting down. "Now really, Mr. Townsend," she said. "This kind of talk is hardly appropriate for a church!"

"And the kind of talk that this one was dishing out is?" Townsend demanded. "I'm telling the truth. For what she did to Pierce and to poor Meg, she'd have been slugged long ago if she were a man! I'll be doing a kindness to take her away from Wheelerville without any further ado!" He turned back to Louise. "Pack your belongings and be ready to ride tomorrow," he said, "because I'm the only escort you'll get and if you aren't ready in time you'll be going alone."

Louise stared at him, her face flaming. "Who do you think you are?" she demanded.

"Who do I think I am?" he repeated scornfully. "Well, I'm still not sure what I am. I'm what you might call a 'work under construction'. I can tell you what I was, which is an easier thing. I was pretty much the town bully. I was full of myself. Stronger and bigger than a lot of folk here." He paused and considered. "I don't guess I ever thought I was smarter, though... Anyhow, that's what I was. Then I went to war and fought a couple of years, quit, came back here and tried to take up where I left off. It didn't work out, and I saw I'd been wrong. I'm on a different path now, and we'll see what I become if I live long enough. Maybe it'll be something good. Meanwhile, you want to get out of here safely, and I want to go toward Macon, so I'll take you, and rid this town of you."

"But Lavinia Wheeler has just said that I had to go alone!"

"Don't give me any nonsense about Miss Lavinia," he said scornfully. "If you hadn't done the dirty, she'd never have taken such a line with you. I think she's got it right."

He looked around and raised his voice. "Does everyone here know what you did? I'll tell them. I'll tell them how you tried to drive poor Private Pierce mad, how you went after little Meg and told her she was trash, how you chased her down in the cemetery, right at her mama's grave, and told her that her mama was murdered by Yankees like the sergeant. And I'll tell them all how you wrote to our army and told them that the town of Wheelerville was on the side of the Yankees and housing Yankee troops."

Louise's expression froze.

Townsend looked around at the group. "That, ladies, is why they came swooping down here and took all those wounded men away," he said. "And they'd had an eye to arresting the leaders here, except that Miss Lavinia did a good job convincing them that we all were loyal. This one's been saying that Miss Lavinia threw her out. Well, that's true enough, but Miss Lavinia has too much charity to go shouting about what a viper this whey-faced strumpet is. I'm not as charitable and I've told you now. You're looking at a twisting little snake who can take a good friendship and make it seem somehow foul, who can take a fellow's heart and soul and trample it in the muck, like she did with poor Pierce. And to get even for some wrong she thought she was done by someone who took her in and gave her food and shelter when she was in need, she thought nothing of spreading lies about an entire town that could have led to it being burned to the ground. And she's still lying!"

Mrs. Swithin slowly inserted her needles in the ball of yarn on her lap, wound the extra length around them, and looked at Louise. "You know it is true, Louise," she said. "I can't take your part any more."

Louise looked from Aunt Amabel to Townsend and then at the half-circle of women, some sitting with their needles poised, some gazing at her with shocked surprise. Even then, if Louise could have turned a face of brass upon them, and spoken softly, she might have been able to maintain the doubt in her listeners' minds, but her flaming, furious face as she rounded on Townsend proved her guilt better than anything he could have said, better than the words she was spitting at him. "You trash! In a better place than this you'd be horsewhipped!"

"Showing your colors at last?" he said, folding his arms.

"What do you know of being holed up in a slum, living on charity day in and day out putting up with the airs and graces of a passel of sanctimonious—!"

Mrs. Wigfall rose. "I think we have heard enough, Miss Hamiter," she said. "This gentleman has agreed to escort you to your family in Macon. You had best return to my house and assemble your belongings."

Townsend turned back to the rest. "Miss Lavinia's a virtuous lady," he said. "And Asa Sheppard is a gentleman, and there was nothing ever done that was improper."

Mrs. Swithin said, "I believe that is generally known."

"That's right," Townsend said. "I don't claim to be a preacher, but the Book says to cast out evil from your midst: I suggest you give Miss Hamiter her things and send her on her way. She'll be away from here in the morning."

CHAPTER FIFTY-FIVE

Lavinia had returned to the house with a profound feeling of relief and accomplishment. Louise was no longer a problem and she could forget the woman had ever existed. Or try to. First she would have to burn the trunks, though she thought it best to wait until after Louise had actually left, in case there might be something she wanted.

Soft-hearted, she chided herself. At any rate, she had thought, the problem would soon be behind her. She set about her duties at Fairlawn with a good will.

But Lavinia discovered that the problem of Louise was still very much with her when Judge Prescott called on her around noon, stiff and uneasy, but a little grim as well.

"This vengefulness isn't like you, Lavinia," he had said without preamble.

Lavinia, who had been engaged in reworking the embroidery from one of the dining room chairs, had merely arched her eyebrows. "Then I can add another...benefit from my association with the woman to the tally of the others," she said. "It's quite a list: Gaylord's death, a great deal of Mother's final sufferings, Private Pierce's anguish, Meg's heartbreak, the danger that those poor wounded men are facing at this moment, and my own exhaustion and near-breakdown in 1860. She's fortunate we're both women: if we were men I'd have called her out for this latest evildoing. And you know I'm a fair shot."

"Lavinia," Prescott said.

She looked at him.

"You might as well have taken a shot at her. You're sending her into danger."

"Is that what she's whimpering now?" Lavinia demanded scornfully. "Why, she maintained all this summer that she would be perfectly fine when she left! Sergeant Sheppard was not convinced, but he's gone now and I decided to take her at her word and let her go."

"She changed her mind," Judge Prescott pointed out. "And you ordered her out of Wheelerville."

"I am within my rights," Lavinia stated. "After all that scheming creature did this past summer—let alone over the past five years!—I have certainly earned the right to order her off my property and so I have. You are going too far, Judge, when you presume to condemn me for that. If the bed she made now seems to her to be too dangerous to lie in, that is her problem and not mine."

"She asked to stay," Prescott said.

"No, she did not," Lavinia said with precision. "She gabbled out something about how I meant to kill her. Never did she request my leave to remain." She held up her hand when Judge Prescott started to speak. "No, I would have refused her if she had. I am the mistress of this town and I will not have her here one day longer. I told her that she could go with an escort if she could find someone with the stomach to assist her."

"Do you think anyone will fly in the face of your displeasure?" Judge Prescott asked.

Lavinia set her needle aside. "'Fly in the face of my displeasure', indeed!" she said. "Look at me, Judge. I am nothing more than a small, plain, middle-aged woman. I was a wealthy one, once, but I doubt that counted for a great deal with these folk here; it might have been different in Savannah. What do you suppose they think I'll do? If they have any gumption, they'll follow their consciences, if their consciences point to them helping Louise Hamiter. I suspect they don't."

"Lavinia..."

"No, Judge. I will not lift a finger to help one who has so deliberately spread hatred and pain among those I care for. Let us say no more."

Judge Prescott had stayed and tried to argue with her, but he finally left.

And Al Townsend came to call on her the next morning.

** ** **

Lavinia had been mending some shifts for Meg, shaking her head at the holes the child had managed to tear in the vicinity of her knees. She had looked up as George announced Townsend, and set her mending aside when he came into the parlor.

Townsend was dressed for riding, wearing a pair of good new boots, a new shirt and coat, and a good fur felt slouch hat. He seemed somehow braced to Lavinia, and even a little grim, but he had bowed to her and accepted her offer of a chair.

"I am glad to see you back so soon, Captain Townsend," she said. "I gather you left Sergeant Sheppard and the others well on the way of overtaking the wounded?"

"They were within about two miles," he said. "I wanted to stay for the fun, but the sergeant sent Abner and me back, saying the less involved we were in the illegal end of things, from our standpoint, the better." He added, "I think he was right."

"Most likely," Lavinia said.

Townsend smiled at her and offered a bundle wrapped in a handkerchief. "He asked that I bring you this," he said. "Said he thought you'd understand." He watched as Lavinia opened it. "He told me he'd been working on it this summer, between times."

Lavinia touched the carved mockingbird with gentle fingertips and looked up at Townsend. "There was a mockingbird that sang every evening at the same time this summer. We used to sit and listen to it and talk about the problems with the wounded and with the town, all the while it was singing in the background. I guess the mocker's gone now."

"He'll be back, following the spring, most likely," Townsend said. "That sort always returns." He did not elaborate and instead added with the touch of a frown, "By the way, Abner and I are the only ones who know that the Sarge didn't go off at the first sight of those fellows, like we told the rest. The less the folks here know, the better."

"Even Judge Prescott and Dr. Meacham?" Lavinia asked. She had thought the Judge at least had known.

"Not even them," Townsend said. "Ever since those raiders were hanged and everyone got ugly and blamed Sergeant Sheppard when I didn't let them strangle, I haven't trusted them with any secrets. There's just enough bad feeling to poison things. It's a shame, but that's the way it is."

"I am obliged for the warning," Lavinia said. "And I am sorry it has to be so."

"War," Townsend said. He frowned down at his boots, and finally got to his feet. "Well, Miss Lavinia," he said, "I've got to be going. I came by to drop off Sarge's gift and caution you. Now I'm saying my farewells. I'm riding toward Macon." He looked straight at her. "And

I'm taking Louise Hamiter with me."

Lavinia stiffened. "Is that so, sir?" she said with distaste.

"It is so, Miss Lavinia," Townsend said.

"Well go, then, and God help you," Lavinia said roundly. "If you want my blessing on this venture, you won't have it, but I'll pray for your safety. I can't imagine why–"

Townsend spoke over her without hesitation. "I didn't come to ask your permission to take Miss Louise," he said. "I came to tell you why I was doing it."

"You don't have to explain, Mr. Townsend," Lavinia said. "No doubt you have your reasons."

"I surely do, Miss Lavinia," he said. "But I don't like the way you're looking at me and I'd hate to have you thinking ill of me all over again."

"I never thought ill of you," she said.

"Think back," he said. "You were one of those who thought me a deserter when I came back after two years in the army."

Lavinia drew breath to deny it, then she paused, remembering. "I have changed my mind since then," she said after a moment. "I'm sorry I misjudged you. It was wrong of me to make assumptions where I didn't know everything."

"Oh, you didn't misjudge me," Townsend said with the touch of a smile. "You see, I changed my mind, too. I never meant to desert, exactly, but I knew what I was doing, and I thought at the time I was doing wrong. Well, anyhow, there it is, and everyone was right about me. The point is, I don't want you thinking ill of me, though I don't care about the rest of them, and that's why I'm here."

Lavinia sighed. "Tell me, then," she said.

Townsend said, "I was at that place where Sarge found Meg's folks that night. I don't wish that on anyone, man, woman, villain or saint. So I'd have taken her anyhow, just to ease my own fears. But I'm heading that way to do some things that have been hanging fire for a while, and it's not out of my way. I'll be taking her away from here, to bother us no more, and I'll be protecting her, too, so it's worth the doing. I wouldn't mind your blessing, if you'd care to give it, but I'll understand if you can't. She caused a lot of grief here, before the war and later..."

Lavinia had lowered her eyes midway through Townsend's speech.

She raised them to his when he finished. "Don't be foolish, Mr. Townsend," she said. "You have shown me what a vicious creature I've been, myself. Take her away, and thank you and God bless you. Come back safely—and never fear I'd ever think ill of you."

Townsend smiled at her and got to his feet. "You set me at rest, Miss Lavinia," he said. "I can go with a clear mind."

"Go with a..." Lavinia repeated. She looked at him with eyes that suddenly seemed to see clearly. "Mr. Townsend, where are you going?" she demanded.

"Toward Macon," he said.

"Why?"

He hesitated, then nodded once. "I'm going to the army," he said. "General Cobb's in Macon, and they've been calling for men... I'm going to offer to join up again. They may want to arrest me, or whatever. I left without their permission, after all, and I did swear an oath when I joined... But, anyhow, it seems to me that the Confederacy needs me, and I've got to do what I can."

Lavinia was frowning. "But..." she began."Mr. Townsend, you know–you must see–that the Federals will win this war. It's all over now but the dying."

"That doesn't make it right for me to stay here," he said. "I figure, once you know what's the right thing to do, then the only thing is to do it as quick and as thoroughly as you can."

Lavinia had to look down.

He smiled with a touch of compunction. "I've made you sad," he said. "I didn't mean to, I promise. You've had so much on your shoulders the past months, and I didn't realize it till late. Well, I don't want you to worry more than you have to. Things will work out all right, you'll see. And meanwhile I'll be getting the Hamiter woman out of your hair." He got to his feet. "We're leaving in an hour, maybe," he said.

She rose and went to him. "Mr. Townsend," she said.

He looked at her.

She took a deep breath. "You're one of the finest men I have ever known," she said. "I want you to know this."

"I take it kindly, you saying so," he said, taking her hand and raising it to his lips in a courtly gesture that seemed somehow to suit him. "Good bye, Miss Lavinia. I might not see this town again for a time.

You keep yourself safe."

CHAPTER FIFY-SIX

The wind whirled along the alley of oaks, setting the crisp brown leaves to clattering. The afternoon sky was banded with dark clouds that parted occasionally to reveal glimpses of blue. Winter was setting in with a vengeance, Lavinia thought as she bent over the wine-colored chrysanthemums that flanked the front steps. And it was not even the middle of November.

She could hear music and singing inside the house: Callie playing the piano for Meg, a lively reel that she had not heard Callie play in years. She could hear Meg's delighted laughter in response and the patter of her feet on the floor, a lighter, livelier echo of the wind-tossed oak leaves.

Lavinia straightened and gazed down at the flowers, cupped in her hands as though, like goblets of wine, they might spill and bleed their color. Beyond her, in the middle of the alleyway, lay a blackened patch, the last reminder of Louise Hamiter.

Lavinia smiled, remembering. She had stood on that very spot the morning Louise had left Wheelerville with Al Townsend, five days before. She had watched George lay pitch-pine kindling around the pile of trunks, wood hoarded against a cold winter. She had watched him strike a match against the nearest trunk and touch it to the kindling, and she had watched as the flames had climbed up around the trunks and eaten into their wood and fabric sides until the trunks had collapsed and spilled out dresses and shoes, bottles and fans across the alleyway.

Lavinia had watched Louise's belongings burn until the last scraps of blackened fabric had twisted and tumbled away in the updraft and all that had remained was a pile of heat-warped brass fittings and some assorted buttons. George had raked those up the next morning, whistling, and dumped them in the manure pile outside the stable.

Louise was gone now, and there was nothing to bring her back to mind, not even the daguerreotype that Gaylord had carried with him when he joined the army, that had been sent back with his body after his death. Lavinia had tossed that into the fire, as well.

Lavinia brought the flowers to her nose, savoring their sharp, spicy scent as the wind rose and tugged at her skirts. Louise was gone, and so was everything she had tried to mar. The ballroom had been set to rights, the cots folded and put away, the floor swept and waxed again, but Lavinia could still seem to see the rows of beds that had stood there.

Another dancing song came rippling from the piano.

Lavinia turned to look at the house over her shoulder. She could see Meg through the window. As she watched, the child looked up, dimpled, and blew her a kiss. Lavinia caught it and blew one back, smiling.

She had heard at last from her friends in the Georgia government. Meg was the last of her family, and was the heiress to a modest property south of Atlanta. Lavinia had spoken with Judge Prescott, and now she was awaiting word that her adoption of the girl had been approved by the government.

Callie was playing and singing 'Annie Laurie' now. The odd sour note indicated that Meg was trying her hand at the keys.

It had been an eventful several days. Her letters, fired off to the authorities right after the departure of her wounded, had hit home, drawing visits from several high-ranking officers and government officials, and then a full apology. But her soldiers were gone and the house was echoingly empty without them.

She raised her eyes to the alley of oaks and thought of the verse that she had read her Bible the night before, the first vision of Zechariah the prophet:

I saw by night, and behold a man riding upon a red horse, and he stood among the myrtle trees that were in the bottom; and behind him were there red horses, speckled and white...

There was no use sighing, she thought. Asa Sheppard was gone. And yet, she thought, watching the wind in the trees, he might very well return. Who knew what the future would bring, good or bad? It could as easily be laughter, contentment and heartsease as disaster and heartbreak. If she had learned anything during Asa Sheppard's stay, it had been that courage and gaiety might very well carry the day. She gazed along the alley where it curved away east as the wind rose, heightening the rattle of leaves until it sounded like hoofbeats. The tossing russet leaves were glinting and swaying, the shades of brown shifting and solidifying until they gleamed bright chestnut in the sun.

And then, in the flash of time it took to draw breath, she realized that the patch of red-brown was Asa Sheppard's tall chestnut mare, carrying him down the alley of oaks at a smart canter.

Lavinia flung the chrysanthemums aside with a glad cry, caught up her skirts in both hands and ran to him across the brown grass as he leapt down from the saddle, caught her up and swung her around, laughing.

"You came back!" she gasped through the joy that seemed about to choke her. "Oh Asa, you came back!"

"I had to, Lavinia," he said, still holding her up above him. "I never had a chance to tell you properly that I love you!"

She was still breathless from being spun around, still laughing down at him. Her breathing eased, caught, and her hands came softly up to frame his face as he set her back on her feet. "Oh Asa," she said as the piano tinkled into silence in the parlor. "You never needed to tell me. I knew it all along. I was lost without you. Welcome home, dearest."

"–And I wanted to ask you to marry me," he said, smiling down at her.

Her hands stilled beside his face.

He caught her right hand between his and brought it to his lips. "I've wanted to ask you for months," he said over the sound of the door opening behind them and the swift patter of running feet.

✳✳   ✳✳   ✳✳

"The mockingbird's silent, now," Sheppard said. They were standing in the fast-falling darkness, gazing up at the willow tree. It had taken a wonderfully festive meal, a bedtime story, being tucked in and kissed good night to still Meg's joyous wrigglings. George and Callie had ceased to hover only after supper, when Callie had repaired to the smaller parlor to tend to her darning and George had gone off toward the stables to talk with the rest of the Fairlawn Free Militia, who had come back with Sheppard. The last of the crickets were sounding in the growing darkness, and the distant mountains were visible only as an irregular boundary between the shadows of the land and the growing multitude of stars.

It had been an odd evening, seeming almost as though nothing had changed, as though they had returned to the days before the raiders came, when the war had been far distant. No one had spoken of Louise, and aside from a quickly spoken assurance to Lavinia that the wounded men were safely behind Union lines and none the worse for their journey, the urgent cause behind Sheppard's departure more than a week earlier was not touched upon. But the reality of the days and times had been there nevertheless, underlying all that was said and done at dinner and afterward like water moving silently and unseen beneath the thin ice on a winter-bound river. One falling leaf too many, one pebble tossed heedlessly, one word, one careless echo, would shatter the smoothness and reveal the dark, swift current.

"He's gone for the winter," Lavinia said, tucking her hand more warmly into his arm.

"Winter always ends," Sheppard said. "He'll be back."

Lavinia shivered slightly and drew her shawl more closely around her. "I have the one you carved for me," she said. "That will remind me"" They walked together in silence for a moment, watching the stars grow in number in brightness, one by one. "There," she said, turning toward the east. "Orion is rising now. Winter's almost upon us."

"I remember the first time I saw a southern night sky," Sheppard said. "It was such a deep blue, it seemed to vibrate. Blue, shading paler till, at the edge of the west, it was the color of a peach. It was beautiful, and I found myself wishing that I had someone to show it to..."

"Maybe we'll have time to watch the sky when this war is past us," Lavinia said quietly.

"If we can, in years to come, we will," Sheppard said. He drew her hand from his arm and held it for a moment. "Lavinia," he said, and then paused, gathering words.

She returned the clasp of his hand and waited.

"I want you to know that I loved Sarah with all my heart," he said. "I want you to know that I tried to be the best husband I could be for her."

"I knew that, already," Lavinia said. "You didn't have to say it."

"But Lavinia," he said, "You also must realize that—that Sarah's memory—holds no threat to you. I'll always love her, but I think maybe that's what made me able to love you as much as I do. Will you marry me?"

She looked up at him and suddenly smiled. "You've known the answer since before you formed the question, Asa Sheppard," she said. "Asa!" as he went to one knee on the ground. "Now what are you doing?"

"Yes or no, Lavinia," he said. "I must have your answer: will you marry me?"

She began to laugh. "Get up, Asa, and stop being so silly! Yes, I'll marry you! I'll marry you in front of everyone, in Savannah or in Wheelerville, and be happy to be your wife. I'll go with you to New York or stay here with you, whichever is best. Does that satisfy you?"

He pushed himself to his feet and smiled down at her for a moment before taking her in his arms. "Perfectly," he said, tipping her startled face up to his. "Now we're properly betrothed, I can kiss you like I wanted to all these months."

** ** **

"We trailed the wounded for about a day after I sent Al Townsend and Abner back," Sheppard said later that evening as they sat before the fire and drank tea that Callie had brewed for them out of their precious, dwindling store. "It was the easiest thing in the world to ambush the wagon train, and after the first shot, the mounted men made a break for it."

"Did they get away?"

"Several did," he said. He paused to take a sip of the tea and then lift his eyebrows at Callie. "There's ginger in this," he said.

"It's good for the stomach," Callie said, stretching a stocking over the porcelain darning egg and frowning at the holes in it. She had smiled upon Sheppard and Lavinia as they came in, listened to Sheppard's announcement that Lavinia had agreed to marry him, remarked that it had certainly taken him long enough to ask, and then suggested that Lavinia pour the tea. "And ginger goes well with honey," she said. "I thought we should enjoy it." She anchored the stocking with a finger and took a stitch.

"You say they got away," Lavinia said. "Did they see you?"

"I suspect one or two saw me," he said. "I don't think they caught a good look at the others."

Callie was weaving the needle in and out of the stocking. "Why was that?" she asked.

"They were hooded," Sheppard said. "We talked it over as we were following, and we decided it would be best if those fellows didn't know what they were dealing with. There have been enough instances of Negroes being mistreated, I didn't want to give them any reason to continue it. As it happened, most of the escort fled without even looking."

"Did you pursue them?" Lavinia asked.

"No," Sheppard said. "We weren't looking to exterminate them, just get the wounded away. Their leader was killed, though."

Lavinia set her cup down with a click. "I am sorry to hear that," she said. "Though he was not guilty of trying to behave in any sort of way calculated to make anyone think him a gentleman!"

Sheppard looked at her with the hint of a smile as he offered his empty cup for a refill. "I heard he called you a liar," he said.

Lavinia lifted the teapot, steadied the lid with a fingertip, and filled Sheppard's cup. "He was a soldier obeying orders," she said.

Sheppard said nothing further as he opened the honey jar, took the spoon and trailed a slow, golden stream of honey into his tea.

"He was a very rude one," Callie said.

"He may have had his reasons," Sheppard said. He took a sip of tea and then set the cup and saucer down. "He had a letter... I will be calling on Louise Hamiter tomorrow." He frowned at the changed quality of Lavinia's smile. "What is it?" he asked.

"Louise Hamiter is gone," Lavinia said.

"Where did she go?" Sheppard asked carefully.

"As far as I know, she is in Macon now," Lavinia said.

Sheppard drew a long, slow breath and reached into the breast pocket of his jacket. He took out a folded piece of creamy stationery, discolored at one side with a smear of dirt. "We found this on the leader," he said, offering it to Lavinia.

Lavinia pushed her spectacles down on her nose unfolded the letter, and looked at the mark on the front. "Bathsheba said it looked like a butterfly," she said. "The child has more imagination than I do"

"Then you knew about it?" Sheppard demanded.

"Oh, yes," Lavinia said. "That is, we knew there had been a letter, and from the way that fellow was talking, we were pretty sure what it said."

"When I left?" Sheppard pursued.

"We knew about it the day they took the wounded away," Lavinia said. "Bathsheba caught a good look at the letter that Capt. Fullam had in his hands, and she remembered it from that last group of letters she brought out to that Mr. Adams the day he left for South Carolina. Louise had given it to her, and had spoken rudely to her when she did so, so she had very good reason to remember; and there was the ink spot, as well. She came to me after the wounded left, and told me everything."

And you let Louise go?" Sheppard asked.

"I drove her out," Lavinia said. "I ordered her off my property. You know I'd wanted her to go for months. I told her to pack what she wished to take and said that everything she left behind would be burned. She complained to me that I was being unkind, and started giving directions about her escort. I pointed out that I had not approved an escort for her. Ultimately, she left, though it took her two days to do so."

Sheppard was frowning. "That dark patch in the road" he said. "It looked as though there was a bonfire" His expression cleared slightly. "Did she go alone?" he asked.

Lavinia lifted her cup and saucer, turned the cup so that the handle was to the right, took up the cup, and sipped from it, smiling. She set it down and looked up at Sheppard. "No," she said. "Mr. Townsend went with her."

"That was charitable of him," Sheppard said.

"It was on his way," Lavinia said slowly. "He thought to do us a kindness by taking her away from here."

"He was right about that," Sheppard said on the edge of a sigh. "Certainly one less worry. I'll thank him when he gets back."

Lavinia's smile faltered slightly. "He wasn't sure when that would be," she said.

Sheppard's brows drew together fractionally, but he nodded. "I guess you can't be sure about anything," he said. "But if I do see him, I'll give him thanks. Meanwhile, I guess I'd best look into starting up patrols again. I'll talk with Toby and Caesar in the morning."

CHAPTER FIFTY-SEVEN

Sheppard sat back in his saddle and frowned southeast. He could feel the bite in the air; winter was coming on. Another week, maybe two, and the cold would be settling in. He turned his collar up and swept his gaze over the fields lying beyond the stand of trees that sheltered him. Wheelerville was in better shape than most places, he thought. They had been able to grow crops and gather them with hardly any interruption. There would be grain enough for the winter, and some meat to spare. If the war didn't sweep back over the town, they would be in a fair way to weather the coming winter. Better than other towns he'd passed through in the last several years.

Dixie shook her mane and snorted, her breath forming wisps of steam that faded in the air. Sheppard patted her neck with easy affection. "I know, girl," he said. "It's cold for down here. Cold for New York, for that matter, but we'll be going in soon."

He turned again to gaze southeast toward Atlanta, his attention caught by some motion in the distance. A lone rider, approaching slowly. He reined Dixie back into the cover of the trees and watched.

A tall man on a gray gelding; Al Townsend, coming back from Macon, no doubt. Odd: Lavinia had made it sound as though she hadn't expected him to return.

Sheppard frowned and watched more closely. Townsend looked windblown and tired, and his gray was moving quietly on a loose rein, his head down. Sheppard could see a blanket roll on the saddle behind Townsend. His pistol was holstered, and while he was looking around, he seemed preoccupied.

Sheppard moved forward and waited.

Townsend caught sight of him and drew rein for a moment. From where Sheppard sat, Townsend suddenly looked a little grim, but he was smiling as he touched his horse to a trot and came across the field to Sheppard. They were gripping hands a moment later.

"So, you're back, then," Townsend said. "Looking fit to whip a regiment, too! I'm glad to see you! I was wondering if you'd make it here."

"I had to," Sheppard said. "I had an assignment to finish."

"Of course," Townsend said with a smile. "I'd have done the same."

They sat in silence for a moment, watching the wind shake loose the last of the summer's leaves and send them whirling to the ground. "I hear you took the Hamiter woman away," Sheppard said. "Is she gone for good?"

"You could say so," Townsend replied. There's a story there, but it'll keep till I call on you and Miss Lavinia later today." He paused, "Did she tell you what business I left on?"

"No, she just said you went to Macon," Sheppard said.

"She must have thought I wasn't coming back, then," Townsend said thoughtfully.

Sheppard looked at him.

"Another story, Asa," Townsend said with the hint of a smile. "I'll tell you both this afternoon. Will you be back...say, before sundown?"

"I'll ride back with you right now, if you like," Sheppard said.

"No, give me an hour or so," Townsend said. "I'm just coming in, and there's some things I need to do pretty fast in town."

** ** **

"We went toward Macon for two days," Townsend said that afternoon. "She was sulky all the way, since I told her I wasn't interested in hearing how ill-used she was, having all the facts, as you might say. Actually, she was mad as fire at me for having told all the ladies of the town just what she'd done to make you throw her out, and you should have heard her on the subject. I just said I believed in calling things as I saw them, and she was lucky that she had me to take her."

"She went quietly, then?" Sheppard asked.

"Let's just say she didn't exactly pitch a fit," Townsend said. "She had a lot to say, though." He was sitting on the in the parlor late afternoon sun, enjoying a cup of coffee—Sheppard had brought more back with him —and catching up on news. Now he looked thoughtful. "I got an earful, and it made me think a little less harshly about her," he said.

Lavinia looked scornful.

"I can't understand people, some times," Townsend said. "She's poor. Did you know that? I guess her family supported the Confederacy and put their money where their mouths were, and now it's all gone."

"All of it?" Sheppard asked.

"Pretty much," Townsend said. "It's all the Yankees' fault, you know, just ask her. Everything that happened to her, from Gaylord Wheeler going into the army and dying to the fact that her family's business is on the rocks thanks to the blockade. I just let her talk and didn't listen too hard. I don't know why she kept that all inside her. Pride, maybe."

"I'd heard something about it," Lavinia said thoughtfully. "But if she'd mentioned it to me she might have received some sympathy... Did she think we'd view her as poor white trash?"

"Probably," Sheppard said. "It explains a lot, like why she was so hard on Meg."

"It explains but it does not excuse," Lavinia said. "So, Mr. Townsend, you delivered Louise Hamiter to Macon."

"Not exactly," Townsend said, stretching his booted legs out before him and crossing them at the ankles. He smiled at Lavinia's expression. "I told you there was a story there," he said.

"What do you mean?" Lavinia demanded. "Wasn't her family there?"

"They were," Townsend said, "and I gave them word, not that I think it made them very happy. No, she left me half a day's journey before we got there. It was worth my life to get away, too."

Lavinia sat forward. "Did she get killed?" she demanded.

"No," Townsend said. "She sure didn't. But she almost got me killed." He looked at Sheppard and Lavinia and smiled faintly. "Well, you see, we ran into some cavalry," he said. "I'd seen signs of horses around about Cartonville, and I was being careful. I'd heard tell of some units sent out by Sherman, under a fellow named Kilcullen, working their way south, round and about. I'd heard they had an eye to pretty women, so I was being careful since I'd pledged to get Miss Hamiter safely to her folks. Well, we got to a spot where I thought we could stop to water the horses, and I told her to get out of the wagon and wait among some trees while I took the horses to a stream. She did, and I did, and when I got back there she was talking to a group of bluecoats. They were a rough-looking lot, but there were some officers with them, and one of them had a general's stars on his shoulder-straps. There was a really fine traveling-coach in the middle, with the doors open. I guess the general had been traveling in that."

Sheppard was frowning. "They were regular cavalrymen, then?" he asked.

"From what I could see, they were," Townsend said. "The general was standing by Miss Louise and talking up a storm, and they both looked up and saw me. She gave me the sort of smile you'd expect to find on a rattlesnake's face, if it could smile, and said, 'That's one of them, sir! A Reb through and through, and he was abducting me because I expressed sympathy for the Union!' The general heard that and nodded to a couple of his boys, and they took off after me."

"No!" Lavinia exclaimed.

"Oh, yes," said Townsend. "I abandoned the wagon, jumped on my gray, and took off like a shot with them right behind me. I managed to lose them."

"So you left Louise with them?" Lavinia said.

"That's right," Townsend said. "I didn't feel right about it, so I made my way back that night, going the roundabout route, and was able to track them to a nice house by the roadside. There was a light on in one of the back bedrooms. From what I could hear, Miss Hamiter was in with the general and wasn't wasting her time." He paused and added, "And from what she was saying, she knew what she was doing, so to speak."

Sheppard was scowling. "Wait," he said. "This general—was he on the short side, with reddish whiskers?"

"That's right," said Townsend. "Stringy-looking fellow with a loose mouth."

"That was Hugh Kilcullen, all right," Sheppard said. "He considers himself a lady's man, and he's little better than a raider, himself. General Stanley had him dismissed because he didn't like his style. He went with another division, and has been foraging and scouting, from what I heard when I took the boys back."

"Well, he and Miss Louise were thick as thieves by the time I got away," Townsend said. "She was sporting finery taken from some houses along their way, and she was riding with him in that traveling carriage. I could hear her laughing... I went to her family in Macon and told them what happened. I don't think you need to worry about her any more."

"She's ruined," Lavinia said, appalled.

"I suspect she was 'ruined' before she came to Wheelerville," Sheppard said. "But why she would go with a fellow like Kilcullen..."

"I think she had an eye to her main chance," Townsend said. "She knew her name was mud in Wheelerville. I'd done my part to open everyone's eyes to what she'd done. I guess she saw what was coming, figured the Yanks would be winning, and thought to get in good with them."

Lavinia was gazing unseeingly before her. She slowly set her cup down. "Do you suppose," she said, "That Louise would bring him back here, to—to destroy things?"

Sheppard surprised her by smiling. "She could try," he said. "But one of the things General Stanley did when we brought the wounded to his lines was to write up orders to be sent to all the other armies under Sherman, to be given to all units. The orders concerned Wheelerville and Fairlawn. No matter how besotted Kilcullen might be with Louise Hamiter —and I can't imagine that he would stay that way for long —he wouldn't dare go against General Stanley's orders, especially since there's a good chance they'd been approved by Sherman himself. I think you're safe, Lavinia. And you certainly will be as long as I'm here."

Townsend was looking down into his coffee cup. He raised his eyes and said, "So what happens next, Sarge?"

"I stay here," Sheppard said. "I'll turn myself in to the enemy when they come to Wheelerville. I'll show them the Order for the Safeguard and request safe conduct." He tried to smile. "Who knows? Maybe I'll get it."

"And maybe not," Lavinia said bleakly.

Townsend set his cup down on the glossy, inlaid wood of the small table beside him. He paused, tracing the marquetry pattern with a careful fingertip. "Oh, you'll get it, Asa," he said, looking up. "That's why I'm here." He saw their expressions and gave an odd smile. "*I'm* the enemy," he said. "I'm a captain of cavalry now, and I'm here just long enough to get a company together before heading off after Sherman's crowd. I'll honor the Order and get you to safety. And I'll take you myself."

Silence fell after he spoke, and he paused before breaking it.

428 · DIANA WILDER

"Here," he said at last, taking a folded paper from his breast pocket and handing it to Sheppard. "Here's my commission, so you can see I'm on the up and up."

Sheppard opened it and read, then handed it to Lavinia. "So you went to Macon to join the army," he said.

"I did," Townsend said. "I concluded I had no choice, and there were a lot of things hanging on what I did, including what was going to happen to you. I heard they were recruiting there, so I went to them, gave my history, and they said they could use me. I told them about you, by the way, once I saw how things lay. They gave me their approval to deal with you like it's supposed to be. It seems Miss Lavinia wrote some letters that made them think. They were also interested to hear about the Wheelerville Guards."

Sheppard looked straight at him. "And the Fairlawn Free Militia?" he asked.

"Do you know?" Townsend said, "I didn't think to mention them. Guess I'm just getting old." He met Sheppard's gaze with a level look of his own.

Sheppard nodded. "This war," he said. "You find yourself facing folks you'd rather have as friends."

"I know," Townsend said. "I know." He lifted the cup again, drained it, and set it down with a touch of finality. "Wars have to end, eventually," he said. "And there are some friends who'll always be able to count on me. That's a promise."

"I never doubted it," Sheppard said. He took a deep breath. "Well," he said, "Since we're being official, Al, I surrender myself to you. And I'd best show you the Order."

Townsend waved the suggestion away. "We can pretend you've done it," he said. "I've seen it before, and I don't need to see it again. And as for surrendering yourself, we'll consider that done, too. So you can stay where you are for the time being; we'll arrange to get you to safety as soon as possible. It's little enough that I can do, but what I can, I do with a good heart."

"You've done more than enough, Al," Sheppard said, holding out his hand. "I thank God for a friend like you."

** ** **

"I'll send Abner to fetch you when we're ready to go," Townsend said. He was standing on the steps, holding the gray's reins. "It'll be in the morning, probably early. There's bigger forces coming fast, and I can't say when they'll be here, but I want to be well away from here with you before then. I rode hard and fast here just to make sure you'd be safe." He looked from Sheppard to Lavinia. "It'll give you a chance to set things in order. I just wish I could give you more time."

"You're giving me more than I expected," Sheppard said.

"I don't deal in quick trips to prison camps," Townsend said. "Miss Lavinia—"He paused as she came down the steps and took his hand in hers. "I'm sorry things have to be like this."

She was pale and seemed somehow withdrawn, but she smiled up at him. "You have nothing to regret," Mr. Townsend," she said. "You have shown yourself to be a true gentleman through all of this."

Townsend grinned suddenly. "Well, Miss Lavinia," he said, "I surely wish my Ma could have heard you say that!"

"I'll tell her when we meet in paradise," she said with a touch of tartness. "And maybe...Alan...you can drop the 'Miss' now."

His grin gentled to a smile and he bowed to her, then turned to Sheppard. "Till tomorrow," he said. "Abner'll fetch you, as I said. I think he's got some things he wants to say to you."

"Tell him I'll be waiting for him," Sheppard said. He shook hands with Townsend, then let go, and gave him a boost to his saddle. "Good bye, Al," he said.

"Asa." Townsend touched the gray's sides with his heels and left at a trot.

Sheppard turned to see Lavinia gazing after Townsend with wide, somehow blind eyes. As he watched, she turned slowly, her hand to her throat, looked over Fairlawn's facade, and then turned back to him. "Tomorrow morning," she said. "So soon..."

"It'll give me time to set things in order, as Al said," Sheppard said. He looked up at the sky. The sun was westering now; maybe four hours of daylight left.

"Asa..." Lavinia's voice was hushed, shaken. "I'll marry you to-night, if you want." She hurried on, her voice quivering when he did not reply. "Reverend Parsons can come here and perform the wedding. There's time..."

"People will talk," Sheppard said.

She looked up at him, white-faced, with two spots of color on her cheeks. "I don't care," she said. "I said I'd be your wife. I want to marry you, Asa. I love you. We have time, before you go back to that war."

"No, Lavinia," he said. "We're going to have a life together, not just a night. You're going to have a real wedding, out of your house, for all your friends and family to see, just like you said. I know you care about being proper, and I know you do care what people say, no matter how brave a face you put on things. There's going to be no hole-and-corner activity here; I'll take you to wife properly, and it will be a happy day for us both."

"But the war—!" she said.

"It's always been there," he said. "It never stopped, though we forgot about it for a while. It brought us together, and I don't think it will separate us. I'll come back to you, Lavinia. I will: I promise it on my honor!"

"But this is the only night—!"

Sheppard took her hands in his and held them firmly, but with a smile. "It takes more than a wedding night to make a marriage, Lavinia," he said. "It's worth waiting for: I'll be the best husband for you that I can be, and you'll be a wife any man could adore. There's nothing you can do in the next day that'll make me love you any more than I already do."

"But if you don't come back..."she said.

"I will," he told her. "I promise."

CHAPTER FIFTY-EIGHT

Abner Wigfall came with the dawn, apologetic to Lavinia for being there so early, awkward with Sheppard when he offered his weapons.

"Gosh, Sergeant," he said, "You haven't used them against us so far, and they surely gave you reason for a while there, so I guess you could keep them."

"That may be," Sheppard said, "But you'd better take them anyhow and keep them safe till we part." He smiled at Abner's expression and added gently, "It's all part of the drill, son."

Abner nodded and accepted the pistol and the carbine. "You got your reloads for this?" he asked, lifting the carbine and eyeing it, then setting it down on the floor beside his chair.

"What I have left, yes," Sheppard said. "It's not a whole lot."

"Those raiders took a lot out of us," Abner said. He flushed slightly, catching the double meaning of his words, but did not change them. "Sarge..." He trailed away.

Lavinia, who had been silently treasuring every remaining moment with Sheppard, caught his expression and rose with a smile. "I would do well to make sure that everything's been packed and ready," she said. "And I know Meg will want to say her farewells, so I'd best get her, too." She left the room, pausing at the door to smile at both of them. They heard her a moment later going briskly down the hallway and then up the stairs.

"I'm glad they sent you," Sheppard said after her footsteps had faded away. "I can't think of a finer fellow for the job."

Abner's flush deepened and he looked down at the carved arms of his chair. "I don't like the job," he said, tracing a carved scroll with his thumbnail. "They should never have made it needful."

"Abner," Sheppard said.

Abner looked up.

"This is what's supposed to happen," Sheppard said. "When the enemy troops move through, I'm supposed to go to them and request safe conduct to my own lines. That's what Captain Townsend is doing for me. Others might not have done so."

"That jackass fellow that came through and took Higgins and the rest away," Abner agreed with a flash of annoyance. It died after a moment. "Well, I just wish we didn't have to do it."

"So do I, Abner," Sheppard said. "I'll be leaving behind people who are like kin to me now. And you're one of them."

Abner looked up at him, a startled smile touching his mouth.

"If my sons grow up to be like the man you're shaping to be, I'll be pleased and proud," Sheppard said. "When your pa comes home, he'll be happy to see how you've come on."

Abner was looking at his hands again. The shy smile was still in place, but it faded. "Did you hear?" he said. "Mr. Townsend is raising a company from here."

"Is he, now?" Sheppard asked. "Are the others going with him?"

"Most of the Wheelerville Guards," Abner said. "Mr. Wallins, Mr. Pickens...Jack Toombs... They didn't have to join—Mr. Wallins is a blacksmith, and Mr. Toombs is a wheelwright—but they did. Mr. Townsend came in yesterday, around noon and called a town meeting. He told us he was in the army and was raising a company, and they all had a chance to join. He didn't prettify it, either: he said things were rough and it looked like we probably wouldn't win, but he said that he wanted to go because it was the right thing to do. They mostly signed up."

"Well, I can't say I'm glad to hear it," Sheppard said slowly. "But I'm not surprised."

"I wanted to go," Abner said. "He wouldn't let me join."

"Too young?" Sheppard asked sympathetically. "No," Abner said. "He-he told me he wanted a levelheaded fellow to take care of matters here. I asked him to let me go, but he said it again. So here I am."

Sheppard looked thoughtful.

Abner drew a long, shaky breath. "So now I have to stay here," he said, the words coming out in a rush. "Shut up here, safely, with a bunch of sancti-sanctimonious people, while everyone else goes and fights and does their duty..."

"He's right, you know," Sheppard said slowly.

Abner looked at him.

"You're not high and dry and safe here," Sheppard said. "There's going to be fighting, with the main armies going after each other to the north and to the west. Captain Townsend is taking most of the able-bodied fellows of fighting age with him. And that will leave this place open to attack from the sort of riff-raff and scum that we fought this summer. It'll be dangerous, and if I were the one setting things up here and taking a troop of cavalry away from here, I'd finger you to be the leader for the town."

He smiled at Abner's miserable look and added gently, "I know: no blaring trumpets and floating banners. But you don't have them in a war, anyhow: take my word for it. And no one who knows will call you a coward."

"But I'm old enough to fight!" Abner objected.

Sheppard lifted his eyebrows at him.

"I am! Fifteen years old in a month!"

Sheppard sat back and looked at him. "Do you remember when there was first talk of setting up a militia, Abner? Remember how I said everyone had to swear an oath, or I couldn't help them?"

Abner lowered his eyes. "Yes, sir," he said.

"And do you remember how you came to me and offered to take the oath. As I recall you said, 'Someone's got to fight, and it can be me!' You were willing to help out any way you could."

"I remember," Abner said. "But I'm not sure..."

"Captain Townsend was sure," Sheppard said. "And I'm sure, too. It's an important job and you can do it. I said you were shaping up to be a good man: it would make me easier knowing you're here. Between you and Judge Prescott and Dr. Meacham, the town will be in good hands."

"Do you mean that, Sarge?" Abner asked.

"I mean it, Abner." Sheppard said. "Every word." He paused and listened. "Miss Lavinia is coming back," he said. "I need to speak with her alone, just for a couple minutes. Will that be all right with you?"

"Sure, Sarge," Abner said, rising as Lavinia came back into the parlor. "That's fine."

Lavinia was slightly flushed, and her eyes were bright. Meg was with her, holding her hand and rubbing her eyes with her other hand.

"Everything's ready," Lavinia said. "Here's the order General Stanley wrote up, Abner. I'm giving it to you, to hand to Captain Townsend when he comes."

Abner got to his feet. "I'll go to watch for him, Miss Lavinia," he said. "He told me he'd be coming here with some others, and they'd leave from here."

"I thought we'd be going from the town," Sheppard said.

"He changed his mind," Abner said. "He told me he thought things through and decided that the less he had to do with the townsfolk, after the last couple problems, the better. He said he thought you'd understand."

Sheppard nodded. "I do," he said. "It's better this way." He smiled at Abner as the boy left the room, then looked at Meg. "Well, peanut," he said.

She let go Lavinia's hand and went over to him. "You're going away," she said through a long yawn.

Sheppard smoothed her rumpled hair and dropped a kiss on her forehead. "Yes," he said. "I have to leave with Mr. Townsend. He's going away, too."

"You'll be back," Meg said. It was not a question. "You can take me galloping then, and the wicked bitch won't be here."

"Margaret Emmeline Benton!" Lavinia exclaimed.

"It's all right," Meg said. "I'm telling the truth, and Aunt Callie said that if you tell the truth, the angels rejoice

"It depends on when and how you tell it," Lavinia said.

Sheppard firmly squelched his laughter, lifted the girl in his arms, and gave her a resounding kiss on the cheek. "That's for my little girl!" he said. "You be good and mind your mama while I'm gone."

"I will," Meg said, squirming a little. "I always do. Can I watch Mr. Townsend come?"

Lavinia and Sheppard traded looks. "Go ahead, dearest," Lavinia said.

Meg gave Sheppard a quick hug, and then went skipping out the door.

"How does she know?" Lavinia asked.

"I have no idea," he said with a smile. "But she could be a soldier with those premonitions."

Lavinia went to him and took his outstretched hand. "Time is moving so swiftly now," she said. "And the spring and summer seemed so golden and endless."

"And all I want to do now is to stop time, somehow," Sheppard agreed. "I just have to remember that the time will pass while we're apart, and we'll be together for always."

"For always," Lavinia said. "Always." She released his hand and trailed her fingers along the sleeve of his jacket. "I made you two more of those," she said, trying to smile. "And a fur-lined coat. I spent last night lying awake, counting up the things I'd packed for you, hoping you wouldn't have to use them, but knowing you'd be glad of them. The fur lined coat, the gloves, the stockings the—Oh, Asa!" She stopped with an exclamation of dismay and grief, put her arms about him and held him as though by doing so she could hold war, winter and solitude at bay. "I don't want you to leave," she finished, her words muffled against his collar.

"I don't want to leave, either," he said, holding her as tightly. "You've been my strength and my joy when I thought there would be no more. Leaving you is the hardest thing I've had to do."

Sounds outside intruded; approaching hooves, voices.

They clung a moment longer, then parted. "They're coming," Lavinia said. "It's time."

Sheppard nodded and took a deep breath. "We'll say our farewells here, then," he said. He paused, then added, "Lavinia, I...don't think I'll be able to write to you. I think my army is leaving Georgia, and I don't know where we'll be going or what we'll be doing."

"I know," she said. "I thought of it last night. I wish there were a way. I'll write you every day, and you can read my letters when you return."

"Listen, Lavinia," he said. "I'll get word to you somehow after the war is over. Give me six months. I'll be here, or I'll write to you within six months of a peace being reached. If you don't hear from me by then, you'll know I'm no longer alive. But I will be back: I promise it!"

She went to him and lifted her face to his. "I'll hold you to that promise, Asa," she said. "And I'll wait for you as long as I have to."

** ** **

They were smiling as they walked arm in arm through the front door and stood waiting on the steps as Al Townsend rode toward them at the head of his company, with Judge Prescott and Dr. Meacham beside him.

Abner stood at the foot of the steps, beside George, who was holding Dixie.

Sheppard nodded to Meacham and Prescott. "Good morning, Judge," he said. "Dr. Meacham."

Judge Prescott's expression was at once grim and grieved, but he bowed to Lavinia and nodded to Sheppard.

"All right," Townsend said, reining his horse around. "You all are here and you all are listening. Sergeant Sheppard has spent the past half a year in this town under orders to provide protection to Miss Lavinia's property. The order's been here for anyone to read it. Well, he's done more than that: he's helped to train our militia, he's helped to fight off some of the worst folk ever to walk this earth, and he's been a friend to all of us. He's never raised a hand in anger—except when I threw the first punch—and I don't think any of you will say any different." He looked over at Judge Prescott. "Is that right, Judge?" he asked.

Prescott nodded.

"Well, then," he said, "For those of you who don't know how a Safeguard works, I'll tell you. When the army comes through, he is supposed to go to the leader of that army, or the highest ranking officer there, show him the order, which I've got right here, and ask for safe conduct to his own lines. I'm the highest ranking officer here, and I say we'll give him the escort, and consider it our duty to do so. The folks in Macon agreed with me when I put the situation before them. Now does anyone here dare to say otherwise?"

Dr. Meacham shot him a look. "Stop acting like you're going to rupture yourself, Al," he said. "We all know Sergeant Sheppard."

"Well, some folks haven't acted that way," Townsend said. "That's why we're having this meeting here and not in town, and why we're leaving from here."

"I know, Al," Meacham said. "I don't think any of us is proud of what happened. None of us had anything to do with the removal of those wounded. And don't look at me like you think I did!" He turned to Sheppard and held out his hand. "I would like to say that I'm grateful, Sergeant, and I wish you well. I count it a privilege to have known you, and I wish we weren't parting in this fashion."

Sheppard gripped his hand, released it, and was suddenly surrounded by all the Wheelerville Militia, thumping his back, shaking hands with him and, in one or two cases, quickly embracing him. Judge Prescott was wiping his eyes, and Callie, standing on the porch beside Lavinia, was twisting her hands in her apron.

Prescott cleared his throat with a little more force than usual. "Well, Sergeant," he said, taking a document from his breast pocket, "I've written up a letter to send with Captain Townsend, to whomever it may concern, outlining the good you have done and requesting, in behalf of the government of this county, that every courtesy be shown to you. It may serve to help."

Townsend took the letter from him. "It might at that," he said. He looked around, took a deep breath. "Well, folks," he said, "I'm taking custody of Sergeant-Major Sheppard of the Federal Army, according to the order given back in May. We'll ride for the Federal lines —I think they're a day's journey northwest of here —and then we'll join General Hood. Abner Wigfall, here, is my deputy in this town, and he'll be working with the Judge and Dr. Meacham. He's a good young man, and I think I'm leaving this town in good hands between the three of you."

Abner's white, strained expression eased a little, and he smiled shyly at Sheppard, who clapped him on the shoulder.

"Are we ready?" Townsend asked. "All right, then: mount up!"

Sheppard looked over at Lavinia, who had come down the steps to stand beside him. He took her hand in his, bent and kissed it. "Miss Wheeler," he said, "I'm your servant, always." He looked up at Callie and bowed to her. "Miss Callie, you take care of yourself and keep me in your prayers!"

Callie nodded wordlessly.

Lavinia watched as Sheppard gripped George's hand, accepted a boost into the saddle from Abner, and gathered his reins. "Take care of yourself, Sergeant," she said. "And come back safe and well."

He smiled down at her. "I will, Miss Wheeler," he said. "That's a promise you can hold to."

She looked beyond him to Townsend. "Captain Townsend?" she said.

He rode over to her and bent down. "Yes, Miss Lavinia?" he said quietly.

She quickly stretched up to kiss his cheek. "God bless you, Alan," she said. "Go safely and come back."

"I'll take that as an order, Lavinia," he said quietly with a smile. He straightened and frowned at the group. "All right, everybody," he said.

"We've said our good-byes, so let's move on out. Mount up!"

"Bye, Papa!" Meg called above the creak and jingle of harness. Lavinia put her arms around the child and watched the militia form ranks. She smiled at Sheppard as he blew a kiss to Meg and then took his place beside Townsend.

"Move out!" Townsend called.

The militia turned, headed down the alley of oaks. Townsend and Sheppard waited until they had passed, then turned and joined them.

Lavinia watched Sheppard ride down the long alley of trees, and when he turned to wave to her she raised her hand and waved back, and continued to wave until the rattling, red-brown leaves seemed to swallow him up and he was gone.

When there was nothing more to see and the wind was curling knife-edged about her shawl-wrapped shoulder, tugging loose strands of her hair, she went into the house and firmly closed the door against the coming winter.

CHAPTER FIFTY-NINE

December came on with a vengeance, blasting Fairlawn with window-rattling fury while Lavinia sat by the fire and combed her hair and heard of the terrible fighting through Tennessee while General Hood's Army of the Tennessee followed close upon Union General Schofield's line of march as he raced to join General Thomas in Nashville. She heard of the fighting and as her hands drew the comb through her hair she seemed to see a thousand ways in which a cavalryman might fight and die in Tennessee.

She made no comment when Savannah fell at Christmas, and only smiled when she received word that her family's house had been spared any damage and was being guarded by Federal troops.

Meg had outgrown her summer clothes and needed new winter-weight ones; Lavinia went into her trunks and took out fine woolen garments, which she cut down to fit the girl. Sky blue gabardines, a holly green Melton cloth coat, a rose-colored muslin. She worked calmly over the clothing, and when she finished them, she took out her mother's black silk dresses and altered them to fit her.

"You're dressing like a widow," Callie said, aghast.

Lavinia had only smiled at her over her needle and thread. "Or a respectable, married woman, Callie," she said. She stitched away at the black silks and taffetas, washed and starched the cuffs and lace collars, and braided her hair into a crown. She pushed her spectacles back on her nose and dimpled at her reflection, reflecting that Asa would love it that way.

The city of Columbia, South Carolina, burned in the middle of February after a winter that had passed on the tide of Sherman's destructive march through the Carolinas. She heard of cavalry actions up and down through Alabama and was silent.

The leaves began to burst out of their buds in late February. She gazed upon the misty green and thought back to the time they were russet and gold, covering her last view of a rider on a red-brown mare.

She touched the onyx brooch at her throat and wondered if he would be riding her when she saw him again.

There were so many buried in the cemetery in Wheelerville. So many had not come back. John Toombs, Sam Wallins… Letters came from Al Townsend from time to time, notes he wrote for Meg, telling amusing tales of camping and riding. Meg always seemed to know when a letter from him had arrived, and she would ask George or Isaiah to take her into town to get it.

** ** **

> *My dearest Asa,*
>
> *It is odd to read back over these pages and see how close you have been to my thoughts during all this long time, as close as though you had never left Wheelerville. I have so much to tell you.*
>
> *Meg is my daughter now. The Benton family has been exterminated. George Benton, Meg's father, was killed in battle, and his father, brother, sister, wife and baby murdered as you saw. She speaks of you often, and of late I have caught her gazing down the alley of trees.*
>
> *I remained at Wheelerville during this last long winter. I know you said that I should go to Savannah this winter, but I thought of you in Nashville in all that ice and freezing rain and I had no heart to go where it was warm and snug. I remained here and watched winter sift down over the mountains and blanket the hills and fields, so silent and so cold.*

Lavinia looked up from the page, her eyes traveling across the bright green lawn and down the alley. Her mind turned the tossing green leaves back to autumn russet, and she seemed to see a chestnut mare cantering up along the alley, but it was all so distant and so small, as though she were looking back and down through layers of time. She smiled at the memory, dipped her pen, and wrote,

> *The winter has worn away, spring and summer past, and now September is half gone. So many things have changed.*
>
> *I seemed to see you, sometimes, Asa, holding your hands*

over a fire, smiling at your fellow soldiers, rubbing down Miss Dixie. I thought of you and I thought of the coat I had made for you, and prayed that it was keeping you warm.

The war is over now, and the people are returning in one way or another. Mr. Wallins died outside Chapel Hill, and no one knows where he is buried. John Toombs is a name on a grave marker set beside the one where you placed those flowers a lifetime ago. The name is there—he was reported as having fallen in the fighting around Petersburg—and then, some months later, he came back here, as alive as you and me, inclined to laugh about the entire affair. But there are other names in our cemetery that you would recognize.

Abner Wigfall guarded Wheelerville and never complained, just as you and Mr. Townsend ordered him. In this war there have been many heroes, and I think Abner may well be one. His father came back just two weeks ago. We learned that he had spent half a year in a prison in a small town in New York called Elmira. He managed to escape, and made his way back to General Lee's army just in time to participate in that last campaign that led to the surrender of the Army of Northern Virginia. How strange it must be for him to remember leaving a child behind, and to come back to a grown man. If Abner were my son, I would be so very proud of him.

Alan Townsend came back, grimmer, grayer and somehow fine-honed, like a well-balanced sword. It is almost as though he has somehow made peace with a part of himself that had shamed him before. He comes here every afternoon, to make much of Meg and to sit with me and talk. How strange that I had once thought him uncouth. No one here knows that he left the armies for the final time as a colonel.

General Stanley came to visit. He has been assigned to oversee the occupying army here. I believe he is well liked in Georgia, though there are some who speak pointedly about 'Yankee trash'. I don't see that they are the ones who did any fighting to speak of.

She raised her head and looked into the tossing leaves above her, remembering the morning General Stanley had arrived at Fairlawn. The war had brought some good things in its wake, including that friendship. He had been as courtly as ever, and aglow with expectation; his Eleanor was sailing to Savannah, and would be taking up residence there. He had hoped that Lavinia would be able to make her acquaintance when she removed to that city from Wheelerville. Lavinia dipped her pen again.

> *You would be grieved at the changes in the land. Those around me look at their defeated country and wonder why God deserted them. So many women assured their children that God was on their side and would give them victory, and now that the Confederate armies have surrendered, they do not know what to say. I see it in the eyes around me, and there is nothing I can do or say to change the despair that I can almost feel.*
>
> *The vultures are gathering, Asa. With President Lincoln's death, the gates of hell were opened and the cruel scavengers have swarmed southward. In August I received a call from a man who held himself up to be a representative of the government. He came to Fairlawn with a smile and a note requesting payment of the back taxes on Fairlawn and the other properties my family owned, on pain of forfeiture. I thanked him and spoke him fair, and directed that he return in two days with his credentials.*
>
> *After he left, I sent a message to General Stanley, requesting the presence of a ranking officer to witness the transaction. I also retrieved some gold that I had secreted against just such an emergency, and waited for the tax collector's arrival in the morning. You can imagine my gratification when General Stanley himself arrived the next morning, along with General Meade.*
>
> *When the tax collector returned, and had satisfied those two gentlemen as to his bona fides (not an easy task!), I gave him payment in full of all the taxes, both for my family and for every other family in Wheelerville, and secured a written receipt and release in full, witnessed by my two distinguished guests.*

Lavinia smiled at her pen.

> *The 'Government Representative' was not pleased with this development. All that gold, and he could not touch it! But perhaps I am too cynical. The reaction of the Wheelerville people was interesting. There was quite an outcry; no one had expected me to pay the taxes, myself. I have the feeling that perhaps I was too generous for their comfort, or so they thought at one point. There is talk of repaying me in some way, and it would be politic and, I think, charitable, to encourage such an action.*
> *And so the time passes.*

She dipped her pen again and then paused. How she had fretted for the first four months after the surrender! But the months passed, and she had reached a sort of peace and resignation. The six months were not over yet, after all...

> *The weather is now turning toward October, with the skies brightening to an almost unbearable blue. And yet it is still warm enough for me to sit here in the shade and write to you, and to look up from time to time to smile at Meg. She has been talking about having a tea-party for Jesse, Lydia and Caleb, and says it will happen very soon. In fact, she is practicing as I watch her. The child is so often right about things, I can but hope. In the meantime, Asa, I have sewn my wedding dress from a length of ivory silk satin purchased when I was a girl, and I have found my mother's veil of Brussels lace. I thought we could be married here in Wheelerville and then winter in Savannah... We could then return to New York in the spring. Oh, Asa! It only lacks your presence to make all this come true. Six months, you said. And the six months are so nearly expired. I promised to wait for you, and I have done so, and shall do so as long as I live.*

She saw that Meg was smiling at her. She blew the child a kiss, and watched as Meg lifted an invisible teapot, took an invisible teacup in her hand, carefully poured, and set the cup and saucer before her doll. Another invisible cup filled, Meg carefully turned it so that the handle was correctly placed, lifted the cup to her lips...

Lavinia could almost see the china cup, could nearly catch the pink rosebuds painted on the sides— And she seemed to hear the crash of shattering china as Meg sent the imaginary tea set flying, scrambled to her feet, her face aglow, and ran toward Lavinia, past her and on across the lawn

Lavinia set her pen down with shaking fingers, carefully rose to her feet, turned, and stood smiling as Asa Sheppard, Meg in his arms, rode toward her across the wide, green lawn beneath the alley of oak trees.

LIST OF CHARACTERS

Benton, Margaret .... (Meg)Orphan child
Fairlawn .... Wheeler estate
Fullam, Andrew .... Captain, CSA Cavalry
Greene, Sergeant .... 1st Sergeant, Co H, 57th Ohio Infantry
Hamiter, Louise...................... Gaylord Wheeler's fiancée
Haskell, Charles .... Major, U. S. Army; Chief Surgeon
Hayes..................................... Private, U. S. Army (wounded)
Higgins, Geoffrey.................. Private, U.S. Artillery (wounded)
Leary, Private .... Private, Co H, 57thOhio Infantry
Pickens, Edward..................... Proprietor of the Wheelerville store
Pierce, Byron.......................... Private, U. S. Infantry (wounded)
Prescott, Alexander .... Wheelerville's chief magistrate
Reeves, Haller .... Publisher of Wheelerville Gazette
Schuyler, Nathaniel................ Colonel, U. S. Army
Sheppard, Asa .... Sergeant-Major, Ohio cavalry
Skilton, Lawrence .... 2nd Lt., U. S. Army, 57th Ohio Infantry
Swithin, Amabel...................... Lavinia Wheeler's aunt
Stanley, Miles .... Major General, U. S. Army;
Toombs, John.......................... Wheelerville's wheelwright
Townsend, Alan .... commander of Wheelerville Militia
Wallins, Samuel .... Wheelerville blacksmith
Wheeler, Bathsheba .... Freed slave, Callie's granddaugter
Wheeler, Caesar .... Freed slave, Fairlawn blacksmith
Wheeler, Callie (Calliope....... Freed slave, Fairlawn's housekeeper
Wheeler, Gaylord................... Lavinia Wheeler's brother
Wheeler, Isaiah....................... George Wheeler's grandson
Wheeler, Lavinia................... Mistress of Fairlawn
Wheeler, Toby....................... Freed slave, Fairlawn overseer
Wigfall, Abner .... A founder of the Wheelerville Militia

ON SAFEGUARDS

In June of 1988, while attending the 125th anniversary reenactment of the battle of Gettysburg, I bought a replica of a book published by the Government Printing Office in 1863. This book, Instructions for Officers and Non-Commissioned officers on Outpost and Patrol Duty, and Troops in Campaign, is in two parts, the first covering patrol duty and the second concerning directing troops in campaign.

I was working on another novel, set during the Civil War, and this edition, in facsimile, proved very helpful with my research. In going through it, I encountered the following item:

SAFEGUARDS
(from Troops in Campaign, P. 79)

Safeguards are protections granted to persons or property in foreign parts by the commanding general or by other commanders within the limits of their command.

Safeguards are usually given to protect hospitals, public establishments, establishments of religion, charity, or instruction, museums, depositories of the arts, mills, post offices, and other institutions of public benefit; also to individuals whom it may be the interest of the army to respect. A Safeguard may consist of one or more men of fidelity and firmness, generally non-effective non-commissioned officers, furnished with a paper setting out clearly the protection and exemptions it is intended to secure, signed by the commander giving it and his staff officer; or it may consist of such paper, delivered to the party whose person, family, house and property it is designed to protect. These Safeguards must be numbered and registered.

The men left as Safeguards by one corps may be replaced by another. They are withdrawn when the country is evacuated; but if not, they have orders to await the arrival of the enemy's troops, and apply to the commander for a safe conduct to the outposts.

Form of a Safeguard:
By authority of _____
A Safeguard is hereby granted to [A. B____, or the house and family of A. B_____, or to the college, mills, or property; stating precisely the place, nature and description of the person, property or buildings] All officers and soldiers belonging to the army of the United States are therefore commanded to respect this Safeguard, and to afford, if necessary, protection to {the person, family, or property of ___ _____, as the case may be.]
Given at headquarters the _____ day of ____
A. B_____, Major General Commanding-in-Chief By command of the General.
C. D_____, Adjutant General
55th Article of the Rules and Articles of War.
"Whosoever belonging to the armies of the United States, employed in foreign parts, shall force a Safeguard, shall suffer death."

I found this intriguing.

A 'non-effective' soldier is one who is somehow incapacitated, and the requirement of 'fidelity and firmness' gave some indication of the qualifications needed for a Safeguard, and the high regard in which such an assignment was held. I started picturing the reasons that a Safeguard might be needed. This story arose from those imaginings.

When I showed this manuscript to my father, James D. Wilder, who had served in the United States Navy in the Corps of the Judge Advocate General and retired with the rank of Captain, he gave me some excellent background on the use of Safeguards – they originated under Richard the Lionheart – and researched the background to the concept of a Safeguard as it was used during the American Civil War.

The American Civil War differed from any other war fought by the United States of America, once it was fully set up, because the United

States Government did not consider it a war with a foreign power but, rather, an armed insurrection conducted by people who were still citizens of the United States. Territory occupied by the Union armies were officially viewed as United States territory. Once hostilities ceased, the southern citizens were expected to pay the taxes they owed to the government during the years of the war, as Lavinia Wheeler did. Under the wording, above, provision would not apply because the South was still considered (by the U.S. government) to be part of the United States.

It was determined, however, that an exception would be made for this conflict, and so it was done, with property protected by men of firmness and fidelity, sometimes against great odds.

A Note From The Author

Thank you for reading *The Safeguard*. If you would like ore information on it, or my other books, please visit my website at *www.dianawilderauthor.com*.

If you wish to sign up for my newsletter, you can do so on my website. I never share email addresses, and you can always unsubscribe by clicking the link at the bottom of the page.

About the Author

Diana Wilder comes from a family of storytellers and people-watchers. A childhood spent traveling with her military family gave her plenty of opportunities to weave stories around the places and people that she encountered. Her first novel, written on lined paper and barely legible, was a story of the Hawaii of Kamehameha the Great. The Safeguard, born of a lifelong fascination with its period, features several of her ancestors who were in the area at that time. She says it is difficult to be bored when there is history to read and people to write about.

www.ingramcontent.com/pod-product-compliance
Lightning Source LLC
Chambersburg PA
CBHW070831260626
47170CB00007B/2334